Praise for *Steadfast*:

"Lackey works in enough twists and period color to keep things truly engaging.... This is a charming period adventure mixing magic, real and theatrical, to good effect." — *Locus*

"*Steadfast* is the latest installment of Mercedes Lackey's Elemental Masters series. I, personally, have greatly enjoyed all of them.... They are wonderful reads, full of rich imagery and characters you desperately want to see come out on top." — Bookshelf Bombshells

And for the previous novels of the *Elemental Masters*:

"This is Lackey at her best, mixing whimsy and magic with a fast-paced plot." — *Publishers Weekly*

"Richly detailed historical backgrounds add flavor and richness to an already strong series that belongs in most fantasy collections. Highly recommended." — *Library Journal* (starred)

"Fans of light fantasy will be thrilled by Lackey's clever fairy-tale adventure." — *Booklist*

"I find Ms. Lackey's *Elemental Masters* series a true frolic into fantasy." — Fantasy Book Spot

"Lackey has delivered another fine entry to the *Elemental Masters* series.... The storyline and subplots are smoothly woven together and as usual, Lackey's character development is delightful." — Monsters & Critics

"All in fine fairy-tale tradition.... It's grim fun, with some nice historical detail, and just a hint of romance to help lighten things." — *Locus*

MERCEDES LACKEY

STEADFAST

The Elemental Masters,
Book Eight

DAW BOOKS, INC.

DONALD A. WOLLHEIM, FOUNDER

375 Hudson Street, New York, NY 10014

ELIZABETH R. WOLLHEIM
SHEILA E. GILBERT
PUBLISHERS

www.dawbooks.com

First Paperback Printing, June 2014

1 2 3 4 5 6 7 8 9

DAW TRADEMARK REGISTERED
U.S. PAT. AND TM. OFF. AND FOREIGN COUNTRIES
—MARCA REGISTRADA
HECHO EN U.S.A.

PRINTED IN THE U.S.A.

To the programmers and developers of the late Paragon Studios, and the memory of City of Heroes, my second home.

KATIE Langford woke with a start, heart pounding, the sweat of terror soaking her clothing. It took her a moment of paralyzed fear to realize that she was *not* in the circus wagon, she was *not* about to be beaten by her husband again, and at least for this moment she was safe. Safe, sleeping on a sort of shelf-bed in old Mary Small's *vardo,* protected by the menfolk sleeping outside. She could hear their snores from underneath her, sheltered by the great Traveler wagon, and from the bender tents around the wagon.

She took slow, careful breaths as her heart quieted, and she felt her emotions fall back into the curious state of numb apprehension that she couldn't seem to work her way out of. She wondered if she would ever feel normal again—or happy?

Probably not until I know that Dick is dead.

She listened to the snores. Mary Small had outlived her husband, but her sons and grandsons were many, and since Mary had declared that the half-blooded Katie was to be sheltered and protected, her sons would see to it that their mother's word was followed.

This was . . . interesting. Her mother might have married a *gadjo*, she might be *didicoy*, and Katie herself might know no more than a few words of the Traveler tongue, but still, it seemed that for Mary Small, blood was blood.

Perhaps it was something more than that, for Mary had declared she was *drabarni*, she had magic, and so she was to be doubly protected.

Katie could not for a moment imagine where Mary had gotten *that* idea. Magic? The only magic she had ever seen was sleight of hand and outright fraud. Her mother had told her stories of magic . . . but if Katie'd had anything like what had been in those stories . . .

My parents would be alive, she thought, and swallowed down tears. *If I'd had that sort of magic, they would be alive.*

It was dark in the wagon. The communal fire outside had been allowed to die down to banked coals, there was no moon, and they were far from a town. It was quiet, too; Mary Small was a tiny woman in robust health, and slept as quietly as a babe.

Katie breathed slowly and carefully in the spice-redolent darkness of the *vardo,* waiting for the tears to pass, the numbness to settle in again. It was only three days ago she had taken everything portable she had of value and fled the circus—but it seemed an entire lifetime ago. She still could hardly believe that she'd had the temerity. *That* Katie, who'd resolutely taken everything that was due her and run, seemed a stranger to her. After months of being married to Dick, she had turned into a terrified mouse of a creature, afraid to put a single finger wrong. Where had that courage come from? She still didn't know . . . but it hadn't lasted for more than the few hours it took to put some distance between her and the circus.

Once it had run out, then she'd settled into the state of dull anxiety she lived in now. But she had kept going, understanding that after having run, being caught would be—a horror. She didn't dare even think about what Dick would do to her if he caught her.

It had been only a day since she had stumbled on the Traveler encampment—literally ran right into it, since the *vardos* of the Small clan were Bow Tops, painted to blend in with the woodland rather than stand out like the bright red and gold Reading *vardos*. The entire two days before, she had been running, mostly along country lanes and paths through forest, changing her direction at random. Her husband Dick—and more especially, Andy Ball, the owner of Ball's Circus—would most likely assume she would head for one of the nearest towns rather than take to the countryside. They didn't know her at all, nor had they ever made any effort to know her. They would assume she was like the other women of the circus, who knew only the wagons, the tents, and the towns.

Dick would be furious, not only because she, his possession, had dared to run from him, but because she had picked the lock on his strongbox and taken every bit of the money *she* had earned. Or at least, every bit that was left after his drinking; she took only what should have been her salary, and there was still money left in the strongbox when she closed it again.

It was not as if he actually needed her money. The truth was, he generally didn't have to pay for drinks, though he was quite a heavy drinker. Locals in the pubs would buy him rounds just to see his tricks, like unbending and rebending a horseshoe, or tying an iron bar into a knot. He didn't have to pay for whores, either, with farmer's lasses throwing themselves at him.

She wouldn't have cared about that. She *didn't* care about that. She'd only married him because he'd been craftily kind to her after the horrible fire that killed her parents, and because Andy Ball said she had to marry a strong man to protect her now, and who was stronger than the Strong Man himself? She'd been so paralyzed with grief, mind fogged, so alone . . . Andy had been so insistent . . . it had seemed logical. Most marriages among circus folks were arranged, anyway—an acrobat daughter sent into a family of ropewalkers, or off to learn trapeze work. So she'd gone along with it, and found herself married to a man who at first was impatient with nearly everything she did, then increasingly angry with her, then who knocked her around whenever something displeased him.

Of course, it hadn't been bad at first. A slap here, a push there—circus folk were not always the kindest to each other and plenty of husbands and wives left marks on each other after fights. Circus folk drank, and there were often fights.

She'd gone in despair to Andy Ball, who had shrugged, and said "Then take pains to please him, he's your husband, you must do as he says. I told him if he broke your

bones, he'd be answering to me, so stop your whingeing."
And for the longest time, she had believed that it *was* her
fault. After all, her mother and father had never done
more than shout at each other. And none of the other
circus wives were ever treated as she was. She'd been too
ashamed to talk to any of the other women about it, especially when he began to really beat her.

Why had Andy urged the marriage on her? Because
Dick wanted her and he was handing her over like some
reward for loyalty? Because he was afraid to lose his
chief dancer and contortionist?

She'd been part of a three-man acrobatic act; her
mother, her father, and herself. It had been like that for
as long as she had been alive. With her family gone, besides her dancing in the circus ballet, and her contortions
in the sideshow, Andy had come up with a new act for
her. She became part of Dick's strongman act, with tricks
like standing on her hands while balanced on Dick's
palm, and shivering the whole time, afraid he'd drop her.
She would have liked to join some other act, but Dick
forbade it. "You'll work with me or no one," he said, in
that tone of voice that made her shake and imagine that
no one meant he'd strangle her in her sleep.

It was only when she'd been bathing in a stream—she
usually did that alone, to hide the bruises—and some of
the other women had come on her unexpectedly that she
had finally been forced to confront the truth. They'd
been alarmed, then angry, then—afraid. Because while,
one and all, they told her that *this wasn't right,* they also
told her she would have to somehow get away on her
own. No one dared challenge Dick. He could snap any
other man's neck without thinking about it.

At least their words had snapped her out of the fugue of despair and fear, and gave her the courage and the strength to run. The opportunity had come when a lot of rich men had descended on Dick and plied him with drink far stronger than he was used to. He'd been so dead drunk that nothing would have awakened him, giving her plenty of time to pack up all her belongings, steal the money, and get a good head start on him. As a child she'd been a woods-runner, and in summer, her parents had often spent entire weeks camped out, hidden, on someone's private land, living off it. Unlike Dick, she didn't need a town to survive. But she was counting on the idea that he would think she did.

It had been while she was following a path through the woods on some lord's enormous estate that she had stumbled on the Travelers. The old woman had started with surprise as she appeared in their midst. She'd snapped out a few commands from the porch of her *vardo* in the Traveler tongue, and one of the young men had seized Katie's wrist before she could run.

"Don't be afraid," he'd told her, in a lightly accented, warm voice that caressed like velvet. *"Puri daj* has seen you are of the blood. She says you are *drabarni,* and that you are afraid and running. We will hide you."

The accent, and the words, straight out of her childhood, when her mother had whispered Traveler words to her, had somehow stolen her fear away—and besides, at that point she was exhausted and starving. Cress, a few berries, and mushrooms she had gathered had not done much for her hunger. The old woman had directed that she be brought to the fire, given an enormous bowl of rabbit stew, and draped with a warm shawl. She'd fallen asleep where she was when the bowl was empty. They'd woken her enough to guide her into the *vardo,* where she'd fallen asleep on a little pallet on the floor. When night fell, one of the women had awakened her and pulled down this shelf-bed, which she had climbed into to fall asleep immediately again. It was narrow and short, and must have been intended for a child, but she was small and it fit her.

Today she'd been given things to do—mending Mary Small's clothing, since the old woman's eyes were too dim to thread a needle now—and wash pots and dishes, freeing another of the women to go out and forage in the forest. The men went out and came back with food and word that the circus folk had passed through the village, asked if anyone had seen a girl like her, and moved on without stopping to set up.

"They're in Aleford," one of the boys, last in, had reported. "Set up there. Moving on in the morning." He had eyed her, then. "What did you do, that made you run?"

"My husband beat me," she had told him, the first time she had told anyone but Andy Ball, the shameful words surprised out of her. He had told her never to tell. He had told her she deserved it. Even now, it was almost easier to believe he was right, he'd said it so often.

"Ah," the boy had said, and spat to the side. "A curse on a bully that strikes a woman, unless with wanton ways or shrewish tongue she drives him to it."

"The *drabarni* is neither wanton nor shrew," Mary had proclaimed from the porch of the *vardo,* though how on earth she could know anything about Katie . . .

Her words settled things, it seemed, for the boy spat

to the side again and repeated his curse, without the conditions this time.

"What is it you do with the circus?" someone else asked. So far none of them but Mary had told her their names, but it was one of the four other women in this clan.

To answer that, she showed them, bending over backward and grabbing her ankles with her hands, straightening up again and going into a series of cartwheels so fast that her skirts never dropped to show her legs at all. "And I dance," she had added simply as she finished back where she had started and clasped her hands in front of her.

"Good," Mary had nodded. "Then you can do that while the boys play music. And we will teach you your mother's dances. You have the Gitano look about you and we are Gitano. Now it is time to eat."

And now she was spending her second night under the canvas top of Mary's *vardo,* which seemed to be the place they had decided she was to stay. At this point she was content to do what they told her to. It wasn't only her body that was exhausted, it was her mind.

A rumble of thunder in the distance suggested what it was that had woken her; a moment later a gentle rain pattered down on the canvas top of the *vardo.* There was a curtain she could use to draw across the front of her shelf, and she did so. A moment later three of the boys came up the stairs, their bedrolls over their shoulders. They squeezed themselves together on the floor, and before she would have believed it possible, they were asleep again, on their sides, arranged like spoons in a drawer.

And the rain lulled Katie back to sleep, secure in the presence of her protectors beyond the gently waving curtain.

Everyone said this was going to be the "perfect summer." April had been unseasonably warm. So was May. It was now June, and quite beyond "unseasonably warm"—in Lionel Hawkins' estimation, though he would never use such language in the presence of a lady, it was bloody damned hot.

He lounged at the stage door of the Palace Music Hall in Brighton, wondering if he should try and see if there was a sylph about willing to fan in a bit of breeze. But that would mean actually stepping outside, in his stage costume, attracting the inevitable attention of the horde of small boys lurking out there, hoping to sneak in. That would put him in the position of either having to show them a little sleight of hand to satisfy the little beggars, or scare them away with a show of Turkish Fury and a bit of flash powder. Too much work, either way.

Not with only an hour to showtime. He *might* get away with stepping outside if he was in the persona of Antonio Grendini or Professor Corningworth, but not as Taras Bey, the Terrible Turk.

At least the costume was cooler than most, consisting of a pair of ballooning silk Turkish pants, a wide silk sash, a vest, a turban, and nothing else but some greasepaint. *Glad I still look menacing, and not like some fat carpet-seller,* he thought to himself, as one of those small boys peeked in the door, squeaked, and retreated at his scowl before the doorman could chide him to step away. This was not his *favorite* act, but it appeared he had chosen it wisely when he'd decided who he was going to play for this season. If it got any warmer, the music hall was going to be unbearable at afternoon rehearsals for anyone in a heavy costume. He thought about the wool suits Grendini and the Professor wore, and grimaced. No. Not until hunting season, if then!

Unlike most of his kind, Lionel did not do "the circuit," moving from music hall to music hall. Lionel remained in place, forever installed at the Palace. He didn't change his location, he changed his persona and his act instead. This enabled him to have a house of his own, possessions that did not need to be portable, the luxury of days off that were spent enjoying himself, and the equal luxury of a cook-and-housekeeper who left a lovely dinner on the table waiting for him when he got home, saving him from eating greasy and dubious meals in pubs. It also enabled him to collect large-scale props and effects that very few other magicians outside of the great metropolises could own or use. Transporting big effects was expensive, and the risk of damage was always real. His effects all lived in his warehouse, and only needed to be moved once a season.

This settled life also meant he saved money. It was much cheaper to keep your own place than it was to live in short-term lodgings.

He had many personas, and was always creating more. There was Taras Bey, with his sword-tricks and more ways to dismember a lady than Torquemada, Lee Lin Chow who specialized in silks, doves, and Chinese cabinet effects, Antonio Grendini who performed large illusions, Alexander Nazh the mentalist, Professor

Corningworth with his sleight of hand, and Saladin the Magnificent who conjured spirits and apparitions. He'd considered adding an escapist routine, but decided that at his age he just wasn't flexible enough any more. Besides, Grendini already had one big "escape" trick, and he didn't want to repeat it. He had also considered a mediumistic act, but didn't like the idea of duping people into thinking he could speak with their beloved dead.

There was a smell of hot cobblestones from the alley—thankfully no worse than that. The doorman, Jack Prescott, a sturdy and upright man—if battered and much the worse for war—did a fine job of keeping people from using the area as a privy while the music hall was open. All on his own he had taken to sluicing down the area with water and a broom before everyone started arriving for rehearsals. That made things much more pleasant for everyone.

Prescott turned, as if he had sensed Lionel's thoughts—which he might have, since both of them were Elemental Magicians; Lionel of Air, and Prescott attuned to Fire. Lionel offered him a cigarette. Prescott took it. Lighting up was never a problem for a Fire Mage. Prescott was a handsome man, despite the lines that pain had carved into his face, and he was clearly still every inch the soldier. His brown hair was short and neat under his workman's cap, his neckcloth tied with mathematical precision, his jacket, hung up on the back of his chair, unrumpled. His shirt had been ironed, and it looked as if his trousers went into a press every night.

"Did you get up to London for the coronation?" Lionel asked. Edward VII's coronation had taken place in May, and Lionel remembered Prescott had talked about going there and meeting up with some of his old mates from his regiment.

Prescott shook his head. "By the time I thought about it, the only rooms you could get were little garret holes up three and four flights of stairs. I couldn't face stumping up and down a dozen times a day with this." He tapped his cane on the side of his leg, rapping the wooden peg that took the place of the limb he'd lost in the last gasp of the Boer Wars. "Not to mention what they wanted for a few days was more than I pay for my flat for a month. I shudder to think what everything else was costing, though I suppose I might have been able to eat in the regimental mess, still." An errand boy ran up with a package. Jack signed for it.

"I'll take that," Lionel offered, and Prescott handed it over.

"Don't get excited, it's beards for the comic acrobats," Prescott said with a grin. "Not candy for that pretty little can-can dancer."

Lionel snorted. "My assistant Suzie is better looking."

"Which is why she's getting married," Prescott reminded him. "Have you found a replacement yet?"

Lionel sighed. This was the bane of his existence. You wanted a pretty assistant, but pretty assistants had the temerity to go off and fall in love! *I'd hire an ugly girl, but then I would have to cast the illusion that she was pretty—and then face her wondering why men were interested in her when she was* on *stage but not when off.* "Not for lack of trying. She'll stick until I do, though. She's a good girl, Suzie is."

"I'll keep my eye out for you," Prescott promised as Lionel turned to deliver the box of beards. "Sometimes a dancer turns up at the stage door looking for work, and for the Turkish act, a dancer would do."

Not for anything else, though, Lionel thought glumly as he made his way back to the dressing rooms. He didn't often regret his decision to remain in one place and change his act while everyone else around him was on the circuit— but in the matter of getting and keeping good assistants, his mode of life was a handicap. When a girl was only dealing with stage-door beaus, who inevitably thought she would be easy, it wasn't so hard to keep her. Because you moved every four to six weeks, it was less likely she'd meet anyone *but* a lot of cads, except the lads in fellow acts. And the lads in fellow acts very often had sisters, wives or mamas that were fiercer than mastiffs at protecting their own. But when you stayed put, well, it gave her the chance to meet someone with more on his mind than improper advances. A local girl had family and friends here already, she might have had a beau or two when she'd hired on. Knowing the town, she had a lot more opportunities to meet nice fellows than someone who was transient. So far in his career, Lionel had watched a full half-dozen good assistants walk down the aisle with Brighton boys.

On the other hand, since all of them were *still* local, all of them kept themselves in good fettle, and all of them still kept in touch—in an emergency, he knew he could count on at least half of them to be willing to put in a few nights or even weeks in the old act.

Still, that slight advantage was far outweighed by the disadvantage. Not for the first time, he wished that he could finally get a good, *permanent* assistant.

And while I'm dreaming, let's dream one that's got some real magic in her too.

He'd had two of those; it had been blissful, knowing that he wouldn't have to watch for some slip to betray him in his act. Lionel was more than just a stage magician; Air Magic was the magic of illusions, and his act was generally more than half *real* magic as opposed to stage magic. Floating and flying small objects? All done with the aid of sylphs. Levitating? His apparatus hardly needed to bear the weight of a good-sized goose, since the sylphs aided there as well. Bending and shaping the air meant he didn't have to depend on physical mirrors. In general he didn't need more than half of the physical apparatus of a conventional stage magician. But you had to be careful when you had an assistant who might notice that there was a lot more going on in the act than you could account for by normal means.

He squeezed his way along the narrow corridors. Space was at a premium in a theater. The more space backstage, the fewer seats up front. Finally he arrived at the appropriate dressing room. Beards delivered, he went back to his own.

As the only resident performer, his room had a well-lived-in look, and a great many more creature comforts than those afforded to the transients. As a result it was very popular for lounging, and he discovered the current "drunk gentleman comic" sprawled over his shabby but comfortable armchair when he arrived. There was a matching couch, but evidently Edmund Clay preferred to hang his legs over the arm of the chair and lean his head against the back.

"I don't suppose you have any mint cake in that sweets drawer of yours, do you?" that worthy asked as he took his seat at the dressing table to put the finishing touches on his makeup.

Lionel opened the door with a foot. "Only hard peppermints, but help yourself."

"Thanks." The comedian did so. "I should know better than to eat at the Crown. I try to remind myself every time we come to Brighton, and I always forget."

"Well, stop taking those lodgings right next to it," Lionel told him.

"But they're cheap *and* clean!" Edmund protested. "How often does one find *that* particular combination?"

"Not nearly often enough," Lionel admitted. "But in this heat, you really should avoid the Crown, or you're likely to get something more serious than an upset stomach from all the grease. Look, there's a Tea Room about half a block north—"

"Tea Room!" Edmund interrupted him. "And sit there amid a gaggle of—"

"Do shut up and stop interrupting me," Lionel snapped crossly. "Who is the native here, you or me? It serves cabbies. Nice thick mugs of proper strong tea, nice thick cheese sandwiches. You can't go wrong."

"Oh well, in that case," Edmund replied, and set to sucking on a peppermint. Lionel went back to putting the finishing touches on Taras Bey.

There was a perfunctory tap on the door and it opened. "Lionel, are we doing the basket trick first, or the—oh, hullo, Edmund!"

"Hello, Suzie," the comic said, looking up at the pert little blond wearing an "Arabian" costume that served double duty when she worked the chorus during the

Christmas pantos. "Your veil's working loose on the right side."

"Oh golly, thank you," the assistant replied, and hastily refastened the offending drapery. "If I weren't about to leave poor Lionel in the lurch it would be time to think about a new costume, I guess."

"But you *are* about to leave poor Lionel in the lurch," Lionel said heartlessly, watching her in the mirror. "So you'll just have to keep mending it. I'm not buying two new costumes for the Turk act in one season. And yes. Basket first. Then the Cabinet. Then I saw you in half. It's working better with the audience that way."

"Right-oh!" Suzie said brightly, and scampered off to fix her outfit after blowing Edmund a kiss.

"Well, that peppermint seems to have done the trick—"

"For heaven's sake, come back with me for dinner when the show's over," Lionel ordered. "Mrs. Buckthorn said she's baking me a hen; I can never finish a whole one by myself, and this is no weather to go saving it for tomorrow. I'd probably poison myself."

"Don't have to ask me twice," Edmund said complacently. "Right, getting on for curtain time. Break a leg."

He swung his long legs over to the floor, got up, and sauntered off. Lionel could tell from the sounds in the theater that the curtain was about to go up. He finished the last touches on his makeup, stood up, and thrust his two trick scimitars through the hangers on his silk sash.

Why, oh why, did Suzie have to get married now?

Jack Prescott listened to the hum of the theater behind him, and kept a sharp eye out for little boys trying to sneak in. From now until curtain-down, that would be his main task. Not overly daunting for anyone, even a fellow with only one good leg to his name. The alley out there was like an oven; even though the sun was down, it still radiated heat. If you weren't moving, if you accepted the heat the way he had learned to in Africa, it felt good. Or maybe that was just his talent as a Fire Mage talking; Fire Mages always seemed to take heat better than anyone else.

He lit another cigarette and inhaled the fragrant smoke. Tobacco caused no harm to a Fire Magician, who could make sure nothing inimical entered his lungs—nor to an Air Magician, who could do the same. And the tobacco seemed to help a bit with the ever-present ache of his stump.

He poked his head out of the door, and looked up and down the alley. Even the little boys had gone now, discouraged by the heat, and knowing there would be no more coming and going from the door until the show ended. A real play or a ballet or some other, tonier performance would give the actors, dancers, and singers a break now and then to come to the stage door, catch a smoke, get a little air. A music hall tended to work you a lot harder. Acts often had two or three different sets and had to rush to change between them. Only star turns appeared once a night. Lionel was a star turn, even though he never appeared anywhere but here; he was just that good. But his assistant Suzie did double duty in the chorus behind a couple of the singing acts for a bit of extra money, so Lionel, being the good sport that he was, did the same as well.

Jack sat down on the stool propping the door open for

a bit of air, and rubbed the stump. It always hurt. He wasn't like some fellows, he never got the feeling he still had a leg and a foot there. He didn't know if that was bad or good. He did dream about having two legs again, sometimes . . . but except for the ache, and the difficulty in doing some things, he reckoned he wasn't that badly off. There were others that had lost two limbs or more. Or worse, come back half paralyzed. Or blind. At least he could hold down a job—a job he liked, moreover. Alderscroft in London had arranged it when he'd come back an invalid, through the secret network of Masters and magicians. It had taken time to arrange, virtually all of the time he was in the hospital recovering and learning to walk again, but hunting for a job on his own would have taken a lot longer.

The only other magician here was Lionel, so Jack wasn't entirely sure *how* the job had come about, only that the offer had turned up in the mail, inside an envelope with the address of Alderscroft's club on it. That had been about two months after the hospital had given him the boot and he was pensioned out. At that point, he'd jumped on it; he'd been staying with his sister, but they'd never been all that close as kids, and her husband had been giving him looks that suggested he was overstaying his welcome.

He'd expected that, of course. In a way, he'd been surprised it hadn't happened sooner. He was a lot older than this, his youngest sister, and he reckoned she had mostly offered to let him stay out of a feeling of obligation. He couldn't move in with his older sister, the one he was actually close to—she was living with their parents, in *their* tiny pensioners' cottage, and there wasn't room for a kitten in there, much less him. They weren't the only children, but all his other siblings were in service. He'd have been in service himself — he'd been a footman — if he hadn't joined the Army.

And of course, no one had any use for a one-legged footman.

Behind him, he could hear the orchestra in the pits, and the reaction of the audience. Out there past the door, if he strained his ears, he could hear the sounds of motorcars chugging past on the road beyond the alley and the vague hum of the city. The heat was keeping people out later than usual. Probably, between the excitement of being on holiday and the heat, they weren't able to sleep. Well, it was intolerable heat to them; having been in Africa, where you slept even if it felt like you were sleeping in an oven, it wasn't so bad to him. He knew all the tricks of getting yourself cool. Not a cold bath, but a hot one, so when you got out you were cooler than the air. Cold, wet cloths on your wrists and around your neck. Tricks like that.

But if it got hotter, and all his instincts as a Fire Magician told him it was going to, people would certainly die. They didn't know the tricks. They'd work in the midday heat, instead of changing their hours to wake before dawn, take midday naps, and then work as the air cooled in late afternoon. It was going to be bad, this summer. He'd have to see if he could do anything with his magic to mitigate things in the theater. At least, he and Lionel could get together and see what the two of them could do.

He'd have to be on high alert for fires in the theater too. In fact, when he'd been hired on, that seemed to have been the chief reason he'd been taken.

"Says here you have a sense for fire," the theater manager, old Barnaby Shen, had said, peering at the paper in his hand.

"Aye, sir. Maybe just a keen nose for a bit of smoke, but I'm never wrong, and I never miss one." All true of course, though it was the little salamander that told him, and not his nose. That had saved his life, his and his mates, more times than he cared to count in Africa. Knowing when a brush fire had been set against them, knowing where someone was camped because of their fire . . . even once, knowing when lightning had started a wildfire and the direction it was going in time to escape it.

He hadn't really even been a combatant, just a member of one of the details set to guarding the rail lines. The Boers rightly saw a way to be effective with relatively few men by sabotaging the rail system, hampering the British ability to move troops and resupply, and at the same time tying up a substantial number of Tommies by forcing the commanders to guard those lines.

It was a weary, thankless task, that. Kipling had got it right. *Few, forgotten and lonely where the empty metals shine. No, not combatants—only details guarding the line.* A handful of men to patrol miles of rail, never seeing anything but natives, and those but few and far between.

He'd cursed his luck, the luck that kept him out of real combat . . . until new orders had come down that made him grateful to be where he was.

They'd almost left him, the salamanders, when he'd first turned up in Africa, and the orders came to burn the Boer homes and take the women and children left behind to the camps. They hadn't left only because he'd escaped that duty right up until the moment he'd gotten injured, by getting assigned to patrol. But he'd heard about the camps from other men in the hospital. Camps where half the children starved to death, or died of dysentery, and the women didn't do much better. Fortunately—he supposed, if you could call losing a leg "fortunate"—he'd never had to either burn a home out, or drive the helpless into captivity. He hadn't even lost the leg to a man. It had been a stupid accident that got him, a fall and a broken ankle that went septic, far from medical help. When you were on the rail detail you were pretty far from help, and his commander reckoned it could wait until the weekly train came in. So he'd waited, in the poisonous African heat. By the time he had got that help, all that could be done was to cut the leg off just below the knee, but by that time he'd been so fevered he hadn't known or cared.

He was well out of it all at that point. He hadn't realized just what a horror this so-called "war" was when he'd joined the Army. Hadn't realized he'd be told to make war on women and children. Hadn't known he was going to war for the sake of a few greedy men, and diamonds, and gold.

Hadn't realized just how vile those men could be.

Hadn't realized that the leaders back home hadn't given a pin about the lives of the common soldiers they squandered. That he and his fellows were no more to them than single digits within a larger number on a marker they shoved about on a map.

He knew by the time he mustered out, though.

He was bitter about it, but he tried not to let the bitterness eat him up. There were plenty of things to be thankful for. That he'd never been forced to make war on the innocent. That he'd escaped the sickening horror of guarding the camps where his own country was murdering children by inches. He told himself that he had no blood directly on his hands, and no deaths on his conscience.

And he was grateful for this job that he had held since. The people here at the Palace were kind in their own ways. He had a *decent* job, one he liked, with people he liked. He had money for books, and the leisure to read them. If his magic wasn't strong, it was at least useful.

In the end, he had it better, so much better, than some of the other shattered shells of men that had come out of that war. Yes, he had a lot to be thankful for.

And when bitterness rose in him, when his stump ached too much, that was how he burned the bitterness out. The flame was not high, but it was clean and pure. And in the end, what more could a man ask for?

2

KATIE had been with the Smalls for a month now. The Travelers had supplied Katie with clothing. Walnut had stained her skin darker, and some concoction of Mary Small's had made her dark hair closer to black. She knew all the names of everyone in the clan at this point. Only Mary and her sons and one of the brides were pure Gitano, rather than mixed-blood—which probably accounted for the reason why Katie, with her mixed blood, was welcome among them.

Katie had settled into an emotional state she could only think of as exhausted wariness. Not wariness of the Smalls—the only time she felt safe was when they were all hidden away in some patch of forest and tending to their camp—but somewhere, deep inside, she was still certain that Dick was not only still looking for her, he was getting angrier the longer she was gone.

But from the Small wives—though they didn't talk much, Katie had been given a certain silent reassurance. Good men did not beat their wives. All of the Small wives were proud of their husbands, proud of the spotless condition of their *vardas,* proud of their swarms of children, but they were not in the least afraid of their husbands. There were things that a wife should not do—look at other men, nag, be dirty—but within days they seemed convinced, without Katie saying a word in her own defense, that Katie had never been guilty of these things. Therefore they accepted her, and their ranks parted to include her.

The four wives of the Small clan were Beth, Sally, Bessie, and Celia. All four were married to Mary's descendants. Celia was the lone Gitano among the girls, and the dancer. Her husband didn't much care for her dancing for the *gadjo,* although he understood it was needful, and was just as happy for Katie to take over that particular job for a little.

Celia was married to Joe, one of the two musicians. He played the guitar. The other musician, a fiddler, was Bert, married to Sally. Beth's husband was Robert, the father of Joe, and Bessie's was David, the father of Bert. That was the four married couples. There were six more unmarried men: two of them, Harry and Paul, were two more of Mary Small's sons, and the remaining four, Charlie, Fred, George, and Jack, were her eldest grandsons. And there was a swarm of children, great-grandchildren, that Katie still didn't know the names of.

The men—in fact, all of them—treated her with a little of the same deference and respect that they gave the matriarch; they seemed to accept that this "magic" that Mary Small claimed Katie had was as real as the sun on their faces, and at the moment, since they didn't ask anything of her except to dance and tend to Mary Small's needs, she wasn't inclined to argue with them. If that made her more welcome, all the better.

She learned the swaying, sinuous dances of her mother's folk from Celia, combined the movements with what she already knew, and performed in the firelit circle for the *gadjo* who came to gawk at the encampment, get their fortunes told by the other women, and buy old Mary's potions. As ever, learning dance and movement came as easily to her as breathing. She was already better at the Gitano dances than Celia was.

She never left the camps. Even if the men had not warned her that she would be harassed at best and molested at worst by the village men, she would not have left the camps. First of all, circus folks were just as likely to be harassed and molested if caught alone as Travelers, so she knew better than to go strolling about through a village, and secondly, the last thing she wanted was to somehow be spotted by someone who knew her. Her disguise wouldn't fool one of her fellow performers in the least. People who knew how to spot familiar features through greasepaint were not going to be fooled by a little stain.

For the first time since her parents died, she felt relatively safe. But only relatively. She couldn't continue with Mary Small's clan, and they all knew it. Winter would come eventually, and with her taking up the bunk, they were three places short of the number needed to sleep all of the unmarried men—for obviously they could not sleep in the same space as a strange, unmarried woman to whom they were not related. It was always possible that they would inadvertently cross paths with the circus, and the little troupe of Travelers could not possibly defend themselves against the mob of circus roustabouts Andy Ball would unleash on them. Worse, Dick would probably kill one or more of them, and the law would do nothing about it. She knew this. They knew this. This was only a respite until they got far enough away that it would be safe for Katie to buy a train ticket to somewhere further yet.

But where?

She decided to consult with old Mary one night before the matriarch went to sleep.

For the first time, she was invited into the cupboard built at the back of the wagon that held the big bed that had once slept Mary and her husband and whatever baby she was nursing. It had a curtain across the end to close it off from the rest of the wagon, like the curtain across her shelf-bed. Right now the curtain was open, and Mary was tucked, cross-legged, with her back to the wall. Katie sat on the edge of Mary's bed, on the faded quilt patiently patched out of the last bits and pieces of worn-out clothing, and waited as the Traveler pondered the question.

"You must make your own way," Mary said at last. Her old eyes were very bright as she regarded Katie shrewdly. "Yet your gifts are . . . not common. You could not work in a shop, or serve in a pub. While this could be a problem, it can also be of benefit. Uncommon gifts are sometimes in demand. But at the same time, you are no great dancer. You are very good, but I have seen great." She nodded wisely, and Katie had to nod in return, if she were to examine herself honestly. Her heart sank. What was she to do? Where was she to go? Not another circus, certainly! Andy Ball would find out immediately if she joined another circus.

But Mary was continuing. "You need a place where the circus will not go, because there is so much else there to entertain crowds that they will make a poor showing. Yet you need a place where there are *small* entertainments, where you might find a place." She pondered again. "Brighton," she said at last, with an air of finality.

"Why Brighton?" Katie asked, quizzically. It was true that the circus had never gone there. *"Too much bloody competition,"* Andy had grumbled.

"It is a seaside resort. Many small theaters. Many places like sideshow booths. Many opportunities for you. Surely one of them will take you. It is a place where you can even perform in the street, as we do, sometimes. For that you would need only yourself and a cloth for people to throw money." Mary made the pronouncement as if it was already an accomplished fact, and really, Katie wasn't inclined to argue with her. Her logic was sound.

The walnut stain had already faded from her hands and face; the next day, under Mary's instruction, Katie turned and mended her clothing until it not only looked respectable, but she probably could not be told apart (on the train at least) from a little country housemaid going on a well-earned trip to her family.

The next town held a train station, with the line going straight to Brighton. To the Travelers, the signs could not have been clearer. Katie was meant to go to Brighton. And then they left her at dawn on the platform of the station with only the briefest of farewells.

When the ticket-booth opened, she bought her one-way

ticket to Brighton. The stationmaster in his official blue uniform seemed incurious, even though she wasn't a native of this village and he certainly must have wondered where she had sprung from. But she sat quietly on the platform, holding the bundle that contained all her worldly possessions and the provisions the Travelers had wrapped up in carefully saved butcher-paper for her, and that seemed to be enough for him to leave her to her own devices.

In all her life, she had never been on a train. All the traveling that the circus had done had been under its own power; the horses that pulled the circus wagons and the living-wagons did double duty, helping to erect and take down the circus and performing in the acts. She was a little nervous, and kept one eye on the station clock. Three trains arrived and departed before hers pulled into the station, and at least the stationmaster took the time to leave his post and gesture at her to let her know for certain it was hers. She went all the way to the rear, scuttling along as fast as she could, until she came to the third-class carriages. They were very old, and the windows had been put all the way down, but as warm as it had been, that was not exactly looming large as a defect in Katie's mind.

She took the first open door and the first empty seat, squeezing herself into the corner next to the window so as to make the most room for anyone else who might come along at the next station. There were only a few other people in the carriage, and all of them seemed to be dozing. None were in her compartment. At the very back she could just see what appeared to be an entire family arranged along the back bench. She was barely in place when the conductor came along, closing all the doors with a *bang,* and the train started again.

She quickly came to the conclusion that, on the whole, she preferred riding in or on the front bench of a wagon.

Although the countryside sped by at a rate that was alarming to someone who was used to plodding horses that could not be urged to a speed faster than an amble, the entire carriage shook, rattled, and swayed on the rails. The hard wooden bench on which she sat was no worse than the driving bench on a wagon, but it vibrated under her, and every shock to the carriage was transmitted in a most unforgiving way to the bench.

This was not an express. That fact had been made very clear to her when she purchased her ticket. Expresses were more expensive. So they had not been underway for very long—not nearly long enough for Katie to get used to the speed—before they began to slow again and pulled into another station.

More people got in this time. Katie was alarmed when some stocky young men looked into her compartment, but two older women who might have been their mothers took one look at her and hustled them along to another. To Katie's relief, it was a trio of old women and a younger one with a baby that got in, ranging themselves along the bench. They proceeded to talk among themselves, a conversation that sounded as if it had been resumed from one begun as they had waited, all about pregnancies and births and weddings. With them sitting bulwark between her and any strange men, Katie allowed herself to relax.

Stop after stop punctuated the morning. Katie discovered by dint of listening and careful observation that the door in the middle of the blank wall led to a lavatory, and she was glad to make use of it, finding it a far cry from the primitive privies set up at the circus. It seemed the height of luxury to her; she recognized how to use it from reading magazine advertisements for such things. She wondered what it would be like to have such a little room right in your own home, with, perhaps, a bathtub that wasn't made of canvas and didn't have to be set up outdoors! She was tempted to linger, running her hand along the cool, clean, white porcelain of the wash basin, admiring how water came from the tap . . . but there might be someone out there waiting, and she didn't want to draw attention to herself.

She did thrill in washing her hands and face not just once, but twice, before she left.

As the hour neared noon, each time the train stopped, she began to notice people hawking food and drink at the windows of each car. She gazed wistfully at the bottles of lemonade and burdock, but contented herself with a paper cup of water to drink with her bread and cheese. She kept her eyes on her own food as the party around her bought ham sandwiches and lemonades and chattered on, oblivious to her presence. Or, perhaps, politely ignoring her, so she wouldn't feel her poverty too much.

If the latter, well . . . that was kind of them.

It was early evening before the train pulled into Brighton at last. She had gathered up her bundle and was about to leave the compartment, when one of the old women that had shared it with her turned back.

"Go here, ducky," she said, with a kindly smile, pressing a little rectangle of cardboard into Katie's hands. "Not to worry, it's safe as houses." Then she rejoined her party, as Katie paused to look at the little printed card.

Mrs. Brown's Boarding House for Working Girls, it

said, and listed the rates. Katie stepped down out of the carriage and onto the platform with a sinking heart. If this was how much it would cost to live here . . . her scant supply of money would not last three days.

One of the sylphs was hovering just over Lionel's mirror. She looked like an Art Nouveau illustration, with her butterfly wings and her flowing hair and garment—such as it was—and she made Lionel smile a little. The sylphs came and went as they chose for the most part, only in the most extreme and emotional of occasions could a mere Elemental Magician actually *summon* one. But they liked Lionel, and they were positively addicted to performing and being onstage. In fact, he often had more of them volunteering to help than he actually needed! Not that he ever turned them down. It made more sense to take them all and let them sort themselves out than it did to turn some down and risk that they would never turn up again.

"You look sad, magician," the creature whispered, curving her head on its long neck down to regard him solemnly.

"Well . . . I'm in a bit of difficulty," he confessed. Carefully, in simple terms, he explained that Suzie was leaving, as the other girls had left him, and that he had not found someone to replace her.

Not that his advertisements hadn't brought answers—but all of the girls that had turned up were utterly unsuitable. One had turned up this morning, in fact, with the torn-out advertisement in her hand. Even though she had only credentials as a dancer from the chorus of a review, in desperation, he had tried her out anyway, only to discover that there was no way she was going to fit inside the apparatus. She just wasn't flexible enough in the right places.

The sylph teased up the scrap of paper from where it had been left on the corner of his dressing table. Lionel was so dispirited he didn't even object—not even when she whirled it around like an autumn leaf and then whisked out the window with it. Let the creature play with her toy; he'd learned he got better results from his sylphs when he indulged them. And it wasn't as if he needed a torn-out copy of his own advertisement.

With a sigh, he went back to cleaning and arranging the things on his table, a little ritual he liked to go through before he got ready for the performance. Some people sang little songs, some people tied a lucky charm somewhere about their person. Some played over a hand of solitaire. He liked to make his dressing table mathematically precise and neat as a good housewife's.

As he did so, he wondered why the sylph had been so intrigued with the bit of paper in the first place.

Katie had been wandering the seaside streets of Brighton for more than an hour, feeling entirely dazed. It was true that there was a dazzling array of entertainments here—*too* dazzling, really. It seemed that every time you turned, there was someone else clamoring for your money. And to Katie's weary eyes and increasingly depressed heart, they all seemed far more sophisticated than anything she had done in the circus.

Certainly they were all dressed better than the shabby

little gauze costume and tights she had in her bundle of belongings. How could plain white gauze, which looked fine and bright in the light of the circus tent, compete with spangles and glitter, artificial jewels and tinsel? It seemed impossible that she would make any money at all, displaying her tricks by herself out on the Boardwalk. She didn't think she could dance out here either, although the Gitano dances she had learned might have done well; she needed music to dance to.

It seemed equally impossible that she would find a job among the dancers she saw here. They all had dance routines that were nothing like the circus ballet performed. All bounces and kicks and tossing of petticoats—she could probably *learn* such things quickly, but these people wouldn't want someone who needed to learn, they would want someone who already had mastered such steps.

She turned a corner to find herself staring at the back of a huge, muscled man—and froze in panic for a moment. *He's found me! He tracked me here and he found me!* she thought, before the man turned around—and it wasn't Dick at all. It *was* someone who was almost certainly a strongman in a show, but he had a sweet face, with puppy-like eyes. She flattened herself against the wall of the building anyway as he passed, her bundle clutched to her chest, and felt too limp to move for many minutes when he had gone.

It was going to be suppertime soon, as her stomach reminded her. She wondered where she could possibly find the cheapest food here. Concern knotted her stomach as much as hunger. *Maybe if I followed some of the performers—*

Her thoughts were interrupted by a scrap of paper—

It caught her eye as it danced toward her like a butterfly, and then suddenly lodged itself in the cleavage of her gown. Annoyed, she fished it out and was about to throw it away, when she realized it was an advertisement torn from a newspaper. Curious now, she read it, excitement growing with every word.

Wanted: Female Dancer or Acrobat. Position open as assistant to stage magician. Must be slender, limber, and fearless, prepared to work hard, eager to learn. Apply to Lionel Hawkins, Palace Music Hall.

She could hardly believe it. This seemed like a miracle—too good to be true—

But what did she have to lose by answering it? The worst that would happen would be that the position had been filled, and she could ask at the music hall about cheap lodgings and food. At least she knew there *was* an opening, or had been when this advertisement had been torn from the paper!

Bit of newsprint clutched in her hand, she slipped in among the crowds, looking for someone who could direct her to the theater, hope rising in her that Mary Small might have sent her to the right place after all.

The girl in the alley caught Jack's attention mostly because she wasn't the usual sort to be lingering at a stage door. She was small, lithe, and dark—Gypsy, he'd have said, or part-Gypsy. She was dressed neatly, and was very clean, but her clothing had seen a lot of use and wear. She peered at the open door with a hesitant look on her face, and he stumped out to where she could see him.

"Something I can do for you, miss?" he called. He half

expected her to bolt, but instead, she looked a little relieved, and hurried toward him.

"I was told to come to this door—" she said, holding out a scrap of newspaper. "—there is a position open?"

He recognized it at a glance for what it was—Lionel's advertisement. When he looked back up at her, her little face shaded with hunger and apprehension, she continued. "I am a dancer and an acrobat," she said, in a hushed voice with an inflection of doubt, as if she was afraid he wouldn't believe her.

But he hadn't been the doorman of this theater this long without knowing how to judge who was a performer and who was not.

"The show's on now," he said, in as kindly a voice as he could manage. "But the position is still open, and it's getting a bit urgent to fill it. Here—" he handed her a ticket for the gallery. "Why don't you run along to the front, watch the show and rest your feet, and come back here after? I'll make sure Lionel sees you, and you'll make a better impression if you're rested."

For a moment he thought that she might take that as rejection, but after a moment of hesitation, she accepted the ticket and squared her shoulders. "Thank you," she said. "I will come after the show."

And with that she turned and went back into the oven-hot alley.

For one moment, seeing the doorman in his respectable suit, Katie had been tempted to flee. But then she had seen that his eyes were kind, but pain-shadowed, and that he had only the one leg, and felt a stirring of pity for him.

He hadn't been haughty with her either, and took her statement for what she was at face value. When he offered her the ticket, though, she almost refused. She was getting quite hungry now, and she would gladly have traded that ticket for a penny bun—

But she didn't know where to get one here. And at least she would be able to sit down and rest.

And . . . she had never actually *been* in a theater before.

She thanked him, and went around to the front, presenting her ticket at the booth. Already she was feeling very much out of her depth. She was not used to buildings this tall, and they were all around her, towering over her like mountains. The Andy Ball Circus confined itself to entertaining villages and small towns; the tallest building she had ever seen, an old Tudor inn of the sort built in a square around a courtyard, was only two stories tall. This theater was four!

Once inside, she wasn't allowed to linger in the lobby, but ushers directed her to a set of stairs, and then up and up to the highest floor. She came out at the back of the top gallery, a full four stories above the stage, where she gasped and put her back tight to the wall. It was so high she felt dizzy for a moment, the bright lights on the stage dazzled her, and it seemed too warm and stuffy. She was afraid to move for a moment, until the usher, getting impatient, hissed at her to "just sit anywhere."

Moving gingerly, she shuffled sideways along the wall until she came to the corner. She could see that the chair in front of her was empty, so she groped for the back of it, and took it.

Only then did she really look at the stage, and felt

dizziness come over her again. She had never, in all of her life, been so far from the ground.

It took her a good three acts to recover, as she clutched her bundle on her lap and peered shakily at the performers below her.

It was the acrobats, and the dancers that followed them, that finally shook her out of her nerves. The acrobats were not as good as she was—the dancers were doing the same bouncy-kick, skirt-tossing routines as she had seen out on the Boardwalk, but when you managed to look past the tinsel and glitter, their costumes were a bit . . . tat. They certainly wouldn't bear close inspection—unlike those of the boardwalk dancers, who looked gaudy, these costumes seemed nearly worn out. And when she watched more closely—well, as "close" as this lofty perch allowed—she could see the little tricks both the dancers and acrobats were using to make it look as if they weren't taking shortcuts. If this was what the magician was looking for, well . . . she could do this! She could do better than this!

She relaxed a bit after that, though the smell of food and beer from the tables down on the main floor made her hungrier. Next, there was a man who appeared to be drunk, and his antics on stage made even her laugh, and then the curtain opened on the magician himself.

He was *nothing* like that. Not the least bit shabby. In fact, he was a little terrifying. If she hadn't known his Christian name, and been well acquainted with stage makeup, she'd have been perfectly ready to believe he was a genuine Turk. He looked powerful and fierce and quite prepared to cut his pretty assistant into any number of bits on the least provocation.

And he did just that—he seemingly ran swords into her, sawed her in half, chopped her into six pieces, sent her from one cabinet to another across the stage, and finally, made her climb a rope he managed to levitate right up into the air, from which precarious position she waved at the crowd and vanished from full view, leaving the Turk to roar with impotent anger and rush off stage, presumably to search for her. It was quite the performance. Katie was captivated. But part of her had been paying attention to every little move that the assistant had made, and she had no doubt, no doubt at all, that she could duplicate what the other girl had done.

Then came a lady dressed up as a man who sang some sentimental ballads, and the dancers came on again, then two performing dogs, a lady comic singer, a dancing couple, a clown, the dancers, and finally a man who led the entire theater in singing popular songs, then everyone came out, took bows, and the curtain came down. Katie waited for everyone to clear out of the gallery so she wouldn't attract anyone's notice by pushing in among them; as she stood, once again with her back to the wall, she realized once the magician had come on, she had quite forgotten that she was hungry. Now her stomach contracted painfully.

Well, she had gone without food for longer than this before. There had been times, before her family joined the circus, that had been quite lean indeed, and those suppers gleaned from the woods had been all that stood between them and starvation. Sternly, she told her stomach to behave itself, and edged along the wall to the exit.

She made her way carefully and quietly down the stairs, trying to keep from drawing attention to herself. It wasn't hard; the people leaving were all happy, having had a grand time, and some were even singing scraps of the songs that the last performer had led them in.

It had been near sunset when she first entered the theater; now it was full dark. The lobby was brightly lit with gas lamps, but outside the doors, there was nothing but dark and shadows. She got outside, waited a little more for the crowd to thin, then hurried back down the street to what she had been told was the "stage door." She was a little nervous about entering a dark alley all alone, but as she turned the corner, she realized she need not have been. There was a bright gas light at the stage door, and the alley itself was actually crowded; a laughing group of women was just leaving, all in a surge of skirts and feathered hats, and it appeared there had been at least one young man—sometimes two or three— waiting for each of them. She flattened herself against the wall of the theater to let them pass, and made her way toward the door, where the one-legged man was waiting, peering anxiously into the darkness.

His face cleared when he saw her, and he smiled. "Ah, well done! I was afraid you might have had second thoughts about the job. Lionel is fearfully anxious to audition you, would you feel prepared to perform for him right now?"

Her heart jumped with nervous elation. But although before she had seen the performers here, she might have wondered *why* he was anxious to audition her, now she had no trouble imagining the reason. If the common sort of dancer in this hall was all he'd had to choose from, it was no sort of choice at all. There was no place in this man's act for someone who didn't put out full effort,

every time. Or who tried to cheat her way through a pe
formance. "Of—of course," she stammered, and he stoo
aside for her as she climbed the steps and entered a ver
tall, but incredibly narrow corridor. A young, blond lac
in a neat green walking dress with matching hat was ju
approaching them, and the one-legged man hailed he
with relief.

"Suzie! This is the dancer who wants to audition fo
Lionel. Would—"

The young lady didn't even let him finish what he wa
about to say. "The girl that wants to try out for assistant
Golly, that's a bit of all right, you turning up before I lef
Come on, ducky, I'll take you right to the boss!" Sh
seized Katie's elbow, even though there was scarce
enough room for one person in the corridor, much le
two. "I'll get you to the stage—oh wait, would you hav
a bit of a costume with you? That'll make it all easie
than trying out in street clothes."

"Y-ye—" Katie hadn't even gotten the whole wor
out before Suzie was hauling her off like a mother wit
a toddler in tow, chattering the whole time. She poppe
Katie into a room crammed with dressing tables, mirro
and hanging costumes, waited while she slipped into he
gauze skirt, mended tights, and tight bodice, took posses
sion of her clothing and bundle, and chivvied her ou
further along the corridor, and finally, before she wa
quite ready, out onto a bare stage with a couple of brigl
footlights shining up on it.

There was the magician, half in, half out of hi
costume—without the turban, or the huge, fierce mou
tache, and with the greasepaint wiped off, but still in th
voluminous crimson pants and wide blue satin sas

"Here's the little dancer, Lionel!" Suzie called cheerfully, as the magician turned to see who had intruded. "Hire her quick so I can get married!"

The magician snorted good-naturedly, and turned to Katie. "All right then, my dear," he said in a kind voice that reminded her oddly of her father. "I can see by your costume you're no stranger to performing. What is it you do?"

"I'm an acrobat, m-mostly," she stammered, and before he could command her to do anything—or she lost her nerve—she went through one of the shorter routines she did for the circus, a combination of tumbling and contortion, with a little dance thrown in for good measure. She had not realized that there was a pianist still in the orchestra pit until a few notes started right after she did; the man was good, he picked up the rhythm of her performance immediately, and ended when she did, with a flourish as she pirouetted.

"Well!" Suzie said, admiration in her voice. "I'm off! I can't wait to tell—"

"Not so fast," the magician said. "Go wheel out the sword-basket, you little minx."

With a laugh, Suzie went offstage, and returned pushing the basket in which she had been impaled with swords on its wheeled pedestal before her.

"Now this is how it works," Lionel said, leading her over to it by the hand. "You get in here." He gestured to the giant basket, as Suzie helpfully pushed a little stair up to it. He led her up the stair by the hand, and she stepped into the basket. Having seen the act, she dropped down inside. Lionel leaned over and whispered to her. "Some of the swords have collapsible blades. Some you can just avoid. See the slots for them?"

When she looked at the inside of the basket from where she crouched inside, she saw that, rather than being a real basket made of coiled rope, it was a cunning imitation of one, made of much sturdier material that had pre-made slots for the swords in it. "I'm going to go very slowly so you can get your skirt out of the way," he whispered in further explanation. "I don't want to ruin it for you. As limber as you are, you should have no trouble with this. Ready?"

She wasn't, but she nodded. He popped the top of the basket on. In the next moment, she heard him utter the fearful roar that the "Turk" had given as he ran a great sword through the basket.

But true to his promise, the sword was inserted slowly, and she had no trouble avoiding it. She realized in the next moment *why* he uttered that roar each time he drove in a blade—it told her *where* the sword was coming from. And he was right—it would certainly take a *very* limber girl to fit in the spaces among the blades, but it wasn't that difficult for her.

"I say, Lionel, I rather like you doing it slowly like that," said the pianist from the pit, as he played. "It looks ever so much more menacing."

The swords were withdrawn, the top of the basket taken off, and she popped up, breathless and flushing. Without warning her, Lionel's hands encircled her waist and he lifted her out and put her on the floor. "And light as a feather," the magician said, approvingly. "Tell your lad you're posting the banns, Suzie." He grinned at Katie. "You may consider yourself hired, my dear—ah—what *is* your name?"

3

"K-KATIE," she stammered. "Katie Langford. I—"

But he had plunged his hand into that sash and come out with a pocketbook, from which he was extracting some pound notes. "You'll be needing lodgings of course, so we'll just advance you your first week's pay." He shoved them into her hands before she could blink. "There you go! Now, Suzie—"

Suzie rolled her eyes. "Yes, yes, all right, I'll see she's put up. And fed, *I'm* starving and she must be too." The girl took possession of Katie's elbow. "Come on, ducks, let's get you respectable again, and it's off to the boarding house."

"But—" Katie said feebly. Suzie ignored her, and towed her back off to the little dressing room. It was like being in the circus again, back when her parents were still alive and Katie had been allowed to change with the rest of the circus dancers and acrobats. Suzie had the bodice undone in a trice, was pulling off her gauze skirt while she was doing up her corset, and between them they had her tidy in half the time it usually took her to dress. "You're the size my sister used to be," Suzie said, as she gently shoved Katie ahead of her, down the now-mostly-deserted hall to the stage door. "I have an entire trunk of her things in my room I've been dying to be rid of."

"But—won't she want them back?" Katie asked, now completely bedazzled by the swift turn of events.

"She got pregnant and too plump to wear them, and besides, she's a farm wife now and she's got no use for 'em. Coo! That gives me a capital idea!" Suzie went on. "You can share my room till I move out of it! That will give me plenty of time to coach you!" She waved at the doorman. "Jack! This is Katie Langford, and she's hired. As soon as she has the routine I'll be off with my boy, so don't let anyone take advantage of her!"

The doorman pulled the brim of his hat. "Wouldn't think of it, Suzie. Welcome, Katie. Rehearsal is at ten."

Suzie gave Katie no chance whatsoever to reply. Down the street they went, but not very far, not nearly as far as Katie would have thought. They cut down an alley to a quiet cul-de-sac, and it was obvious what their goal was: the only building in the circle that was still brightly lit up. There was a sign above the front door: *Mrs. Baird's Theatrical Lodgings For Ladies.*

"Boarding house," Suzie explained, tugging on Katie's arm when she hesitated, pulling her up the stairs to the door. "It's cramped-small, but lovely. Four shillings six a week, breakfast and supper included. Come on, I have a lovely room."

There was a heavenly smell wafting down the passage, but Suzie urged her up a narrow stair, past two landings, and unlocked a door on the third.

Maybe Suzie thought her room was cramped for space, but by the standards of someone who had lived most of her life in a caravan it was impossibly spacious. There were two narrow little beds, a wardrobe, a tiny dressing table, a chest at the foot of each bed, and one at the window. One of the beds was covered in odds and ends; Suzie cleared it swiftly and dropped Katie's bundle on it, then hurried her downstairs again.

This time they followed the passage to the back where there was a room containing a single enormous table with women and girls crammed all around it and a woman presiding at the end—

A woman that, had Katie not been circus folk, would have caused her to stare and stare, because she had a beard that would have done any man proud, and every inch of skin that could be seen was heavily tattooed.

The company was chattering at the tops of its lungs. Suzie had to shout to be heard over them. "Mrs. Baird! This is Katie! She's taking my place at the Palace! She'll be having my room in a week or so!"

The bearded visage nodded. "That's all right then!" Mrs. Baird shouted back. "Four shillings six a week! Breakfast and supper, and we have supper late, after closing! We'll settle up in the morning!"

"See, I told you, all settled," said Suzie, who nudged at the end girl on the bench nearest her, who obligingly squeezed over enough to give them both room. There were plates in a stack at their end of the table, and cutlery and cups. Suzie passed what was needed to Katie, took some for herself, then dished out soup from a big tureen in the center of the table while someone passed Katie a basket of thickly-sliced brown bread and a dish of butter. Someone else filled a mug of tea and handed it to her.

After that, Katie didn't think of anything except the food in front of her. No one seemed to be counting how many slices of bread she took, nor how many times anyone refilled her bowl of soup. Not that she was greedy, nor that she stuffed herself, but it was lovely to be able to eat your fill when you were hungry, and leave the table feeling sated.

Girls left the table and more girls replaced them. Katie watched and saw that it was the done thing to take your dirty dishes with you. She and Suzie took theirs and left them with a cheerful little red-faced maid in an apron three times too big for her who was washing away with all her might.

"This way," Suzie said, tugging at her when she turned to go back to the front of the house and the stairs. "You'll want to wash up every night when you come home. You can't get all the greasepaint off at the theater, and Mrs. Baird likes her linens to be nice."

And sure enough, Suzie pulled her to the room of Katie's dreams, a room with a row of deep washbasins, and three big bathtubs along one wall, all fed by pipes like Katie had seen in the loo in the train. Without being prompted, Katie stripped herself almost half nude and gave herself a good wash in one of the basins, while Suzie did the same.

"Usually I take the time to go upstairs, put on a dressing gown, and come down here for a *good* wash-up," Suzie said, as they went in single file up the stair. "But it's awfully late and you look knackered."

"I am, a bit," Katie confessed. "It was a long day, and I didn't think I'd see a job at the end of it." She gazed in wonder at the two pound notes clutched in her hand.

"I'll show you where to get a decent bite at lunch, not that nasty, greasy pub food. Breakfast here is always the same, oatmeal and toast and fruit." Suzie sighed dramatically. "Mrs. Baird is Scottish, you see, and you cannot convince her that breakfast should be anything else." She opened the door. "Have you a nightgown?"

Katie blushed. "That's almost all I have besides my costume," she admitted, shamefacedly.

"Well, no worries about *that*. My sister, I swear, spent every spare penny on clothing, and now she can't wear any of it!" Suzie chuckled, and shut the door just as two more girls came trudging up the stairs, chattering like sparrows. She flung open the window, and along with the breeze came the distant sounds of celebration. That was all right; Katie had learned to sleep through the sounds of celebration while still in her cradle.

This must have been a bed for a child, it was so small; that was why two of them fit in the room. But she and Suzie were both small, and fit the beds neatly.

She slipped out of her clothing and into her threadbare nightgown, and then tumbled into the bed. She didn't even hear Suzie get into hers.

She had expected she would wake before Suzie did—she *always* woke up at the crack of dawn, long before Dick, in order to get out of the caravan before he woke. Fortunately she didn't have to cook for him, for all the circus people ate together in common, and Andy Ball took the cost of it out of their wages.

But she didn't wake before Suzie did; in fact, it was Suzie who woke her, humming to herself as she unpacked the trunk at the window.

She raised herself up on her elbow and stared as Suzie held up a skirt. "These will all fit you," Suzie said, glancing over her shoulder. "And a good thing, too. Much longer and they'd be so old fashioned that people would stare at you like some sort of Guy."

"I can't—" Katie began. "I mean, you don't even *know* me. Why are you being so kind to me?"

Suzie turned and sat abruptly down on the side of the bed, and took Katie's hand in hers. "Because, ducks, once upon a time, two starving girls who had just lost their mum and da got taken in by a bearded lady, and taught how to do some dance steps, and were gotten jobs down on the Boardwalk."

"Mrs. Baird?" Katie asked, incredulously.

Suzie nodded and let go of Katie's hand. "Besides, Lionel hired you right on the spot, and I have never, *ever*, known Lionel and Jack to be wrong about a person. So! Let's pick out a gown for you that you're not going to die of heat in, go down and make things straight with Mrs. Baird, and have breakfast. Then it's off to the theater."

The gown was clearly not new, but Suzie's sister had taken good care of her clothing; it was oyster-colored linen trimmed with blue piping, very neat and a little nautical. Suzie chose a biscuit-colored skirt and shirtwaist, and the two of them helped each other with their corsets. Katie felt quite different, wearing something like this, a gown she would never have chosen for herself. Almost as if she was entirely another person.

Mrs. Baird, attired in a crisp linen shirtwaist and walking skirt, was sitting in her office, her ledgers spread out before her, her beard neatly arrayed over her chest. It looked like a lustrous skein of brown silk. She smiled when they came in, accepted Katie's pound note, and counted out the proper change; Katie ran upstairs to put most of it away safe, then knotted the sixpence into a corner of her handkerchief and put the latter safely in a petticoat pocket.

Then she ran back downstairs and they went in to breakfast, which was, as Suzie had promised, oatmeal and toast. But there was plenty of both, and there were fresh strawberries for the oatmeal and marmalade for the toast, and anyway, it was much the same as the circus breakfast except that Mrs. Baird's oatmeal wasn't burnt on the bottom. Mrs. Baird didn't stint on the tea, nor boil it till it was bitter and nasty, nor serve leaves steeped so often the "tea" was barely colored water. She wasn't stingy about the sugar and milk, either. Katie was getting the sense that she was going to get good value for her boarding money.

The table was not quite as crowded this morning as it had been last night, but girls and young women kept trailing in one and two at a time. As soon as she and Suzie were done, they took their dishes back to the kitchen, where a different, slightly older, but equally cheerful girl was washing away mightily.

After that, they went out into the streets, and in a few moments were at the theater. Katie could see she would have no difficulty remembering the way back; it really was supernaturally convenient. Her head was spinning as she contemplated her luck. How easy it would have been to get into a place where the landlady was abusive, or worse, a pander! It was almost as if some good spirit had been guiding her from the time she arrived in Brighton. The doorman was already on duty, and smiled at them both, touching the brim of his hat to them.

He looked as if he had been a very handsome man before pain and grief had etched lines in his face, making him look older than he was. *I wonder how he lost his leg?* Katie took care to smile back at him. From his bearing, she guessed that he must have been a soldier. She knew, vaguely, that there was a war going on . . . in Africa? Had that been where he'd been hurt?

The theater felt emptier this morning, probably because the acts that knew their parts in their sleep didn't feel the need to turn up to rehearse this early. The corridor was *still* quite dark, and a bit claustrophobic for someone who was used to the vast expanses underneath circus canvas.

"Let's go to wardrobe and see if we can't find something in the Aladdin panto costumes that you can use for now," Suzie said, as they threaded their way past the dressing room. "Here—"

She paused, and there was a set of stairs, just off the corridor, that Katie hadn't realized was there. They weren't regular stairs, not wooden stairs with landings; they were made of iron and wound in a tight spiral, taking up very little space. Down they went, ending in a corridor that was a good bit wider than the one above it, and then left, and into a room filled with costumes on racks, and lit by a long line of somewhat dirty windows up near the ceiling, where a sewing machine was clatter-ing away, vigorously pumped by a middle-aged woman in a neat little bonnet.

"Mrs. Littleton!" Suzie called, and the clattering stopped as the woman looked up. "This is the new girl that's taking my place. Lionel wants to order a costume for the Turk number for her from you, but until you fin-ish it, is there something in the panto costumes she can use? She fits my sister's old things a treat."

The costume mistress looked Katie up and down. "I should think so," she said. "Wait here."

She vanished into the forest of racked costumes and returned with something bundled in her arms. All that Katie could tell was that it came with a pair of volumi-nous pantaloons. "This is one of the Sultan's page boy outfits. It will do," Mrs. Littleton said, thrusting the outfit at Suzie. "Make sure it comes back without any damage. Watch them swords and other nasty things. Now, hold still." Before Katie could move, the woman had whisked the tape measure from around her neck and was measur-ing her at all points, writing the measurements down in a little leather-bound book she pulled out of a pocket of her apron. "What's your name, gel?"

"Katie?" Katie replied hesitantly.

"Right then. It'll be a week, them Eye-talian acrobats paid me to do them all new suits, and they come first. Tell Lionel I'll finish this new slave-girl frock in a week, and he's to pay me right away, and after that if nothing urgent comes up, I'll do up all the others he'll need for her be-fore he's done with the Turk season."

And with that, she sat back down at her machine and went back to sewing. Clearly, they had been dismissed.

They both went out of the wardrobe room, pausing to let a stagehand go past with a piece of scenery—which explained why the corridors were wider here, if things were stored on this floor.

Suzie handed over the costume to Katie, who took it reflexively, and the two of them went back up the stairs and to the dressing room. "Here," Suzie said, sitting Katie down at one of the tables. "This is mine, and you might as well have it. We can share until you're trained and I can leave." She showed Katie where and what all the makeup was; Katie already knew more than enough about the matter to know what to do with it, and said as much. "I worked in a circus—" she began, and Suzie laughed.

"Well, as long as you weren't a clown, then you should be all right."

Then they got Suzie into enough of her costume for a rehearsal, and Katie into the page boy outfit, which consisted of a pair of red bloomers and a billowy yellow blouse with a red vest all embroidered with spangles that snugged tight around her chest with front lacings. Like most acrobats she was . . . rather flat. When she looked at herself in the mirror, with her hair up, she *did* look a good bit like a page boy. Certainly not like pretty Suzie, in her slave girl finery . . .

"There, that looks good enough," Suzie said.

"Is this going to be all right?" she asked, doubtfully. "I look like a boy."

Suzie laughed. "Lionel is more than good enough that he doesn't need a pretty assistant to distract the eye," she said proudly. "A page boy will do as well as I will. Come on then—Lionel will be waiting, I can promise you. He goes to rehearsals more than a preacher goes to church."

Katie followed her mentor back into the cramped corridor, and from there to the stage, and sure enough, there was the magician, in ordinary clothing with his shirtsleeves rolled up, fussing with the sword-basket.

Lionel had been utterly astonished to see one of Jack's salamanders riding along on the would-be assistant's shoulders when she had turned up to audition. And within moments, it was quite obvious that *she* was utterly oblivious to its presence.

It seemed that the fates or the Elementals had decided to dump an entire barrel of good fortune on him at once. The girl moved easily and freely, she was small and lithe, and—

Well, that certainly explained why Jack had been so eloquent in his insistence that Lionel run his eyes over this new applicant immediately. He'd even stumped his way up to Lionel's dressing room to insist on it, though Lionel had (as usual) had people hanging about, and Jack had not been able to be specific about why he was so anxious. There was no doubt, whatsoever, that if there was *any* chance she was suitable, he should take her on no matter how long it took her to take to the act. An unawakened Fire Magician was certainly not going to turn up at the stage door every day.

He was delighted to see she was clearly a dancer—her costume told him that. Typical little gauze skirt and bodice, useful for a thousand roles, depending on what you decorated it with. Not only was it fitted to her, personally, it was far too worn for her to be anything but a dancer with plenty of experience. Her little routine was quite good—to be honest she was better than every other dancer currently working here at the Palace, although she was not going to set the world on fire at the Paris Opera Ballet. He was even more delighted when she performed some acrobatics and contortion. She was better than those blasted Italians, and he had been getting so desperate he had been thinking strongly of recruiting one of them, though he preferred female assistants.

She was smart, willing, and flexible—and quite desperate for a job, desperate enough to jump right into the sword-basket and let him run the trick on her without a moment of hesitation. By the time she was done, he was convinced, and hired her on the spot. Certain that her desperation for a job indicated an empty pocketbook, he advanced her the first week's salary. He was not going to chance losing her because she was picked up for vagrancy, or have her fainting at a performance from hunger. The salamander, who had been watching the entire time, flicked its tongue out with satisfaction, spun around in a circle, and vanished.

After Suzie and his new assistant had left the stage, Lionel shoved his props back into their proper places and headed for his dressing room. He wanted to talk to Jack—badly. But before he did, he needed to get out of the Turk rig.

As usual, as if the universe was conspiring against him, there were half a dozen people who just *had* to see him after the performance. When he finally dispensed with them—including the agent who was frantic to sign him, and could not understand why he didn't *want* a season at the Hippodrome in London—the theater was nearly empty except for the cleaners.

Jack must have known that Lionel would want to talk, however, for the doorman was waiting patiently for him, though he had donned his hat and coat.

"You are coming back with me for supper, old lad, and nothing you can say will change my mind," Lionel announced as he approached.

Jack smiled crookedly. "I rather thought as much. Don't go charging ahead as you usually do. I'm too tired to keep up with you tonight."

Lionel nodded, and they left together, Jack pausing to lock the stage door behind himself and turn off the gas lamp.

They said nothing as they walked, slowly, to Lionel's little house, with Jack's wooden leg making an odd thump on the cobbles as they walked. It was near enough that Lionel never took a cab unless the weather was utterly foul. Jack's flat wasn't that much farther off, by intention; he'd looked for a place close to Lionel's as soon as he'd been hired at the music hall. Only Earth Mages tended to be recluses. Other Elemental Magicians preferred to be reasonably close to one another—there was safety in numbers, and when darkness came calling, it was good to have your allies within shouting distance. Lionel made sure to dine with his friend at least once a week, sometimes—usually in winter—more often. Fire Mages used up more energy than Air, and he wanted to make sure Jack got at least a couple of properly hearty meals during the week.

Even this late, there were plenty of people on the streets. Most were men, or paired women. The only single women out at this time of night were those who did a private sort of entertaining, and the families who came here to holiday were generally worn out at the end of an evening performance and already back in their lodgings by the time he and Jack left the theater. There were still plenty of bars and pubs open, though, and smaller music halls than the Palace, the sort where the songs were not the sort you wanted your wife to hear, and the can-can dancers might not be wearing knickers.

Lionel shuddered at the notion that the girl he had just hired might have been reduced to *that*. It wasn't just that such work was degrading (which it was) and filthy (which it was) and led down darker paths (which it did), it was that desperation could do bad, mad things to an Elemental Mage's mind, and of all the unawakened Elemental Magicians you did not want trudging down the path of despair, the highest on the list was the Fire Mage. When a Fire Mage went out of control, emotionally, even an awakened and trained one could do a great deal of damage. If an unawakened Fire Mage went out of control, and awakened during the process—

Well, there were many fire brigades that had been faced with catastrophic, unexplained fires that would, had they known Elemental Magicians existed, have discovered a somewhat grisly answer to their many questions. "Spontaneous human combustion" was what they called it. Temperance lecturers ascribed the phenomenon to drinking too much, although they never had an explanation for why it also happened to teetotalers.

He shook himself out of his dark thoughts as a trio of drunk sailors lurched past in the street, singing. *Disaster averted,* he told himself, and felt relief. Suzie would take care of the girl, get her settled in safe lodgings, see to what she needed. Reliable little Suzie! If only she'd been a mage . . .

Well, she wasn't, but with her good heart she was a treasure he would sorely miss, the more so since she'd been with him longer than any other assistant that *was* a mage.

He and Jack turned down a little lane connecting two larger streets. Both sides of the lane were lined with two-story dwellings, wedged-in and dwarfed by the three- and four-story townhouses of the two streets themselves. Those towering townhouses were owned by very well-to-do families of what might be called the "upper" middle class who could afford a second home for summer, and didn't care for either the country or conventional watering spots like Bath. This was where the wife and kiddies came for the summer, both for a bit of fun and to avoid the perilous climes of London, and where the good, hardworking husband came for his holiday. All except for this lane, whose occupants, with the exception of Lionel, were white-haired and elderly.

This lane was where his house was—outright bought and owned, like the townhouses, rather than rented. There were only half a dozen of these little places, three to each side of the street, and all were at least two hundred years old. Their proportions were a bit broader than the townhouses, although the ceilings were a bit low. He often wondered how they had survived the conversion of Brighton into a holiday resort, when the little houses like them had been knocked down and replaced with the grander townhouses. Perhaps the explanation was simply that the owners had refused to sell at any price, so here they were, hemmed off and overshadowed.

For someone like Lionel, being hemmed off and over-shadowed was anything but a handicap. After all, he was gone most of the day, so why would a lack of sunlight bother him? And the relative darkness in the morning, when he was sleeping long past the hour when most were awake, was just what he needed.

The little scrap of a back garden that belonged to his house had been left to go wild, and whatever could flourish nurtured only by the rain and the little sun that got down there did so, and what didn't, died. The fact that it had ended up becoming a tiny wilderness pocket of shade-loving plants was a happy accident. Birds loved it, and he even had a resident squirrel.

He'd completely renovated the inside when he'd bought the place, so he had all the conveniences of the most modern of flats, including laid-on gas, a boiler for hot water, gas fires instead of coal, sound indoor plumbing, and floors that did not tilt in every possible direction. He didn't care that he had no view, it didn't matter that the inside needed artificial lighting even at midday. The fact that those tall buildings on either hand also muffled the noise of the city was something he had counted on, and more than made up for the shadowy interior.

The house was the middle of the three, with a door right on the street, so poor Jack hadn't any stairs to climb. The modern gaslight at the door had been left lit by Lionel's housekeeper; by its clear beams he unlocked his door and waved Jack inside.

There were no smells of cooking, other than the lingering aroma of fresh bread. The housekeeper was very old-fashioned in her cookery habits, and saw no reason why they should buy bread when she could make it.

That lack of cooking-scent meant that the supper laid out for him in the dining room under the hygienic metal domes he insisted on would be cold. Probably Sunday's ham, which was quite fine with him, and which Jack would enjoy.

The two of them moved to the back of the house and the little dining room attached directly to the kitchen, where the domes gleamed in the center of the table. With a faint sigh, Jack sat down immediately; Lionel whisked off the domes to reveal what lay beneath. As he had suspected: ham, some cold sliced tongue, some rather lovely cheese, onions, pickles of various sorts, radishes, some lettuces, and a fresh, round loaf of bread.

"That looks heavenly," said Jack with approval. Knowing what his friend and fellow magician liked, Lionel was already making him up a sort of plowman's lunch without being asked, even as Jack passed him plates and cutlery from the stack waiting on his side of the table.

There was beer as well, but that was in a little barrel on the sidebar. Lionel pulled them each a pint before he sat down himself.

"All right then," Lionel said firmly, before taking his first bite. "Time for you to be talking, my lad."

"Not much to say," Jack replied, picking up a piece of Gloucestershire, eyeing it for a moment, then eating it. "The girl turned up with one of your sylphs flitting about her, so at first I thought she might be Air, but then one of my salamanders flashed out and attached himself to her, so I knew she was Fire. Unawakened, of course, but if a salamander's taken to her, the power is there. She had a scrap of paper with your advertisement on it and asked if the job was still open. I told her yes, gave her a ticket to the show so she'd stop here, and told her to come back when it was over. Then I went to let you know."

He paused and dabbed some mustard on the ham, folded it in bread, and ate that while Lionel pondered. Lionel remembered the sylph making off with a similar scrap of advertisement; had *she* been responsible for the girl turning up?

More than likely—probably. Unlike a Master, an Elemental Magician couldn't actually command Elementals to do something, and half the time, when he *requested* something of them, they ignored the request. But Lionel had always gotten along well with his sylphs, and knowing he was truly in desperate need of a proper assistant, it looked as if they had finally decided to assist him.

"She's Traveler, or Gypsy, or I'll eat my hat," Jack continued, the lamplight making gold out of the few silver threads in his hair. "Not that there's anything wrong with that. Plenty of magic in Traveler blood, and no sylph or salamander would take to her like they have if she was bad." He ate a hard-boiled egg while he thought. "Did she seem . . . nervy to you, though?"

Lionel knew that as an Air Mage he was not as sensitive to emotions as Fire or Earth would have been. "I couldn't tell," he said truthfully. He thought a little more. "It did seem . . . I got the impulse to act rather like her old dad, just to keep her soothed, if that makes any sense."

Jack nodded, and ran his finger around the inside of his collar, loosening it a little. "I've never known nor heard of a Traveler or a Gypsy to leave the caravans of their kin unless they were running from something. And this is a girl, alone. It does point to her running away."

"She's not just any girl—" Lionel pointed out, then took a pull of his pint, and tapped the wood of the table to emphasize his words. "This is a trained acrobat, a trained dancer—trained enough she likely had a good job somewhere. In fact, I know it; that rehearsal dress of hers looked like a costume, it was used, and used often and hard. Could it be *that* she's running from?"

"Circus, maybe," Jack mulled. "Circus uses dancers around the horses—around the elephant, if they've got one—and in the parade and chorus numbers. Dancers always double as something else. And she does acrobat tricks." He turned his beer glass in little circles on the tabletop. "A girl like her, maybe alone in the world . . . a hard man would find it easy to take advantage of her, and most circus men I've met with are hard men."

It disgusted him, but Lionel had been in show business more than long enough to know Jack had probably hit the answer. After all, the kinds of girls he'd been getting, answering his advertisements, had not been . . . the nicest of young ladies. His sylphs hadn't much cared for them, and neither had Jack's Fire Elementals. So how was it that suddenly, the perfect assistant came calling out of the blue? *Because she isn't all that perfect. She comes with a past.* "I think you've got it." Lionel nodded. "Some circus owners can be brutes. Could be she ran off and broke her contract." He ate the last of his ham, and followed it with a pickled carrot. "I'll operate on that assumption until she tells me different. We're going to have to break it to her that real magic exists, and train her."

Jack barked a laugh, and drained his pint. "That went without saying. I knew that the moment I realized what she was. There are no coincidences when it comes to magicians, Lionel. I think your sylph brought her here. You know how things are; if the sylph brought her here, so far as *they* are concerned, she's our responsibility and we'd better see to it that she gets sorted out."

The elephant in the room finally having been acknowledged between them, they were able to dispense with it for the moment, and go on to homelier matters. When Lionel finally let his friend out the door, things were pretty much settled between them. They would wait and see how the girl managed, and only force the issue on her if it appeared she was being obstinately blind to the genuine magic going on around her.

He locked his door and made his way back to his bedroom, turning out the lamps as he did so. *I'm glad that at least I don't have to deal with this alone. Jack might not be a Master, but he is a damned fine Fire Mage. He can be the one to really train her. I just need to be the one to be ready to jump in if he gets in over his head with this.*

And Jack would be the one to try and coax the tale of her past out of her. Having Lionel, her employer, demand it of her might only frighten her. But Jack was an equal, and was friends to everyone in the theater. She should see that almost immediately, and with luck would come to trust him.

It was as good a plan as they could come up with, at any rate.

4

THE magician seemed pleased with Katie's costume, which fitted better than she thought, and was as easy to move in as any of her circus costumes. If this was an example of the Wardrobe Mistress's work, she had no fear now that the new costume would be a hazard.

"Excellent!" he exclaimed on seeing the two girls in the wings. "Now, I have a plan for the two of you, to slowly break young Katie in on the act. What I want from you, my dear young lady, is to caper about while you watch, carefully, what Suzie does. That is what you will do in the first few shows as well."

Katie looked at him thoughtfully, trying to think in her mind what her character should be. She had learned about *character* from one of the clowns, who had pointed out just how different each of the clowns was, and how each of them represented a distinct personality. After that, except when she worked with Dick, she had tried to do the same. So . . . it was clear from watching Lionel's act that the magician liked telling a sort of story. How could she fit herself into that story? "I can caper, right enough—but am I on *your* side, or hers?"

Either of those would do, really. Just so she had a side to be on. There would be a lot more enthusiastic capering if she were on the magician's side, though.

His eyes gleamed. "Excellent question. Which would you prefer?"

It occurred to her in that moment that she was rather tired of performing as a frail little flower. Being a bit of a devil would be a relief. "Your side, sir," she answered, and thought a bit more. And then, another idea occurred to her. "Be good if I could wear a domino, or some other devilish mask . . ." The mere thought of being able to don a mask almost made her knees weak with a sudden sense of relief and liberation. If she wore a mask, even if Dick or Andy came looking for her, they'd never recognize her. All she had to do was keep her head down when she was outside the theater, and they would *never* find her!

"Capital idea!" the magician applauded. "The more devilish you look, the better. That way, when you take Suzie's place, no one will recognize you. All right then, Davey, let's have a full run-through. Ladies, with me."

He led them off into the wings, then nodded to the pianist, who banged out the opening chords of the magician's music with a will. She already knew this tune from last night; quite a lively piece that would be easy to dance to. On impulse, Katie ran out ahead of Lionel, who was pulling the "reluctant" Suzie along by ropes looped around her wrists. She did a series of leaps and tumbles across the stage, cartwheeled back, and ended up at Lionel's side as he pulled Suzie to the table on which the "magic carpet" was lying. As Katie mimed evil laughter, the magician mesmerized his victim with a few passes of his hands, and laid her down on the carpet. And Katie rolled over to stage front, keeping on the floor, but starting a series of slow contortions as she watched the proceedings. Her job, after all, was to distract, so that no one noticed whatever trickery the magician was doing to perform the illusion.

From out front last night, the carpet had appeared to levitate itself. But that had been when the backdrop curtain had been in place. Now, it was painfully clear that Suzie was lying on a board, over which the carpet had been draped. From the other side of where the curtain would be tonight, a burly stagehand inserted an iron bar under the board and with a clever mechanism and a lot of main strength, made Suzie "float." And when the magician had passed a ring around her to prove that she wasn't being hung on wires? Simple manipulation of the hoop in such a way that it *seemed* as if the hoop was passing over her twice, when in fact, the magician was manipulating the hoop to avoid the bar. Now that she was up in the air, Katie capered about as she watched this, like a devilish little monkey, clapping her hands and somersaulting, and pausing now and again to turn herself into another knot.

The "flying carpet" didn't look very comfortable for Suzie; it wasn't nearly as long as she was tall, and her head and legs draped over either end. Well, it more or less had to be that way, Katie supposed, otherwise the hoop couldn't make the passes around that bar.

Suzie came down again, the stagehand pulled out the bar, and the whole apparatus was wheeled away to the side as the magician woke his victim back up again. Katie darted in, tugging at Suzie's gauzy pantaloons, pretending to pinch her, and generally making a nuisance of herself to cover the sound of the apparatus being taken away backstage.

The magician now brought out a lamp, and conjured up a "genie" out of it—a square of scarlet silk, knotted so that it vaguely resembled a figure, that danced about in the air, while Suzie wheeled in the next apparatus, the sword-basket. Since Katie already knew how this worked, she now imitated a cat chasing after the dancing silk, and eventually Suzie joined chasing it, with more graceful, dancing movements. For the life of her Katie couldn't see how the magician was doing what he was doing, but that didn't matter. She understood that *her* job was to provide enough distraction to the audience that if Lionel slipped, they wouldn't notice his manipulation.

The "genie" whisked back into the lamp, and the magician turned his attention to Suzie again. With threatening gestures, he forced her into the basket while Katie leapt and tumbled about with glee. With every thrust of a sword, Katie shouted, jumped, and clapped her hands. And when Suzie emerged unscathed, she pounded her fists on the stage in rage.

The magician seized her, bound her with ropes, and forced her into a cabinet. He closed the cabinet doors, whirled it around four times, and opened them again, and she was gone! He closed them again, whirled the cabinet four more times and opened them, and there she was! Katie still couldn't see how this one was done, but she rejoiced at her "master's" triumph in a spiral of cart-wheels.

And now came the finale. Lionel threw a rope up into the air, which remained, stiff as a pole, hanging in midair. From here, Katie could see that a stagehand had caught the rope and somehow fastened the end of it to a stout hook in the overhead scaffolding. With threats, the magician forced Suzie to climb the rope, but when she got to the top, she began making rude gestures at him.

As the magician raged at her below, and Katie imitated him, there was a blinding flash and a puff of smoke and Suzie vanished as the rope dropped to the ground.

Except, of course, two very strong stagehands had actually pulled her quickly up into the scaffolding with them and let the rope drop.

The magician ran off stage, raging, as Katie followed, imitating him, and the piano player finished with a few crashing chords.

"Well *done,* by Jove!" the magician exclaimed, and the piano player stopped playing to applaud. "Just repeat that tonight and we'll be fine!"

"Too bad you can't keep both of them," the pianist said with enthusiasm.

"Not a chance, you cheeky monkey!" Suzie called down, on her way down out of the scaffold. "I told my Harry we can set the date, we've already had the banns read, and that is that!"

The piano player struck his chest with one closed fist. "Crushed! Again!" he cried. Katie was surprised into a giggle.

"Now, lads, let's wheel the cabinet out so Katie can see how that one is done," Lionel ordered, and the stagehands brought the box back out again. And of course, once Katie was inside it, she saw how shallow it was compared to the outside dimensions. Of course, since it was painted black inside, it was impossible to tell that. She understood immediately what he was doing as she braced herself inside the cabinet. There were *two* sections to it, one with her in it, and one empty. When Lionel opened the cabinet door on her side, she stepped out again.

"Now, let's run through the tricks with you doing them, while Suzie coaches you," the magician ordered. "You'll be fine bouncing about as you did just now in the shows, but making the illusions appear flawless takes some work."

A great deal more work, it appeared, than she had thought from her one stint in the sword-basket last night. Timing was everything, and so were balance and the ability to hold absolutely still. They managed to go through all of the big illusions twice—very shakily—when the magician called a halt.

"I don't want you two fainting of hunger," he said. "Off with you. Be back in an hour and we'll find Katie a mask before the first show."

The two girls hurried back to the dressing room, which was starting to fill with other girls. They changed into street clothes, Katie made sure she still had the handkerchief with the remains of her pound knotted into it, and they headed for the stage door.

The doorman was at his post, of course, with a bottle of lemonade on his desk and a brown-paper-wrapped sandwich waiting beside him. "Can we bring you anything back, Jack?" Suzie asked, as they squeezed by a couple of men chattering in some foreign language.

"I'm fine, thanks, dearie." The doorman smiled warmly at Katie, who flushed a little and returned the smile. It occurred to her again that he was a handsome man, and that the strands of gray in his hair had probably been put there by pain, and not by years. "How did you fare, Miss Kate? Pleased enough with the job?" His eyes twinkled. "Reckon you'll stay?"

"It's—lovely, thank you," Katie stammered, shyly. "Really lovely!"

"Just you watch out for them Eye-talian acrobats," he cautioned her, as they stepped down into the alley. "They pinch!"

"And how *do* you like being a magician's assistant?" Suzie asked, as she guided Katie to the left and down the walkway, which had started to get a bit crowded, as compared with the morning.

"It really *is* lovely," Katie confessed. "I like bobbing about like a little ape, and making a bit of a Guy of myself. I really like being able to make things up to get into a character, and to make up my dances and acrobatic turns. Would Master Lionel be annoyed if I made things up when I take your part?"

Suzie laughed. "Bless you, no, not as long as you hit your mark with the music. You can do anything you like in between your marks. And if for some reason the apparatus is being balky, he'll signal the orchestra to repeat, you follow that. It's only happened twice since I've been with him, and never with the Turk act, but having someone that can do more than prance about and pose the way I do would be jolly useful. Nothing like being able to tie yourself in a knot to distract people from apparatus troubles."

Katie skipped out of the way of a large man with a very red face who was evidently in a great hurry, and nodded.

"*How* did he make that silk dance about, though?" she asked, furrowing her brow in puzzlement. "I could not work that out."

"I never have, and I've been with him two years, ducks," Suzie laughed. "And he won't tell me! Some things just have to remain a mystery."

Jack felt Lionel approaching long before the magician appeared at the end of the corridor. At this point, people were arriving for brief run-throughs with the band—the group of musicians employed by the Palace was far too small to be called an "orchestra." They would have to be a bit careful of what they said, but the two of them had worked together for so long that they were used to speaking in a sort of code that sounded perfectly ordinary to anyone who might have been listening in.

"Satisfied with the new assistant?" he asked, when Lionel took up a spot just inside the doorway where there was a good breeze. He handed Lionel the second bottle of lemonade and another paper-wrapped sandwich, faithfully delivered by one of the lads that regularly ran errands for the hall.

"Quite. She's quick, observant, smart. She'll never set the world on fire as a dancer, but she's *good,* better than those goat-footed prancers in the chorus, she's got fantastic timing and good musicality. She should have the tricks down within the week. I can't ask more than that of an assistant." Ah, the things that Lionel did *not* say. One of the most glaring was that he didn't mention the "genie" illusion, which was no illusion at all. The bit of flying silk was manipulated by one of Lionel's sylphs. And the girl hadn't seen the little thing.

Yet.

"Perhaps when she's settled in, I should take her to see the fireworks," Jack said in measured tones. "Or out to a bonfire picnic."

"Both," Lionel decreed. "If she doesn't enjoy those, she's not the girl I think she is. Actually on that note, I'd like you to see if you can draw her out on the subject of her past, because she wants to wear a mask onstage."

Jack raised an eyebrow in surprise. *Most* performers preferred not to go masked onstage. It was, quite frankly, dangerous, especially for a dancer. Masks, however unrestrictive and closely molded to the face, still obscured one's vision. And it was not just the danger of a misstep that made performers shun masks, it was the danger of getting too close to the footlights. Performers had been burned, and even killed, doing so.

"I'll do my best, but wouldn't Suzie be better suited to that?" he asked.

"I'll put a word in with Suzie myself," Lionel promised, finally popping the cork on his lemonade and taking a long drink. "But you never know. She might feel safer confiding in you."

I'd like her to confide in me, Jack thought, a bit wistfully—surprising himself with the thought. "Well then, I'll see what I can do," he promised.

"And I'll go find the girl a mask and get into my rig." Lionel tilted the bottle at his fellow Elemental Mage in salute, and headed back down into the bowels of the theater, leaving Jack to wonder what it was about the new

girl that had made him think of her as a *girl,* and not a
performer . . .

Katie pelted after Lionel in a feigned rage, feeling a bit
giddy with the shouts and cheers that followed her offstage. Of course, she was used to applause—but this
somehow seemed—bigger.

Maybe it was the size of the audience. When she performed in the sideshow tent with Dick, the audiences
were not very large. When she'd performed with her parents at fairs and market-days, although there were a lot
of people, the number who could actually see her at any
one time was smaller still. And when she performed under the main tent, she was never the star, she was never
even close to being the star, she was just one dancer
among the half dozen, and more often than not, they
were all in support of one of the thrill acts.

So that might have been it. But whatever the reason,
the cheers and shouts left her feeling breathless and
flushed and very excited.

Suzie caught her shoulders as she tumbled into the
wings, and the two of them hopped up and down for
sheer excitement for a few moments. "That was *brilliant,*" Suzie crowed. "Really, really brilliant! I was actually a little afraid of you out there!"

Lionel had found her a fez and a soft leather mask that
looked a bit like a monkey. It fit very well, and scarcely
restricted her vision at all. She had dredged up all of her
memories of the circus monkeys—a vile-tempered lot,
not that she blamed them, given how their trainer seemed
to think that "training" meant "tormenting"—and had

put every bit of her heart, soul, and energy into acting the Turk's demented "pet." She'd done so well that not only had she caught a couple of whispered "well dones" during the act, but the limelight had actually followed her and not Suzie while they were supposed to be distracting the audience.

"I am an evil little monkey," she giggled back, then fanned herself with her hand, and pushed the mask up onto her forehead. "Oh, I need a breath of air after that."

"Remember, you can't change," Suzie warned her. "And don't forget curtain call. I have to go change for the dancing-act."

Actually getting changed was the last thing on Katie's mind; the costume was cooler than her street clothing. But she was perishing for a drink of water, and she desperately needed a loo!

Surely one didn't "go" out in the alley . . . she turned to ask Suzie, but her mentor was already gone, running off to change into a fluffy gown for her turn in the chorus behind one of the dancing acts.

Jack will know, she decided, and made her way to the stage door.

They always wanted to know because somehow that was always the one thing everyone else forgot to mention; Jack knew the moment that he saw Miss Kate slipping her way past hurrying performers exactly what she needed. "Down the spirals, past Wardrobe. There's a Gents and a Ladies," he said, before she opened her mouth. "And if you go to the other side of the stage from here, and take what looks like a door into the orchestra pit, it actually comes out at the bar. Water's free, beer's not."

A look of gratitude suffused her face, and she beamed at him before turning and hurrying back the way she had come. He chuckled.

A salamander zipped up the side of his desk and curled up in the empty inkwell, blinking glowing eyes at him. He cupped his hand over the top of it, and felt it vibrate with pleasure. "So you like her, then, eh?" he whispered to it, when he was sure he wouldn't be overheard in the general din.

The salamander nodded. Jack smiled a little. That was a good sign. He hoped *this* girl would stick around and not go get herself married. Or at least, if she was going to get married, it ought to be to someone in the theater. Not one of the other acts—that would just take her away after the season. But maybe one of the stagehands, or the barkeepers, or a musician. Davey the piano player would be a good choice, he was a steady lad. Lionel himself—well, he was long in the tooth, but you never knew with women. Sometimes they favored men old enough to be their fathers.

He laughed at himself then. He was really turning into an old woman, sitting here, trying to be a matchmaker just so Lionel could keep the new assistant! They didn't need to get her married off to keep her. They only needed to get her to understand that there was real magic out there, and once she got a taste of it, the only way she would leave would be if she got called away by the Old Lion—which had happened to the first of Lionel's assistants with the gift of magic—or if she fell in love with another Elemental Mage—which was what happened to the second.

Third time is the charm. We'll hang onto this one, I'm sure of it.

By the end of the second performance, Katie was limp with exertion, but practically fizzing with excitement. This was the first time she'd actually enjoyed performing since her parents had died.

She took the final bow with the entire company, holding hands with one of the Italian acrobats on one side, and Suzie on the other, with the footlights blazing up in their faces and the band thundering out the overture as hard as they could. Applause at the circus had never been like this.

They all ran offstage, and then milled a bit while people filed into the corridor for the dressing rooms. The Italian paused for a moment in the wings with her as she caught her breath.

"You are a fine tumbler, *signorina*," he said graciously. "Not so good as the Famous Fanellis, but good!" And before she could thank him, he pinched her bottom and scampered off before she could squeal.

"I warned you!" Suzie laughed from behind her. "Didn't I warn you? Never let those lechers get within reach of any part of you!"

"Well, that was my lesson learnt," Katie replied ruefully, as they joined the crush heading for the dressing rooms. "Oh, but I am *knackered*. Is it going to be like this every night?"

"You did twice the work I did," Suzie pointed out. "All that tumbling and dancing and running about. The only time I do anything that strenuous is when I go up the rope." They squirmed their way into the dressing room; since Katie had her mask, she didn't need to use greasepaint, so she left the stool and dressing table to Suzie while she wiggled her way into her street clothing using as little space as humanly possible. "Honestly," Suzie continued, "That is the worst part of the act. I am always terrified when I go pulling myself up that rope. I don't know how you managed to do it without fainting in rehearsal today."

"I was in the circus," Katie replied, as some of the other girls muted their chatter a bit, the better to overhear her. "I had a notion I might try rope dancing—you know, the sort where you climb a rope and do contortion and acrobatics on it? So my father used to string a rope in the trees when we camped for me to practice on. I didn't like the fast unwinds, though, and you have to do those if you're going to have a good act."

"Fast unwinds?" one of the other girls asked.

"You know, where you wind the rope or the silk around your waist, then let go and unspool yourself like string on an unwinding bobbin and stop just short of the ground." She mimed it with her hands. "It made me dizzy, and I never wanted to go as fast as you have to if you are going to have a good act. So all I kept out of it was the ability to go up a rope like a monkey." She shrugged. "That was useful, still, since I could always help with the tightrope and trapeze rigging."

Suzie shuddered. "I could *never* do that," she declared, wiping the greasepaint from her face with a lotion-soaked cloth. "Not *ever*."

Katie just shrugged again, and hung up her costume in its proper place. The other girls seemed a bit impressed, though, at her daring. But it hadn't seemed like daring at the time; she'd been enthralled by the rope and silk-dancers, and had longed with all her heart to be able to do what they did. To dance in mid-air, free from the earth! She would have loved that.

But there had been no one to teach her properly when she was young, and that was a skill that needed learning very young indeed.

Still, who would have thought that her rope climbing would come in so handy!

She and Suzie chattered away about the act all the way back to the boarding house, where Mrs. Baird presided tonight over some sort of delicious white bean dish. Katie couldn't remember having eaten anything with beans in it that tasted this good.

Scrubbed clean and pleasantly exhausted, Katie had only time to reflect on her incredible, almost supernatural good luck in getting this job, and this place, before she dropped like a stone into a well into a deep, dark, and dreamless sleep.

"There's a sort of gentlemen's agreement among the music halls," Suzie explained, as they hurried to the theater the next morning. "The good ones, anyway. The bad ones never close, but the good ones give us one day off a week. It depends which hall you are at, which day off you get."

Katie nodded at that; the circus did that too. It was called "going dark," probably for the logical reason that none of the evening illuminations were done that lit up the tents, or the front of the music hall.

"At any rate, our dark night is tomorrow, so we'll have a day off. I'm going off with my boy, but did you have any notion of what you would like to do?" They had just reached the stage door as Suzie said that, looking at her a bit anxiously.

Truth to tell, Katie didn't have the slightest idea of what she wanted to do. She knew she was going to have to live frugally; that salary was not bad, but things were more expensive in the city, even if she *had* been gifted with an entire wardrobe for nothing.

"Actually, Lionel wanted me to tender an invitation to join him at his house for luncheon, Miss Kate," Jack said, putting a hand briefly on her forearm to make her pause for a moment. "I generally join him there on our dark days. It's quite pleasant, we have a nice card game, his housekeeper joins us if we have three to make a fourth."

Katie had hesitated until he mentioned the housekeeper; she felt some relief. A girl alone with two men — well, if the housekeeper joined them, that wouldn't be so bad.

"I've gone over heaps of times," Suzie said with relief. "If we don't play cards, we go over what we'll do in the next season, and make changes just to keep the act fresh from the last time we did it." She winked at Katie. "I guess he's going to keep you, if he's asking you to luncheon!"

"I will, then," she said decisively, and when they got to the stage for rehearsal she told the magician herself.

"Beef or ham?" was all that Lionel asked, as he set up the sword-basket.

Goodness! She hadn't had either in such a long time — except for wafer-thin slices of ham, now and again, between thick, thick slices of bread, as a treat. "Ham?" she said tentatively, hoping she was choosing the cheaper of the options. She didn't want to appear greedy.

"Ham it is," said Lionel, and sent her into the basket again.

As she fitted herself in where the swords wouldn't reach her, she realized she was smiling in the hemp-scented gloom. This was unexpectedly—fun. She had been overjoyed at the job, pleased to be dancing and tumbling and not trying to set up at the seaside with her acrobatics and a scrap of cloth, and the last several days of the show had been the most glorious she had ever experienced as a performer. But the last time she had actually had *fun* in performing had been when she was a child, and had no idea that the occasional hard times she and her family went through were anything but adventures. There had been no anxiety about making enough money to eat, or repair the caravan, or buy the wool and cloth so that her father could have a warm winter cloak and jumper, his old one could pass down to her mother, and her mother's could be cut down for her.

Now, this was fun. Amazing fun. The magician was gentle in his corrections, and enthusiastic in his praise. She was almost as good at most of the tricks as Suzie now, and better at the climactic rope trick at the end. The hardest one for her was the flying carpet; it was very hard for her to lie perfectly still and trust that the stranger on the other end of the apparatus was going to be able to lift her up and down safely. It felt entirely too much like being at the mercy of Dick's strength.

This time, at last, she fitted herself through the swords with perfect ease when Lionel was going at full speed.

When she popped out of the basket, Lionel was very pleased.

"Suzie," he said, "Day after tomorrow, Katie here will be the victim. Do you think you can be my *evil* genie?"

"I won't be as good as Katie is at being your imp," Suzie laughed, with a toss of her blond hair. "But I can add some black to the costume with some scarves, do the evil-queen makeup from the Snow White panto, and make wild gestures. We can do a full run-through that morning."

"Good. Six nights of good shows with Katie as my assistant, and you may take your leave of us when you please," Lionel told her, and she actually jumped up and down, clapping her hands with glee. "By that time, Katie's slave girl costume will be done, and the act will be back to normal."

Katie felt actually giddy. She truly had not expected to be in this position so quickly, once she had realized how much work was involved in being the magician's assistant.

"Are you still wanting to wear a mask?" Lionel continued, turning to Katie—and suddenly she went from giddy to sober, and cold. What if he didn't *want* her to wear a mask? What if someone from the circus came in here? What if there was a performer out there in one of the other shows, or on the Boardwalk, who had known her and her parents before they joined the circus? Performers talked, and word could spread to the most unlikely of places, and Dick could find out where she was by so many means—

"Because I rather like it," Lionel continued, and she felt faint with relief. "I think it gives a properly mysterious air to the act. I don't want you to do so if you feel it restricts your vision, but a pretty little mask, with the bit of veil fastened across the bottom of it? It would not only look exotic, it would solve the problem Suzie always has of her veil coming loose. One less thing to worry about."

"I would *love* to wear a mask," she said fervently.

"Good then, it's settled." Lionel gave a decisive nod, which Katie had noticed that he always did when he was satisfied with something. "You two scuttle along and get your luncheon, and go talk to the Wardrobe Mistress about that mask and veil before you come back for the last run-through." He made a shooing motion with his hands, and the two of them went off to the dressing room to hurry on enough of their street clothing to be respectable.

Many of the girls sent out for luncheons, as Jack and Lionel did, but Suzie was just as concerned with saving pennies as Katie was, and she knew the best places to eat cheaply and well. Today she guided Katie to a little cockle stall, where they ate their fill of shellfish so fresh they were still moving when plunged into the steam for a quick cooking. The proprietor was Welsh, and Suzie insisted on them having something he called "laver bread" as well. "It's *good* for you," she insisted—and Katie, who had eaten much more dubious things than an oatmeal cake mixed with seaweed, was not inclined to argue with her. Besides, to her mind, it was delicious. The stall owner seemed utterly delighted that they liked his "delicacy."

"Welsh caviar, that is, girls!" he told them urging second helpings on them. "Welsh caviar!"

"Think you can find your way back here?" Suzie asked, as she always did. Katie nodded. She'd always had an unerring sense of direction, and not even the twisty little "twinnings," the alleys among the fishermen's shacks that required you to go in single file, confused her. "Good. Now, listen . . . I am fairly certain Lionel is going to use luncheon tomorrow as a reason to ask you *all* about yourself." Suzie craned her neck to look earnestly into Katie's face. "Please don't try to lie to him. He can *always* tell when someone is lying and he never forgives that."

That took Katie just a bit aback for a moment, and she thought hard before she answered. *Do I . . . should I . . .*

Suzie obviously took her silence for exactly what it was. "Listen to me . . . no matter what you've done, what scrape you've been in, I *promise* you, if you haven't actually broken the law too much, Lionel won't care as long as you *tell* him!"

That surprised an answer out of her and she spoke before she intended to. "I never broke any laws!" she said, breathlessly. "But . . . I'm trying to keep away from . . . someone . . ."

"Then *tell* them, tell them everything!" Suzie urged. "They can't help you—and they will!—if you don't tell them."

But when Katie thought about Dick . . . his hideous strength, and his boundless rage . . . all she could do was shake her head. *Oh no,* she thought. *It isn't them that would be protecting me. It's me keeping him off them.*

5

"TEA, lemonade, or squash, Miss Kate?" Jack asked politely, as Lionel skillfully carved the ham. He could tell by the girl's expression that this was the first time she had ever been presented with a meal like this one, a proper "Sunday dinner" type meal, although it wasn't Sunday. It reminded him every time he shared dark-day dinner with Lionel of the meals in the little farmhouse where he had grown up. Proper country meals, made by a farmwife, born and bred. Meals were the fuel on which a farm ran, and a good farm served up good meals, never stinting anyone.

Even though this was summer, the hottest summer Jack could remember, the housekeeper and cook would not have dreamed of serving a cold dinner. Mrs. Buck-thorn, Lionel's housekeeper, was a proper country cook, and she was cooking for someone she considered to be a "gentleman," so it was a gentleman's dinner. The only difference between her meal and one that would be served in the house of a prosperous merchant was that her meals were served farmhouse style, with everything on the table at once, and people helping themselves.

The aroma was enough to make a dead man rise and walk to the table to join them, at least as far as Jack was concerned.

Katie gazed on it all with wonder. The meal began with a bit of clear soup, then on came the rest: ham with a succulent honey glaze that glistened in the dim light that came in through the dining room windows, the green peas with butter melting over the top of them, the fluffy mashed potatoes heaped in a bowl like a great mound of steaming snow, the cabbage, apples, and onions baked together into a succulent mass, the brandied carrots shining like gold, the big dish of pickles lying cool in their juice, the fine loaf of fresh-baked bread, the dish of sweet butter, and jewel-like dishes of apple and currant jelly. The poor girl hardly knew where to look next as her gaze wandered over the laden table.

"Tea, please," she said in a soft voice. Then she smiled tentatively and a little shyly at them all. "I feel sorry for Suzie. She can't be having nearly as good a dinner as this one."

Savory aromas swam about them . . . and Jack chuckled. "Her beau's half-owner in his parent's oyster-house, and it's a big, prosperous one. She'll be tucking into lobster about now, I should think, so don't feel sorry for her. It'll be just as good a dinner. Seafood, not ham, but just as good."

Lionel gestured with his knife and fork that he was ready, and served the ham as Mrs. Buckthorn passed him plates. Jack filled the rest of Katie's plate for her; he had the feeling she would just have put a little potato and a few peas on it otherwise. Mrs. Buckthorn and the maid sat right down with the rest of them—an anomaly in any other household, where the servants would eat separately, but this was no ordinary household. For one thing, Lionel wouldn't hear of his housekeeper eating in the kitchen when all he had was the housekeeper and her little niece, who served as maid-of-all-work, and for another, Mrs. Buckthorn was a very, very minor Elemental Magician herself. Just enough to be aware of the magic and the Elementals, but that was more than enough for Lionel to consider her as an equal who happened to take his wages. As for Mrs. Buckthorn herself, she was farm-bred and saw no difficulty, for servants always ate with the family on the farms. Servants were considered part of a farmhouse family, at least on good farms.

Katie, of course, would never have been around anyone who had servants, so she wouldn't know how unusual this was.

Lionel was very careful which of his assistants he had invited to dark-day dinners; some of them would have been shocked, for oddly, it was often those who were poorest who had the most rigid ideas about what was, and was not, "proper." It was odd, but it was often so.

Unless, of course, they were born and raised entertainers, who had no set ideas of any sort of household etiquette, for they rarely had servants, and almost never had houses. Rooms in a theatrical boarding house, or flats rented by retired theater people, that was what they had. Servant and master etiquette was as loose among entertainers as it was among farm folk.

In deference to Mrs. Buckthorn's finer feelings, they bowed their heads while the housekeeper uttered a brief blessing. Then they all gave proper, thoughtful respect to the food, and Jack got a great deal of pleasure from the happiness on Katie's face as she ate. He rather thought that Lionel did too.

There was a very nice breeze cutting right through the house, and as wild as the back garden was, it held an untamed old-fashioned rosebush that had taken over one entire corner. It added its scent to the savory aromas of the food.

They kept the conversation to extreme commonplaces—and compliments to Mrs. Buckthorn, who dimpled like a girl over them. They discussed the show, some of the back-stage goings-on, whether the summer was going to continue to be as hot as it was now, and Mrs. Buckthorn held forth at length on Queen Alexandra, for whom she had enormous admiration.

There was Eton Mess for dessert, and Jack thought that Katie might perish on the spot from pleasure over the sweet. When they were done, Mrs. Buckthorn set to clearing the remains back to the kitchen, and Lionel led the way to a peculiar back parlor that shared the back part of the ground floor with the kitchen.

The one delightful thing about this overshadowed house—particularly *this* summer, which was proving to be unnaturally hot—was that because it was in near-perpetual shade, it remained deliciously cool while the rest of Brighton baked. The back parlor had exceptionally large windows, which Lionel had made to be able to open completely, with gauze curtains fastened over them to keep out the dust and flies while allowing in the breeze. There was also a French-style door.

The garden, as overgrown as it was, held the cool as well. There were two trees, the enormous rose-bush, vines of some sort that rambled all over everything, and between the shaggy bits of lawn, the remains of a little gravel path that led to a birdbath that Mrs. Buckthorn kept filled. Jack wondered what the more prosperous neighbors thought of the pocket wilderness on the other side of their garden walls. Well, the brick and stone walls were pretty high; probably they couldn't see anything but the trees and shaggy rosebush.

If they know, they are probably having quiet furies about it. Of course, if they knew their neighbor was in the theater, they would probably be fulminating over it every Sunday dinner!

Lionel also had ceiling fans of the sort that were found in Indian bungalows, but rather than being powered by a small native boy, these were set in motion by an ingenious clockwork that Mrs. Buckthorn wound up every morning. Lionel tripped the mechanism as they entered, and the flat fans began lazily swaying back and forth with the mechanism ticking pleasantly away.

Everything about the parlor was light and cool; the wallpaper was a pattern of twining green acanthus vines on white, the furnishings were all of white wickerwork with cotton cushions that matched the paper, the tables of metal—more twining acanthus vines—with glass tops. The table nearest the window had been set up with cards and four chairs, but Lionel didn't immediately repair to it.

"Now, until this moment, Katie," Lionel said carefully,

as he lowered himself onto a padded wicker settee, "We have let your skill speak for you. But as I have invited you into my house, and into my trust, I would very much like it if you would reciprocate by giving us your trust. Would you do us the great favor of telling us just where, exactly, you come from and where you learned your dancing and acrobatics. Hmm?"

Katie hesitated a moment, and her face went very still. Jack could imagine her mind racing, and he couldn't blame her for her hesitation. If she was running from something, she probably had plenty of reasons to be wary.

Lionel had used that "there, there," sort of soothing voice, that a parent would use to assure a child that it was perfectly all right to tell everything. Into the silence of hesitation, Jack put in his own words.

"Really, Miss Kate, you've seen how much the act *needs* you. You needn't worry that Lionel is going to run you off; we just want to know a bit more about you. It doesn't matter where you come from, not really. You could be a little Hottentot, or a Hindoo beggar, and it would be all the same to us. What matters is that you be honest with us, you see? Show people can't be too nice about pointing fingers; plenty of people who come to see us think we live lives of terrible immorality—and some-times they're right." He chuckled a little, hoping to put her at her ease. "Honestly, the number of times I've had to cover for a husband or a daughter having a gay old time with someone they shouldn't have been with don't bear counting. We *know* you aren't a thief now, whatever you might have had to do in the past. Short of murdering someone, I can't think of anything you might have done that would cause us to turn you out." He smiled into her troubled eyes. "And as for us, if we'd meant to do you mischief, we had plenty of opportunities, yet here you are, safe as houses, full of a good ham dinner and in a lovely chair and with lemonade when you want it. And you'll notice, there's a French door, right there—" He pointed at the door that led into the bedraggled garden. "—and neither of us is spry enough to keep you from it, if you cared to bolt. So." He leaned back in his own chair. "Why don't you tell us what sort of cuckoo we're fostering?"

Her face had gradually begun to clear as he spoke. After all, everything he had just told her was perfectly reasonable and sensible, and as she thought about it, he reckoned that she realized everything he had said was true.

"I'm—half Traveler," she said hesitantly, and waited for their reactions. When all they did was nod, her face lost some of its worry. There were not a lot of Travelers on the music hall circuit, but there were some. Jack knew of an entire enormous family of singers, guitarists and dancers from Spain—or so they said, you could never tell with Travelers. But their music sounded Spanish to him, and they did that foot-stamping sort of dancing that he vaguely associated with Spain.

Maybe they were Gypsies, not Travelers, strictly speaking. He also vaguely knew that not all Travelers were Gypsies, and not all Gypsies were Travelers, *or* cared to be taken for Travelers.

"Ma was the Traveler, Pa was an acrobat. They met at a horse fair, and they just fell right in love there on the spot." Her eyes softened when she said that, and Jack smiled a little. "He properly asked to court her, but when her people wouldn't take him, as mostly Travelers won't take outsiders, she ran off from them and back to be with him. When she did that, by Traveler law, she was spoilt, and her good name was just right gone, and since she didn't have any brothers to come after her and beat him for it, just her father, then she was cast out."

"He was a lucky man, from what I've heard," Lionel mused. "Travelers can be hard men, and they don't take to having their women interfered with."

"Well, Ma was a lucky woman, for a spoilt Traveler girl will never get a husband, and will have to live and tend to her parents all her life, and do all the work," the girl replied, then shrugged. "Well, Pa taught me the acrobatics, and Ma taught me dances, and I learnt more from every dancer we traveled with."

That, Jack thought, explained a great deal about her dancing skill. Had she learned one discipline and been taught in it in a proper school, she might have been great. Stupendous, even. She surely had raw talent, and must have a knack for picking things right up. But without proper training, her dancing was something of a muddle, and even he could see she'd never get out of it now. The more was the pity. But on the other hand . . . it meant she was versatile, and that was certainly what Lionel needed.

"Things started to get hard though," she continued. "It was getting hard for us to make money at fairs, with so many other new things coming along to take peoples' pennies. We were small, and . . . and people would want to go see a Hindoo dancer, or Chinese acrobats, even if they weren't as good as us. So we joined a circus. That was easier. We could always count on eating. I learned a lot of dancing there. There was even a girl who danced on her toes, who said she was a—a—bally-dancer."

"Ballet," Lionel corrected, gently. Katie nodded.

"Aye, that was what she said. I learned that. That's *hard!* It looks so floaty and graceful, and the circus people, they liked me to balance that way on one leg a lot, and it really hurts!" Unconsciously, she rubbed at her leg through her skirt, as if in memory of the aching. "But after a while, it wasn't so bad. And we did all right in the circus, even if we were working harder, better than being alone." She sucked in a long breath. "We went to another circus when the first one had a row between the owner and his partner, and we didn't want to get caught up in the middle of it all. The owner gave us a good name, and this one was bigger. They had a lion tamer and an elephant. They gave us a sideshow booth as well as work under the canvas. We thought it was good."

She started to tense up, her eyes got very bright, and two of Jack's salamanders suddenly appeared at his feet, ran to hers, eeled up the legs of the chair, and settled in on either side of her—to comfort her? That was what it looked like! It didn't take that to tell him that what was coming was very painful, even tragic. She'd gone quite pale, and her throat showed strain as she swallowed.

She ducked her head, and clasped her hands tight in her lap, oblivious to the salamanders cuddled up next to her. When she spoke, her voice was tight and choked with grief.

"Early February, it was. We were at a big Traveler horse fair. I don't remember much, only that Ma and Pa were tired, and since we were doing the shorter show with the smaller company under the canvas, for-bye it was so cold, they just did the sideshow, and then went to bed in the caravan early while I worked the big show. I just come out of the tent, when I hear, *Fire!* And—" She choked back a sob. "It's our caravan . . . our caravan, on fire, all roaring up high, like a rag soaked in oil. I ran there, I tried to get in . . . at least they told me I tried, and my dress was all burnt afterward, but I couldn't get in, and the fire was just roaring, roaring—they pulled me away—"

Her voice was so full of agony, Jack wished she would break down and cry, so he would have an excuse to go to her, try and comfort her. But other than that one choked-back sob, she showed no signs of being about to give way.

But she took several long, shuddering breaths, and then she was far too tightly in control of herself again. Hands still clasped in her lap, she looked up. Her face was as pale as the white wicker, and her eyes glittered with unshed tears. The two salamanders pressed into her like a pair of anxious dogs.

"I don't remember much about the next couple of days. When it was over, in the morning, I remember going to look at the caravan. There wasn't anything left. Everything was burnt, down to the axle. All that was left was the horses. I—"

She hesitated for a very long time, and that wariness came over her again. She dropped her eyes, and Jack and Lionel exchanged a glance. Without saying a word, the look they exchanged told each other what they both knew was coming.

The next thing she said would be a lie.

They'd been showmen for too long not to be able to read when a lie was coming.

"It was just me, and that wasn't enough of an act, so

they turned me off," she said. "They gave me a little money for my horses, and told me to find someplace else. They couldn't afford me a new caravan and all, and I wasn't good enough to be a star turn that could get such a thing on credit."

No, they didn't send her off, she ran. Maybe the owner tried to drag her into his bed, maybe he mistreated her, maybe someone else in the circus tried to take advantage of her. But she ran. She was never, ever turned off. Jack was as certain of that as he was of his own name. *Even if she wasn't good enough to be a star turn, there should have been someone in the show that would give her space in their wagon, and she could have joined another act. The clowns, even—acrobats make good clowns. Look at her! She's tight as a banjo-string with fear even now! Someone in that circus terrified her—terrifies her still. That's why she wants to wear a mask on stage. She's afraid whoever it is will one day find her again.*

"Well, bad luck for them, and good for us," Lionel said lightly. "There, now, that was simple enough, wasn't it? Thank you for telling us about yourself, Kate, and you needn't have worried. I promise that you've a place in my act for as long as you care to keep it. And the more fools to that circus for not trying harder to keep you."

She shuddered at that—though she did her best to hide it.

And being kept was the very last thing she wanted, Jack thought, grimly.

"Thank you, sir," the girl whispered.

"Lionel. I told you to call me Lionel." The magician made a *harrumphing* sound. "All that sir nonsense makes me feel like an old man!"

Finally, she laughed. It was strained, but she laughed, and the two salamanders relaxed, stretched themselves, and vanished in a poof of sparks.

Mrs. Buckthorn appeared at just that moment, with perfect timing, and a tray with tall glasses and a pitcher of lemonade. "Well, gents," she said with a laugh. "Are you ready to be beaten soundly by an addled old woman and a wee bit of a girl?"

Katie looked up at the housekeeper; she was still pale, but swiftly getting her color back. "I would not be all that sure of my skill at cards, Mrs. Buckthorn," she said, shyly. "I know bridge, and whist, but not very well."

The housekeeper put the tray with the glasses and pitcher down on the side table and took her accustomed place with her back to the windows, taking up the cards and beginning a shuffle. "That's all right, dearie," she said. "I'm good enough for both of us."

Jack laughed and took his usual chair, next to the table with the drinks, his wooden leg making a thumping noise on the wooden floor as he limped to his place. Lionel sat across from him, and Katie across from Mrs. Buckthorn, and they began a brisk game of bridge.

Despite her assertion to the contrary, Katie was quite a good player, easily Mrs. Buckthorn's equal, and Mrs. Buckthorn had been playing the game for longer than Jack or Lionel had been alive. This actually didn't surprise Jack at all; card games were the best way to while away the time for showmen everywhere, and he had never seen a circus where someone hadn't been playing cards, somewhere. He and Lionel put up a valiant fight, but to no avail. Of the four games they played that afternoon, they prevailed in only one of them.

Much to his pleasure, and Lionel's, Katie seemed to have completely forgotten her earlier distress, or at least, it had passed from her. She was happy; she laughed a great deal, and smiled a lot, and even ventured to tease Jack a little. Not Lionel, though; she continued to treat him with grave respect. Jack decided that was a good thing; she didn't seem to be afraid of him, but she wasn't showing any of the less palatable traits she could have had, given her background. Circus folks were not the most polite, and Travelers—well, Travelers could be known for their insolence.

Then again, the salamanders had liked her from the moment she had shown up. And they had shown a certain distaste for a couple of the assistants who had been inclined to be pert and insubordinate.

Lionel would not put up with much of that. He might be easy to work with, and he might be kind, but he would not tolerate outright disrespect. And he absolutely would not tolerate laziness or slackness. His act relied on discipline, and the moment someone showed a lack of discipline, they soon found themselves corrected. And if the corrections didn't "take," they soon found themselves looking for other work.

That was, in Jack's opinion, as it should be. The act *could* be very dangerous. He had to be able to trust his assistant, and his assistant had to be able to trust him— and above all, they had to both be accurate to a fault.

It was beginning to look as if Miss Kate was going to be able to uphold Lionel's very demanding standards with grace.

As the evening turned to sunset, the quartet finished the last game, and Mrs. Buckthorn wordlessly handed

Lionel the cards to be put away in their case, then took the empty glasses and pitcher back to the kitchen. Katie was quick to take the hint.

"I'll be getting back to the boarding house," she said, standing up, and waved Jack back to his place when he started to rise. "I can go alone, it's not bad for a girl alone this early, and I know my way. Thank you *ever* so for a lovely dinner, s—Lionel," she added warmly. "It was . . . I don't think I've ever had a meal so good. It was like eating in heaven."

"Well, you may as well get used to it, my dear," Lionel replied, rising. "You are invited here for dinner with Jack every dark day. I like the company, Mrs. Buckthorn loves cooking for more than just me, and I think it makes us something of a family. We won't always be playing cards, though, because some times I will be needing to work on new illusions, but perhaps then Jack can show you some of Brighton."

"I'd enjoy that," Jack said gravely, before she could answer.

"In fact—" Lionel said, as if the thought had just occurred to him, rather than being something he and Jack had already plotted between them, "—I have a capital plan. Next dark day, you come here for dinner, Jack can borrow my little trap and show you the city a bit, then you both go down to the Pier to watch the fireworks after sunset, come back here for a spot of supper, and he can take you home in the trap! It will probably just be cold tongue and chicken, but I always say Mrs. Buckthorn's chicken is as good cold as it is hot."

She looked for a moment as if she was afraid to say yes, so Jack added a little more incentive. "Please do," he said. "I'll have a few errands to run anyway by then, and the trap and an extra set of hands will make it all that much easier."

"All right then," she agreed, flushing a little. "If I truly will be useful."

"You truly will," Jack promised, and rose long enough for Lionel to see her out of the room and out the door.

He could hear them talking in the hall as they made their way to the door; he assumed Lionel was putting a little more persuasion into play. All to the good. He might be able to figure out why so far she wasn't seeing the Elementals. Usually Elemental Magicians began seeing them in mid-childhood.

He was back to his favorite chair by the time Lionel returned.

"Any surprises?" Lionel asked, as he lowered himself to the settee again.

Jack shook his head. "Honest as a new penny right up to the point where she talked about leaving the circus. And I will take any wager you care to make that it wasn't because she was turned out."

"Because the owner tried to drag her into his bed, more like," Lionel growled, echoing Jack's own thoughts. "Blackguard. I hate him already and I don't even know him."

"I was thinking—given how shut-mouthed she is about it—it was less *tried* and more *succeeded*," Jack rumbled, feeling anger rising inside him and ruthlessly shutting it down. Anger was dangerous in the Fire Mage. Fire Elementals were very quick to respond to emotion, and the violent emotions sometimes caused them to act on their own with unfortunate results.

"What about that fire, though, the one that killed her parents? It almost seems too much of a coincidence that it was a fire that they died in, when she's Fire. I admit that troubles me." Lionel looked at Jack hesitantly, as if he expected Jack to react badly to the statement.

"Huh." Rather than making him angry, the suggestion that Katie's power might have had something to do with her parents' death caught him off-guard. "That never occurred to me. She didn't give me any hint that she was unhappy with her *parents.* On the contrary, they sounded like a loving family, and she was certainly grief-stricken enough."

"Well, it's something we should consider," Lionel pointed out. "What if she'd had a quarrel with them that night? What if she'd taken up with a young man they didn't approve of? You *know* what happens when Fire Mages are not aware of their power, and are caught up in emotion."

Jack didn't *like* it, not the least bit—but Lionel was right. It *was* something they had to consider. "I don't think it was—no, I *know* it wasn't deliberate," he said at last. "Salamanders won't abide someone that's used their power to kill on purpose. They might get worked up on their own and think to *help* someone and cause harm, but they won't go doing harm on the mage's behalf without being forced. Other Fire Elementals might, but not the phoenix, not the salamander. She had two of them snugged up against her like a couple of cats."

Lionel pondered this, drumming his fingers on the arm of the settee. "The only way I can see it is if she somehow has rage inside her that we haven't seen yet," he said. "Something that attracts the darker forces. Daemons, for instance. Or Imps."

"If she could do that," Jack snorted, "Anyone that tried to force her would be cooked."

"How do we know he wasn't?" Lionel countered. "Maybe that was what she's afraid of. Maybe that was why she ran. First her parents die in their caravan in a fire, then maybe the man that forced her? I'd run too."

Jack liked that even less, but he had to admit that it was a possibility that fit the little that they knew. "All right then. I'll keep a tight eye on her, and I'll see if I can get my Elementals to talk to me." Mostly, they didn't ... but sometimes, if he offered something enticing enough, they would. "But it still doesn't feel like a fit, to me."

"Plan for the worst, hope for the best," Lionel said, and stretched out his legs. "And now, old man, how about a good smoke?"

Katie walked back to the boarding house with a great deal on her mind. She hadn't expected Lionel to want to hear about her past—it was when he'd first hired her she'd expected the interrogation, not nearly a week later!

It had startled her into being more honest than she had intended. She really hadn't wanted to say anything about her parents' deaths, but she found herself doing so before she could stop herself.

She'd just *barely* managed to keep herself from blurting out how she'd found herself married to Dick. Although she still wasn't quite sure how she'd found herself married to Dick. That entire time was a blur, as if she had been moving through some kind of a dream, a waking nightmare. No matter what she really wanted, when

Andy Ball said she was to do something, she'd found herself agreeing. She scarcely remembered the brief ceremony in front of some Non-Conformist minister, with only Andy and the lion-tamer as witnesses. The entire wedding night was a blank. And then—one day, it was as if she had woken up, expecting it all to have *been* a nightmare, except that it wasn't, and she *was* married to Dick, and her parents *were* dead.

And would it have been so bad to tell them?

She found herself flushing painfully at the thought, and ducked her head down to keep people from seeing it. What would they think of her, those two fine men, to hear that she'd married that brute with her parents' ashes barely cold?

They'd think you were afraid, alone, and desperate.

Maybe they would—and maybe they wouldn't. And right now, she didn't want to take the chance on the latter. She didn't want them to think she was—bad. She didn't want them to think that maybe she'd flung herself at the handsome strongman as soon as her parents weren't around to do anything about it, and only regretted it when she found out what sort of a bad bargain she'd made. She didn't want to hear *you've made your bed, now lie in it.*

She didn't want them to decide she was wrong for running away from her lawful husband, and try and send her back . . .

That made her grow cold and hurry her steps. Yes . . . that was it. Because they *were* men, no matter how kind they seemed to be, and men backed up other men. And Dick was her husband and she belonged to him. No matter what he did to her, she'd willingly married him, and he had rights.

It's your own fault, you don't try to please him. Yes, she knew people would say that, for people did. Never mind that she'd tried every way she could think—they still said that, and meant it, and would turn her away.

She reached the boarding house, and sat quietly at supper with the earliest of the girls. Suzie wasn't back yet, but she had told Katie not to wait up for her. Katie decided to take the opportunity for a real bath, since she'd be able to think while she soaked and washed her hair without anyone trying to chatter or gossip with her.

She soaked until the water was tepid, then worked soap through her hair, and rinsed it, rinsed it again, then wrapped it all in a towel and wound the towel up tight, squeezing the water out of it. It was then that the idea sprang full-blown in her mind.

I'll get a divorce!

Her hands continued to work, automatically, but her mind suddenly felt full as a beehive with the idea. She knew about divorces from the papers, of course; even in the circus, there was gossip about famous ones. She knew how you got one—you proved infidelity, and there was certainly plenty of proof of *that* with Dick. It would take money, though . . . lawyers were involved, and lawyers, so she had heard, cost a lot of money. It might take having someone catch Dick with one of his women. But . . .

I can get a divorce. I can save the money, and I can get a divorce and I'll be free of him forever!

Then . . . yes, then she would be willing to tell them. When she could prove before a judge that Dick was a *bad* man, and that no good woman would want to be married to him. And once she was free, she could tell them, tell them everything.

Yes. That was the answer!

She squeezed the last of the water out of her hair, wrapped herself up in her dressing gown, and hurried up the stairs to the room she shared with Suzie. Her friend still was not back—though really, it was only sunset— and she sat on the edge of her bed, combing her wet hair dry, thinking about it. Holding the idea in her mind, like an egg to be hatched.

Finally she looked up at herself in the peer-glass across the little room. "I will get a divorce," she said aloud, to see what it sounded like.

It sounded ... perfect. And her reflection beamed a huge smile back at her.

I will get a divorce. And then, that beast will never touch me again.

6

"I THINK we should have a toast," Lionel said, raising his glass, as the others paused in their pursuit of succulent roast hen, and looked up at him. "Really, this is double a momentous occasion, and it deserves a toast. So! A toast! To our Suzie, who is about to be launched upon the sea of matrimony, and our Katie, who is about to become my full assistant at double the wage I hired her!"

"A toast!" Jack echoed, and Suzie and Mrs. Buckthorn raised their glasses and drank, as Katie stared at them all with her mouth slightly open.

"What?" Lionel said, feeling extremely mischievous. "Did I forget to tell you? You haven't been my full assistant until now, so you've been on trial wages. Plus, when Suzie leaves, you'll be responsible for the whole of the room rent, unless you want to allow in a second girl, so in all decency I really have to increase your salary."

He had to laugh to see her going pink with pleasure and surprise. So did the others. "The only thing I am *terribly* annoyed at, Miss Minx," he continued, turning to Suzie, "Is that you are having the dreadful taste to get married on Saturday, when we have three shows. Which means we can't see you properly shackled."

When Suzie had announced the date, she *had* been very contrite. "I can't keep apologizing, you know," she said, with a shrug. "It wasn't up to me, it was up to my lad's parents and the padre and their church. That was the date that was available for everyone."

"Everyone *except* your very good friends in the business," Lionel grumbled. "Poor Jack will have to represent us all, since he's the only one that could get a few hours off."

"Well, you know you can come to the wedding breakfast, and it's not going to harm a thing to skip the morning rehearsal," Suzie countered. "It's not as if you would really enjoy sitting through the ceremony, and you know it, you old pagan."

"But I can't make you and the groom vanish at the altar," the magician protested, eliciting a giggle from both Suzie and Katie, since both knew that the groom's parents, particularly his mother, would probably faint dead away if he did that. Not to mention that, short of arranging for a trap door at the altar, there was no way he *could* do that, even if they let him.

"Still bloody unfair," Lionel muttered, causing Mrs. Buckthorn to rap his knuckles with the handle of her knife and exclaim *"Language!"*

"I'll do the proper, Lionel, don't worry," Jack told him. "I even got my uniform cleaned and all the medals polished."

They continued teasing Suzie all through the meal; she answered them back with plenty of amusement. Lionel enjoyed every minute of it, with a touch of melancholy. Suzie had been one of the best assistants he had ever had, barring the two that had been Elemental Mages themselves. He enjoyed her cheerful personality and he was going to miss her.

On the other hand, she clearly loved her "boy," and her young man adored her. His family loved her too, and they had a good reputation in Brighton.

And it wasn't as if she was going off to Australia or something of the sort. She would be right here, and would probably drop by to see how they were all getting on.

Still, this was the last time they would be together like this. He had made it clear that she and her new husband were invited to turn up for dark-day dinner whenever they chose, but that was hardly likely — well, except, perhaps, when winter came. Everything slowed down when the holidays were over, including custom at the oyster-houses.

"I really must go," Suzie said at last, with regret. "Now you make *sure* you turn up for the wedding breakfast or I shall be *really* cross with you!"

Lionel gave Jack a quick glance, and Jack took the hint. "Katie and I have errands to run in Lionel's trap — did you want us to take you anywhere? It's pretty hot."

But Suzie shook her head with a laugh. "The day I can't walk to the seaside it would have to be hot enough to boil water." She got up, and so did Jack. Katie followed suit. "Let's all go and leave Lionel to wallow in sloth in his back parlor."

"Wallow in sloth!" He feigned indignation. "I am going to be working on a new illusion in the workshop, I will have you know!"

"Well then, we'll leave you to it," Jack replied, and the three of them said good-bye to Mrs. Buckthorn and took their own way out, leaving him contemplating the table for a moment as Mrs. Buckthorn got up to clear it.

I hope Jack can trigger something in that girl, somehow, he mused. *The sooner she realizes what she is, the safer we will all be. Having a Fire Mage that doesn't know what she is about is a bit like having a bomb that has failed to explode sitting near you . . .*

Then he shook himself out of his reverie and headed for the workshop. If Katie would just cooperate . . . he'd had an idea for a whole new act.

The little livery stable where Lionel kept his pony and trap was just at the edge of the range that was comfortable for Jack to walk in weather like this. The wooden leg made everything twice as hard as it had been when he was a whole man. But he wasn't going to feel sorry for himself—not when it meant he had the company of Katie for the entire afternoon.

She had done up her black hair on the top of her head, though a few little tendrils had escaped and were curling around her face in a very attractive manner. She was wearing a white cotton dress of the sort he thought they called a "tea gown," and a wide-brimmed hat. He thought she looked enchanting. You couldn't recognize the little imp she played onstage in the lovely young lady walking slowly at his side as he stumped along.

He was wearing clothing suitable for running errands in the heat; nevertheless, he was mortally glad when they reached the livery stable. The little pony was lethargic and not particularly happy about being out, but Jack didn't intend to push him, just let him amble along at his own pace. After all there was no hurry in these errands. It would be fine if they were done sometime around sunset.

Katie immediately went to the pony's head, whispered in his ears, and scratched gently under his jaw. She kept this up for several minutes, and when she was done, the pony shook his head, and perked up, no longer looking so sullen.

She smiled at his odd look. "I'm a Traveler, remember?" she said—quietly enough that no one would overhear, because it was very likely anyone who did would have a severe prejudice against Travelers. "We've always had a way with horses." Then she looked a little sad. "I miss Buttercup and Belle. I hope they're all right."

There wasn't much he could say to that, so he just nodded sympathetically. "Would you rather drive?" he asked instead. Because it occurred to him that if she missed the horses, she might like to drive.

But she smiled, and shook her head. "If you've driven him before, he knows you on the reins."

He helped her into the little cart, heaved himself in, and picked up the reins and clucked to the pony, and off they went at a nice slow amble.

"What's his name?" Katie asked, as they kept to the side to let faster traffic pass.

"Paddy," Jack told her. "Allegedly—at least, according to Lionel—he's a Connemara pony from Ireland."

Katie craned her neck a little, and examined the pony from her seat as the little fellow ambled along, all good nature now.

"You know, I think he is," she said at last. "Mostly, anyway. He has the temper and the personality. Connemara ponies are often white or gray, but I've seen duns and bays."

Well, if anyone would know it would be a Traveler, he assumed. She made clucking noises and laughed to see the pony's ears flick back to listen to her.

When they got to the first shop, before he could do more than pull the pony up at the front, she turned to him. "Just tell me what you want," she said. "I'll run in and get it, and you take Paddy around to where there's shade."

"That's a kindly offer for both of us, and I'll take you up on it," he replied, with surprised gratitude. He simply handed over his money to her, gave her the list, and took Paddy around the corner while she jumped down and stepped into the shop.

He soon learned that there was another advantage to having her do his shopping. She was in and out much faster than he would have been, and that was after allowing for his missing leg. It was very clear that being a pretty girl meant that shopkeepers—male ones, anyway—attended to her very quickly indeed. The afternoon wasn't even over before she had taken care of his errands and Lionel's too.

So they made one more stop, got some bottled lemonade, and gave Paddy a bit of a treat by driving out along the road beside the seashore. The air was much cooler here, and the pony perked up considerably. When they found a good place to pull over, within sight of the ocean, but with some shade trees and a bit of a stream winding down to the ocean, they did.

Jack would have left Paddy harnessed up, but Katie took that out of his hands, swiftly unharnessing the pony, removing his bit, but tethering him so he could graze beside them under the shade and still be in reach of the stream. He cropped lazily at the turf, or took a few mouthfuls of water, while they spread out rugs and a couple of cushions to sit on to keep her white frock from getting spoilt by grass stains and drank their lemonade.

He told her stories of being in Africa. The good ones, not the ones with bad memories attached. Like the time one of his mates got a mad notion for milk in his tea, and nothing would dissuade him from trying to find some. How he went out, day after day, as they patrolled the rail track, and how finally, one day, he came back triumphant with a goat he'd bought from one of the tribes.

"Oh don't tell me!" she laughed, as he described the little cockney Tommy being pulled along by a half-wild African goat that had its own notion of where it wanted to be. "He bought a billy!"

"No, they took pity on him, they sold him a nanny, but not so much pity that they sold him a *nice* nanny," Jack chuckled. "They sold him the meanest, most cross-tempered old goat I ever saw in my life. Another lad and I that had some country upbringing showed him how to milk her, but you had to truss up her head tight, and keep one hind leg off the ground when you did it, and half the time she still got bites and kicks in on you. He lost more milk than he ever got, what with her kicking over the pail all the time, but he had milk for his tea, by Jove!"

She told him stories of roaming with her parents, before they joined a circus. Of flitting through the forest like a little fairy when they camped, learning how to creep up so quietly on a hare that she could almost touch it before it bolted. He wondered if she had ever seen Elementals as a child. It wasn't unusual for those with the magic to do so—though as they got older, they often repressed the memories.

He couldn't tell if she had; if she was editing her recollections, it wasn't obvious. But he could practically see the wild little thing in his mind's eye, her hair all loose, wearing one of her Pa's shirts as a frock with a ribbon around the waist, feet innocent of shoes, as she scampered along forest paths, gorging on berries, gathering nuts, making dolls out of leaves and twigs and bunches of grass. The Elementals would have been enchanted by her. They loved children, and the good ones always worked hard to protect a child from the bad ones.

"Half the time I came back with my hair full of leaves and flowers and feathers I'd stuck in, and my poor Ma would spend an hour untangling it and combing it all out," she said, leaning back on her elbows and watching the waves lap on the shingle a few yards away. "She was always afraid I'd try swimming in a pond and drown, but I never did."

"Try swimming, or drown?" he asked, teasingly.

"Both." She shrugged. "I like a nice hot bath, as does anyone, but I never learned to swim, and I never wanted to. That's not that unusual among Travelers." But she shivered a little, and he knew why.

He nodded. *Exactly what I would expect from a Fire Mage. Generally you can't get them to swim under less than a death threat, and sometimes not even then.* Water was the inimical Element for Fire, after all, as Earth was for Air.

Eventually they ran out of conversation just as the heat got just short of oppressive. Thinking slowed, as if Jack's thoughts were pushing through treacle. Paddy the pony found eating grass to be too much work, had another long drink from the stream, and laid himself down on the turf. Jack found himself staring mindlessly at the ocean for a good long while, and when he finally looked over at Katie, she was doing the same. Fire Mage though he was, he had always found the sound of the waves soporific.

He wasn't sweating at all, of course. He rarely did. That was one of the little gifts of being a Fire Mage.

"Was it this hot in Africa?" she asked, finally.

"Hotter," he replied. "The trick is not to fight it. You sort of accept it, let the heat become a part of you." At least, Fire Mages did that. The trick probably didn't work for anyone else. But for the Fire Mage, any source of heat was a source of energy, and short of being shoved *into* a fire—and often not even then—it never did them any harm.

"Actually," she said thoughtfully, "That doesn't sound all that difficult. I always liked the summer, and being warm. It was winter that was hard for me. If I could have wormed myself right into the stove in the caravan, I would have."

"It's still like that for me," he told her. "Winter nearly kills me, every year. My housekeeper is a good sort, like Mrs. Buckthorn; she always tucks three hot bricks into my bed before she goes to bed, so it's warm when I get there, or the walk back from the theater would undo me."

He was feeling lazy, but not uncomfortable. He was in that state that his old mates used to call "baking like a lizard on a rock," with envy. He waited, glancing over at her sideways, now and again, to see if she would manage it. Because if she did, she would be that much closer to realizing her power.

He actually saw it happen; not so much a change in her expression as an over-all sense of relaxation that became pleasure. Like the moment when you have been sick, and suddenly aren't, and can relax and enjoy the sort of pleasurable release that just having been freed from illness brings with it. Or when you have been fighting to get something accomplished, and finally manage it, and can bask in the feeling of getting it done.

"Oh," she said, with mild surprise. "This is . . . lovely, actually. I think I used to do this when I was a child. I don't ever remember being *hot* when I was little, at any rate."

"You'll get better at it," he promised. "I used to march all day with a bloody great pack on my back, whilst my mates were dropping like they'd been poleaxed. After a while, even when we're doing a matinee and the footlights are blazing up at you, and the limelight blazing down, you still won't feel anything but comfortable. Africa was not bad for me, that way."

"Do you miss it?" she asked. "Africa, I mean."

He shook his head. "No, it's too alien, and too barren. I'm sure the natives love it, but that's their home. When I think of home, I think green fields. My mates, I miss." He thought a little more. "Mind, there were some good moments there. And there's a . . . a strange kind of beauty about that part of the world. When the sun sets, and the mountains are aglow as if they're on fire . . . with the sky above them like the heart of an emerald, and the flats below a dark sea of velvet purple . . ." He sighed. That— yes, that he missed, missed dreadfully. There was no violent, gorgeous, *fiery* equivalent in England, except on very rare occasions. The "red sky at night" that allegedly was the "sailor's delight."

"But the loneliness was enough to murder a man," he continued. "It was you and your mates, and nothing but desert, a few natives, and once in a while, a train howling through. And once or twice a week, one of them trains stopping to toss off your mail, your supplies, and the papers. If the lads were married, and some of them were, their wives would ride out on the train just for a few minutes of talk. Imagine that . . . seeing your wife for only a few moments a week, and then all alone with the heat and the beasts and sometimes, rarely, some fighting."

There was long silence, then. "That sounds . . . rather like torture," she said, finally, and when he looked over at her, she was shaking her head. "I can't even imagine it. I mean, us Travelers spend all our lives right in each other's laps. We never get away from each other and never want to."

He sighed. "It wasn't so bad for me. I never had a sweetheart, and I've always been a bit solitary. But, it was still bad. Men aren't meant to live like that. Sometimes they go peculiar."

"Peculiar" was a polite way to put it. Some turned slovenly and slack. Some became even more rigid and tightly regimented than if their officer was a martinet.

Some you could hear sobbing quietly when the shift was supposed to be sleeping. And once in a while, a man would just run off, never to be seen again.

"No ... I don't think I miss it all that much," he concluded. Then chuckled. "Though this summer, it seems Africa misses *me.*"

She laughed at that, and didn't ask any more questions about his service.

Finally the sun began going down at their right hands, the air had begun to cool at last, and it was time to harness Paddy up and begin the slow ramble back to Brighton. They weren't in a great hurry, and neither was Paddy. He'd eaten enough of the tough seaside grass to content him and he wasn't particularly anxious for his hay. His hooves made a nice even clopping on the hard road; Jack had thought about driving him back along the sea to help him stay cool, but this pace wasn't making him sweat, so they stayed on the road.

It was dark, and just about time for the fireworks, as they neared the Pier. And now, Jack had a bit of a quandary. Should he take the pony back to the stable, then both of them walk to the Pier? Or should he find a boy to hold the pony?

The quandary was solved when, as they passed the point where people were starting to gather for the view, he spotted a boy he actually knew, one of the lads that ran errands at the music hall. The young fellow was already holding two horses, and was perfectly happy to hold Paddy for a couple of pennies. Problem solved. The purchases were securely stowed under the seats behind a bit of a plank door and could not be seen, so there was no need to worry about theft from the trap, either.

Jack offered Katie his hand, but she barely needed it, alighting from the trap with an ease he envied. They joined the slowly gathering crowd at the edge of the water who were preparing to enjoy the nightly show. Vendors moved among them with trays suspended from their necks that held cones of fairy floss and bags of nuts, lemonade and beer, boxes and bags of sweets. Jack got another lemonade for each of them, but he knew from experience that after baking in the sun all day, no Fire Magician was ever going to be tempted by snacks. The heat and light from the sun itself seemed to replenish those whose Element was Fire.

Having lived here as long as he had, he knew where the best places to view the fireworks were, and they weren't where the majority of the visitors had gathered. Of course, the majority of the visitors were chary of going too far down on the beach; they couldn't see well there, despite the illuminations, and they didn't know the tides. Visitors were always afraid of wetting their shoes and spoiling the leather with salt water. He did know the tides, and he also knew the trick of looking for where the pebbles reflected light—that was where the waves had washed them. He took Katie's elbow and guided her down to the shoreline. The tide was going out; if they stood right where the pebbles were wet, they'd get the best view and not have to worry about getting washed by a wave.

"Have you ever seen fireworks?" he asked her.

"Little ones, the sort that children set off at Guy Fawkes," she said. "Nothing—"

And that was when the first of the skyrockets went up. Brighton was famous for its fireworks displays that went on all summer long, and no expense was spared to make them as spectacular as possible. Jack listened to Katie suck in her breath and "ooo" and "ah" with the rest of the crowd, and in spite of the fact that he was deucedly uncomfortable, standing out here on the pebbly beach with his wooden leg pressing achingly into his stump, he was glad he had thought of this.

Although next time, he was going to think ahead and find a place to view the fireworks from the trap, or some other place where they could sit. A café, maybe. She'd like that.

He just wished he was as good at thinking of some way to get her to realize her power. . . .

And that was when it happened.

Runaway skyrockets were uncommon, and the displays were shot off from the end of one of the piers just to keep runaways out over the ocean and away from the crowd. Probably no one would have realized that *this* one was coming straight for them under most circumstances.

But Jack was a Fire Mage, and he spent most of his energy keeping himself aware of what Fire was doing when it was around him. And he had just spent the afternoon "topping up" his well, so to speak.

So when the thing unaccountably made an abrupt right-hand and downward turn, and came straight for them, all his senses went alert at once. Which was a very good thing, since they had no more than seconds before it would reach them and burst.

The entire afternoon had been a great deal of fun for Katie. For one thing, she had never before owned the sort of clothing that would allow her to just walk into a nice shop and buy something without harassment. She greatly enjoyed doing that at any time, but knowing she was running needful errands for Jack and Lionel made her happy to be able to help them as well. She greatly enjoyed simply having the money to buy what was on her list, without having to think about counting her pennies as she did even now, when she had what she considered to be a generous wage. And it was rather nice to be treated as a welcome customer rather than "a filthy Traveler."

She hadn't realized how much she missed the presence of horses until she met Lionel's pony, Paddy. Connemara ponies were highly desired by the Travelers, for their good temper and willingness to work. Paddy wasn't happy about the heat, but she told him they were going somewhere cooler in Traveler horse-tongue, and he seemed to understand. He recognized her immediately as a Traveler, and accepted her at once. Having his soft nose under her hand made her feel completely at ease.

She also hadn't realized how much she missed being somewhere other than inside four walls. Granted, she didn't feel as suffocated by buildings as most Travelers did—she knew from her mother's stories that there were Travelers who broke into a sweat and nearly died when they were confined inside a gorger building, which made being thrown in gaol a terrible torture for a Traveler. But still, she missed the open, she missed the green, and once all of Jack and Lionel's errands were run and the purchases tucked in a secure box beneath the trap's seat, and they were out on the open road, she felt the oppressiveness of *walls* fall away from her.

However, once they stopped, she discovered an entirely new source of . . . unease. And it was completely unexpected. She'd never been this close to the sea before. In fact, she had never actually seen the sea, only heard about it.

It was fascinating, in an "oh, look at that *thing* that is monstrously huge, and could swallow you up without thinking about it" sort of way, and she was glad that Jack kept them up on the grass and well back from it. It wasn't the openness of it—the moors were just as open, and she felt at home there. It was as if some part of her had decided that the sea was probably an enemy, and wanted her to get well clear of it.

She managed to convince that part of herself that the sea wasn't going to suddenly rear up, come rushing up after them, and wash them away. The sea itself only seemed to exude a sort of warning after a while, and she wondered if this was nothing more than her own common sense, reminding her that she didn't know how to swim. Once she had convinced herself she was in no danger, she was able to concentrate on listening to Jack's stories of Africa.

It was hard to imagine at first, but he was good at describing things, and his words managed to paint a picture in her mind of a vast place, lying under a burning sun, parched and yet beautiful in its way.

She wished she could see it.

She was able to picture the natives quite clearly, though. She'd actually seen men from Africa at the bigger Fairs—there had been an African fire-eater at one, a couple of tiny, frightened people called Pigmies at another. She'd felt sorry for the Pigmies, and had been a little frightened of the fire-eater. He had been fierce and wild in his demeanor, and she had wondered what ever could have brought him to England. She imagined the goat-herding natives as being something like that fire-eater, only less aggressive.

He was the one she thought of, as Jack described the Hottentot warriors, the fighting natives he had encountered in the course of guarding the railway line. Very black, very tall, very proud, with patterns of scars picked out all over their faces and bodies. The fire-eater had worn ordinary clothing, but Katie imagined Jack's natives draped in robes of burnt orange, umber, and yellow. Fire colors, for people living under an unforgiving sun.

Now and again, he paused, and she revealed a little more of her own past to him. It was strange, how she had trusted Jack and Lionel from the very beginning, as if they were kin. She wished she dared tell them everything, but she knew she couldn't say anything about Dick yet. Not until she was free. But at least now she knew how to *get* free, and was on her way to doing so.

Keeping her ears open at the music hall, she had discovered that one of the singers was supposed to be divorced; it had taken every bit of her courage to approach the woman, but when at last she had, she found that the lady was sympathetic and a fount of information.

Katie had made sure to catch her one afternoon when she had come in uncharacteristically early. She had tapped on the door of the woman's little dressing room, and when invited in, had slipped in quickly and closed the door behind herself.

The room was as crowded as the dancers' dressing room, with costumes hanging everywhere, even on the walls, a divan crammed in beside the dressing table and stool, and a changing screen cutting off one whole corner. It didn't smell of sweat or dirt though, and it was clear that the room was kept spotlessly clean even though Katie knew that the singer smoked cigarettes.

"I—wonder if I could ask you something?" she stammered, and the woman looked mildly surprised. "Some advice?"

"Well, I'll do my best, dearie." The singer was the older woman, who performed somewhat rowdy, racy comic songs at the end of the show. Something about her inspired confidence in Katie. In a way, the lady reminded Katy of some of the nicer circus wives, the ones that took care of the daily chores around the circus so that the performers could concentrate on their acts. "I don't know what advice an old hag like me can give a pretty little thing like you, though."

"It's about . . . divorce," Katie had blurted, flushing painfully. "I wondered if—you knew how to get one."

"Oh well! Now *that* I can help you with." The woman lit herself a cigarette and gestured to Katie to take a seat on the divan. Katie lowered herself down onto it gingerly, taking care not to crush the flounces of the dress laid out beside her. "Four men I married and divorced, so I have some practice in it, you could say. Well, shall I begin at the beginning?"

It took a bit of time, with a lot of diversion into ". . . and such a handsome bloke, but a right bastard . . ." but the gist of it was fairly simple. The singer—Peggy Kelly was her name ("Though I'm too fat and old to be called Pretty Peggy Kelly anymore")—knew the answer to one of Katie's most important questions. That is, she knew to the penny how much this was going to cost. She also knew an amenable lawyer right here in Brighton ("I used him for two of the four, and the only reason I didn't use him for the other two was because I had to sue in London courts or miss my show dates.") and from everything Peggy said, the man was sympathetic to a woman without wanting to get his hands all over her, and if he was a trifle too fond of the bottle, he liked and understood show business people.

And Peggy knew exactly how to go about getting that divorce in the first place, without ever alerting Dick to the fact that it was going on.

"It's no use going into court and crying that he beat you," Peggy said—and when Katie winced, she nodded with sympathy. "Married to a brute, eh, ducks? Well, unless he kills you, the law's on his side." It was said with calm acceptance that made Katie hang her head, flushing with shame.

Peggy took one finger and put it under Katie's chin, making her look up. "Bright side, ducks. We can get you clear by other ways. But first, you have to tell me all about it. Don't hold nothing back, there's not a bloomin' thing you can tell me that I haven't seen or been through."

This was not what Katie had intended when she first came into Peggy's dressing room. But the older woman, though she looked like a caricature of a low-class barmaid, past her prime and with nothing more profound in her head than the next pint, the next bloke, and the next new hat, turned out to be kind, shrewd, and worldly. She nodded as Katie told her story, without any judgment. "I can't say I've known more than one or two Travelers in my life," Peggy said, "But since a lot of the things that nose-in-the-air people say about Travelers are the same things they say about me, I reckon there's about the same amount of truth in 'em. You and me can be friends, ducky. Like that Kipling man says. Sisters under the skin!" And she *meant* that. She was as warmhearted as Katie's own mother, and Katie could feel that warm-heartedness in every word she said. No wonder she was an audience favorite!

When Katie got to the part about the fire, and agreeing to marry Dick, Peggy frowned fiercely. She asked Katie some pointed questions about those foggy days following the fire. Katie wasn't sure why she was asking these things, but at this point, she trusted Peggy, and answered them. Peggy didn't say anything . . . but Katie could tell she was thinking hard, and wondered why.

Still, since Peggy said nothing, Katie soldiered on with her story.

". . . and then I took the train to Brighton, I found an advertisement, and came here," she finished. "The advertisement was Lionel's, of course."

"Hmm-hmm." Peggy sat back in her chair and folded her hands over her stomach. When she was on stage, her bulk was constricted into ample curves by a corset that looked to have been designed by railway bridge engineers. Here in her dressing room, inside of the folds of a dressing gown that looked like a waterfall of lace and ribbons, her body was allowed to expand. "Well then. We'll have to go the same route that I did, ducks. We lie."

Katie gaped at her, unsure of how to interpret that.

Did Peggy expect just Katie to lie? Or could she possibly mean—"We?" she faltered. "You—"

Peggy laughed, and reached over to pat her hand. "You may be a thievin' Traveler, but you're a bleeding babe in the woods when it comes to law courts. I'm not about to let a little gel like you—much less one that's our Lionel's assistant!—go into the den of snakes alone!" Her eyes gleamed with both amusement and anticipation of a battle. "Besides, that blackguard that shackled you sounds like my second, and I'm always game to take down a wife-beating bastard, I am. So now, this will be as simple as anything. You sue for divorce on grounds of infidelity. I lie and say I caught him bedding my maid. She lies and says he did. That's all we need, we have two witnesses and one of them was the one doing the bedding. My maid'll cry and say he cuffed her and laughed at her when he was done, and that'll be enough for the judge to believe. Can he read, this man you're stuck with?"

Katie felt dazed. How was it that Peggy had come up with this story so quickly? "I don't think so," she said.

Peggy laughed with glee. "All the better then. We'll hire a feller to give him a bunch of old newspapers with the legal stuff shoved in the middle of it, and like as not he'll just use the papers to light the stove with." She nodded.

"But your maid—I don't want to—she'll be spoilt—" Katie objected weakly. She couldn't for a moment imagine why the maid would ever do such a thing for her.

Peggy tossed her head back in gales of laughter. "Oh bless your heart, she's spoilt herself a dozen times over before this! Two of my four, she served as the key to get me out of their noose. No, we'll just need a date and a place where the blackguard might have bedded a girl or three, and it'll have to have been one where we were playing somewhere nearby. I'm partial to a Fair, and I'd be just likely to take a dark day off to go see one, if it was close."

Before too very long, they'd come up with a date when the circus was within an hour's jaunt of Bath, where Peggy had been playing the Crown and Castle. "Now, there we go, deary. It's just a matter of you saving up your pennies. My maid will need a little present of about five pounds." Peggy's eyes twinkled with mirth. "Can't ask her to lose her honor all over again without a little present, now, can we? I swear, she should make this a second income, that she should."

Katie nodded her head, feeling quite as if the entire situation had taken the bit between its teeth and run off with her.

"And you need to save up for the solicitor. He'll want his money in advance, these legal-lads always do. He'll take care of everything else, I'll advise him about what the fellah needs to serve the papers, and he'll get the right bloke to do it so your bully-boy gets served without knowing."

Katie felt a little like a leaf caught in a gale. It was a *good* gale, and it was certainly taking her where she wanted to go, but she didn't seem to have much say in what was happening.

"Why are you doing this for me?" she asked, finally.

Now Peggy's shrewd and calculating gaze softened, and again she reached out to pat Katie's hand. "Because a long time ago, there was a bawdy old gal that dressed up in trousers that did the same for me, when she found me crying in a corner. Don't you worry, ducks. Everything will work out fine."

She had already been to see the solicitor, who had agreed to the same fee Peggy had quoted. Now it was just a matter of raising the money, but as she and Jack rolled along in the trap, heading back to Brighton, she felt more hopeful and more like her old self than she had before her parents died. She was on the way to being free of Dick. She had a lovely room to live in, and good food to eat, and a good job with a good boss. She had friends!

And now they were going to cap off a wonderful day by seeing fireworks!

She'd heard them going off at night, of course. You couldn't miss them, not even being deep inside the music hall at the time the displays were put on. But as she had told Jack, the only fireworks she had ever seen were the Roman candles, squibs, and crackers that settled folk in villages let off at their Guy Fawkes bonfires. Those were pretty and a lot of fun to watch, but these were supposed to fill half the sky. She believed that. She believed the colored pictures she saw on the posters in shop windows and nailed to posts. The Brighton fireworks displays sound like a war from inside the theater, and she could hardly wait to see them.

When they arrived, Jack found one of the little boys that ran errands for the music hall waiting to hold horses for people who had little carts and traps and riding horses, but wanted to get down to the beach to see the fireworks closer. Brighton beasts were used to the noise and light, of course, and unless something else startled them, were not going to get spooked by a skyrocket. It was perfectly safe for the boy to hold as many as half a dozen horses, three to each arm. Paddy didn't seem the least nervous; in fact, when he realized he was staying with the boy, he relaxed into a hipshot pose and put his head down a bit to doze.

They left Paddy and the trap with the boy, and Jack steered her down onto the beach with one hand politely on her elbow. She was a little worried for his wooden leg on the uneven, pebbly surface, but he seemed to manage all right. She kept feeling, though, as if it was she who should have been putting *her* hand under *his* elbow to keep him steady.

Being right down next to the ocean, though, made her stomach a bit uneasy. There was that feeling again, as if all that water plainly did not like her, and would do her a mischief if it could. Jack had bought them both more lemonades, and she kept sipping the sweet-sour beverage to ease her nervous dry mouth, but that didn't help the sensation of being in a place she didn't belong, and a place that was not particularly happy about her *being* there. It was almost as if the sea was haunted by sullen ghosts that were just waiting for a chance to do her a mischief. It wasn't a logical or rational feeling, but she couldn't deny it was there.

All that fled away, however, with the first rocket.

It looked like a flower made of orange fire, blooming across a quarter of the night sky. She was entranced by the beauty, and even reached out unconsciously to touch it. She completely forgot her discomfort as she stared at the display, and rocket after rocket discharged its beauty, red and gold, orange and blue, green and white, into the black sky while the flat sea beneath reflected the colors.

She was vaguely aware of a band playing out on the Pier, and of the exclamations of those around her, but only dimly. She felt almost as if she was *drinking* in the fire and the colors, as if this was satisfying something deep in her soul that she hadn't even been aware was hungry until now.

And then, between one moment and the next—it all went from glorious, to terrible.

She felt it; she couldn't tell how she knew, but suddenly, out of nowhere, she was struck with absolute terror, the terror of the fox that suddenly hears the hounds, or the bird that finds itself trapped on the ground. Somehow she knew—in a heartbeat—that they were in terrible, horrible danger. Stark, breathless fear transfixed her, coursing through her like lightning. They didn't have time to move. She *knew* that. Peril was racing toward them out of the sky.

And then, Jack . . . did something. Just as she instinctively flung up her hands in a futile, but desperate attempt to ward off what she *knew* was coming.

A plume of fire erupted between him and the ocean, and out of it burst a swarm of little lizards. Except these little lizards were made of fire, and had eyes that glowed like white-hot coals. They swarmed over him, and started for her—

As a spray of fire fanned out from her hands, and turned into a fan of fiery feathers, as a pair of *birds* made of fire spread their wings between her and—

The runaway rocket hit the lizards and the birds and burst, sending showers of burning balls mostly out to sea, but also over their heads and to either side of them—balls of white hot flame going everywhere—

Except where the two of them were standing.

People were screaming and running away. *She* screamed, and ducked, as the birds cupped their wings around her and arched their necks over her. Everything was fire and darkness, screaming and terror.

And then, as quickly as it had started, it was over. The beach was dark again. There was no one for yards around but her and Jack.

And they were standing there completely unharmed, as the fiery lizards and the flame-birds disappeared as if they had never been there in the first place.

7

THE salamanders came at Jack's panicked call to shield him and Katie.

But Katie, it seemed, didn't need shielding, as a pair of phoenixes flashed into being all on their own to protect *her*.

That was all that Jack had time to take in. Then there was fire and choking, acrid smoke, and explosions all around them, and briefly, before the salamander batted it away, a wire of pain biting into his arm from a bit of burning metal.

Then, it was over, and they were engulfed in a moment of absolute quiet, in which the only sound was the waves on the beach and the distant band on the Pier. And then the noise started again, as the crowd rushed back toward them, expecting horror and finding commonplace, two people standing there completely unharmed.

It was incredible. No one believed it. *A miracle!* shouted someone, but Jack just grabbed Katie around the waist and pulled her into the crowd while it was still milling around. He was sure of only one thing; they needed to get away while things were still confused enough that they had a chance to. Peoples' eyes were still dazzled enough that once they were *in* the crowd, no one knew they were the two that had survived the barrage of fire. The salamanders and phoenixes had deflected all the fireworks out to sea; not even the rocket casing remained.

While it might have seemed good publicity to be the ones that had somehow come unscathed from what could have been a terrible accident, it was the last thing that Katie would want. Such publicity could bring whoever it was that she feared so deeply hunting for them. There would be pictures in the paper, and reporters wanting interviews. Sooner or later, someone would find out Katie was a Traveler, and there would be police assuming she was a thief, or that she had somehow caused the accident herself to try and get some money out of the city.

No, they needed to get away, and quickly. Let the crowd search, they would be long gone.

Katie was still limp with shock, and didn't even object to his rough handling. He worked them both through the crowd as quickly as he could, while behind him, he heard the shouts.

"Where are they?"

"They were there a moment ago!"

No one imagined they would want to get away from the interest of the crowd on the seashore—and the police and fire who were now pushing their way *toward* the spot as Jack and Katie went in the opposite direction.

Who wouldn't want the attention of having barely escaped death? Who wouldn't want the congratulations, the fame, their names in the paper?

Only us, Jack thought, and broke through the edge of a crowd that was getting denser with every new arrival. He worked his way up to the street, and to their faithful boy, still holding the horses and Paddy, but craning his neck as hard as he could to try and see what was going on down by the water.

"Didja see, sir? Didja see?" he demanded, when he recognized them.

Jack laughed, and he hoped it didn't sound as shaky as he thought it was. "Only a runaway skyrocket, lad. Didn't hit anyone, thanks to the Grace of God, and bounced back out to sea."

"Oh . . ." the boy said, briefly disappointed that there had been no carnage, no horrors. Jack laughed again, weakly. Boys were like that . . . loved talking about people bursting into flames or exploding, or being blown up into a thousand bits. Loved to think about it, as long as they didn't actually see the reality. He remembered being exactly like that at this boy's age. Stories about fighting, cannons roaring, stories about the American Wild West and Indian massacres, anything wild and bloody just fascinated him and made him and his friends act it out. Actually he had still been a little like that when he joined the Army. He didn't get it knocked out of him until he'd seen the reality of war. His imagination hadn't been good enough to get past the exciting explosion and flames and whizzing bullets part, and into the part where there were scattered limbs, burned flesh, and the bleeding bodies. Girls never seemed to be like that. Girls were nicer creatures than boys, really. Or maybe their imaginations were better.

He gave the lad his penny, got a still-shocked Katie up into the trap, and clicked to Paddy, who knew there was only one place they could be going now, and broke into a trot to get there.

Katie felt . . . stunned. Nothing made any sense. The world didn't contain lizards and birds made of fire that protected people from skyrockets. It *didn't.* No matter what stories her mother had told her at night, huddled in the cupboard-bed in the caravan, or sitting beside a campfire. That was all silliness and magic, like the little people she used to pretend she saw in the forest, the ones with goat-hooves and horns, or the tree-girls, or the tiny flying ones with butterfly and dragonfly wings. Even if she thought she used to see lizards and birds like that in the campfire, that was all a child's nonsense. It had never been real. Children could convince themselves they had seen anything, that a bush was a lion and a cloud was a dragon.

But these things had been real; there was a slight scorch across the linen of her skirt at ankle-length to prove it. Her hair and dress stank of gunpowder and chemicals. It had *happened.* She had seen it with her own, adult eyes, and so had dozens of witnesses. They had almost been killed by a runaway rocket, and things out of her childhood daydreams had appeared out of nowhere to save them.

It was impossible.

It was real.

She vibrated between the two, unable to accept that imaginary creatures had just saved her life, unable to deny that they had. She was so numb that she just allowed Jack to hurry her through the crowd and away from the site of the impossibility, let him practically throw her into the trap. But finally, as they got into a side street where it was quiet, where Paddy's hoofbeats echoed cheerfully among the buildings, she seized his arm and shook it violently, making Paddy pull up, confused.

"What just happened?" she choked out.

Jack licked his lips. It looked as if he was thinking of a thousand different answers, but the one that he decided on was a single word.

"Magic," he said, in a tone that brooked absolutely no argument.

"But it—but then—but you aren't—" she began, thinking that surely, surely he meant something like what Lionel did—except, of course, illusion wasn't going to shield a person from a rain of fireballs!

"Katie, *hush,*" he said sharply, grabbed her wrist and gave it a little shake. "It was magic. Real magic. Now hush, and hear me out."

She couldn't have said a word now if she'd had to, they were all stuck somewhere in her throat. So they sat there in the trap in the empty street while Paddy pawed the cobblestones impatiently, and he told her impossible things.

How there were four kinds of magic—"Elemental Magic," he called it—Earth, Air, Fire, and Water. How some people could use this magic. How there were magic creatures that were made of this magic. How he and Lionel were able to use it, that he could use Fire and Lionel could use Air.

How she could, too. How the fiery birds coming out of nowhere to protect her proved it. How the fact that she could *see* them proved it.

"You don't think anyone else saw them, do you?" he asked her. "Did you hear them shouting about the phoenixes and the salamanders? No, of course you didn't. They only saw the skyrocket. Only you and I saw what came to protect us."

She didn't want to believe him, but the only other explanation was that she had gone mad.

She kept shaking her head *no* and he kept saying *yes*.

"Are you going to be all right?" he kept asking. "I don't want you to get into your room and have hysterics alone, I need to know if you are going to be all right."

Finally, when she realized that what he meant was that he was actually going to *take* her straight back to her room at the boarding house, if she was going to be all right, she managed to shake her head yes.

He turned Paddy's head, much to the pony's disgust, and as she sat there on the seat of the trap and shook, he took her home.

Lionel must have been waiting at the door, listening for the sound of the pony and trap, for he practically flew out of the front of the house the moment that Jack pulled the cart up in front of the house. "What in the name of God happened?" he asked, sounding frantic. "I felt something *horrible,* and my sylphs were out of their minds! My—"

Jack waved a weary hand at him. "Let's get the things into the house, then if you don't mind, could you take the trap back to the stable and walk back? I don't think I'm up to it."

"Good God man, you stink of—" Lionel shut his mouth. "Obviously you are all right, and obviously Katie is all right or you would have sent a message. Get in the house, get some soup in you, it's waiting on the table. I'll be right back."

Jack lowered himself out of the cart, and limped heavily into the house, his stump aching worse than it had in a very long time. He thought for certain that the evening's near-disaster had killed his appetite, but when he smelled the heavenly aroma of thick chicken soup, he realized it had not. The heavy tureen had kept it piping hot, and he was into his second bowl when Lionel returned.

Now that the rawly ravenous gnawing in his gut was quieted—and he should have realized, working that much magic, that fast, was going to burn a *lot* of energy—he described to Lionel what had happened.

Lionel sat back in his chair, light from the gas lamps showing his features clearly. "Good Lord," he said. "Good Lord. And she—manifested."

"A pair of phoenixes," Jack told him. "I didn't have to protect her at all."

"And she *saw* them."

"She saw *everything.*" He blew out his breath in a sigh. "And all I can say is, thank heaven she's poor and depends on the job at the music hall, or I very much doubt we would see her tomorrow. If she weren't poor and desperate, she'd probably be packing to leave right now."

Lionel passed his hand over his face. "Well," he said, finally. "At least she didn't incinerate anyone."

"In fact, my salamanders just kept me from being turned into cinders. Her phoenixes deflected the worst of the rocket back out into the sea." That little detail had only come back to him as he'd talked. He finished his soup and the last of his bread, and pushed the bowl away, reaching for his beer. He very much felt as if he had earned it.

"Now what do we do?" Lionel said at last.

"I suppose . . ." Jack paused for thought. "I suppose that very much depends on her."

Katie would have run up the stairs and hidden in her room—except that the moment she opened the door of the boarding house, the smell of Mrs. Baird's good soup struck her a blow and she nearly doubled over from hunger. And once again she found herself vibrating between two things that she desperately wanted to do. She desperately wanted to run up and pull the covers over her head—and she desperately wanted to eat.

Hunger won, although she kept absolutely quiet while she ate three bowls of thick pea soup. Since everyone else was chattering gaily away, no one seemed to notice—or if they did, they probably thought she was melancholy over losing Suzie to matrimony.

As soon as she had eaten, she scuttled up to her room; this morning she *had* been sad that she was going to be in it all alone—it was the first time in her life that she'd had a room all to herself, and it felt alien and not-right. But now . . . now she was intensely grateful. And she *did* throw her clothing onto the other bed, huddle herself into her night-dress, and pull the covers over her head, to curl into a ball and shake.

Because . . . if all this was real . . .

Then besides all those childhood memories of little folk in the fields and forests, and strange things dancing in the fire, there were other memories she *did not* want to face.

Memories of running to the burning caravan, and being driven away from the door by fiery birds that protected her from the flames and tried to keep her from going in. Memories of beating on the door—a door that would not move so much as an inch—with fists surrounded by flame-lizards. Memories of being pushed, back, and back again by the little lizards, who had kept her from trying to break down the door, until real, human hands seized her and dragged her away.

And oh, she did not want to see, she did not want to remember!

But she did, and she cried, and cried, and cried, until she could scarcely breathe, until she was all out of energy and all out of thoughts, and fell at last into a sodden, grief-filled sleep.

She woke a little earlier than usual, feeling heavy, empty, and starving. Her eyes were sore, her cheeks were sore, and every muscle felt cramped.

Not a good omen for a performance day . . .

"Oh, Mother Mary," she said, almost starting to weep all over again. Of all the things she didn't want to do right now, facing Lionel and Jack, much less a crowded music hall, was at the top of the list.

But she didn't have a choice. There were bills to pay. She needed to eat. And—

For one very brief moment she toyed with the notion

of just packing up and fleeing. Finding a job somewhere else . . .

But then, good sense came back to her, because really, where else could she go that Dick wouldn't have a good chance of finding her? Mary Small had sworn that Brighton was the only place safe for her and . . .

And . . .

Mary Small said I had magic.

Could this have been what the old woman meant? Had Mary Small herself had a touch of this—stuff? Her head began to spin. How many other people had this? Jack said he and Lionel did . . . did Suzie? Anyone else in the music hall?

Oh God . . .

The gnawing in her stomach finally drove her out of bed. She washed her feverish face in the basin on the dresser and bathed her eyes, hoping to take some of the soreness out of them. She pulled on her clothing, wincing a little at the faint scorch-mark on the bottom of the skirt. At least being left out overnight had aired the gunpowder smell out. At least as far as she could tell . . .

Suzie had left some of her things behind, and one of them was a bottle of lavender-eau-de-cologne. "I can't bear lavender, you have it," she'd said. So now, just to be sure, Katie sprinkled it liberally on her dress before she put it on.

When she came down to breakfast, the entire table was abuzz—but not, as she had feared, with the story of the miraculous escape of two people from a runaway firework, but with rumors of a railway strike. Relieved that no one was going to be asking her about her outing, she ate in a hurry and rushed out of the boarding house, only to find her steps lagging, as she didn't really *want* to go to the theater....

And most especially, she did *not* want to face Jack.

She waited just outside the alley, though, for a big knot of the dancers to come. They all shared the same boarding house—another, not unlike Mrs. Baird's, but that catered to dancers—and they tended to arrive and leave at the same time. Of all the professions in the music hall, it seemed that men were under the impression that the dancers had the most easily negotiated virtue. Of course ... they were mostly right, the men. The dancers weren't paid very much, and it wasn't as if they were going to be able to put anything aside for their old age. Given that the general opinion was that they were no better than they should be *anyway,* plenty of them figured they might as well be hung for a sheep as a lamb, and took advantage of that reputation to get as much out of the stage-door beaus as they could. But some were not particularly anxious to trade their slightly shabby virtue for anything less than a wedding ring. Those traveled in packs of four to six, and *never* went out with men alone. Or at least, not until they found someone willing to marry them.

One such pack came around the corner before she had waited too long, and she added herself to it. She managed to get past Jack without him being able to do more than see she was there, and into the dressing room.

And suddenly, surrounded by all the things that were normal and everyday, she started to wonder if maybe she hadn't imagined all of that. Perhaps she had fallen and struck her head, and the entire incident had been a sort of fever dream. After all, as she listened to the dancers chattering away, she didn't overhear *anything* about a runaway skyrocket. Surely that should have been something of a sensation by now....

As she put on her rehearsal clothing, she started to feel embarrassed. Poor Jack ... what must he have thought, when she started babbling about lizards and birds? He surely couldn't *really* have told her all that nonsense about magic. He must have been trying to talk sense into her ... or maybe she was just imagining that there had been any sort of conversation whatsoever.

She hurried out to the stage; thanks to waiting for the gaggle of girls, she was a little late, and Lionel was looking a bit anxious when she turned up.

"I'm sorry I'm late," she said.

"I heard about your—accident," Lionel said, sounding unusually tentative. "Jack told me. Are you all right?" She flushed.

"I clearly made a right fool out of myself," she replied. "At least I can put that down to a knock on the head rather than drinking too much—all we had were lemonades. I'm fine now, and I'm ready to work."

Lionel looked at her oddly, but didn't say anything more, just started the run-through of the act. For her part, she tried to behave entirely as if nothing at all had happened, and aside from a couple little hitches with the equipment, the rehearsal went fine.

Well, fine except that Lionel kept asking if she was certain she was all right. It made her nervous, and she wondered just what it was Jack had told him—and what she had told Jack!

Finally, when she was helping him arrange the equipment in the wings for the matinee, she asked, nervously, "Are you having second thoughts?"

"About?" He turned to look at her, his face surprised.

"About whether—I'm a good assistant—" she faltered.

He laughed, and it sounded surprised. "No, no, nothing of the kind. I just want to be certain that you are feeling all right."

"I'll be better with a bit of luncheon," she said, trying to sound perfectly well and at ease. "I'll be right back."

She hurried into her street clothing and whisked past Jack a second time. She really did *not* want to know, now, what had happened after that skyrocket . . . went awry. Surely it could never have come too near them. Surely what had happened was that it had burst too close over the water, and she had been startled, and fallen, and hit her head. That was the only rational explanation.

And surely a good, strong cup of tea and a thick, commonplace sandwich would drive the last of the boggarts away.

"Lionel, I need to speak with you!" A voice trained to bellow out slightly bawdy songs so they could be heard all the way to the back of the uppermost gallery arrested Lionel in his tracks as he hurried after Katie, intending to catch her before she escaped the music hall. He turned.

Peggy Kelly ambled her way across the stage toward him, making her leisurely way, the plumes on her hat bobbing, her ample bosom making her look like a ship in full sail. It would have been unspeakably rude to just run away from her, so he waited, but not patiently. He really needed to get hold of Katie, take her somewhere that was quiet, sit her down, and make her understand that *none* of what had happened last night was due to a hit on the head! Of all the possibilities he and Jack had discussed last night, this was not one of them!

But Peggy Kelly had other plans in mind. "Come along to my dressing room, you reprobate," she said, fondly, but in a tone that warned him she was not going to take any argument from him as she took his arm. "I have a few things to discuss with you. And no, before you ask, it cannot wait."

Inwardly, he groaned, but he put a good face on it, and allowed himself to be towed off to Peggy's dressing room. It was one of the better ones here, as befitted someone who was a "star turn." Small, of course, but Peggy's dresser and personal maid had made the most of it. She motioned to him to take a seat on a surprisingly comfortable chair, lowered herself onto a divan, and whisked a napkin away that was covering the little table between the two. Somewhat to his mild surprise, there were two bottles of beer there, and a plate of extremely nice pub sandwiches.

"Now, eat, and listen to me, and don't interrupt me until I am finished," she said, helping herself to a sandwich and one of the bottles of beer. "That new assistant of yours—she's—"

"—I know, she's a Traveler," Lionel said impatiently, and started to get up. "Peggy, if you don't mind—"

"But I *do* mind, and you can set yourself right back down, my lad!" she said sharply, so sharply that he did as he was told. "Now I *told* you not to interrupt me! That's not what I brought you here to talk to you about! You think *I* have anything against Travelers?" She snorted. "That little Traveler gel has herself a very great burden of fear and troubles on her, and you need to know why, and you need to know *now* before the troubles come here, as they might."

Lionel listened, growing increasingly astonished, as Peggy laid out in no uncertain terms all of Katie's "troubles." He was a little irritated that after all of his kindness to her, the girl hadn't come to *him* for help, but only a little. After all, he was a man, and he might be expected to take the man's part in this; it was more natural for her to confide in a woman, once she knew she wouldn't be condemned out of hand for running away from her husband. And Peggy was well known to be a divorcee. It was logical for Katie to have gone to the older woman, really.

"Well?" Peggy asked, watching him shrewdly when she had finished.

"Well, clearly we are going to have to help her," Lionel replied, a little nettled that Peggy would doubt his support. "You needn't ask, we shall. By Jove, when I think of a brute of a man beating that poor little thing that must have been half his weight, well, it's a damn good thing that I can't get my hands on him, that's all." He felt his lip curling with contempt. *And it is a damned good thing for me that my powers wouldn't extend to harming him. However provoked, Alderscroft would hunt me down like a mad dog if I used them that way.* "I think that explains why she was so happy to wear a mask on stage—she doesn't want to chance anyone recognizing her." He licked his lips. "Divorces aren't cheap, are they?" he ventured.

The plumes on Peggy's hat bobbed as she nodded. "Not cheap, no. And if she's not going to decide she needs to starve herself to save for it, *you* will need to find a way for her to make a bit more money." Peggy made it quite clear with her attitude that he had *better* come up to the mark and do so quickly, or he would be answering to her.

"Of course, of course. . . ." That was the least of his concerns. He didn't think that Katie was overreacting by wanting to wear a mask on stage. She knew this fellow better than anyone, and she would also know exactly how possessive and persistent he would be when his "property" bolted. "Peggy, just how much of a brute was—is—this fellow, could you tell from what she told you?" He was actually rather anxious to know the answer to that question. He might have to find a way to restrain Jack from hunting the man down and shooting him when the doorkeeper found out.

"Not as bad as my second," Peggy said complacently, and turned her sandwich around a bit in her plump, pink fingers so she could bite a corner off of it. "It sounds as if he only knocked her about a little bit; it was his strength that did the hurting. But she's right terrified of him, and I think he's brutish and stupid enough that if he's drunk or in a temper, he's quite likely to try and kill her for running away. At the very least, if he's drunk or angry, he won't hold back his strength, and might kill her by accident. I'd keep that from Jack, if I were you. He's taken a fondness for her, and she for him, if my old bones are right."

"Oh your old bones are not wrong . . ." He chewed on his lower lip, took a drink of beer, and finished his own sandwich. "Well, let me think this over. Really the best, first thing we can do is get her free of this brute. Since that takes money, well, then money we must find. Maybe something will turn up in the way of an extra job for her.

She's already in the chorus, but that pays almost nothing . . ."

"You're a good lad, Lionel. You'll think of something." She patted his knee and finished her beer, the lace flounces on her sleeve fluttering like the wings of a butterfly—or a sylph. "Now you run along back to your dressing room. We've a matinee to get ready for."

"Good gad, is it that late?" he asked, startled, and looked at his watch. He'd entirely missed a chance to get Katie alone. There would be absolutely no time between the matinee and the evening performance. He would never be able to catch her after the evening performance if she decided to bolt back to her boarding house. "Blast. It is. Well . . . thank you, Peggy."

"You just do right by that little gel," Peggy warned him. "No woman deserves to be knocked about like a stray dog. I won't hear of it. She's your responsibility, now that you know what's what."

"I will," he promised.

Back in his dressing room, he looked up to see a sylph perched on his mirror. "Well now what do I do?" he asked the little thing, who cocked her head to peer down at him. "The girl has talked herself into believing none of what she saw is real. *And* we have to figure out a way for her to earn *quite* a bit of extra money. I don't suppose you have any ideas, do you?"

The sylph shrugged, and vanished in a *poof* of sparkling magic. He sighed.

"Of course not," he grumbled, applying himself to the business of getting on his makeup. "And it's not as if I was one of those poncy Masters with pots of money sitting around like Alderscroft. God above knows *that* would solve everything, one way or another."

The show went well, and Katie enjoyed her turn with the chorus dancers; the blond, pink, and white wigs they wore in their three numbers were a good disguise, and she was always kept at the back to fill out the group anyway. Suzie had held that particular job as well as that of Lionel's assistant, and she had seen to it that Katie got her audition before anyone else had a look-in. Katie was better than any of the girls in the chorus, but was also clever enough to look only as good as the best, so she wasn't put up front.

The more she convinced herself that it had all been due to a silly bump on the head, the better she felt. After all, she'd come to no harm, and all she'd managed to do was embarrass herself. She began to feel a great deal less strained and anxious, and in between the matinee and the evening performance, she even managed to get out to talk to Jack, making certain to catch him at a moment when there was no one about.

He was all alone at his desk, looking very much cooler than the performers who had slipped out for a smoke and a pint, and when he saw her coming, she was relieved to see he didn't look at all put out with her.

"I'm horribly sorry, and I hope I didn't embarrass you too much," she said, a little breathlessly. She did *not* want him to be upset with her in any way. He and Lionel had been so kind—and she had come to enjoy those dark-day dinners with both of them so *very* much. She had friends again, friends that didn't look down on her for being a

Traveler, friends that talked to her like an intelligent person and not an object. They knew she was a Traveler; she didn't want them to start thinking she was touched!

The doorkeeper blinked, looking confused. "Excuse me—embarrass you?" Jack faltered. "I don't understand—"

"When that runaway skyrocket came so close and I must have slipped and hit my head," she explained. "Or maybe a piece of it hit me. I mean, I don't remember, but I wouldn't if it had hit me hard, now, would I? I—well, what I thought I saw doesn't matter, I just hope—you can understand it was all a sort of fever dream, right?" She looked at him pleadingly. "I hope you don't think I was raving mad, or that I was making things up to—to get attention."

Emotions passed so swiftly across his face that she couldn't read them, but to her great relief, his expression settled into one of kind concern. "Of course not, and all you did was babble a little. I don't remember you falling or being struck, but then I was a bit distracted, you might say. I know you were scared, and I was worried for you. I should be the one apologizing to you for not getting you seen to. If I'd known you'd been struck, I would have had you off to a doctor! I drove around for a bit to make sure you were going to be all right, but you insisted on being set down at Mrs. Baird's boarding house, and I reckoned that you'd be all right there. Is your head sore?"

"Not a bit—" For a moment that confused her. Because if she had hit her head badly enough to have seen—things—shouldn't it be sore? But she resolutely shoved the thought away. She must have hit her head. Her father always said she had a hard head. He said it came from her mother's side. He must have meant that literally as well as figuratively.

"It's all right then. The next time we go and watch the fireworks, we'll do it from Paddy's cart." He patted the top of her head as if she had been a child, and oddly, she didn't resent it. "I hope you'll be the one forgiving *me* for not seeing you'd come to a mischief. No dizziness? You were all right on stage?"

She nodded, relieved. "Right as rain. I remembered what you were talking about, down at the shore, how you would just accept the heat when you were in Africa, and I tried that when it started getting too warm out there. It worked! So thank you ever so, for that."

He made a little bow, with one hand to his heart. "My pleasure. But if you were getting warm out there, best you go toddle off to the bar and get some tea or water. And here—" He pulled out a little packet from his desk, which proved to have three hardboiled eggs and salt in a twist of paper in it. "—eat these, and if you can't eat them all, share 'em with one of the other girls. Heat makes you not want to eat, but you ought to anyway."

She accepted his gift. "Thanks, ever so. You are always so good to us, Jack!"

He smiled.

Feeling much more at ease now, she ran back, first to the bar to get that tea, and then to the dressing room, where she shared the eggs with two of the other girls. The barmen were partial to the girls, and always gave them bread and cheese along with the tea, although they weren't supposed to. With bread and cheese, three hardboiled eggs was really far more than one person could manage, and besides, she knew there would be plenty of soup waiting for her at supper.

It also made the chorus girls more friendly. You could never have too many friends in this world.

Lionel slipped out of the alcove where he'd been hiding, listening to Jack's conversation with Katie, once the girl had gone. He and Jack had hoped she would come try and confide in the doorman, but he was disappointed with how she had already managed to convince herself that what she had seen was a complete hallucination. He shook his head with mingled irritation and sympathy. "Hit her head!" was all he said.

Jack shrugged. "You can't blame the girl for not wanting to believe," he pointed out, as he offered Lionel an egg from inside his desk. "Think about it—she's never seen magic before, or if she did, it was something she made herself forget as soon as she was old enough to realize no one else could see it. You and I at least had it in the family, and our fathers made sure to make us understand about the magic from the time we could first see the Elementals. What's she had?"

"A worse time than we'd thought, apparently." While Jack listened, increasingly appalled and angry, Lionel outlined what Peggy Kelly had told him.

When Lionel was done, Jack was grinding his teeth so hard he finally had to force himself to stop and get a bit calmer. He might not be a *Master,* but the anger of an Elemental Fire Mage was nothing to be trifled with. While he couldn't command his Elementals, they did respond to him, and they were just as likely to go out hunting for something to take *his* wrath out on as they were to react with indifference. In fact, given that they had elected to start showing themselves to the girl, they were *more* likely to look for something to hunt.

"Right, then," Jack said, after several steadying breaths. "Well. Right now, not much we can do about that bastard she's shackled to."

Lionel made a sour face. "True. At least, not much we can do about her situation until she confides in us."

"When it comes to getting her more of the ready, well, our hands are pretty well tied, no matter what Peggy thinks," Jack continued. "There are only so many jobs in this hall, and she's taken all the ones she can legitimately take. I don't think it's a good idea to let her hunt more work outside this hall."

"Nor do I!" Lionel replied with alarm, and wiped his forehead with his handkerchief. "No, the only solution is to find her more work here, but—"

"Exactly so. But. *Unless,* of course, some opportunity for her to make more money happens to land in our collective laps." Jack drummed his fingers on his desk. "Which . . . it might. Your Elementals and mine now know about this, know that we need to find her a way to get enough to get shed of that bastard. Hers have known all along, but might not have realized that money was part of the solution. Well, now they do know, and the Elementals of three mages, plus the mages themselves combined, often have the effect of changing luck merely by them *wanting* it to change."

Lionel blinked at him. "I—didn't know that—" he said slowly.

Jack laughed. "Why do you think old Alderscroft has that bloody White Lodge of his? It's not just for going after the big things. It's for bending luck the way he wants it to bend. Which, largely, is to keep ordinary folk from finding out we exist, but sometimes he bends it to help someone out, or bring about something that's good for mages in general. One of his cronies told me. Almsley, I think he called himself." He thought back to his encounter with Almsley . . . must have been Almsley Senior, the man had been older than Jack. And a Duke, to boot. There'd been a little something he'd wanted help with and only a Fire Mage would do. Jack had been a bit young to help, so he never found out what it was. Almsley'd been a damned fine chap, nothing high and mighty about him, polite as you please to Jack's Pa, and no ordering anybody about. The sort of fellow that made you want to help him because he was a good man.

"Heard of him. Never met him. Well . . ." Lionel took out his handkerchief again and mopped his forehead with it. Jack felt sorry for him, this heat was really punishing the Air Mage. "All right, there's this. The gel's seen her Elementals. They're not going to let her *un*see them again, no matter how much she tries to tell herself they came from a knock on the head. So we need to be ready for when she gets her second encounter."

"Fire Elementals are an impatient lot," Jack observed, grateful that at this moment there was no one trying to get in or out of the stage door, so no one to overhear them. "They won't put up with being ignored for long. I'm a little surprised they waited this long."

"Probably the minute she's alone, then." Lionel gave Jack a look. Jack sighed, knowing what the look meant.

"All right, I'll hang about outside her boarding house in case it's tonight," he promised. His leg was going to hate him for this.

8

BY the time the evening show was over, Katie was feeling almost as happy as she had been yesterday afternoon, when she and Jack had been out watching the sea and drinking lemonades. The show went well, Jack had not been offended by her nonsense, and his little trick of dealing with the heat had actually left her feeling more refreshed than tired when they took their final bows and all trotted off to their various dressing rooms.

She waved off Jack's offer of taking her to supper; she was well aware that his purse wasn't all that much heavier than hers, and he'd already treated her to lemonades yesterday. "I've paid for Mrs. Baird's supper, thank you, Jack," she said cheerfully. "Given I've paid for it, I'd rather eat it!"

"Can't argue with that logic," he replied, and turned to deal with a drunk who wanted in the stage door to meet with a "Dorrie." Katie saw his kind every night, men with enough in them that they convinced themselves one of the girls in the show had been making eyes at him and him alone for the whole night.

As was her usual habit, she waited at the corner until she joined with a knot of girls going on their way in her general direction, trying to look as if she was part of the group. When they drifted off in a different direction from the one she wanted, she joined a family group of a husband and wife and several older daughters. And when they made a turn in the direction of some family boarding houses, she was within sight of Mrs. Baird's and felt safe in hurrying the remaining distance on her own.

The soup tonight was a lovely spinach soup, and as usual, there was Mrs. Baird's perfect bread to go with it. Some of the other girls were acrobats from another of the music halls, and when she ventured a comment on something one of them had said about how to best execute a tumble across a smaller stage than they were used to, they accepted her immediately into their conversation. It was like being back at that first circus again, the one that had been so much friendlier than Andy Ball's.

She didn't miss Suzie much at all. It was a pity these girls would be gone in another few weeks, but at least until then, she had someone she could compare notes with. When she finished washing up and went upstairs, it was in a singularly contented frame of mind.

Which meant that, when she had closed and locked her door behind her, and turned to light the lamp, the surprise of finding that the lamp already *was* lit—and, apparently, by the fiery little bird inside it—was a cruel shock indeed.

Even more of a shock was to turn and see a trio of glowing lizards winding in and around the logs in the unlit fireplace.

Before she could react, one of them leapt right out of the fireplace, ran up her arm, and sat on her shoulder, staring into her eyes with its own glowing, white orbs.

She froze; even her thoughts came to a standstill.

It flickered out a flame-tongue at her, caressing her cheek with it. It should have burned her. Instead, it felt like a cool breeze.

It stared deeply into her eyes. *"Remember..."* it hissed. *"Remember..."*

Images flashed across her memory—the ones from that horrible night. The caravan, already fully engulfed in flame, as if someone had doused it in paraffin oil before setting it ablaze. The absolute *lack* of cries from inside. Herself, rushing for the wagon, up the stairs, and pounding on the door with both hands, calling her parents' names. The fires licking around her, and creatures exactly like this, twining around her, protecting her from the inferno. A larger bird, springing up out of the flames, actually *pushing* her away from the door, as she screamed and tried to get past it, tried to reach for a door handle that was white-hot.

No!

She didn't want to see. Didn't want to know. Didn't want to understand that by the time she saw the caravan in flames, her parents *must* have already been dead, or she would have heard them inside.

And she did *not* want to see these hallucinations, these creatures out of her own mind, right here in her room. They *must* be hallucinations! Because if they weren't—

If they weren't, then it might have been that she could have controlled the fire and saved her parents. And for some reason, she had not.

That was what she didn't want to face, most of all.

With a tiny cry of despair, she brushed the lizard from her, wrenched open the door, and raced headlong down the stairs, and out into the street.

The room that had been a shelter to her was a shelter no more, and all she wanted was darkness and a place to hide.

A little salamander popped out of the bowl of Jack's pipe as he stood on the corner, quietly smoking. The door to the boarding house flew open, and, warned by the appearance of his own Elemental, Jack was not surprised to see Katie, eyes streaming tears, running blindly down the stairs and into the street.

And, fortunately, right toward him. Fortunately, because as fast as she was moving, he didn't think he had a prayer of catching up with her.

She didn't even see him and he was able to reach out and catch her as she stumbled past him. "Gently, Katie!" he said, before she could lash out at him. "It's me, Jack . . ."

She didn't fight him, which was a mercy. She didn't go limp, either, or fling herself at him. Instead, she just stood there, looking as if she was so caught up in what was going on in her own head that she was oblivious to everything around her.

They had to get somewhere safe. He had to bring her out of this, and make her understand and accept what was going on with her. Frantically, he tried to think of somewhere he could take her where they could talk and be private. Some place she would feel secure. Not, good gad, his own rooms at his little flat. Not the parlor there either, nor Mrs. Baird's parlor. It was too late and too far to go to Lionel's—

The music hall . . . He had the keys. He could take her to Lionel's dressing room. She'd feel safe there.

"Come on, Katie," he said. "I know somewhere we can go."

It must have been well after midnight when he finally got some sense into her and out of her; Jack had not bothered to take out his watch to check the time, for fear that she would interpret the gesture as being he was tired of dealing with her. He was tired, but not of dealing with her . . . exhausted, really, but so was she.

But finally he got through to her. He convinced her she wasn't insane. He showed her everything he knew how to do, from requesting Elementals to come to them—and fortunately they were more than anxious enough to oblige—to creating fire in his hand, lighting a lamp, shielding them both within a dome of Fire-energy—

Every trick he knew, really. And then, somehow, he coaxed her to try a little. Just the usual; make a flame dance on the tip of one finger, coax a salamander into her hand.

Finally, he heard the full story of that terrible night when her parents had died from her own lips. He didn't know if he would *ever* be able to convince her that there had been nothing she could do to save her parents, but at least he was sure of one thing.

Whatever the cause, it hadn't been her doing.

Both of them exhausted, he walked her back to her boarding house. Mrs. Baird was not the sort to render judgment on the girls that lived there, not as long as they didn't actually bring men to their rooms. So as he suspected, the kitchen door had been left off the latch, and she could slip inside and make her way back up to her room without anyone the wiser.

And as for him, well, no one cared at what hour a man came home.

Katie woke up to find herself lying fully clothed atop the bedclothes . . . and with a curious glowing lizard nose to nose with her.

If there was ever any chance that she was likely to wake up doubting what Jack had shown her last night, having a salamander lying on one's chest like a friendly cat was the one thing that would explode all possible doubts.

She started to sit up, and the salamander scampered down her body and up onto the bedpost, where it sat like some sort of brass ornament, watching her.

"Good morning," she croaked hoarsely.

The creature bobbed its head to her.

It continued to watch her as she changed her clothing and washed herself. Doing so didn't make her feel less exhausted, but at least it made her feel less sticky.

When she opened the door, the lizard vanished in a poof of sparks; she knew now that it would come back when it chose to, and sometimes, when she asked it to. It occurred to her as she made her way slowly down the steep staircase that she had never had a pet before.

Which led to a new question, among . . . hundreds, really. But the one foremost in her mind was a rather simple one. Were these Elemental creatures more like pets, or more like companions?

So many questions, and she was not sure if it was right to ask about them. Was she supposed to find these things out for herself? Jack hadn't said anything last night about what she was to do about all of this. Was someone supposed to teach her? Were there books? *I don't read very well* . . . In fact, she could just about blunder her way through a basic primer. How could she be expected to read a complicated book?

If this was something that supposedly you just *knew* how to deal with then . . . well, she didn't. No instructions had turned up in her sleep last night.

She was so absorbed in thinking about everything that had happened that she paid almost no attention to what she was eating and was as quiet as the proverbial church mouse. The other girls didn't notice at first, but finally one of the acrobats stopped chattering to her mates and took a good look at her.

"Are you sickening for something?" the young woman asked in alarm. "You look *terrible*. Like you didn't sleep a wink."

"I didn't, or mostly not," Katie confessed. "I had horrible nightmares." That was safe to say, everyone had nightmares from time to time. And this was almost true. Her own memories were worse than nightmares.

"Well at least you weren't screaming," said one of the others. "Blackpool, one of the girls in our house was an awful screamer when she got the horrors. So thanks for that, and sorry you didn't sleep."

"It must have been the heat," Mrs. Baird said, coming in from her office. "Hold still, lamb—"

The landlady put her wrist against Katie's forehead before Katie could say anything. "Well, you aren't fevered. It was probably the heat, and I swear the air don't move in this house at all at night. You'll be all right. I don't suppose a bad night ever killed one of us entertainers."

"It hasn't killed me yet," Katie said, with a hollow laugh. "It was just nightmares, you know how it is, you start up out of them and don't want to go back to sleep for fear they'll come again, worse. I'll come straight back from the evening show, have a wash-up, and go to bed. That'll set me right."

"And we'll be having something cooling tonight for supper, instead of soup," Mrs. Baird promised, looking about at the rest of the girls. "Cucumber and cress sandwiches, perhaps?"

"Oh, yes, please!" begged the girl who had noticed that Katie looked exhausted. Katie tried not to smile. Cress sandwiches might mean "high class" and "high tea" for girls in a city, but they had been the court of last resort for her family in the summer, when she and her parents were short of the ready. Cress might be a luxury in town, but cress could be found wild growing near streams, and if you cut your bread thin enough, you could make it go a long way . . .

But Mrs. Baird wouldn't be cutting paper-thin slices of bread, and there would be plenty of butter on those sandwiches. Cress and cucumber would be a welcome change for everyone, even Katie.

"This summer heat is only going to get worse, I fear,"

the bearded woman said, shaking her head. "I had better go talk to my greengrocer, and the fishmonger, and we'll start eating cooler things, not so heavy. Fruit and tomatoes and toast, perhaps, instead of oatmeal. Cooler suppers. If it's soup, it'll be a cold soup. I can't have you girls having nightmares over my food."

Now, Katie hadn't said a *word* about that, but it seemed their landlady was perfectly capable of deciding that somehow she—or rather, the supper she had served—was responsible for a night of bad dreams.

Well, no harm done, even if it wasn't the truth. Katie had to admit that food that wasn't so heavy would be a welcome change, since the city was baking this summer.

The landlady let her go off with a word of admonishment that if she felt faint she was *not* to let her master badger her into anything other than "having a nice lay-down." "Suzie told me you work harder than anyone, dear," Mrs. Baird told her before she let Katie escape out the door. "There is no point in you fainting on stage. And you let him know I said as much."

But when she got to the theater, and onto the stage for the usual rehearsal, the last thing she expected was Lionel waiting for her just inside the door. "Come with me," he said, before Jack had a chance to say anything more than a simple "good morning." He grinned and crooked his finger at her. "You know the act now as well as Suzie ever did, so this morning, you and I are going to go plan our next act."

She looked at him, confused, as others pushed past them on the way to their own tasks. "But—"

"But the acts change in the fall, and while I normally would just make some slight alterations in this one—

since at this season, the odds that anyone outside this theater would even *know* that mine is the only act that doesn't change are very slim indeed—you are exactly the sort of assistant I have been needing for *quite* some time, and I want to put an entirely new routine together. I've been working on some new illusions, and it is time to invent another persona and retire an old one for a while. Down to the basement, Katie. I have everything we need down there." Lionel turned and headed for the little spiral staircase, and Katie really had no choice except to go.

Not that she minded. The basement was the coolest place in the building, and right now, any place that was cool was on the top of her list for places to be.

The basement, besides being the home of the Wardrobe Mistress, was the site of storage room after storage room, and even a couple of workshops. One of them—the largest, as Katie later came to find out—belonged to Lionel. There were some distinct advantages to being the only performer who remained with the theater year round, it seemed.

"Here we are," he said, opening a door on a room lit by windows up near the ceiling. "This is where I store my large-scale apparatus, and where I construct new apparatus. Two of the scenery carpenters and I have a very good arrangement in that way. Anything I can draw out in neat plans, they can make." He brought her to a shabby willow armchair and sat her down in it. "Now, Jack tells me that he had a long and serious discussion with you last night. I hope I am not going to have to try and talk you out of that delusion that you were having hallucinations. Magic *is* real, my dear, and I make my living based on that fact."

Despite being told multiple times last night by the doorman that Lionel, too, was one of these ... magicians ... and that he, too, had odd little creatures about him, Katie hadn't quite believed it. And she still might not have believed it, if at that very moment, she had not seen a tiny, mostly-naked winged lady flit down through one of the open windows above and hover above Lionel's head, looking interested. She was gorgeous, like a little bit of animated jewelry, and quite as shameless as Eve.

Katie managed not to shriek. But she did gasp "What is *that?*" and point at the tiny thing.

Lionel tilted his head up; his eyes lit and he smiled, for once showing a bit of his age as the skin around his eyes crinkled. "Oh, that is a sylph. She's an Air Elemental, just as the salamanders and firebirds and phoenixes are Fire Elementals. I get sylphs, mostly, some pixies, a zephyr or two. The Air Elementals that *I* seem to attract are all very like the illustrations of a fairy tale book, except that they are quite without shame. Their idea of suitable garments is not to wear any at all, so get used to it, no point in being shocked. They simply don't understand why the rest of us bother with clothing."

Well, being in the circus, and now the music hall as she was, Katie could hardly afford to be shocked. The girls didn't exactly change their costumes under sheets, after all. In fact, it was more of a surprise when they managed to make it to the stage with everything properly fastened up. Katie peered up at the sylph, who peered down at her with equal curiosity. Her little rainbow-wings fluttered and her hair drifted all about her as if it were made of smoke, or spider-web, and not like hair at all. Katie smiled up at the sylph tentatively, who reacted with a giggle, clapping both her hands over her mouth, before zooming up into the rafters.

Lionel waggled his fingers at her, getting her attention again. "Now then. Let's get down to business, shall we? As my assistant, you are something of a partner in my undertakings, and since you are also a magician, I should very much like you to be a more active partner than Suzie was. So to begin with, we need a theme. Something that will allow us to use your salamanders to effect."

"Wait," she said, confused now. "I thought only you and I and Jack could see them."

"That's true," he replied. "But as you saw, they can both *make* fire, and protect you from fire. So . . . I should like to do something that makes use of that."

She thought about that. "You already have the Turk costume. Could you be a Djinni?" she hazarded. "I thought Djinnis were always appearing and disappearing in a flash of fire. I know you said your flashpots are unreliable which is why you don't use them much, but would they be more reliable if my salamanders were to ignite them?"

"I had considered a demon or devil, but many magicians use that theme. I like this." He picked up a pencil and a notebook and began writing. "You could be my assistant Djinni, then . . . we could use the floating illusion, make it a flying carpet, and your salamanders could set fire to the hoop I circle you with. That might make a very effective ending."

"You could start by just setting things spontaneously on fire," she observed. "Candles to start with, then those flashpot things." She sighed. "It'll be awfully hot on stage, though."

"But it won't be summer then, it will be fall. At least our costumes will be light." He was making more notes, furiously. "We can use a great many fire effects, since the salamanders will be triggering them, and I won't have to rely on mechanicals. People love fire effects."

"But . . . can we actually count on the salamanders to do all this?" she asked, now worried, because Jack had made it very clear that the Elementals came and went when they chose and could not be coerced.

But Lionel laughed. "Bless you! They're natural showmen. They love being on the stage, and they adore setting off bursts of paraffin oil, flash paper and flash powder. Well look, there's one of them on the back of your chair, just ask him."

Katie swiveled her head so fast she nearly did herself a mischief, and sure enough, there the little lizard was, flicking a flame-tongue at her. "Well?" she said to it, not sure if she should be feeling foolish about addressing a lizard as if it was a human. "Would you like to be in the show? More than one of you? Would you like to set a lot of things on fire for me?"

The lizard bobbed its head comically at her, and with obvious enthusiasm.

"You see?" Lionel said, and went on with his notes. She held out her hand to the lizard, who scuttled onto it and curled up in her palm, eyes blinking sleepily. "The trick for us who are mere magicians is to make things interesting for our Elementals, so they enjoy being partners. Yours are easy to reward, actually, the mere fact of being able to trigger real fire is in itself the reward for them. Be good to them, and they will be good to you."

She ran a finger along the salamander's back. It was

quite warm, though not painfully so, and it seemed to enjoy the caress.

"I believe," he continued, still scribbling, "that my rusty juggling skills—"

"Oh, I can juggle three balls," she offered, still absorbed in examining the salamander in her palm. As she peered closely at it, it seemed to her as if every scale on its body was rimmed in a thin thread of fire. "Not more, but if three will do—"

"Then you will juggle three balls of fire," he replied with glee. "I'll pull fire out of hats and other containers instead of rabbits or doves. Possibly we can do something with an escape from a box surrounded by fire. I'll look into that. Floating first, then a fire-based escapist trick, should put quite the cap on the show."

He put the notebook away. "Now what we need to think about at this point is how we are going to change the current act. Air Magic is known for illusions. I've been using some all along—mostly at the end, where I make you vanish from the top of the rope. But now that you know what I do, we can—well, we can do what I did with the last assistant I had who was a mage. We can cut you in half, and separate the boxes—that usually needs a second lady, or some rather unconvincing clockwork feet—but I can make an illusion of moving feet. It would be madness to try and teach you new tricks in the middle of the season, but what we're doing is going to be *my* illusion, and all you will need to learn are your new cues."

She nodded. After all, she already knew how to fit herself into his apparatus, this wouldn't take that long to learn.

"We'll add an escapist trick in couple of weeks. It's a version of the 'liberated dove' illusion—and in our case, it really will be an illusion. The 'you' that will be in the cabinet that collapses will be an illusion, you'll actually be in the other one . . ." At her puzzled look, he laughed. "I'll show you with the doves on dark day, and we'll start work on it the day after."

"Is it your sylphs that make the little silk-creature fly?" she asked.

He nodded. "They can't lift much, about as much as a breeze can. They've been assisting with your levitations, and no one the wiser, although that stagehand does keep asking me where I get such thin assistants." They both laughed at that.

"Feeling more comfortable with all of this?" he asked.

She considered that for a moment; considered the salamander in her hand. It blinked up at her, contentedly. "I—am!" she said, a little surprised at herself.

"Well, that is the best thing I have heard next to your turning up in the first place," he chuckled. "Now, let's get back upstairs. We still have time to get a run-through in."

Now that she knew what Lionel was doing, she was a little amazed that she had been so blind to it. The gasp when she disappeared at the top of the rope—it always came *before* the stagehands grabbed her wrists and hauled her up into the flys. How could she have missed that?

Well there it was; now she knew, he was concealing her with a flash of illusion where another magician would have used some sort of mirror-trickery. That actually made her far less anxious than she had been before; it didn't all depend on *her* to pull off the trick.

It was payday, so once she had changed after the evening performance, she made her way to Lionel's dressing room. He would get his pay packet from the owner, who also served as his own accountant, and he would pay her out of his pay. It was an equitable arrangement, and convenient for the owner. At this point, Katie had been doing this for weeks, and she wasn't expecting anything more than to get her packet, perhaps exchange a few pleasant words with Lionel, and be off to the boarding house.

She certainly wasn't expecting to find the music hall owner half-collapsed into one of Lionel's chairs, and lamenting at the top of his lungs, shaking what looked to be a letter in one hand and beating his fist on his knee.

"I'm *ruined,* I tell you!" Charles Mayhew cried. "All the advertising expense! All those playbills! And what will I have to show for it? Nothing! A cancellation notice and an empty top-spot on the bill! I'm *ruined!*"

"Get him a beer, will you?" Lionel begged her as soon as he spotted her head poking cautiously in the door. "And run right back. Oh! Bring Peggy. The more old heads we have on this, the better."

She did as she was asked, fetching a beer from the bar before it closed out, and getting Peggy from her dressing room still in her dressing gown. At this point Mayhew's lamentations were approaching epic proportions, as he could be heard down the hall. Peggy took charge of the beer and shoved her way inside, as the rest hovered at the door.

The noise had attracted others—mostly old hands—

and from one of the stagehands, Katie finally got the whole story.

It seemed that this spring the arrival in London of a lot of Russian dancers had made everyone go mad for that sort of thing—and if you wanted any sort of popular show, well, you had to at least have someone with an "ov" or an "aya" or an "ova" at the end of his or her name, and a claim to be from that part of the world. Mayhew had secured for himself a "Russian ballerina" for the rest of the summer season, and had expected to pull packed houses even though the heat would otherwise lead folks to seek their entertainment somewhere cooler.

Now, however, the "Russian ballerina" had canceled....

She had pled injury, but Katie had a notion that she was just going to change her name, book through another agency, and collect a larger pay packet than she could command from Charlie Mayhew.

This left Mayhew with what really *was* a disaster. His top act—one he was counting on being there in two weeks—was gone. This late in the game, he was never going to get a really *good* act to take the ballerina's place. He couldn't ask the current top act to stay on— well, he could ask, but of course, the Italian acrobats were already booked elsewhere.

Her heart went out to him ... and sank. This was going to affect all of them. The box office was going to suffer. They were all going to suffer ... even the acts that were moving on in two weeks could wind up suffering, for a bad box-office in the summer would have a knock-on effect for quite some time. Mayhew might not be able to afford them next summer. They'd likely have to take jobs somewhere less pleasant, or less lucrative.

No wonder so many of the performers and staff were crowding around the dressing room, looking worried.

"Katie!" she heard Peggy bellow from inside the dressing room. "Ducks, if you're out there, squeeze yourself in!"

She blinked, but obeyed, as the others made space for her. She couldn't imagine what on earth they wanted with *her,* but—

"Here she is. Ah good, still got them toe shoes on," Peggy proclaimed. "Lionel, hoist her up on that table."

Before she had any idea of what was going on, Katie found Lionel lifting her up at the waist onto a small round table, putting her above the floor. She was surrounded by Peggy, Mayhew, and Lionel, all seated, and several other old hands who had crammed into the dressing room.

"All right, then, ducks," Peggy said, her hands folded across her midsection. "You know that twiddly business you do in the morning to limber up before anyone gets here? Do that for us, will you?"

That business was something Katie had never thought anyone paid any attention to—a combination of dance and contortion she did while the piano player warmed up. She generally did it off in a corner, to keep out of the way. When had Peggy seen her at it? And why on earth would she want Katie to do it now?

Well . . . *maybe because I'm good at it* . . . It was something she had practiced at the behest of her parents, who wanted her to make a solo act of it eventually. It was far more elaborate than anything she had ever done with her husband; she had kept him from ever seeing it, because . . . because she had wanted something for herself alone. She had wanted something that she absolutely knew she was good at.

Well . . . if Peggy liked it, it might be good enough for a solo act. Maybe good enough to put at the bottom of the bill and shove everyone else up a slot, so there would at least not be the dreaded *gap*.

She took a deep breath, caught her balance, and began.

Unlike the circus contortions, which were flashy and lively, this was slow, graceful, deliberate . . . and very, very difficult. She began by slowly bending over backward, sliding her hands down along the backs of her legs, until she placed them flat on the top of the table. Then, just as slowly, she raised her legs into the air, balancing on her hands, scissored her legs slowly, did it again, knifed them, bent her knees and arched her back, balanced her toes on the top of her head. She held that for a good couple of breaths, then put her feet flat down on the table again, one on either side of her hands, and slowly stood up. Then she brought her left leg up behind her, reached back and caught her ankle in her hands, and pulled her leg right up over the top of her head, balancing on one foot. Then she inched her way in a slow circle, still with her leg held up over her head.

She never stopped moving, never paused for a moment, as she went through contortion after contortion. She never gave anyone the "pause" that would signal a moment of applause. The whole routine took about ten minutes, and when it was over, she was dripping with sweat, and the room was so quiet you could have heard a pin drop.

She ended as she had begun, standing with arms outstretched, looking down at Peggy and Mayhew, and very aware of Lionel behind her. Finally, she lowered her arms.

The people packed into the dressing room uttered a collective sigh.

"Give that child a towel, one of you!" Peggy ordered, breaking the silence. "And come down off the table now, ducks." As Katie took the offered towel, and obeyed, Peggy turned to the theater owner. "Well?" she demanded.

Mayhew chewed furiously on his moustache. "Well . . ." he said, doubtfully. "It's a damn good act. But it ain't *bally*—"

"It is if we say it is, Charlie," Lionel interrupted. "Seriously? All people know is that *Russian Ballet* is some sort of dancing, and is something they haven't seen before. If it looks like dance, and we dress her up right, her act will be taken as whatever we say it is. Plus I have another couple of ideas I know Katie can pull off if you'll give her the chance."

Wait—what? Katie paused in mopping her face to stare at him.

"Charlie," called a girl from the door. "Everybody in the chorus *knows* she's heaps and heaps better than the rest of us. She'd make us all look like fools if she cared to, but she's a trooper and fits hersel' roight in. You oughter give her a chance."

"Well. . . ." Mayhew chewed on his moustache some more. Finally he turned to Lionel. "If you two can give me a three-routine act in a week—"

Caught in shock and amazement, Katie listened dumbly as Lionel promised she would—somehow!—

throw together a three-dance act in a week, and fiercely negotiated a rate for her that practically made her head spin.

Panic flooded her at that. How would she *ever* be able to put together two brand new dance routines in two weeks' time—much less dance routines that would pass for this *Russian Ballet* business? Her mind went absolutely blank. It was impossible, completely impossible.

But then—then everyone *else* began coming up with ideas!

One of the Italian acrobats suddenly sprang to his feet, smacking himself in the forehead with the palm of his hand. *"Bah, imbecile!"* he exclaimed. "Guiseppe, we have just the thing! The ribbon!"

His brother made the same gesture. "Of course! I know just-a where she is!" He jumped to *his* feet, wormed his way out of the dressing room, and evidently dashed off somewhere. Lionel looked around at the bodies cramming his dressing room. "Let's move this to the stage," he suggested. "If we're going to come up with something for Miss Kate, it might as well be there."

By the time all the interested parties had shuffled back to the front of the house, Katie reckoned that the "interested parties" numbered about a quarter of the folks that worked there. She could understand why some of the musicians and stagehands would feel intimately concerned over the financial well-being of the music hall, but what surprised her was that Peggy and a few others of the better traveling acts were as well, people who had no reason to worry, even if Mayhew came a-cropper over this.

But Charlie's a good master, she realized, quickly. He

was fair in his pay and his hours, fair in how he ran his hall, and people liked working for him. If Charlie went under, whoever took this venue probably would not be nearly so nice.

By the time people had arrayed themselves over the stage and in the seats in the orchestra pit, the acrobat had returned with what he had sought.

"Our sister, she saw this thing, wanted it in the act," Guiseppe explained, unfurling what looked like yards and yards of silk ribbon from the end of a wand. "It never fit, and then she made Mama happy and got married to a nice clerk from Napoli. It-a works like this—"

He demonstrated, and Katie fell instantly in love. Guiseppe made the ribbon form into spirals, swirls, circles . . . it was *magical!* She took it from him, and started her contortion routine again, only this time, framing it with the intricate patterns of the swirling ribbon.

Mayhew hooted, and began applauding. "Now *there's* the ticket!" he exclaimed, as Katie broke the usual pattern by getting up on her toes and pattering backward, trailing a curlicue of ribbon behind her, then executed four turns with the ribbon encircling her. Then she circled the stage in a series of jump-turns, swirling the ribbon around her, stopped in the middle, and spun like a top with the ribbon orbiting her. "Now *that* looks like *bally!*"

"I think we can sell that as Russian," Lionel said, as she spun to a stop. "Seriously, Mayhew, I have *seen* these Russians, and there's a fair amount of their act that's based on gimmick, and this is just the right sort of gimmick to work for us. That Pavlova girl—one of her little dances, she pulls her skirt up around her like a flower closing petals for the night, another one she's supposed to be a swan dying ... I'm not saying she's not a sensational dancer, because she is, but our audience don't care about sensational so much as spectacle."

Katie played with the ribbon without actually dancing with it, listening while they talked.

"I've seen the Russians, too, Charlie," Peggy said. "Katie's no Pavlova, but the long and the short of it is, this ain't Covent Garden either. Our people want something pretty and fun, and our Katie can give 'em that, without needing a genius in toe shoes."

That actually made Katie feel a lot less anxious. She remembered what Mary Small had said about her dancing ... well, if she was supposed to come up to some sort of impossible standard, she might just as well tell them it wasn't going to happen! But produce something pretty and fun ... yes, she could do that.

Lionel watched her playing about with the ribbon as she worked out how it moved. "We should go through the panto costumes and see if we can find some fairy wings or somewhat for Kate, and with that ribbon, there's the second third of the act right there." He got up and paced a bit, watching her. "First routine—living statue. Just her and some drapery, and a white light on her. Second routine—fairy, with the ribbon."

"All you need then, is the last third," Peggy observed, tucking her frothy dressing gown around herself.

"Well, let's see if *this* won't do that."

Hearing the familiar voice of Mrs. Litttleton, the Wardrobe Mistress, everyone turned to see her laboring onto the stage beneath what looked like a giant cloud. She dropped the whole thing on the stage at Katie's feet, then stooped down to pluck at the folds. "Anyone remember four years ago, that horse-faced Meg Farmer, how she came back from Paris and wouldn't have it but I make up this costume? Twenty yards of silk tulle, if it's an inch, and she could no more manipulate it like that Loie Fuller wench than I can fly."

"I remember she nearly strangled herself on it," Lionel chuckled. "The general impression I got was a lot of flailing about."

"She danced like a cow," observed one of the chorus girls, the one who had been nice about Katie's dancing. "And that was without putting on that set of sails."

"Ah, here we go!" The Wardrobe Mistress evidently found something, and before Katie was quite aware what was happening, she found herself swathed in yard and yards of ethereal fabric. She felt rather as if she was the center pole of a tent—

"Here—" she felt something like the ribbon-wand thrust into each hand, except that these wands were attached somehow in all the fabric. The Wardrobe Mistress stepped away a bit, and eyed her. "All right, Katie, see what you can do with that. Move the wands about. Something like those skirt-dances I've seen Travelers do—start slow, see what you can do with it."

But Katie found her attention caught by something up in the light above the orchestra pit. She stared upward, manipulating the wands a little, but not really paying attention.

It was one of Lionel's little sylphs, but this one seemed to have more of a sense of modesty than the others, for it was swathed from neck to below the ankles in what looked for all the world just like this voluminous gown the Wardrobe Mistress had enveloped *her* in. And as soon as Katie's eyes lit on the little creature, she began to dance with the fabric—

Katie watched her, fascinated at first, and then, as she watched, she understood *immediately* just what it was she was supposed to do! As the sylph moved, making every movement as exaggerated as possible, Katie imitated her. It was exactly like learning a new circus dance number, where you followed the one girl who knew how to do it. This was exactly what she needed—if she could *see* what it was she was supposed to be doing, she could almost always imitate it.

She started out simply, turning first one way, then the other, leading the turns with her arms, the wands in her hands pulling the fabric along behind like wings. The more the costume answered her, the bolder she became, sweeping her arms up and around in huge serpentine gestures as she turned and twisted.

"There now!" applauded the Wardrobe Mistress. "That's much more like the thing. Don't that Fuller woman have all manner of lights and things on her when she dances, Lionel?"

"That's what I recall," Lionel observed. "I think we could manage with a couple of magic lanterns and some plain colored slides."

"And I think that's the third part of the act," Mayhew declared, levering himself up out of the chair he'd taken in the pits. "All right, boys and girls, I applaud you all. Ruination is not staring us in the face, and I dunno how to thank you except that there's not a man jack or woman jill of you that's going to pay for a beer at my bar for the rest of your last two weeks."

Spontaneous applause erupted at that pronouncement, as the Wardrobe Mistress helped Katie out of the strange gown and hung it up so that all the folds fell correctly.

"Now, let's get ourselves to our beds. Good night's work. Harder work for you to come, Miss Kate." Mayhew tipped two fingers at her. "Hope you're up to it. You've got an act to build."

9

TWO weeks. Katie had to turn a few vague movements into three dance routines in two weeks. She'd have completely given up in two days, if it hadn't been for Lionel, Mrs. Littleton, and Peggy, who all took it upon themselves to help her. Mrs. Littleton spent all of the first day tinkering with the voluminous gown, fussing with the many layers until it suddenly settled down and behaved itself, as if it was made of magic.

Although . . . that wasn't entirely Mrs. Littleton's doing. Lionel's sylphs helped. They seemed to like the idea of buzzing about inside the thing, adding lift right when it was most needed and making sure nothing got twisted up.

It was Peggy who decided that the dance with the dress should be called Dance of the Fire Lily, and the magic lanterns should project red and yellow on the folds as she twisted and flung them around. With that theme in mind, Davey, the piano player, came up with some wild music of a sort that Katie had *never* heard of in her life—although Peggy rolled her eyes and said "Good Gad, Davey, not old Samson! Really?"

"The band knows it by heart," Davey replied, pounding it out on the piano, as Katie worked out moves to it.

"They should, since every skirt-dancer and kootch-dancer from here to Blackpool thinks it'll make her act *class,*" Peggy snorted, and sang through her nose. *"Neener neener nee-ner, neener neener nee-ner. Neener neener neee-ner, neener neener neee-ner!"*

"Pay no attention, Katie," Lionel advised her, as she faltered. "Davey's right, it's the perfect music, and if it's familiar, that'll be all to the good. Let's not forget who brings down the house every night by singing 'She Sits Among Her Cabbages and Peas,' now, shall we?"

Peggy made a raspberry at him, but said no more on the subject of the music for what Katie was coming to think of as the "Dress Dance." Because goodness only knew, it wasn't *she* who was the star of the thing, it was the dress.

Davey picked out perfect music for the other two pieces of the act as well. Something bright and sprightly for the Fairy Dance with the ribbon—Lionel said it was by a gent named Mendelssohn—and something slow, dignified, and pretty that Lionel said was by a fellow named Glook, or something like that. A strange name, but Katie couldn't pay it any mind when the music was so nice. Davey wouldn't let anyone in the band play the Statue Dance piece except himself and the flute-player, he said they'd just hammer it out like it was the acrobat music and ruin it. The same went for the Fairy Dance, it was just Davey and the flute player and a couple of the fiddlers.

For the Fairy Dance she used her old dance dress, but Mrs. Littleton came up with a pretty spangled bit of gauze to wear over the top of it, some spangled gauze wings, and a masked headdress that had beaded wire curlicue things on top of it. She just had to make sure the ribbon didn't get tangled in the curlicues—but that was where Lionel's sylphs came in again.

Mrs. Littleton managed the cleverest thing for the Statue Dance—an all-over white body stocking like weight lifters wore under their leopard skins so they wouldn't be indecent, and over that, long, slender pantaloons and a bit of a tunic belted in at the waist. So no matter how she twisted herself up, there wouldn't be anything improper showing.

With that, she wore a white wig and dusted her face and hands with white powder so she looked like a proper statue, like rich people had out in their gardens, or nice theaters had arrayed out front.

She was awfully glad that Lionel had given over the idea of starting rehearsal for the new act for the fall season, because things were absolutely mad, trying to work out the dancing act *and* make sure she got in at least a part-rehearsal on the magic act every day.

Charlie was going to get his revenge on the perfidious "Russian Dancer" who had canceled on him, too. He left the playbills *exactly* as he'd paid to have them printed up. After all, what was the woman going to do? Complain? She was the one who had canceled so she could make more money in London under a different name—she couldn't do anything about Charlie using her old name without exposing her fraud.

So Katie was being billed as "Natalya Bayonova, the brilliant Russian Ballerina, straight from the Ballet Russe de Moscow." There wasn't any "Ballet Russe de Moscow" so far as any of them knew, but then, that hadn't been *their* choice of name in the first place. And anyway, as Peggy said, "No one coming to a music hall for some fun is going to know the Bally Russe de Moscow from the Bally Russe de Blackpool, and as long as they get something they ain't seen before, nor will they care."

As Katie fanned herself with a scrap of scenery board, it occurred to her that there was something peculiar in the fact that the hottest summer anyone could ever remember was also being known as the "Summer of the Russian Dancers." Russia was cold, wasn't it? She wondered how the *real* Russian Dancers in London were dealing with the heat. Poor things, she pitied them; they didn't have the tricks that Jack had taught her, the Fire Magician ways of making the heat invigorate you. This morning over breakfast some of the girls had been talking about how horses and even people had been dropping dead in the streets of the heat—not here, but in London and other towns. At least Brighton had the advantage of a steady sea breeze to keep the heat from killing people.

Charlie was scarcely the only impresario in Brighton to be featuring a Russian act, although in some cases connecting "Russian" to the "act" was something of a strain. Charlie had merely been the first to catch wind of how popular the Russians were going to be and act on it—and look where that had gotten him! He thought he'd bagged a good headline act, and then the act had abandoned him and his theater! She wondered how many other impresarios were going to find themselves in the same situation before the summer was out. The lure of a lot of money quickly might well overcome the risk of finding people unwilling to hire you once the craze was over.

The biggest and best music hall in the city, The Coliseum, had what Katie supposed to be the genuine article. After all, a theater that boasted the likes of Dan Leno and Little Tich could probably afford Anna Pavlova herself, if she wasn't already booked in London. The ballerina's name, Irina Tcherkaskaya, sounded genuine enough, at least to Katie. Katie had looked over the playbill from The Coliseum, and the dancer's program sounded quite original—"The Dance of the Polivetsian," "Saber Dance," "Dance of the Rusalka," and "Scene from Swan Lake." They all sounded like solo pieces from larger ballets.

The Brighton Music Hall also had a Russian Ballerina that was probably at least a real ballerina, if not a real Russian. She was billed only as "Marina," and her bill listed "Tzarina Dance," "Bayadere," and "Scene from Sleeping Beauty."

Just about every other theater and music hall had *something* that was supposed to be Russian. It was when you got down to this level that Katie had some severe doubts about the authenticity of any of the dancers, much less their performances. After all, look at her: she knew *she* was an outright fraud.

And putting some poor can-can dancer in a fur hat and fur-trimmed dress was not going to make her Russian, it was only going to make her faint with the heat.

According to Jack, there was plenty of that going on in the lesser halls. Mrs. Littleton had reported a run on rabbit fur to the point where there wasn't any to be had in the entire town, and wouldn't you know it, there were at least three different "Russian Cossack Choruses" being billed in halls smaller than this one.

The smart thing, of course, if you couldn't get a real Russian dancer, was to cobble up some act around a dancer that was something *like* the acts that were in all the papers coming down from London. As long as you could get your hands on a reasonably good ballerina, one that might actually have seen Pavlova and the Ballet Russe, Peggy was right; people would pay to see the act and wouldn't complain.

And that was what other halls larger than Charlie's but smaller than The Coliseum were doing. You could read the playbills in the papers, and it was actually rather funny. There were enough "Dying Swans" populating the stages to have put a serious dent in the supply of white feathers and down—and Lionel had made the joke that if only the Swans would just *die* there'd be roast bird in every kitchen in Brighton.

There was even one comic version of the "Dying Swan," according to the girls at the boarding house, who'd seen it on their dark day and had come back convulsed with laughter. One of the male comics whose act was to be in a dress had got himself a swan costume made up and staggered about the stage scattering handfuls of chicken feathers before falling over, kicking his legs in the air, and taking a good long time to "die." Katie hoped she would get a chance to see him.

There were "Ghosts" of various flowers flinging themselves into and out of the wings—"Ghost of a Rose," "Ghost of a Violet," "Ghost of a Lily," "Ghost of a Daisy" . . . and to add a pleasing variety to the mix, some dancers were crossing the flowers with the swans and creating "Dying Rose," "Dying Lily," "Dying Camellia." How one was supposed to create an impression of a dying flower, she had no idea. Not to mention that with all these creatures dropping dead on the stage, it was not creating the atmosphere of fun and laughter you were *supposed* to find in a music hall . . .

Oh well, she supposed the other acts just had to make up for it.

The various kootch- and skirt-dancers down on the Boardwalk, not to be left out of the craze, had relabeled themselves "Russian Harem Girls," "Russian Cossack Slaves," and "Russian Sword Dancers." They didn't actually *change* anything, of course, just put up new signs. And it wasn't as if the men that crowded the kootch-tents were actually there for the *dancing*.

I'd actually like to see the real thing, the real Russian dancers, she thought, wistfully, waiting for the dog act to finish its last run through the hoops and the curtains to close so she could run out and take her pose on the pedestal for the Living Icon number. She hadn't any notion of what an "Icon" was supposed to be, other than it was some sort of Russian art . . . but then, neither would anyone out there in the audience. Lionel had picked the name, and she trusted it looked all right on the playbill.

As Peggy had reminded her over and over again, just

before the singer took her leave of the house regulars and went on to her next booking—what mattered was only that people got their money's worth, even if they had no idea what it was that they wanted. It was never about reality in music hall. "All those people out there, all they care about is that they see something they ain't never seen before in the middle of the fun they know and like. Then they can go home and say *Coo! Mazie! I saw one of them Rooshans when we was on 'oliday, and she didn't half make me eyes stand out in me head!* And by the time they get done with the telling, you wouldn't recognize your own act."

Well, that was true enough. Every one of the people out there in that audience was perfectly willing to believe that she and Lionel were some sort of wild Turkish magicians, and that *all* the magic was perfectly real. They all believed that the Clever Cow actually counted things, and not that the Cow's handler signaled how many times she was to paw her hoof by tapping her with a wand. They believed with all their hearts that the Drunken Gent comedian was going to tumble into the band pit at any moment, and that the swords the latest juggling act was tossing through the air were sharp enough to shave with.

Given that, believing that Katie was a Russian was scarcely a stretch for them.

The dogs ran off, the trainer ran off collecting their hoops as he went, and the curtain closed. One of the stagehands ran on from the opposite wing, placed Katie's platform, and waited while she ran on from the other side. He lifted her up onto it, she took her pose, and waited.

This was it. This was the moment when they would all see if the hard work of the last two weeks was going to pay off. This would be the very first performance before an audience that was not of her peers.

The curtain parted. Behind her, the backdrop was plain black. The curtain only parted halfway, leaving her framed in red velvet against the black. The limelight burned down on her from above. She stood absolutely motionless, and should, she hoped, look like a white stone statue in the middle of the stage.

The crowd hushed its noise. That was a very good sign; music hall crowds were a noisy lot, this wasn't like a theater, where people were expected to sit quietly in seats. The best seats in the music hall were the ones at the tables, where people drank and ate and were jolly, and expected to be able to enjoy everything about being there as loudly as they liked.

It was good that they were quiet at first, since the flute and the piano were so quiet. *Gluck,* not "Glook," was the name of the fellow who had written this pretty piece. "Dance of the Blessed Spirits," it was called. The lads made a very good thing of it, all things considered. Katie was quite proud of them.

Now, Katie had changed her routine from the warm-up she had first showed Charlie to something that looked better from the house. She waited, remaining perfectly still, for four bars of the music. Then, before anyone could start to get restless, she slowly, agonizingly, brought her right leg up, gliding her heel against her left leg, until she caught it in her right hand. Then she slowly straightened the leg, bringing her foot up right over her head and holding it there.

Still holding her foot over her head, with her back arched, she inched herself around so that she presented herself sideways to the audience. She let go of her foot, dropped it back down to the platform, and slowly began to bend over backward.

Now, as she had first envisioned this act, it was going to be one seamless piece of contortion work. But Charlie—who knew his audiences better than he knew the whims of his own wife—persuaded her to put pauses in there.

And now she understood why he was right to do so.

The first time she did one of her pauses—at the end point of the first of her extreme contortions, where she was balancing herself on her hands with both of her feet resting on the top of her head—there was an actual *whoop!* from someone at a table very near her, and the applause that erupted gladdened her heart.

Before she was half done with the act, she knew it was going to be a success. There was enough "pepper" in it to make men enjoy it, but not so much that their wives would be angry with them for looking so hard at her, and not so much that anyone would be afraid for their children to see it. The act was difficult enough that it impressed people and would make them talk about it. And it was different enough even from circus contortion that people would not be disappointed.

When the curtain closed on her, she knew two things for certain. Charlie was not going to regret taking a chance on her, and by the time the fall season was upon them, she would have enough money to be rid of Dick forever.

She had to change immediately; two of her three

numbers were in the first half of the show, so that there was time for her and Lionel to perform the magic act before her final piece. She ran back to the dressing room as the chorus dancers streamed onto the stage for the first of the musical numbers *they* did. It was the usual can-can; you couldn't have a music hall show without a can-can. Coming right after her quieter act, it would liven everyone up again, and even though the chorus girls were a pretty average lot, they were lively enough, and people were disposed to like them.

So, first came the high-kick number, then the Drunken Gent, then the Breeches Girl singing a sentimental ballad, and then it was time for Katie to do the Fairy Dance, the one with the ribbon.

She squeezed past the comedian and reached her door, which even had her name on it—her name, not the name of the faux Russian she was supposed to be. She and Lionel had been very, very firm on this: there would be no dressing-room visitors for her. Katie could no more counterfeit a Russian than she could convincingly pretend to be a countess. The best way to continue the illusion was to absolutely forbid dressing-room visitors. Jack could, and would, keep them out. There was no bribe big enough to make him allow anyone back to the dressing room to see her.

That edict had made Charlie happy, since there was always the chance she might become *too* popular, and some clever booking agent might lure her away to another hall. It had made Katie happy, because she was quite well aware that the gents in the audience often reckoned that a gal who'd show skin on the stage wouldn't put up more than a token bit of resistance—

easily overcome by money or presents—to allowing that skin to be handled.

The thought had nearly put Katie into a panic, until Lionel insisted she must keep up the mystery. She trusted Lionel . . . she trusted Jack . . . she trusted that Mrs. Charlie would be down on Charlie like the Archangel Michael if *he* interfered with a girl . . . but she didn't trust any other man.

She opened the narrow door and whisked herself inside; she might be at the top of the bill, and at least she was getting her own dressing room, but she still didn't have the sort of advantages that someone like Pretty Peggy did. No dresser of her own, no little servant that could manage things in the dressing room. No one waiting in the wings to help her get things on and off, or even to carry any of her props. The only reason she had a stagehand to lift her up onto the posing stand was because he had to carry it out there in the first place.

She *could* have someone like that, of course, if she cared to pay for the help. But every penny she spent on having a servant was a penny she couldn't put toward being rid of Dick. It made her feel sick, to think that he could, at any time, turn up and take her away, and she would have no choice but to go with him. That he could do anything he cared to with her, and to her, and she had no recourse but to suffer it.

The past few weeks had been like heaven. The thought of going back to hell—

I'd rather die, she told herself, as she closed and locked the door of her room behind her.

At least having her own dressing room—tiny as it was—meant she could keep all her costumes hung up and tidy, and not have to worry about the other girls moving them or putting them in disorder. For the Fire Dance dress . . . that was critically important.

She popped the white wig onto the wig stand, stripped out of the white costume and hung it up. She didn't bother washing the white powder off her face; she used it as the foundation for the half-face makeup for the Fairy Dance—just a pair of rosebud lips and a little pink on the cheeks. On went the familiar gauze skirt of her old circus ballet dress, on went the tight basque, over the tights she was already wearing. There was a hook in the doorframe she used to tighten the laces of the basque; for someone as used to contortion as she was, tying up her own laces was no harder than doing up her own shoes. She pinned the spangled pink scarf to one shoulder, draped it across the front of the basque, pinned it again, and arranged it over the folds of the skirt. She tied on the toe shoes . . . made sure there was some new cotton wool padding the toes. She was very, *very* glad she didn't actually have to get up on her toes more than a couple of times in this routine. She knew that real ballerinas spent most of their onstage time up on the tips of their feet, and she could not imagine putting herself through that sort of torture for longer than a few moments. It might look beautiful . . . but it *hurt*.

She checked her makeup, and listened for a moment for the musical cues of the orchestra. Her timing was good; they were right in the middle of the Drunk Gent. There was plenty of time to shake out the green spangled scarf and arrange it over the rest of the skirt, then put on her butterfly headdress and make sure it was pinned securely in place so that she could see.

She could hear the Sentimental Ballad starting as she finished with the headdress. That gave her enough time to gather up her wings in one hand and her wand and ribbon in the other, and make her way without hurrying to the wings, where Mrs. Littleton was waiting to help her put the wings on.

And then, the Breeches Girl came off, the curtain came down, the backdrop changed to the Garden Scene, the curtain pulled back completely and the music began.

Up on her toes she went, and took a run of tiny, fast steps backward diagonally across the stage while *tiddly tiddly tiddly* she went with the ribbon making spirals in the air behind her. She was supposed to be a ballet dancer, and people would expect to see the toe-work—

Then *turn* and whirl and *big* circles with the ribbon, then *leap* and circle with the ribbon overhead, then back across the stage *tiddly tiddly tiddly*—

It was all fast, done to Fairy Music from a play that Lionel said was very famous, and with a lot of misdirection with the ribbon-work. The ribbon made her dancing look ever so much harder and more complicated than it actually was. She only had to go up on her toes three times in the whole thing, twice to dance backward, and only once to pose with her leg held up in an arabesque. Not that it wasn't hard work! She was essentially running at full speed the entire time; she had to keep moving to keep the ribbon moving. But it wasn't any more complicated in the way of *dancing* than her work with the chorus. Less so, really . . . if she made a mistake or left something out, no one would know except her, and she could make something up to fill in until the next cue.

One last backward *tiddly tiddly tiddly* to give herself

room to run, and then run and *leap* out into the wings again, and it was over!

Well, from the sound of the applause, *this* was exactly what the audience had hoped to get out of a Russian Dancer. As the chorus girls pushed past her to get in place to back the Ballroom Number, she rushed back to the dressing room to get ready for the magic act.

Her dressing room was opposite Lionel's, and he was waiting to unhook her wings for her before she dashed inside to change. She smiled her gratitude at him; it had been his idea to get the wings off her rather than wait for Mrs. Littleton to get finished making sure none of the chorus dancers were going to come apart in mid-kick.

The Djinni costume—and the act—actually felt old and comfortable and familiar after all the heart-in-mouth of the new dancing numbers. She was actually able to relax, even add some little bits of business to throw more misdirection out there at key moments. The eyes were on Lionel, not on her, except when she was the centerpiece of an illusion. Her salamanders were only needed to ignite a couple of flashpots, which they did *beautifully,* and the whole act came off as smooth as the nicest, freshest cream.

Then while the stagehands stowed away their gear, she ran ahead of Lionel, back to her dressing room, to get into the Fire Dance dress.

It was a measure of Charlie's desperation that *he* had paid Mrs. Littleton for the gown—which had never been paid for by the original girl, and as a consequence was Mrs. Littleton's property. But since it wasn't *hers,* and since it was horribly, hideously expensive, Katie was absolutely fanatical about her care for it. It hung up on the wall against a clean dust sheet, and was covered by another when she wasn't actually in it. There were three layers of the gown, and if she hadn't worked out a way to get into and out of it by herself it would have been a nightmare to get into alone.

First, she stripped off all the makeup from the magic act. She had to be absolutely *clean* to get into the gown; the white silk showed the slightest smudge. She pulled off the dust sheet, knelt and lifted up the three layers of the front, then climbed inside the gown while it was still on the hanger. Only when she was safely inside did she pull the hanger out and put it aside, twisting and turning to make certain all the layers of the dress were hanging properly.

She draped herself in the dust sheet to protect the gown, did her makeup, then donned her mask, a form-fitting domino of red leather with three red-dyed feathers sprouting from the middle and arching over her head. Then she gathered up the dress in both arms and made her way back out to the wings.

As the Comic Singer left the stage, she took her place in the middle of it. "Break a leg," he whispered with a wink as they passed each other. She took the wands in her hands, gave herself a shake to settle the folds of the dress, and took a long, deep breath.

Of all three parts of the act, this was actually the one she was least nervous about. There wasn't all that much *talent* involved in this routine. It wasn't really Katie who was doing the dancing, after all, it was the dress. All Katie had to do was make sure she didn't trip, tangle herself up, or get herself into some other disaster.

Once again the backdrop was black, but this time

when the curtain parted, it parted all the way. The dress needed a *lot* of room.

The band crashed into the music with wild enthusiasm and a lot of cymbal- and drum-work. Katie began turning and gyrating, working the fabric of the dress as the two magic lanterns switched from red to orange to yellow and back again. She didn't so much see the sylphs that were helping her as feel them, lifting the folds at the right time, getting just the right amount of air into the layers, adding some height to the tosses of the wands. Katie turned the yards of fabric into flames, into wings, into storm clouds, and back into flames again. She tossed the wands high with every cymbal crash. She spun in place while she made the fabric form into peaks and valleys. Lionel had a cynical phrase for this sort of thing—"chewing the scenery"—but there was no doubt that the audience thought this dance was the best of the three. Loud as the band was, the crowd was louder, until she built up to the final crescendo, gave her wands one last toss into the air, and collapsed on the stage in a pool of fabric as the curtains snapped shut.

The crowd was roaring on the other side of the curtain. Katie was utterly exhausted, but managed to pick herself up off the floor and join the rest for the curtain calls. They took three, which was all that Charlie would allow—he insisted on having plenty of time to clear out the audience, restock the bar, and get all the apparatus set up for the second show.

"Cor! That looked even better than in rehearsal!" the Breeches Girl said in admiration. "How'd you get them little lights to run up and down the dress? I know you ain't got any spangles on it, so it wasn't that—"

Thinking quickly, Katie replied, "It's the silk, it reflects light ever so. Mrs. Littleton is brilliant."

That was all the young woman needed. She nodded wisely. "Ain't every music hall this size has a wardrobe mistress, much less one as good as she is."

Katie nodded, and the young woman gave her a kiss of congratulations, then ran off for her own dressing room. But before Katie could follow, Lionel grabbed her elbow.

"Once you've changed, meet me and Jack in my workroom," he whispered urgently. "We need to talk about what just happened onstage."

10

KATIE would really rather have gone straight to her dressing room, given herself a good wash, and had a bit of a laydown on her little sofa. Perhaps she could ask one of the other girls to bring back some cucumber sandwiches from a tea shop, but if not, she had some bread and butter and a bottle of lemonade. As exhilarating as her first star turn had been, it had also been exhausting. But she knew from Lionel's tone that whatever it was that he needed to discuss, it needed to be talked over *now,* and she had the feeling it had to do with the "lights" the Breeches Girl had seen running up and down her costume.

She hadn't noticed any such thing, but then again, she had been rather busy, and the billowing folds of the gown had rather effectively obscured her vision a great deal of the time. With the scarlet and gold lights from the magic lanterns playing on the fabric, it had been very like being inside a furnace.

She took great care cleaning off her makeup; if she wasn't going to get the chance for a wash between shows, she wanted to be as clean as she could.

And she hoped that they would remember that she only had so long before she would have to get her costume back on for the evening show.

When she made her way down the spiral stairs into the ground floor, Mrs. Littleton's room was quite dark, but Lionel's workshop was heavily illuminated. She ventured in to find Lionel waiting with open lemonade bottles and some newspaper-wrapped parcels.

"I didn't think you'd mind some fish and chips," he said gesturing. "I sent one of the lads for them."

Well, ordinarily it wasn't what she would have preferred; it was hideously hot on stage, and she had just put on the most difficult performance of her life. But it was much cooler down in this room, and she discovered she was starving. She sat down with Lionel and proceeded to devour hot fried fish and chips with all the enthusiasm of any of the pleasure-seekers on the Boardwalk.

"Jack will join us after he has gotten someone to watch the door for an hour or so," Lionel said, after taking a long pull from his bottle. "He is the expert on Fire Magic, not I. But this is why we urgently needed to speak with you. I presume that you didn't notice anything . . . odd . . . during that last dance?"

"I didn't," she admitted, "But the Breeches Girl—ah, I think her name is Victoria Sanderston?—she said there were little lights running through it. I told her it was the special fabric."

"Swift thinking. Yes, there were. I believe, although I do not know for certain, that those were Fire sprites. I have personally never seen them, only heard them described." He frowned. "This is what is troubling. They came by themselves. You aren't a Master, and yet they came by themselves."

She paused with a chip halfway to her mouth. "Is this bad?"

"Well . . ." he shrugged. "I don't know, you see. Jack might. The problem is that you are Fire, and Fire creatures are notoriously emotional. The Elementals, I mean, not necessarily you, personally. They respond strongly to the emotions of Elemental Mages—and more than that I don't know. That is why we are waiting for Jack."

Many hungry days had taught her there was no point in letting worry cause her to waste good food. She finished eating the chip and reached for another.

Jack arrived sooner than she had expected, and sat down and reached hungrily for the third packet of fish and chips without saying anything. Lionel simply forestalled any need to ask questions by describing what he had seen during the Fire Dance.

Jack nodded. "I see your concerns," he said. "and they're real." He turned to Katie. "I'm sorry, my dear," he said apologetically. "I know you are already overburdened with things you must do already, but you and I are going to have to make time for lessons in magic."

She sighed. After what Lionel had said, she had been afraid of something like this.

"You see, the problem is that for some reason, you are attracting Fire Elementals to you to help you without your asking for any to come," he explained.

"Well, you did say that they won't always come even if I ask," she pointed out. "That is why we have the electric sparker to set off the flash powder in case the salamanders are bored."

"But you already asked them," said Jack, finishing the last of his chips and folding the paper neatly into a perfect square. "These sprites came without you asking, and they did exactly as you would have wanted. Now . . . think about this, Miss Kate. What if someone made you angry? On your own, of course, I am certain you would never ask a Fire Elemental to attack the person you were angry with. But what if they did it because they felt your anger? Fire Elementals are emotional and respond to strong emotion. Many of them don't think as we understand thinking. You saw how the firebirds responded when we were in danger from the firework rocket. They simply acted. My fear is that if you are angered by something . . . some other Fire Elemental will simply act on your behalf."

She looked at him quizzically. "What harm could they do?" she asked. "No one can see them but us. They can barely set off the flashpots . . ."

"They could find a pile of old papers, or a tinder-dry attic, or a heap of oily rags," Jack replied, sternly. "And then someone's house could be on fire."

She stared at him, stricken.

"But—you said that if I—"

"I said that if you yourself deliberately caused Fire Elementals to harm someone, the good ones would abandon you," Jack corrected. "But if it was their decision, out of anger, and not yours . . ."

She felt numb; some of that must have shown in her face, for Jack's expression softened.

"This is why I need to give you lessons, so that sort of thing never happens," he said. "It *is* something that can be taught. It will just take time." And now he smiled. "One of the reasons why I'm the doorman here is that I have an understanding with the Fire Elementals. You have seen how easy it would be for a fire to start here in the theater. They will come and tell me if one does."

Well, she didn't see that she had any other choice. "When?" she asked with resignation.

"Whenever we can squeeze in a moment. Between the matinee and the evening performance. On dark days." Lionel smiled at her with encouragement. "You have been so apt at all of this that I am certain it will not take long."

Well, she was glad that he was certain.

Because she was anything but.

Jack went back to his post in a state of bemusement. Normally this sort of thing only happened to children. Elementals were attracted to the innocent, and innocent, young mages, who were not yet conditioned by the parents into disbelief in the wondrous were *very* attractive indeed. So the lesser Elementals were drawn to them; in fact, in the case of a Fire Mage, salamanders sometimes turned up in the dead of winter to warm their beds or dance in the fires of their nursery.

Fire sprites though—those were shy. In fact, he had never personally seen any. For them to not only turn up, but to make themselves visible to ordinary humans, said something; he just wasn't sure what it was.

At least Katie wasn't fighting this. He hoped he would

be able to make it enjoyable for her, as it had been for him as a child.

His father was a Fire Mage; his mother a country farmwife. She was a happy and incurious creature, and he and his father loved her very much. If she even noticed that he and his father sometimes did odd things together, she must simply have put it down to the mysterious ways of fathers teaching their sons, and it simply did not concern her.

His sisters were exactly like her; he wouldn't call them *stolid,* for they certainly weren't that. All of them were very much alive to the ordinary beauties of the farm. They reveled in lambing time, tended the flowers around the cottage with tender care, and often stood side by side in the doorway, admiring a particularly wonderful sunset. They just couldn't see past those things, and didn't care to.

Jack wasn't certain if the way he had been taught was typical for a Fire Mage or not; it certainly was a method that suited him, and, he hoped, was going to suit Kate.

It relied on patience.

As part of his training, his father had taught him how to bring wild birds to eat out of his hand—this was shortly after he had prattled about the things he had seen dancing in the hearth, his mother had laughed at his childish imagination, and his father had known that his son had inherited the family talent. It had been winter, which was the best possible time to make the trick work—and knowing how much mother loved birds, his father had included her in it as well.

They began by making up a straw man, dressed in clothing destined for the rag-bag and draped conspicuously in a cheap, bright-colored shawl that had been given to his mother, and that she had always disliked as "gaudy." One hand was outstretched, and every day they put grain in it. At first, of course, the birds were wary and avoided the straw man, but gradually their hunger overcame them, and they ventured near, and began to eat from the hand. This was when Jack's father took the place of the straw man. He had an uncanny ability to sit perfectly still, and the birds didn't notice the substitution. But the taming was not complete—for the idea was to get *any* of them accepted. So Jack's father had left off the shawl, but brought back the straw man. The wariness didn't last for more than half a day. Then he took the place of the straw man again, but this time, instead of staying completely still, he began talking to the birds. They scattered at the first word, of course, but soon came back.

Eventually, all it took was for anyone in the household to come out of the house and hold out a handful of grain, and the little birds would swarm them the way tame pigeons in a big city would swarm people with bags of bread crumbs. Of course, none of them had ever been to a city, so having wild birds so tame was a wonder and a joy to Jack's mother, and then his sisters.

And in the meantime, Jack had learned the patience it was going to take to coax the Fire Elementals to come out and communicate with him, not just dance for him to see. As volatile as Fire was—and given father's patient skill—it took a lot less time than it had to teach the birds to come.

He had the feeling that Katie had the patience. She certainly had the persistence. It took a very long time to learn the sorts of acrobatics she could do—time, and the willingness to put up with pain until muscles were properly stretched and trained.

Until now she had accepted her gift for magic, but she had not *embraced* it. That was what concerned him the most. If she was going to properly control her ability, and herself, then she would have to do more than come to terms with it. She would have to find joy in it; without the joy, there would be no true control.

Katie hoped with all her heart that Lionel and Jack were not expecting her to turn up for some sort of lesson after the evening performance. She went through her dances in a state of nervous, heightened awareness, and sure enough, she caught sight during the Fire Dance of tiny sparks dancing along the edges of the fabric, moving too fast for her to get a good look at them.

The audience was receptive, and enthusiastic, but not wildly so—they didn't throw their hats onstage, stand on the tables, or even stand up to applaud. Certainly it was enough to make Charlie happy, and to count as a success. She was as wrung-out as an old dishrag, however. This was much, much harder than acting as Lionel's assistant and dancing in the chorus. Still if she hadn't had those "lessons" hanging over her head, she would have been extremely happy. Not only would Charlie keep her act on for the summer, he would probably keep her on as a regular, just like Lionel. The same act would probably do until next summer, and by then, she'd have figured out how to make a new act out of contortion, the ribbon, and the dress.

He's probably going to make me pay him for the dress

out of my salary, though . . . Well, she couldn't blame him; it had been shockingly expensive for all those yards and yards of silk. Enough to make ten regular dancing dresses, for Mrs. Littleton had underestimated the yardage the first time she had brought it out! And she couldn't blame Mrs. Littleton for insisting on being paid for the gown before she allowed it to be used onstage. In her place, Katie would have done the same, and Katie had noted a distinct improvement in the Wardrobe Mistress's attitude since Charlie had paid her for the thing.

I want a good wash-up at least, she thought, as she cleaned the makeup from the performance from her face. She thought longingly of a bathtub full of cool water, and cold fruit soup. Was it so wrong that all she wanted to do was bask in success, and settle in for a well-earned sleep?

She steeled herself for the inevitable, waited until she could hear that most of the others had cleared out of the dressing rooms, then went out to see Jack at the door.

But Jack took one look at her, and shook his head. "You're in no state for a lesson," he said, "And by the time you get your mind wrapped around the idea, it'll be well past midnight. Go home, Miss Kate. Get some supper and some rest. I'll let Lionel know."

It sounded as if he was disappointed in her, but she didn't care right now. She just thanked him and made her escape.

She could not have been happier to reach the boarding house. One cool bath and an equally refreshing supper of the cold fruit soup that she had fantasized about, her window open to the ocean breeze, and she was more than ready to sleep.

And then . . . sleep eluded her. Her mind buzzed, and she tossed and turned, trying to find a cooler spot in her bed. Finally she just took the counterpane and laid it down on the floor; the floor would at least be cooler than her mattress.

Her thoughts wouldn't stay put. She went from reliving her mistakes in her routines, to reliving the moment of triumph at the end of each one when the crowd applauded, to Lionel's little lecture.

She just couldn't understand why it was he and Jack seemed so very urgent about her learning to control this "magic." Wasn't it like acrobatics? If you didn't know how to do a backflip, well, obviously you wouldn't be able to actually do one, would you? So why all the fuss?

But wait . . . they'd said the point wasn't that *she* did things, it was that the Elementals might do things, reacting to her emotions. They had said that was why the Fire sprites had turned up.

But would that be so bad? She wasn't *angry* with anyone; she'd always been excellent at keeping her temper. She'd taken after her father that way, not her mother, who had what her father called a "short fuse." And when it came to Dick. . . .

She suddenly felt cold all over, not hot anymore, because even the thought of Dick was enough to chill her and paralyze her with fear. She had to remind herself that Dick didn't know where she was, didn't know where to look, and by the time he found out, she would have her divorce and if he so much as put a finger on her, she could have him arrested.

It didn't help much.

She felt as if her thoughts were skittering around in her head like so many frightened mice. It was a lot easier exercising physical discipline than it was mental discipline.

There were just too many things she had to do, and people seemed to want her to do all of them at once.

And now that she was chilled the floor was horribly hard. She moved back to her bed, and curled up. There had to be something good she could focus on . . .

Of the three dances, she liked the Fire Dance the best. She was a little ashamed of that because it really *was* the easiest of the three, but she loved the way the fabric just flowed around her, flickering red to yellow and back again as she moved through the light from the magic lanterns. She concentrated on that, putting herself through every step, every movement, every note of the music in her mind. And that, finally, let her sleep.

Even in sleep, however, she was not left alone. Fire creatures moved through her dreams; the salamanders and firebirds that she knew, and other things she didn't. Bigger birds, with long, twinned tails. Tiny things no bigger than her thumbnail that looked, when she peered closely at them, like miniature versions of Lionel's sylphs, only made entirely of something that glowed, though it seemed to give off no heat. There were things that flew about, balls of fire with long tails, and women seemingly made of fire. All these creatures moved through her dreams, and she could sense their curiosity and interest in her. They didn't frighten her in her dreaming state, although if she had been awake, that might not have been true.

She woke at the usual time, and although dreaming so

much at night often had left her feeling more tired than when she had gone to bed, this morning she felt good; rested and energized.

She thought over her dreams, and what Lionel and Jack had told her last night, and the more she thought things over, the more determined she became that she was no longer going to be told what she must or must not do in these matters. She would decide for herself just how much time she would devote to these magic lessons. She was the one who had not one, but two jobs in the show now. She was the one having to perfect the dancing part in a ridiculously short period of time. And it wasn't as if she wasn't grateful—she *was*. But they were asking too much of her. If they kept on like this, she'd have no time to eat or sleep.

She trotted off to the music hall in a new state of determination, planning to arrive early so that she could speak openly with Jack.

And in fact, she literally caught him as he was unlocking the stage door. There was no one else about, and he looked surprised and pleased to see her, and opened his mouth to say something.

But she interrupted him before he could start.

"No," she said firmly. "No, it's too much to ask. I'm sorry, but I am not going to spend every waking moment in these lessons of yours. Dark day, fine. The break between matinee and evening, fine—but only if you'll feed me since you'll not be letting me get my own tea. But *not* after hours, and *not* in the morning. I've rehearsals to do, and I need to *sleep!* And you who have cooks and the like to look after you, did you even think about the fact that Mrs. Baird only serves supper for a little while, and that staying behind for these lessons will make me go to bed supperless?"

The peculiar look on Jack's face told her she had hit the mark squarely. "Well then. Don't think I'm not grateful, for I am. But these creatures have existed around me for all of my life without me getting them so worked up they're dangerous; I expect they can continue to do so for a few weeks more. Meanwhile, I don't think it's going to do anyone any good if you work me so hard I can't think. So you just tell Lionel that, Jack. I need to go practice."

And with that, she held her head and her chin high, and marched right past him and down to her dressing room. She had the feeling that he wasn't in the least convinced, but with her walking away, there wasn't much he could do or say about it right now.

Charlie had brought in a gramophone and records of the music for her three numbers about a week ago, muttering that it was cheaper to have the gramophone than pay a pianist. She changed into her rehearsal dress, warmed up her limbs, and ran through her dances as many times as she could until Lionel arrived for the magic act run-through. The only thing she didn't do more than once or twice was to go up on her toes in the ribbon dance. That part was still hard for her, though she hoped that with more practice it would be a bit less painful.

When Lionel arrived she almost expected to get something of a scold out of him—after all, she had been damned cheeky, leaving word with Jack of what she, who was nothing more than his assistant, would and would not be doing. But instead, he just shook his head ruefully at her.

"You're right, I wasn't thinking," he admitted, after they'd finished their first run-through. "I've arranged for luncheon and tea to be brought here, and if you're feeling up to the lessons, we can have brief ones before and after the matinee. Asking you to add night lessons to that would be absolutely cruel."

That was so completely unexpected—the best she had anticipated was that she would have to stage a battle of wit and persuasion to convince the magician—that she just gaped at him.

"I'm not a complete monster, you know," he murmured defensively.

That awoke something in her that hadn't stirred since the death of her parents. "Not completely, no," she said, dryly, a smile playing about her mouth.

"Cheeky wench," he muttered, and made her go into the basket again.

To her surprise, it was not Lionel and Jack that met her in the workroom at luncheon—which was, as she had half suspected it would be, pub sandwiches and bottles of lemonade. It was just Jack alone. "Lionel is taking the door for me while you and I have our lesson, Miss Kate," Jack said, politely handing over a bottle of lemonade. "Then between the matinee and the evening performance, we're paying one of the stagehands. We told Charlie it's because Lionel needs both of us to help work up the fall and winter acts."

"Does he believe you?" she asked, taking a cheese-and-Bramston-pickle sandwich from him.

He shrugged. "Does it matter? Honestly, I more than half suspect that he knows about our magic, and he'd let us get away with just about anything so long as we protect the hall. I've suspected that all along; my job came at the recommendation of the White Lodge in London, and I fairly well just walked in and Charlie said 'You're hired,' without anything else."

Her eyes widened. "Ordinary people know about us?" she said in surprise.

"Not many." He shrugged. "But aye. Ordinary folk do. That can be right helpful many times. But that's not why we're here." He pointed a finger at her. "You, Miss Kate, have the most dangerous magic of the four. And you can't just shrug your shoulders and say 'Well, I've had it all my life and nothing bad happened, so why should I worry about it now?' because that won't do. That just won't do at all."

Since that was precisely what she had been thinking, she ducked her head a little, guiltily. Still. "Why not?" she demanded.

"Because, it's one thing when you aren't aware of it. That puts a sort of barrier of innocence between you and the Elementals." He sucked on his lower lip a moment. "It's like you have a big, dangerous dog, except you don't know it's dangerous, it's just your dog. And maybe someone comes for you, and the dog attacks. *You* didn't order it to attack, and the dog wouldn't unless he sensed danger. But now you know it's dangerous. So say some fellow comes along and cheats you and you get angry. And the dog knows you're angry and starts growling. And then you don't stop him, and the dog attacks. Did the fellow who cheated you deserve to get his arm bit off?"

She *wanted* to say "yes," because she'd been in places and times when someone cheating her and her parents out of the bit of money they needed to live was just as bad, in her estimation, as being attacked. But . . . well, in the eyes of the law, it wasn't.

Clearly it wasn't, in Jack's eyes. And she didn't want to disappoint him, somehow.

"I suppose not," she said, reluctantly.

"Miss Kate." Jack looked at her sternly. "When you got any kind of power, you're obliged to use it properly. That's what a soldier learns, or at least, the good ones do. A soldier has a dangerous, bad thing with him all the time, a gun. Easy thing to kill with. He has to think about that all the time—not just when he's following orders, but because he has it with him all the time, he has to think about it when there's no fighting going on, and it might be tempting to use that gun in bad ways. Let's talk about that big dog and the fellow who cheated you. You're standing there and the dog is growling at the fellow. You know the dog is going to attack. You got power, you're obliged to use it properly. So what would the proper thing to do be?"

"Grab his collar, I suppose," she said, feeling a bit sulky.

"Aye, and you could say 'my dog don't like it that you cheated me, and my fingers aren't strong, so they just might not be able to hold him,'" Jack pointed out. "And you could say 'you just put the money you cheated me of on the path and go on home and I won't be mad and he won't want to tear your throat out no more.' That's properly using the power. And if he laughs at you, well, you warned him, and if the dog *does* get away from you—really get away, not just that you let it go—it's on his own head, then."

"But that's a dog—" she protested. "He can see the dog, he can hear the dog. I can warn him about the dog."

"And your Elementals are more dangerous yet, because most folks can't see nor hear 'em, and you can't warn 'em without looking like a loony." He folded his arms over his chest. "It's all on *you*, do you see? It'd be as if my gun had a mind of its own. If I wasn't in uniform, and I got mad at someone, and my gun came out and shot 'em."

"Well . . . why is it all right to ask salamanders to come light flashpots, and not these other things?" she persisted. "If the Elementals can think, can't they think for themselves? What if it wasn't just someone who I was angry with? What if it was someone who really was going to hurt me?"

Jack's mind went absolutely still at that point, because this was the closest that Kate had yet come to revealing the existence of her brutish husband. Would she?

He decided it was worth trying to coax her into it. "Is there someone who is really going to hurt you, Miss Kate?" he asked—gently, and without any tone of accusation. "If there is, you should tell me about it, both because of the magic and because I think I can call myself your friend."

She was silent, but she had gone a bit pale, and she wasn't eating the sandwich in her hand, which was very unlike her. She had the healthiest appetite in a female—outside of a country-bred girl—that he had ever seen. It took a great deal to put her off her food.

"Why would it be wrong for the Elementals to get rid of someone that I really knew wanted to hurt me?" she asked, finally. "Someone who'd hurt me before?"

"Because . . ." he sighed. "I'm not sure how to properly explain this. Maybe because we're supposed to do unto others as we'd like to be done by—not do by others as they done to us."

Oh she was a right little heathen, she was. He could see the rebellion in her eyes. She didn't like that, and she didn't agree with it, not one bit. He *could* sympathize, but he shouldn't.

"Let's go back to that dog," he said. "What do you think people do about a dog that has attacked a person— even if the dog was defending the person?"

She shook her head. "I've never had a dog," she said. "I don't know."

"They kill it," he said, bluntly. "Dogs aren't given trials."

"But—that's not fair!" she blurted immediately. "If the dog—"

"The dog has learned it is acceptable to attack a human, and *you* have shown you can't or won't control him," he pointed out bluntly. "Now, perhaps nothing will happen. Perhaps he will continue to be a good dog and loyal, and only attack when provoked or in defense of you. But perhaps he will not. Perhaps, now that he has learned he can attack a human and not be punished for it, he will decide that the next time a human has something he wants, he will take it. Perhaps that human will be a child, or a woman. Constables will not take such a risk, although," he added with a touch of bitterness, "If you are sufficiently wealthy and the dog is sufficiently valuable, they will believe everything you say and merely demand that the dog be kept muzzled at all times. The laws that apply to the rest of us often do not seem to apply to the titled and wealthy."

She nodded, and did not appear shocked at such sentiments. Well, she was a Traveler, after all, and Travelers were well-schooled in the lesson that there were those with privilege and there were those with none—and the Travelers were in the latter group.

"But that is neither here nor there," he continued. "Elementals do not think as we do. We don't know how intelligent—or not—they are. We don't know what the consequences would be for some of them to learn they can harm humans at will. We *do* know that there *are* Elementals of all four sorts that hate humans, and will take any opportunity to harm them."

She gaped at him. "There are?"

He nodded. "Terrible things have happened when such creatures were given the power by a magician or a Master of wicked intent to wreak their will on the world. And we do not know *how* they came to be this way. Did it begin as something as simple as—defending a friend? Like the dog? Once they travel that road, do they turn into something evil?"

"You don't know that they do!" she protested.

"And we don't know that they don't." He shook his head. "I have seen what happens when men who were once good become used to doing terrible things. The war in Africa—I don't pretend to be a politician. I don't know if Britain was wrong to be there, or right. But I do know this; we were ordered to do increasingly terrible things there, we Tommies. They told us that because the Boer men kept slipping off into the bush to fight us, that we had to take all but the barest means to survive from the women and children on the farms, because the farms were clandestinely supplying the men. Then they told us that since that wasn't working, we had to burn the farms out. Then they told us since *that* wasn't working, we had to round up the women and children, throw them into prison camps where they starved, and if they didn't starve, they died of disease."

The words had come hard to him; they came hard every time he had to speak them. He loved his country and his King—then, Queen. He just didn't like what he'd been asked to do. It had made him sick then; it still made him sick, and the fact that he himself had not been *personally* forced to do those things did not make him any less sick about it. Because that had all been luck—and he had seen what had happened to those who had.

Katie really knew nothing of what went out outside of the places she herself had lived and roamed. She'd known there had been a war, and that it had been in Africa—but that was all she knew.

But this man, this fine man who she trusted, and who had become her friend—it was that war that had taken his leg, and from the sound of it, had inflicted an even deeper wound on his spirit.

Then he told her what men like him had been forced to do, and it shocked her to the core. The pain in his voice, on his face . . .

It made her hurt *for* him.

"I never had to do any of that," he was saying, though from the sound of it, he might just as well have done. "I was lucky, or maybe my Elementals twisted my luck to keep me from it. But I knew men who did, and . . . it changed them, Miss Kate. It changed them, and mostly for the bad. Some, it made harder; those were the worst, I think. It made them hard, made them into men who were sure, as sure as they were that the sun came up in the east, that anyone who wasn't British was ... only a little higher than a beast, and deserved whatever the Crown decided to do to him. Self-righteous they became ... and as a consequence, were anything *but* righteous." He passed a hand over his face; his complexion was a little gray. "Some went mad—a bit, or a lot. Their minds just couldn't take the cruelties they were asked to do. Some just deserted, ran out into the bush and either joined the Boers or went native. Most are like me; torn up inside, trying to reconcile what they think they are with what they did."

He shook his head again. "That is what I am trying to tell you, Miss Kate. That is what doing as you were done by does to you. It eats your heart. It's like acid in your soul." He looked into her eyes. "Miss Kate, it changes you. And if it changes you, it changes the Elementals even more. Would you want that? Think of them—if you won't think of yourself, think of them, and ask yourself if you want to change them for the bad that way, and have *that* on your conscience."

Suddenly she found words coming out of her mouth that she had no intention of saying. "I'm married, Mister Prescott," she heard herself saying, her voice gone hard and bitter. "I'm married to a wicked man, a brute. A man who hurt me, and scared me, a man who took the money I earned and spent it on whores and gin. A man who might well kill me for running from him. Are you saying that I don't have the right to defend myself from him if he comes for me? Are you saying I should just lay down and let him beat me or kill me? That I shouldn't let this power I have defend me?"

She couldn't believe she had just said that. She was thinking it, of course, but she couldn't believe she had just come out and *said* it.

She expected him to—well, lecture her, or something. Tell her that she was wrong and she should go back to her husband, that he was her rightful superior and she must have done something wrong to make him beat her. That it was her duty, since she had married him, to be and do whatever he said. That—well, all the usual things.

But he didn't. Instead, he sighed, and looked as if all the pain of the world was weighing on him.

"Miss Kate," he said, wearily. "You still have a choice. *You* know you do. You can ask your Elementals to watch for him and warn you of him, so you can run from him. You can get a divorce, and then if he lays a hand on you, it'll be the law on him. You can take ship for another country—I'm sure you have enough money by now, or will soon. You can hide. You probably have a dozen things you can do, if you need to. Or . . . you can 'defend' yourself by letting yourself get so angry that your Elementals kill him for you, knowing that is what you are doing. And that would be murder on your part, and it would corrupt them. And you know it."

She felt her face flushing, partly in anger and partly in shame. Because she knew he was right.

She hated it, but she knew he was right.

"It's *not fair,*" she said, sullenly and angrily. "It's *not fair.* Why is it that he can do whatever he wants, and I can't?"

"Because you are good, Kate," Jack said quietly, putting one hand over hers as she clenched them together. "Because you are good, and he is not. It's always harder to be good. But it's worth it, in the end."

The touch of his hand on hers was unexpected, and so was the effect. She went very, very still, shocked into stillness by the strange, almost electric feeling that came over her from that touch. It was like nothing she had ever felt before. Everything came into sharper focus, and she was aware of a thousand tiny little things—mostly about him. How gentle his hand was, so unlike Dick's, as if her hands were fragile flowers he was being careful not to crush. How there were lines of pain that made his face look older than he really was—but lines of laughter, and smile lines about his mouth, too. How everything about him was *clean,* trim, and in order—and nothing could have been more in contrast with Dick's slovenliness. Merely looking into his eyes put fire in her veins.

"Kate," he said, so quiet it was almost a whisper. "We care about you. We don't want you lost. We'll help you, but it's you that has to make the choice."

"What choice?" she asked, choking a little on the words.

"Joy instead of anger. Peace instead of hate. Come to your magic like a child would, happy in the new gift, and master it as an adult does, with reason and control. Give over the anger. Let go of the pain so it stops blinding you, and you can see all the other choices you have. I know it's hard, mortal hard, but it's worth it. Trust me."

And she did trust him. Reluctant though she was ... because the anger had been what had saved her in the first place, and propelled her out of Dick's clutches and onto the road. Fear had only kept her paralyzed. Anger had given her strength.

"Anger will burn out and leave you with nothing, Kate," he said, as if he was reading her mind. "These past few weeks—have you *needed* that anger? No. Have you even felt it? I don't think so. And aren't you the better for that?"

She couldn't argue with that, either. It hadn't been anger that had helped her create those dances. It hadn't been anger that had propelled her steps on the stage.

Slowly, she let out her breath.

"I'll try," she said. "I'll try."

And another electric thrill passed through her as he tightened his hand slightly on hers. "That's all I ask, Kate. That's all anyone could ever ask."

11

Jack felt as if he had just fought a major battle as he stumped back to his desk. He was exhausted, but filled with a sense of triumph.

And filled with something else as well . . .

Something he really didn't want to think about just at this moment, when the performers were coming back from tea (or the pub) and he had to guard the door like the proverbial dragon against interlopers.

Already word had gotten around about "the Russian's" performance. This hall was too small to rate a review yet—not unless she generated enough of a sensation on her own. Perhaps the third week in, the papers would get around to sending their reviewers.

But there were people out there buying tickets for the evening performance because of what they had heard in their boarding houses last night. And he knew this, because of what the chorus girls and band members were saying as they trickled in; some of *them* could always be counted on to linger at the ticket booth just to hear what people were saying. It made for great gossip fodder if there was someone they didn't much like.

Or, in this case, if it was someone they liked, like Katie, it made for something cheerful to gush about. Plus . . . well, there was always the chance that if Katie started filling the hall to overflowing, Charlie might put on another couple shows, which would mean more money for everyone. Toffs sometimes hired on part of a music hall show on a dark day to entertain at parties—so far that hadn't happened very often within Jack's memory, but if Katie proved popular enough, that would provide another source of income.

"There's a *line,* Jack, wouldjew berlieve it?" one of the girls gushed as she edged past the desk. "There ain't been a *line* at the box since . . . well, since Charlie managed to get George Lashwood!"

Jack remembered that well. Like too many performers, Lashwood had been a bit improvident, and his solution to the problem was to double-book himself, doing two halls a night—an early one here, then his regular, and an "after midnight" show at the Brighton Hall.

Well, this was a good sign. He wouldn't count on it, though, and he wouldn't tell Katie yet. It might be a fluke. He didn't want to get her hopes up.

Nor to give her stage fright, either.

For a brief moment, he felt a sense of dislocation—not uncommon among Elemental Mages, actually. Here he was, worrying about the box office and popularity of his friend Katie—his friend Katie, who could, if she decided that was what she wanted and persuaded her Elementals to help, probably burn this music hall to the ground. He and every other Elemental Magician led double lives, balancing the "real world" against the other that they lived and worked in. And sometimes that other world seemed . . . insane. Impossible.

Just for a moment, then everything would settle into place again, and he would be back to juggling the two sides.

He was just grateful that tomorrow was a dark day. It could not have been timed more perfectly to get the lesson home to the girl while she was still open to it.

Katie was both glad and sorry that tomorrow was a dark day. Glad because at least she would not have to juggle the magic business with the vastly more important business of properly getting her *job* done. Sorry because she just knew that Jack and Lionel were going to make a full day of it for her. She'd get no rest this dark day . . .

"Lionel's, eight in the morning, Katie," Jack murmured to her as she bid him good night, wishing that she could think only of what Mrs. Baird was going to be offering for supper.

"Eight in the morning. I'll be there," she said, then added rebelliously, "but he had better give me breakfast! Mrs. Baird doesn't serve so early."

Jack chuckled dryly; the sound teased a smile out of her.

"You strike a hard bargain, Kate," he said. "I'll let him know."

And then she was out into lamp-lit streets, which, on

any other summer than this one, she would have thought unusually warm. But compared to the baking heat of the day, well, this was the closest thing to "cool."

She passed a newsboy, still out and crying his headlines. There was a lot about strikes—strikes at the coal mines, threatened strikes at the docks. Then one caught her attention.

A rail strike.

"Holiday towns" like Brighton and Blackpool depended on the railways. It was the only way that people who couldn't afford to keep their own automobiles and carriages could get to the seaside for a week or so. What would happen if there *was* a rail strike? It was no good saying that people that were stuck here would come to the Boardwalk and the halls! They wouldn't be able to afford to—they'd have spent all their holiday money and would frantically be trying to figure a way to stretch whatever they had with them, or to find a way back. The last thing on their minds would be spending more money to go to a music hall.

Was Charlie aware of this? Was Lionel?

She realized a moment later that she was standing still in the street, and people were giving her peculiar looks as they had to get around her. She hurried her steps to the boarding house.

Once there, she discovered that the topic of heated conversation around the table was not any of the impending strikes, but the heat itself. ". . . niver thought I'd be asking to wear *less*," one of the girls was saying as Katie came in. "I'm telling you, they are right daft, thinking we can go prancin' about in fur and all in *this* heat!"

As Katie had suspected, the Russian craze was taking

its toll on chorus dancers and acrobats being asked to pass as foreigners. Katie was all the more happy with Charlie now, who had consulted with Mrs. Littleton and seen to it that his chorus dancers were not going to expire of heat under layers of velvet and fur more suited to the bitterest winter than the hottest summer on record.

The bathroom was very crowded, and for once the girls stripped to almost nothing without shame in order to get themselves at least a cooling sponge bath in a basin, if they couldn't get a soak in the tub. Nor did most of them trouble to do more than wrap the thinnest of wrappers over themselves to go upstairs to their rooms.

Katie counted herself wise that she had taken her bath before supper, rather than after, and went straight up wishing that she was an Air Magician and could conjure a breeze, rather than Fire.

But then she remembered Jack's lessons, and instead of trying to fight the heat, she embraced it, lying down on the still-made-up bed, and reminding herself of how good the heat would feel if it were winter, not summer.

The trick worked, and she fell asleep immediately.

On waking, she felt cool and refreshed, rather than hot and sticky as she had yesterday morning. There definitely was power in Jack's tricks. And . . . maybe there was power in the other things he'd talked about yesterday. Usually she had at least one uncomfortable dream every night, if not a nightmare. Last night—nothing. She'd slept as easily as she used to as a child in the caravan.

Mrs. Baird was only just putting out the breakfast things—Katie had fibbed just a little about that—and Katie was happy to sit down to tea and fruit and a little toast. All that dancing was certainly giving her an appetite; she got up still feeling hungry, and started toward Lionel's house certain that when she got there she could easily eat a second breakfast without thinking about it.

When she arrived, Jack let her in, and she and he proceeded to the dining room to smell the heavenly aroma of bacon wafting down the hall. *Does anything smell as good as bacon?* she thought. Still, she wouldn't have wanted bacon or anything else heavy if she was going to be in the hot theater all day, but they would, presumably, be spending their time here, in Lionel's cool little house, and the bacon and eggs and all the other lovely stuff that was waiting on the sideboard were so welcome that her stomach gave a little growl in anticipation.

Lionel was already eating; Jack had obviously gotten up from his breakfast to let her in. She helped herself and joined them. She had to admit that the male habit of eating in silence and devoting yourself to your food was a rather nice change from the twittering chorus that accompanied breakfast and supper at Mrs. Baird's.

Only when everyone was satisfied and Jack and Lionel were sitting back and nursing cups of tea did anyone speak.

"Today will be a real day of magic lessons, Kate," Lionel said. "We need to show you how to shield yourself, first of all, for if you are feeling very strong emotions, Fire shields will protect the Elementals from your feelings, as well as being able to prevent other magicians from finding you, and protecting you in part from attack."

"Wait—" she said. "Prevent other magicians from finding me? Attack?"

"I told you that you don't want to go down the wrong

path, Miss Kate," Jack replied. "There are those that will take your power if they can, and kill you if they can't have it, for fear that one day you might come to kill them. That's what happens when you go down the wrong path, you see. You start to look at everyone with power as either someone to take advantage of, or as an enemy."

It flashed into her head that this was *exactly* how Dick viewed the world. Everyone he met was either to be used, done away with, or, if they were too strong, placated until he could find a way to get things out of them.

"So, your best defense is not to be seen. Let's go down to the garden room, I'll show you how to see Fire Magic, you might be able to see Air as well, and then we'll show you how to make something out of your magic that will protect you and keep you from being seen." Jack set aside his cup, stood up, and gestured to her to go along ahead of him.

The rest of the morning was spent in that surprisingly pleasant task. When Lionel described what this magical energy was supposed to look like, she had another revelation.

"It's a sort of shimmer around everything alive, isn't it?" she exclaimed. "And drifts of faint color in the air, like oil on water!"

Jack and Lionel exchanged a look. "You've seen this before?" Lionel asked.

"All the time when I was a child. I suppose I just stopped looking for it when we got into towns; it's harder to see there. It's hard to see anyway; easier to not look when it doesn't really mean or do anything." She sucked on her lower lip, furrowed her brows, and *looked* for the shimmer without being asked to. It felt for a moment as if something was fighting her, as if she was trying to open eyes that had been stuck shut, but then there was a sense of something unfolding—and she could see it again!

Jack smiled. "I can tell by your face you've got the trick again," he said. "Now that you can see it, we can show you how to use it."

He showed her how to gather it—to her disappointment, she could only see the red mist of Fire energy clearly—she could only manage a faint blue hint of Air, and nothing at all of Water and Earth. He showed her how to move it about, how to concentrate it, and just the beginnings of how to shape it. Two salamanders watched with silent interest, but neither moved nor interfered.

That was when Lionel decreed that they would break for luncheon and a rest; it was only when he did that Katie realized she was as tired as if she had been rehearsing all morning.

Luncheon had been set up on the sideboard, and rather than being the large, hot meal Lionel usually served, this was a buffet of cold foods. She was grateful for that. She felt . . . oddly warm. Oddly, because she wasn't *uncomfortable,* and it was a peculiar sort of warmth, not like a fever exactly, but as if she herself were containing fire.

And that wasn't uncomfortable, either. Just . . . different.

After luncheon, Lionel decreed a rest, which relieved her. She wasn't at all sure she could go back to work right away. As Lionel and Jack settled into their favorite chairs for a read—and probably, she thought shrewdly, a surreptitious nap—she went out into the overgrown garden with a pillow and a rug.

Throwing the rug down over the thick grass gave her a surprisingly comfortable place to lie down. She did so, and closed her eyes, relaxing and concentrating at the same time as Jack had shown her, trying to "see" what it was that was making her feel so odd. Eventually she drifted into a state of half-asleep, half-awake.

Drifting in a state that was not quite dreaming, slowly, a picture built up in her mind. Her veins, running with fire. Her body, every bit of it hazed with fire. It was as if there were two of her, both contained in her skin, one of flesh and one of fire.

It was . . . fascinating.

It was beautiful.

She could scarcely believe it was her, and yet, in this half-dreaming state, she understood that not only *was* it her, she was going to have to do something to dampen it all down again. She wasn't uncomfortable now, but before too very long she would be. Then it would be painful. Then . . .

And yet she wasn't frightened, because she understood that this was a consequence of handling all the energy all this morning. Somehow she had been accumulating some of it. So all she needed to do now was . . . let it go.

She did, and "watched" it wisp away from her, trailing off like the silk ribbon she danced with in a wind.

And that was when the salamanders reappeared, four of them this time, eagerly leaping to take bites of the power she was letting loose. Eating it!

Well, if they wanted to eat it—she used the tools that Jack had been teaching her to control the stream, shape it and slow it down, making a little pool of the Fire-energy so that they could gather around it and lap it up like cats. The more they drank, the brighter they got, until, by the time she was feeling comfortable in her skin again, they were as bright as red-hot coals.

They turned eyes on her that brimmed with gratitude—then they were gone, and she turned on her side and drifted into a nap of true sleep.

It didn't last long, but it refreshed her tremendously. When she woke perhaps a half an hour later, and took the rug and pillow back into the house, Jack and Lionel were just rousing from their own rest, and looking ready to resume the lessons.

Before they could suggest a start, however, she sat down with them and described what she had felt and done. She couldn't help but notice while she did so, that Lionel kept fanning himself with a palm-leaf fan, but Jack appeared—and she felt—perfectly comfortable.

Lionel listened attentively, but shook his head when she looked to him for an answer or approval. "Air Magic doesn't work that way," he said. "It's the hardest to hold of the four. It sounds to me as if you did the right thing—Jack?"

Jack took a moment in replying, his eyes thoughtful.

"Not what I would have done, but my father always said that if it works right, you can feel it," Jack replied at last, and rewarded her with another of his slow smiles. "Clearly, this felt right to you. So I would say, well done, Miss Kate. I think it was right of you to feed the salamanders with the Fire Magic, too. It shows you are generous, and it shows you can be depended upon to give without asking anything in return. It will make them more generous with you, and more likely to trust you."

"Do as you would be done by," Lionel suggested. "It's important for the Elemental creatures to be able to trust us. Us trusting them—well, you have know which can be trusted, first—but with Fire, that's generally pretty obvious."

Jack made a face. "The only bad ones I've ever seen were the ones that were under the control of a bad magician. But then I don't think that Fire Elementals that had gone to the bad would go after a trained Fire Magician. You don't attack what's strongest against you, you attack the weak."

Lionel nodded sagely; Katie bit her lip a little. So that was what they did? Go after the weak? Children . . . she thought of how as a child she had simply delighted in the pretty things around her that she now knew were Elementals. She would have been easy prey. *Is that what happens, sometimes, when children sicken and die for no reason anyone can think of?*

But Lionel didn't elaborate, and neither did Jack. "Let's see what happens when you continue to work with the Fire Magic, Kate," Lionel said. "Jack will know if you are dangerously overburdening yourself, and we can stop and you can let it drain off from you before we go on."

So, back to work they went. Now the men both taught her how to take that Fire-energy, shape it further, and make it into a kind of shell that would both hide her from another magician and protect her from attack. They told her to imagine blowing a bubble out of it, then think of the bubble as becoming as hard as iron, and it worked! Jack even did some light "attacks" on it, and mostly it held! It was exciting to learn—and it was like dancing all three of her dances back-to-back, twice. By the time she had mastered it, she was ready to drop.

And she must have looked it, for Lionel ordered a halt.

"That's enough for one day," he declared. "Jack will help you practice these things for the rest of the week. You know how it is, you need to be sure of your first tools before you can move on to the more complicated actions. So before we go further, I want you to have mastered these things."

"Yes, Lionel," she said obediently, well aware, from her dancing, that she was just at the stage where she had worked out the steps, but she hadn't gotten them sure in her memory, nor was she doing them at anything like full speed.

The sun was westering now. Not that it was really possible to tell that from this house so much—just that everything was shadowed, and the air here was fractionally cooler as the house moved completely into the protection of the shadows of those around it. The birds in the backyard woke up and got a bit livelier, splashing about in the birdbath. "I," Lionel then proclaimed, "am going to my library to see if there is anything in my books about Fire Magic. It's mostly tomes about Air, but one never knows."

Lionel got to his feet and retreated into the depths of his house, making scarcely a sound—Katie had noticed before this that he walked so lightly it was easy for him to slip up on a person even when he wasn't trying to be secretive. She had no idea where his library could be; so far all she had seen of the house were the garden room, the drawing room, the dining room, and the hall. She marveled a little at one person having all this space to himself—after living in a caravan with two other people most of her life, even her little room in the boarding house felt huge. What did one person do with all this room?

Well, collect things in it, obviously. Like books. . . .

But his leaving left her alone with Jack . . .

There was silence between them, and she wondered what he was going to say. She didn't think she was misreading him. He found her interesting, and not in a sisterly way. And . . . he was so completely unlike Dick, that sort of regard didn't bother her. In fact . . . in fact she liked it. And she rather thought she'd like to have more of it. He fidgeted in his chair. Finally, he spoke. "Miss Kate—"

She interrupted him. "You were calling me just plain 'Kate.' I'd rather you did that, or Katie." She smiled encouragingly at him. "After all, I thought we were at least friends." She hoped she wasn't being too forward. Traveler girls didn't flirt about with boys; a boy might fancy her, but he'd never come to her directly, he'd go to his Da, then the two Das would get together and maybe a wedding would be arranged. That was why she hadn't really fought what Andy Ball wanted for her—he was the nearest thing to a father she had at that point, and what other choice did she have, unprotected by family, and more importantly, her real father? She could have lost her good name without even *doing* anything, and then what would become of her?

Country girls weren't like that—to Travelers, anyone who wasn't a Traveler was "country" or sometimes "house folk." Country girls flirted with boys; she'd seen them, partly envious and partly aghast, until after being in the circus she had more or less gotten used to how country people were, and how some of them didn't seem to care about their good names. So maybe he was used to that? If anything, the music hall, the chorus girls, and even some of the acts were more casual about going together than the circus folks.

But she didn't want casual; she wanted something better. How did you manage that?

He had the most peculiar expression on his face, but it wasn't negative—it was as if a thousand thoughts were going through his head at once, and he was rapidly making up his mind about something.

"Katie, I have something to confess to you," he said, after a long pause, a pause during which her heart began to pound, fearing he was going to say something that would dry up all her budding hopes. "Miss Peggy told Lionel all about your . . . situation . . . after you asked her advice. After all, you didn't ask her to keep it secret, and she thought we should know about it. We'd been putting our heads together, trying to work out how to get you more work and more money, when this Russian dancer affair dropped in everyone's lap."

Now it was her turn to have a thousand thoughts rushing through her mind. She was a little—only a little—angry at Miss Peggy for running off to Lionel. But Jack was right, she *hadn't* sworn Miss Peggy to secrecy. Lionel was her employer, and Miss Peggy might well have thought he had every right to know. Especially if by some horrific chance Dick actually turned up. . . .

The mere idea made her throat grow tight and her heart pound harder than before.

"We never said a thing about it to Charlie nor anyone else," Jack was going on. "In a way, it's a good thing we're all in theater. We've got . . . more flexible ideas than people with settled lives." Whatever he read in her face seemed to encourage him, and he reached out and patted her hand lightly. "I don't think you were wrong for marrying someone you didn't even know, and I don't think you're wrong for trying to free yourself from him. There's more to blame with that circus owner who rushed you into marrying his strongman, and you still in shock and grief, than there is to you. And you're a smart young woman to have run off, smarter still to go somewhere the circus won't. And then, you worked out you needed to get a divorce, who to ask about it, and you've gone about getting there in the most sensible way possible. I really don't know how you've managed to keep your head through all the things you've gone through. I don't know many people who would have. Most would just throw their hands in the air and wait for God or someone to rescue them."

She flushed a little at his praise. It wasn't just the praise, either; it was the brief touch of his hand on hers, and the fact that *he* was praising her. If this was what country girls got, well, she wanted more of it. His hand on hers made her all a-tingle, and the look in his eyes made her think all sorts of things that no Traveler girl should ever think about a man she wasn't married to.

Now more words came, faster, as if he was trying to get them all out before he lost the courage to say them. "Katie, I know you might not want to think of such things as a fellow talking to you like this, because all you know of men is what that . . . foul creature did to you. I know this divorce could take a great deal of time. And I know you aren't free now to even think about possibly finding someone else. But when you are . . . I would consider it the greatest honor . . . it would make me awfully happy . . . if you would consider me . . . letting me . . . pay my attentions to you." He flushed deeply. "I mean . . . honorably of course. Pay court to you, is what they'd say back when I was a boy. If you'd—"

It finally penetrated to her what he was asking, and a startled laugh bubbled up from inside her. For a moment *he* looked startled, then a touch angry and a great deal embarrassed, but before he could take it wrong, the words all tumbled out of her, impelled by a rush of feelings she couldn't define, but which were exciting, breathtaking, and utterly intoxicating.

And at that moment, she was sure, as sure as she knew anything was sure, that this was right. Maybe other people would look at the two of them and shake their heads, but she *knew*. They were meant to be together. The more she thought about it, moment by moment, the more certain she became.

"That would be *amazing!*" she said. "I—I like you better than any fellow I have ever met, Jack, and the more I am with you, the better I like you! I wish you would!"

It was not the most elegant way to respond, but his face cleared, and then he smiled. And he took her hand and kissed it. "Then we can start by becoming the best of friends," he replied. Which was an answer she liked, a very great deal—not the least because it had never even entered Dick's head to be *friends* with her.

"I would like that, very, very much," she said softly,

and did not withdraw her hand, which tingled in a most delightful way where he had kissed it. She would have thrown away her good name a thousand times for this.

Lionel returned to find them holding hands and talking about hundreds of things, flitting from subject to subject, taking it in turns to speak or listen avidly. For Katie's part, she couldn't hear enough about Jack and his past. She could almost see the farm he'd grown up on in her head; often there were farmers like that kind enough to let a Traveler camp on their land for a night or two, or more, if there was something about the farm that they could do. Katie's Da was no tinker, and no strong man, but he didn't shirk work, and often during hop season, the whole family would camp with all manner of folks, Travelers, city people, and wandering workers who came for the harvest, and take part in the hop-picking. From what Jack said, his Da had been the sort that Travelers could depend on to treat everyone fair, and the sort no Traveler was allowed to steal from. She was glad Jack's Da and Ma were still alive so she could meet them. She hoped his sisters wouldn't make a problem because she was a Traveler—though she didn't mind at all being inside four walls, not like some Travelers who couldn't abide it, so perhaps she just wouldn't say anything, and ask Jack not to.

Already, in the back of her mind, there were vague stirrings of plans. They would stay at the music hall, of course. Lionel needed them. Charlie needed *her*, at least for as long as this craze for Russian dancers lasted. She knew Jack had rooms of his own nearby; they would probably be big enough for two, she didn't take up much space. By September, she would have enough money for the divorce. Maybe by the time winter set in things would be quiet enough at the music hall that they could take a week or two to get married and just be completely together for a bit.

And it seemed that Jack couldn't hear enough about her life—or at least the part of it before Dick. He said wonderful things about her Da and Ma, and he even said he used to envy Travelers as a boy, always going somewhere new, and doing interesting things. Romantic, he called it. She doubted that he would have found the going hungry and cold parts all that romantic, but she wasn't going to ruin it in his mind.

When Lionel came in, she saw his eyes take in how closely they were sitting together, and that they were holding hands—and saw little smile-creases appear in the corners of his eyes. But he didn't say anything, he just sat down in his chair and let them separate naturally. For Katie's part, it was also reluctantly. But it wouldn't be proper, nor polite, to act so in front of Lionel, so they both sat back in their chairs, and she folded her hands in her lap to wait and see what he had to say.

"As I expected, my little library was bereft of information on Fire Magic, except in how it works with Air Magic," he said, quite as if he had found them exactly as he had left them, and not "canoodling," as Peggy would have called it.

"Well, that's information we already knew," Jack pointed out, "Since you and I have worked together often enough. You'd think there would be more than that in your books."

"I don't have a large library, just what I inherited from my uncle," Lionel said, "And I haven't had as much time as I'd like to get more books. Most magicians and all the Masters are rather cautious about who they talk to about their libraries, and insist on you coming to them. Then you have to work out if they have a spare copy, or if they'll allow you to make a copy, which, since it's by hand, takes a great deal more time. These books are not the sort of thing one can pick up in a shop."

"You would think," Jack replied, a bit crossly, as Lionel fanned himself, "That the White Lodge would be a little more helpful in getting books out to the rest of us. There have to be *some* good general books about all four forms of Elemental Magic, and it's deuced difficult for those of us who never saw the magic of another Element to try and help out another magician. We don't *all* own family libraries the size of this house, after all! How hard would it be to get a private printing of some of the more useful pieces and offer it to the rest of us?"

Katie could tell this was a long-held grievance of his. She had the feeling it was not the first time he'd made this sort of complaint to his friend.

Lionel shrugged. "Well, we are all mere mages, and rather below the notice of the White Lodge in London unless they happen to need more bodies than there are Masters hereabouts." He flicked the fan in the direction of the garden. "We are the sparrows of the Kingdom, and they are the hawks. It's quite true that they do good work in guarding the unknowing herd from nasty things, but I wish they'd remember we do quite as much as they do, even if we are only eating up the bugs that would spoil the harvest and not fighting the great monsters. But they never seem to unless something happens and they find themselves forced to rely on one of us."

Jack laughed. "Oh, yes, they're all 'Tommy go away' until they need soldiers. And somehow they never seem to grasp that the soldiers do better when they've got the best guns in their hands." But he didn't sound bitter about it. "That's all right; I never had that much teaching out of books. Maybe mere mages learn their magic better and easier by following their instincts and having someone along to guide. Maybe we don't need all the rules and faradiddle the Masters seem to think *they* need."

"It's entirely possible. I've gotten along all my life that way, and so have you. I think we know more about doing a great deal with a very little, certainly. If ever they find themselves cut off from the majority of their power, they'd probably be as helpless as any man you pulled off the street. And most of them are toffs, anyway," Lionel said dismissively. "Reasonable, often fairly likeable toffs, but toffs just the same. It never occurs to them that we're any different from—oh—a valet. Or a butler. Useful but not someone you invite for a brandy and a cigar."

"Hmm hmm," Jack murmured. "Officers and ge'mun."

They nodded sagely at each other. Katie felt a little lost, but then, she often felt that way around men who were great friends—it was as if they had a language all their own. And they forgot, sometimes, that there was anyone else about.

But it seemed after all that they had not forgotten her, because both of them turned to her in the next moment.

"So!" Lionel rubbed his hands together, as if he was getting ready to do some great work. "We've made a good start on some basic things, Katie, but you didn't ask any questions. Do you have any?"

"You already answered the only ones I had . . . about feeling as if I was full of Fire somehow, and feeding it off to the salamanders." She tilted her head to one side, inviting any further information, if they had any.

Lionel leaned back in his chair. "That, I did find something useful about. It seems that, now and again, Air magicians are able to do something similar—and Masters of all four Elements always can. It's something like this. You evidently have the ability to store that magic, rather like storing rainwater in a barrel. Jack merely lets the magic flow through him, rather than storing it, for instance. I do the same. You, however, hold onto a fair bit of it. There comes a point where you are full, and you either have to stop taking it in, or drain it off. Working with magic all day for the first time, you got filled up. You can hold it, but that requires getting used to holding it. I know it made you feel uneasy."

She nodded. "A bit. Like I'd et a bit too much. Like I was restless beneath my skin."

"Well, if you ever have to do something quite large, you'll need to store it for at least a while," Lionel replied, fanning himself. "But for now, you can either drain it off as you did, by offering it to your Elementals, or you might be able to make objects to store the magic in, called Talismans."

"I've heard of those. In stories my Ma told me," she said.

"They're often spoken of in fairy tales—and you will discover as we go along there is a great deal that is true in fairy tales." Lionel gave her a decisive nod. "Making Talismans is useful, since that allows you to keep extra magic about if you need it, but it's dangerous, because such things tend to attract people and things that want the magic for themselves. It's difficult to shield them, impossible to hide them if you can't shield them. Unless you are making some just before a great work, I find they are more trouble than they are worth."

"The Masters feel differently, of course," Jack interrupted. "But then the Masters can do a lot of things we can't, including making shields for things that are permanent and don't need work or thinking about."

Lionel went on. "Feeding your Elementals is useful, since it will cause them to think very highly of you, and will make them more inclined to help you when you need it, but some might consider it wasteful, as opposed to making Talismans, which will certainly be useful to you at some time or other."

She wrinkled her nose. "Not me. I'd rather have friends than things."

"Well said." Lionel looked very satisfied. "And on that happy note, shall we have our tea? I think Mrs. Buckthorn has just finished laying it out."

After tea, they practiced the shields and magic-gathering more—or rather, Katie practiced while Lionel and Jack watched. This time, now that she was aware of it, she could actually *feel* how she was drinking in the magic power she didn't use in making the shields. And when she started to feel tired again, with their encouragement, she called a couple more of her salamanders and fed them—and this time they were joined by a handful of shy little Fire sprites, and a glowing bird.

Once again, when she was done, she was ravenous. "Why am I so hungry?" she asked, as they went in to a lovely cold supper, complete with ice cream. This was a treat that Katie had seldom enjoyed—it was far too expensive for her parents to have gotten for her more than twice, both times being on her birthday, when they had all been at a Fair.

"You're hungry, because it takes *physical* energy to move *magic* power," Jack explained, as they helped themselves off the buffet; lovely cold asparagus, and several kinds of pickles, cress and cucumber sandwiches, cold ham, cheese, cold boiled eggs, sliced tomatoes. "That's why we tell new magicians that they should never do with magic what they can do with their hands. It might look a treat to snap your fingers and light a candle, but it pulls more strength out of you to do that than it would to walk down to the shops, buy some matches, walk back and light the candle with one of those. So, you've been working as hard as if you were dancing, and now you're hungry."

"Couldn't I—I don't know—use the magic? Eat it like food or something?" she wanted to know. "I'd rather eat *real* food, it's much nicer, but it would be good to know if I could."

They all sat down at the table. Mrs. Buckthorn had already eaten, since they had gone past their usual supper time, so it was just the three of them, as the shadows deepened outside, and the bit of sky you could see through the dining room window turned to a darker blue. Definitely sunset. "Supposedly, yes," Lionel said. "Supposedly, there are mystics who can do that. I've never known any, I've never *met* any, and I suspect they need at least a little real food to turn the trick. Most of them are supposed to be in India and China, and it could be like all of those stories out of India and China, all bosh."

"Fair enough," she said, and tucked into the repast.

Jack offered to accompany her back to the boarding house; the idea of him stumping painfully along beside her made her ache for him, but she forced a light laugh. "Oh, no need, and I *know* you two are buzzing inside with all the business you want to discuss without me being here. True?"

The sheepish looks on their faces told her that she had struck the mark fair.

"All right then, tomorrow is a working day, so I will let you get to that, and *I* will get myself some sleep so I am fit for double duty!" She saluted them with two fingers, as the saucy little chorus girls did in their "Only The Admiral's Daughter" number. "Don't stay up too late!" she said, and Mrs. Buckthorn let her out.

She went to bed happy, and dreamed again, dreamed of all those fiery creatures, but this time, they were clearly pleased with her. She walked through a space in which they all had gathered, an arrangement of rocks and gigantic crystals in pleasing shapes, although she couldn't tell from the darkness overhead if she was indoors or out—or if here there was any real difference between the two. The ground was a sort of soft sand without any rocks or sharp things in it. When she entered the space, it was as if she was entering something that was not as special as a party, but not as ordinary as a simple crowd, the sort you might encounter around a village inn.

This time, she was something of the center of attention. The ones that had been aloof smiled at her, or gave the impression of smiling. The ones that had been shy flitted around her. The ones that had been friendly flocked to her like the little birds Jack had described eating out of his hand.

It was the happiest dream she had ever had in her life. It was as if she was at a gathering full of good friends, all of whom were fond of her.

These were the Fire Elementals in their true forms; she understood that now. Waking, she could only see them imperfectly—sleeping, she was somehow able to slip over into *their* world and walk among them. They were pure, innocent in a way no mortal person she had ever met could be innocent, not even a child. Despite the fact that some of them were clearly far, far more powerful than she could even dream, her overwhelming impulse regarding them was to *protect* them.

It was in that moment of realization of how truly innocent these beings were that she knew, this time in her heart and without reservation, that Jack was right. That no matter how much she hated Dick—no matter how much she wanted to be rid of him—no matter how badly he hurt her—she could not bear to let that innocence be ruined by turning them into murderers on her behalf.

Even as she thought that, she felt something . . . enormous . . . looming up behind her back. She turned, quickly, and saw something like a huge, jeweled column reaching upward. Except it wasn't a column, and those weren't jewels. It was a neck and chest, supported by two legs that ended in clawed talons, each talon as long as her arm, talons as clear and glittering as crystal, and the jewels were actually scales covering the creature that sparkled and scintillated with power.

She gasped a little, and her gaze was drawn up and

up—and the creature bent its long, long neck and looked down at her, as flaming wings fanned out to either side of it.

Now she knew what it was. It was a dragon, a white dragon, though it reflected every color she could name and some she couldn't in its iridescent scales. It brought its head down until she was almost nose-to-nose with it, and the hot scent of its breath was in her nostrils. It breathed over her, and her hair floated away behind her from the gentle force of its breath, hot, and spicy.

"Show me your thoughts," the dragon breathed, whispering aloud.

She could no more have resisted that demand than she could have resisted a flood sweeping her away. She felt her mind fall open, and sensed the dragon poring over what it found there, turning over this and that bit, quite as if it was examining its own treasure-hoard. Strangely, she didn't mind; not when it turned over the thoughts she'd been having about Jack, not when it stirred the memories of Dick, not when it reached back and looked through her eyes as a child.

She couldn't have moved if it had set her on fire.

Finally its head rose a little, and it looked down at her through multi-faceted eyes, greater jewels within the bejeweled head.

"You are worthy," it said, then opened its mouth.

Rather than a gout of flames, the raging inferno she had half expected, what came from its mouth was a sort of gentle cloud of white fire, a cloud that settled over her, making her skin tingle, leaving her feeling a hundred times more alive than she ever had before.

"You are blessed with the breath of the dragon," the

creature whispered. *"Care for my children, and you will always be so blessed. Protect my children, and you will always be protected."*

The great wings came around and cupped over her, feeling like a benediction.

Then the white dragon spread its wings wide, and flung itself into the sky, or what passed for sky here, somehow managing to take off without disturbing a hair on her head.

And that was when she woke up.

She lay there for a long, long time as the morning sun shone in her window, trying to work out if that had just been an unusually vivid dream or if it had actually been something real—even though it clearly didn't take place in the real world that she knew.

A little bit of brightness caught her eye, and she turned her head to see a salamander standing on her pillow, staring at her.

Would it—?

Well, why not ask?

"Did I just dream all that?" she asked it.

Slowly, gravely, it shook its head from side to side.

"There really was a dragon?" she breathed, hardly able to believe it.

It nodded.

"And it—"

The salamander nodded vigorously, then rubbed its cheek against hers and turned three times and vanished.

She slowly sat up, and touched her cheek where the salamander had caressed her like a tiny cat.

"Well," she said aloud. "I never."

12

"**W**ELL ..." said Jack, as soon as Katie had left. "I told her Peggy had let the cat out of the bag, and she didn't hit me with your mother's precious toby jug."

"And a good thing too, or my sainted mother would probably haunt you for the rest of your days." Lionel's eyes rested for a moment on the "precious toby jug," a piece of unremarkable china-work that stood about four inches high, shaped like the late Prince Albert, husband of Queen Victoria. The handle was a banner proclaiming the Great Exhibition of London in 1851. It had been his mother's pride, for she had gotten it as a treasured bridal souvenir from her new husband on the occasion of her honeymoon in London to view that same Great Exhibition. For some reason, his mother had been as sentimental about Prince Albert as the Queen herself had been. Hanging on the wall all of his life, there had been a portrait of Albert with a printed black wreath around it, and a black ribbon on top of the frame. The toby jug had been the centerpiece of the china cabinet. As a child, the damned thing had frightened Lionel with its blank, staring eyes that always seemed to be looking at you no matter where you were, and it had haunted his dreams. He was just grateful it had always been kept in the china cabinet and that it wasn't any larger than it was.

For some reason, Mrs. Buckthorn had taken an irrational liking to it, and had placed it in pride-of-place in the drawing room. *I should just give it to her for Christmas,* Lionel decided in a fit of inspiration. *Yes, that's exactly what I'll do. Mother would like that, she only left it to me because I didn't have children to break it.* Mrs. Buckthorn would cherish the wretched thing and pass it on to someone *else* who would cherish it. Possibly one of the small herd of married daughters she had.

"Are you actually listening to me, or has that jug got you mesmerized again?" Jack asked.

Lionel shook himself out of the woolgathering he was doing about the toby jug and turned his attention back to Jack. "Katie actually took what I had to say to her very well," Jack said. "I think perhaps we've been underestimating her. She's got better control of her feelings than I did at that age."

"She's had to," Lionel felt compelled to point out. "Brutes like that beast of a husband take any sort of display of emotion the way a bull reacts to a red rag. It's a sign to attack."

Jack nodded, and Lionel wondered if he should take that as an opening to ask about—well—the hand-holding. It might have been perfectly innocent. It might have been fatherly, or meant to comfort. He doubted it, but it might have been.

But, as usual, Jack shot right past Lionel's hesitation and went straight to the mark. He sighed, and his whole expression softened, and he smiled. "Once we got past her husband, I asked her. She's going to have me, Lionel. Once she's free, she's going to have me."

Lionel would have asked a regular fellow if this wasn't more than a bit sudden—but he knew, as every Elemental Magician knew, that when two magicians were right for each other, there was no such thing as "more than a bit sudden." People who weren't magicians could pother and hesitate, and beat around as many bushes as they liked—and decide, in the end, to break it off. Magicians *knew.* Maybe not right from the moment that they met, but the more time together they spent, the more they were drawn together until it became a literal force of nature that it took a great deal to break. He'd heard of magicians who'd met for the first time on a weekend, and by midweek were in Gretna Green getting married, having no patience for the few weeks it would take to post banns and get a license as most people did.

"Well, that's a relief," he said, lightly. "When you two get married, I won't lose the best assistant I've ever had."

Jack barked a startled laugh. "You selfish git!" he replied, mostly in jest, though with a hint of irritation. "Is that all you can say? Here I've gone for *years,* thinking no woman would ever want to be saddled with a cripple, then I find the dearest, sweetest girl in the world, *and* she's a Fire Magician, *and* she wants me, and all you can think about is that you won't lose your assistant?"

"It's not me she's marrying," Lionel pointed out, and

laughed. "Oh, congratulations, old man. Where would you like to go for a honeymoon? A nice volcano, like Vesuvius? That should suit a couple of Fire Magicians."

"I'll hold you to that," Jack growled. "First we've got to get her free. Of course, since she's said she'll have me ..." A shrewd expression crept over his face. "She can't object to my helping her with that divorce of hers. I've got a nice packet put away for a rainy day. I shan't mind spending it to make a sunny one come faster."

"I'm just a trifle concerned that she's living in that boarding house, though, Jack," Lionel said, interrupting whatever thoughts he was having. "She's very new to the power and she's coming on it very fast. If there should be an accident—all those girls—"

Jack's expression became serious immediately. "Good Gad, I never thought of that. You're right, of course. Things popped up around me all the time when I came into my power, but of course, my father was there to keep them under control, and my mother couldn't have seen them if they'd danced in front of her nose. But who knows which of those girls there has just enough of the magic to be able to get a glimpse of such things? Particularly if they're feeling curious."

"I'm not so concerned with things that people *can't* see, but there are some that people *can*," Lionel replied, and poured them both a brandy. "Fire sprites, for instance, who are having no qualms about turning up on stage with her! What if one decides to go exploring other rooms?"

"Well, how do we get her to move out?" Jack came straight to that point, and it was a good one. "She's comfortable, she's happy, and she's well-cared for. More to the point, the lodging is cheap, and she is trying to save every penny."

"We make up the difference, and don't tell her." Lionel had already made up his mind at this point. "We just tell her about accidents, let her own imagination work for a bit, then tell her we found a little furnished house for her at the same rate Mrs. Baird charges. The drawback will be she'll have to cook and do for herself. The advantage will be she won't have to be back by a certain hour in order to eat or face possibly being locked out. And her Elementals will be able to prowl without sending a house full of girls out into the street, thinking the place is about to burn down."

"How will we—" Jack began.

Lionel just waved at him. "I'll deal with that part. My banker found this house, he can find me another. Besides, once we convince *her,* it'll be three magicians with the same goal again. Remember what happened the last time."

Jack sucked on his lower lip. "A bit frightening how fast it happened, actually," he pointed out.

"All the better in this case. Now," Lionel said firmly. "I thought there was a certain weakness in the way she was handling her shields, but I'm not the Fire Mage . . ."

When Katie came down to breakfast, she found the table full of girls jabbering away at a much higher volume than usual. One of the girls was full of stories about "a dreadful little thing with eyes like fire!" that had looked at her out of the fireplace. Half of the others wanted to hear all about it, the other half were making fun of her. Finally Mrs. Baird herself put a stop to all the jabber.

"There has never been a haunt in my house," she said, firmly. "And there never will be while I'm in it! You, Miss Jenny—you were eating nothing but jam sandwiches last night at supper, and I saw you!"

Shamefaced, but a little bewildered, Jenny confessed that was exactly what she had been doing.

"Well then," Mrs. Baird said, sternly. "It's no wonder you was seeing things and having bad dreams, stuffing yourself with sweet things before bed! You'll be leaving off the jam at night, if that's what's going to happen to you."

Hastily, Jenny promised that she wouldn't stuff herself with jam before going to bed, and Mrs. Baird subsided. But—a thing in the fireplace with fiery eyes? Katie was altogether too certain of what that was, and it rather alarmed her. Why would one of her salamanders or sprites go wandering out of her room—and how was it that Jenny had been able to see it?

She finished her breakfast quickly, then went early to the hall, and caught Jack just as he was unlocking for the day, before anyone else was around.

"One of the girls saw one of my Elementals last night," she said urgently, before he'd even had a chance to greet her. "How could that happen? And why? And—"

"Slowly, Kate," he cautioned her, nodding toward one of the stagehands coming toward them from the alley. "This might be a better topic for later."

She hated to put it off, but he was right, and she knew it. So she retreated to her dressing room and comforted herself with the certainty that if Jack hadn't gotten alarmed, he certainly knew what was going on, and he certainly knew what she should do about it.

The rehearsals went smoothly, although now that the

dance act had been established, Charlie predictably wanted to muck about with it to make it more "peppy," and fussed about looking at the dances from every angle in the hall. Finally though, everyone broke for luncheon, and Lionel told Charlie that "If you don't stop flapping about like a meddling old crow, I am going to turn you into one."

Fortunately, at that point, Mrs. Charlie, who had turned up to run *her* eyes over the new act (and, Katie suspected, make sure Charlie didn't have an unprofessional interest in the dancer in question) decreed that if Charlie didn't take her out for luncheon that minute, she was going to go shopping.

That was threat enough to make Charlie cut the session short, and finally Lionel, Jack, and Katie were able to descend to the workroom and what privacy there was in the hall.

They both listened to what she had to tell them without interruption. Lionel cleared his throat when she was done.

"Well, the obvious reason this girl saw your Elemental was because she *could*," he told her. "Some people have just a touch of magic, enough, when they're in the right frame of mind, to be able to see any Elementals that were about. She might have been reading some penny-dreadful or a sensational novel full of ghosts and devils. She might have been half awake, and thus susceptible. She might be accustomed to having a drop or more of gin in secret before bed. It might even have been the fault of those jam sandwiches." He shrugged. "The main point here is not just that she saw your Elemental, it's that your Elementals clearly regard the whole of the boarding house as safe territory to roam in, and not just your room. That means this might be the first time one has been spotted, but it won't be the last."

Katie bit her lip; this wasn't what she had wanted to hear. "But can't I just explain to them—" she began.

Jack shook his head. "I told you, they don't think as we do. They understand walls as boundaries, but not rooms within walls. Fire Elementals aren't as flitty and forgetful as Air are, but they probably won't remember what you tell them other than 'don't go past the wall.' This is going to be a problem, Kate. It's rather too likely that at some point someone will see one, or a group, and decide the house has caught fire. And you know what *that* will do."

Oh, she certainly did. She felt the blood draining from her face. A house full of young women fleeing in hysteria from a supposed fire? It would draw attention. The one thing she didn't want to do was to draw attention. Any attention. There might be a photographer. Her picture might be taken. If it went in the paper, someone she knew might see it.

Or someone who knew her might see her in the street in the hubbub. And then Dick would inevitably find her.

And even if that didn't happen, Mrs. Baird would start looking for an explanation.

And what if in the panic, someone tipped over a lamp or something and started a *real* fire?

Before she could ask what she could do, Jack was already speaking. "We actually talked about this last night, Lionel and I," he said. "What we'd like is for you to move out and into a little house of your own. Lionel is sure his bank man can find something cheap enough for you—

and at that point, a lot of difficulties become easier. You won't have to worry about anyone spotting your Elementals for a start."

"You also won't have to worry about coming home too late and finding yourself locked out," said Lionel. "Come the fall and winter, if our acts are good enough, we sometimes find ourselves hired out for parties after the second show. Those parties can be late—gents that don't work don't have to worry about getting up in time to be at the shop or office. They pay well, these parties, I can tell you that. The extra pay will let you build up your fund faster."

Well there was no use in pretending that the idea of extra money wasn't strongly appealing to her. . . .

"You also won't have to worry about coming in too late for supper, or oversleeping breakfast," Jack pointed out. "You can do what you want when you want it. You can practice your magic all you like without being interrupted—and practice your dancing if you need to."

It was dreadfully tempting . . . the idea of being able to have a bath no matter how late she came in . . . or make a sandwich and tea and eat it in bed . . .

"But the shopping—" she protested feebly. "When will I ever have time to shop?"

"Just tell me what you want and I'll have Mrs. Buckthorn get it when she does my shopping," said Lionel, instantly. "She shops in the morning before I'm awake to get all the freshest things. I'll bring it along to the hall, and you can take it home that night. Milk, cream, butter and eggs will come to your doorstop with the milkman in the morning."

Well, that settled it, then. She'd seen the milkman turn

up at Mrs. Baird's door every morning, and had marveled how easy it made things once Mrs. Baird had explained it to her. "Wouldn't I need . . . beds and things?" she said, hesitantly. You didn't need that sort of thing in a caravan. Beds and cupboards and everything else were part of it.

"My rooms are let furnished," Jack said with a smile. "Not to worry, that sort of thing is usual, especially in places like Brighton, where there are a lot of holiday visitors. Given the chance to rent a little house for an entire year at a time instead of a week or two at a time during the season and scramble for a renter the rest of the year, a man would be mad not to take it."

Well, they were in a better position to know these things than she was. And the more she thought about it, the more attractive it sounded. No more girls over her head dropping shoes and waking her up. No more lying there listening to two girls talking loudly in the room next door when she was trying to concentrate on the magic. Being able to take her meals when she wanted to—never being too late to get an egg—cool baths when she wanted them—

"If you can find something that's no dearer than what I'm paying now . . ." That was the sticking point of course. She had no idea what a whole house, however small, would cost.

"There are plenty of little cottages that are no more than a room, a bathroom, and a little kitchen," Lionel assured her. "You're probably used to a kitchen even smaller in a caravan."

"There's nothing I can't do with a fireplace and a spirit-kettle, perhaps a spirit-stove," she declared.

"Well then, that's settled. Now...show us those shields, while we still have time for a lesson," Lionel ordered. And she did.

For several days, Lionel's banker sent daily messages telling him that small cottages were not to be had at any price. But then, within the course of a day, everything changed.

And it was the railroad strike that changed them.

Railroad workers, like the dockworkers, had been threatening to strike for many weeks over their wretched pay and hazardous working conditions. Only King Edward's coronation had prevented them from striking earlier this year. But now—despite promises of talks, nothing had changed, and the men were getting desperate. Some had even died, working in the terrible heat without respite, or sometimes, even without drinking water.

They struck, at the height of summer holiday season, knowing that striking now would affect the broadest range of people, including the wealthy, most of whom had given up carriages in favor of first class rail. No escaping from the city on the weekend to cooler country estates. No taking the family away for the more elevated version of the common man's seaside holiday.

This was dreadful for everyone who made his living catering to holiday-makers, but worst on the holiday-makers themselves, many of whom found themselves stranded far from home with no way to get back, or found themselves with no way to get to their destinations.

But it was excellent for Lionel and Katie. Because the morning of the strike—which, providentially, occurred on a dark day—the banker sent an urgent note around to Lionel. *Have prospect, but must leap upon it now,* said the note, and gave him the address of a leasing agent.

Lionel went straight there as soon as he finished breakfast.

It was another brilliantly sunny day, portending more un-English heat, when he walked into the little office staffed only by the agent and a clerk. The leasing agent was just short of tearing his hair out, and so upset was he that he vented his feelings to Lionel, a complete stranger, as soon as Lionel entered the door. "This *strike!*" he cried, flinging his hands wide and scattering papers which his little clerk scrambled to pick up. "It's ruinous! I have cottages with people who won't leave and won't pay any more! I'm having to hire carters to go around to toss 'em out because the constables won't do it! I have people camping in cottage gardens and having to send lads around to throw *them* out! I have cottages going empty because the people that hired 'em can't get here!"

"It's the latter I am interested in, my good man," har-rumphed Lionel, who had donned a long-abandoned persona of "Professor Pennywhistle" to aid him in his ruse. "Need a cottage. Long-term lease. The wife needs sea air. I'm a busy man. Brought her down from Crawley in me trap. Can't abide these filthy railroads. Tried a hotel, *ruinously* expensive. Need a cottage for a year at least. Maybe more, dependin' on how long it takes her to get over her collywobbles."

The moment that Lionel said "Need a cottage for a year at least," the agent stopped his laments and paid instant and complete attention. "I have just the thing!" he said, but before he could proceed to lay out a selection, Lionel interrupted him.

"Don't think I'm made of money! She don't need a palace!" he barked, and named a price.

The agent wilted a little, but came back gamely. They jousted for a bit, before they settled on a price. "It won't be on the seaside—" the agent warned.

"Brighton's on the seaside. Sea air on one side of it is sea air on the other side of it," Lionel said indifferently.

"Well then. Harry—come take the gentleman to see Hare Cottage, Violet Cottage, Li—"

"Which one of 'em has plumbed-on water and a full bathroom?" Lionel interrupted. "And gas. Or electricity. She's not to be hauling coal or wood about, says the doctor." Then he muttered, just loud enough for the agent to hear, "Lot of demmed nonsense if you ask me."

Now, Lionel was very, very good at reading people; he'd had a mentalist act as well as the magic act before he settled into magic-aided-by-Elementals. He'd been gauging this man from his own remarks and attitude as he went along, and very early it had been clear that the agent had a wife that he considered himself to be "saddled" with. He wouldn't dare rid himself of her—divorces were a matter of scandal and respectable people didn't get them. But he resented her, and even though Lionel's attitude was avuncular to say the least, by this point he was entirely on Lionel's side.

"Only Lily Cottage," he said. "It's the best-appointed but it's . . . well, it's out of the way. No amusements nearby, and a walk to the 'bus. It's in a very quiet neighborhood; no shops, mostly professional offices. . . ."

"Perfect!" Lionel exclaimed. "Doctor says 'quiet,' 'quiet' is what she'll get. She wants amusement, she can read her magazines and do her fancywork. She wants anythin' else, well, she can get strong enough to walk to it, eh?"

"You'll have to find a girl, or a char," the agent said, tentatively. "I can suggest several agencies."

Lionel took the cards the agent offered, but of course, he had no intention of hiring anyone. "Done," he said, and opened his wallet to hand over the first six months in rent. He winced a little at the hole this put in his own savings, but reminded himself that if *he* hadn't bought his little house, he'd have been paying that much for some time. Besides, it was for Katie. He signed the lease as "Richard Langford," just to make things easier on Katie so she wouldn't have to remember a false name, and took away the address card and the keys; tonight they could all take the trap over to it and have a look around, then he could have Mrs. Buckthorn put everything to rights.

The agent seemed only too relieved to get the property settled on *someone* in this day of otherwise disaster.

Katie sat squeezed in between Lionel and Jack on the seat of the pony-trap, feeling nervous and excited at the same time. She'd given her week's notice to Mrs. Baird with the excuse that she was taking her act to Blackpool, who had said, kindly, "I'm sorry to see you go, but Blackpool may do better than Brighton if this strike goes on." So that was done. And she was half afraid of what she might find when they opened the door of this "cottage."

Black beetles and wood rot? Earthen floors and a hip bath?

But Lionel had said it was surrounded by professional offices, and lawyers and doctors and so on liked their comforts . . .

Well, one thing was certain. The agent had not lied about it being quiet. Most of the buildings here were newish or newly renovated, with gaslights all up and down the street. They were mostly three stories tall, with shining brass plaques at the highly polished front doors saying whose offices were within.

And then, finally, they found it. A little one-story cottage squeezed in at the *back* of the row of buildings, just as Lionel's own house was squeezed in and overshadowed by others. Clearly it had once been the carriage house for the larger building, which had been turned into offices, but no one wanted an office that would be so dark and gloomy that you would have to burn expensive gas to see even in the middle of the day. From the outside it looked very neat and trim. They tied up the pony at an iron ring that was an indicator of what the cottage had once been, and Lionel opened the door.

It was, of course, dark inside. But they had, of course, come prepared. Jack handed down a lantern from the back of the trap after lighting it, and Lionel led the way inside.

"He said the gas was still on . . . ah, here we go." Lionel moved forward, confidently lighting lamps as he went, while Katie trailed behind.

You could easily see the antecedents of this place, although it *had* been finished up rather nicely. It was all one floor with a loft above where the hay and feed had once been stored; presumably if a family took it, the children would sleep above, in the loft, while the parents slept below. To Katie's relief, the floors were wood, not dirt, nor polished cobblestones. It was all one room; a bed was behind a screen for privacy, there was a bit of a kitchen with a modern gas stove fitted into a hearth, a small sink for washing-up, and behind a partition, a cabinet-bath and a boiler. Well, she wouldn't need that for a while. There was also an indoor, water-flushing loo, like Mrs. Baird had.

For the rest, well, it was obvious that the cottage was not as well cared for as the rooms at Mrs. Baird's. The level of general cleanliness was nothing like as high as Katie's Ma had maintained in the caravan. But it was just as obvious that this would be a very nice, if dark, place to live.

"No one is going to pay any attention to comings and goings here," Jack observed from his spot by the door. "No neighbors to poke into your business. No one asking why there was a man here, when there was only supposed to be a lady. No one asking why the lady was coming back so late at night, if she really *was* a lady."

"Place is filthy," said Lionel, with the air of distaste of someone who is used to immaculate surroundings. "Mrs. Buckthorn will sort it out, though. I'm sure I have some old china and linens of my mothers stored away somewhere; you can have that. Otherwise does this suit you, Kate?"

Over all, the cottage had about four times the space of her room at Mrs. Baird's—and a great deal more convenience. Interestingly, when it came to comfort and luxury—the family caravan had more than this cottage did, but it had all been squeezed into a very small space. And Mrs. Baird's rooms were nicer. But the advantages far overwhelmed the disadvantages. "It's going to be lovely," she said, with genuine warmth. "Absolutely lovely."

Then she grinned. "Especially without the caterwauling of that Irish soprano beside me, and the chorus girl practicing her kicks above me!"

Lionel grinned back. "All right then. Mrs. Buckthorn will have you set up within the week; she'll find out when the milkman comes round and what he has and charges, get this place cleaned up and decent, and stock the pantry. In a week, it will be yours, and we'll move your bits over in the trap."

"A place to practice . . ." she sighed. "That'll be worth it, alone."

As of to underscore that, one of the gaslights suddenly brightened, and a salamander poked his head up over the glass shade.

"It seems your friends approve," Lionel chuckled. "All right. Let's get you back to Mrs. Baird's. Before you know it, the week will be over."

Lionel's words were prophetic, although it was slightly less than that, as the move was scheduled for the evening of dark day. All of her things fit into a couple of second-hand trunks Mrs. Buckthorn had found, which neatly fitted into the back of the trap. It was just Mrs. Buckthorn and Katie this time; the men were coming later after the housekeeper brought the trap and pony back.

It was quiet once again, although it was at least two

hours to sunset, as they tied the pony up at the ring and the two of them pulled the trunks out of the cart and brought them inside. Mrs. Buckthorn showed her how to put a penny in a slot to make the gas flow, and then, once the lamps were lit, waited for Katie's reaction.

Katie could hardly believe the change in this place. The floor and walls must have been scoured, because they were at least two shades lighter than she remembered, and the colors of the striped wallpaper, though faded, were no longer shades of dull blue-gray. There were a couple of homely braided rugs on the floor, and little bits of lace and fabric hiding the battered surfaces of the tables and the worn upholstery of the chairs. The gas stove gleamed. There were proper pans and dishes in the cupboard, and cans and jars and paper packets of food stocked in the pantry. She peeped around the screen, to see that the bed, which had not looked particularly inviting, had been made up with pillows that had not been there before, and a pretty, faded counterpane.

"Mrs. Buckthorn!" she exclaimed. "This is *lovely!*"

"Well, it was a mort'o work, but worth it, dearie," the older woman said complacently. "You just see that you keep it clean."

"I will!" she promised, then listened carefully as Mrs. Buckthorn described the ways and arrival of the milkman, what she was to pay him and how, and how to find the one, lone little shop that supplied some of the basic needs of the men in the offices all around her.

"There's naught much choice, but if you forget something, at least you won't be without your tea for your egg-and-tea," she said, and went on to show Katie where everything was—and in the case of the boiler for the bath, how to use it. For water for washing up, there was a teakettle; the sink would scarcely hold more than a pan, a dish, and a teacup, after all.

"I'll leave you to settle in," the housekeeper said, the look on her face showing that she was satisfied with Katie's gratitude. She let herself out, and Katie set about putting her own few bits in place.

A fancy embroidered Chinese shawl went over one of the chairs to brighten it up. A wooden stool was softened with a cushion. She got out her gown for tomorrow and hung it up to hang out any wrinkles, and put her nightdress on the bed. Then she went about the room, placing some of the little things that she had somehow acquired since she had arrived in Brighton. Lionel had given her a little china Turk with a sword as big as he was, and a pretty glass lamp that burned scented oil. Suzie had given her lace panels she draped over the curtain-rod and the privacy screen, and one of the fancy "boudoir-dolls" that you threw coconuts to win down on the Boardwalk. Jack had given her a stone incense burner and a little iron pot she could keep a coal in for a salamander to curl up around—and just today, several prints to hang on the wall, of fanciful creatures and ladies in long, strange dresses, and a set of embroidered silk scrolls from Japan and China of dragons and phoenixes.

For all that this was a little house, it was not as comfortable as Mrs. Baird's boarding house. And if it had been safe to stay there, she never would have left. There were only four windows in the entire cottage, two at the front, and two at the back, at either side of the front and back doors. She already knew how overshadowed the place was.

But it was nice.

There was one place she hadn't explored yet, and now that she had light and had found the candles, she lit one and pulled a rag rug away from the middle of the floor. There was a hatch there, with a recessed iron ring in it, and she pulled that up.

Why a former carriage house would have a cellar, she didn't know. Maybe it had been dug when the carriage house had been converted to a cottage. She probably wouldn't have known it was there if it hadn't been for Mrs. Buckthorn, nor would she have had an inkling of what to do with a cellar. But Mrs. Buckthorn said that, in lieu of an ice-chest, a nice cool cellar was the best place to keep milk, cream, cheese, butter, and other things that tended to spoil. So down the set of stairs Katie went, to see what a cellar looked like.

Although it was much cooler than the house, she felt immediately claustrophobic, as most Travelers were when confined within four walls. It had walls and a floor made of reused brick, and the only thing down here was a sort of larder-cupboard painted cream and yellow, with doors that looked as if they sealed when you latched them down. She went to it and opened one side. There was a jug of milk there, and a smaller jug of cream, both covered with muslin tied down around the tops tightly. There was a pat of butter in a covered glass butter dish. And there were four fresh eggs in a bowl.

On the other side, there was a bowl with bunches of grapes in it, another with four fresh plums and four apricots, a third with four fresh tomatoes, a water glass with a bouquet of cress, and another covered glass dish with wedges of cheese.

She clearly wouldn't have to ask Mrs. Buckthorn to shop for her for at least four days.

As she went up the stairs and shut the trap door, she was already planning breakfast. She had just dropped it in place when she heard a tap at the door.

As she had expected, it was Jack and Lionel, with a basket. She blew out the candle and set it on a little table that was there, and let them in.

"This is vastly improved," said Lionel, handing her the basket. "I told you Mrs. Buckthorn would work wonders."

"You were right." The basket clinked and was quite heavy; peeking in, she found beer and lemonade bottles. "I think you are pulling a deception on me, however," she continued sternly. "I think the rent for this cottage is *much* higher than my room and board at Mrs. Baird's. I'm not that ignorant that you can gull me."

"I think you should open bottles for all three of us, and we'll explain," said Lionel, not looking the least repentant for his deception.

Since she obviously was not going to get any satisfaction from him until she did, she took the basket to the sideboard, got three bottles open, and brought them all to where the two men had settled into the two chairs, leaving her the lounge. She handed each of them a beer and settled in with her lemonade. She had opened the windows, front and back, and a warm breeze wafted in through the gauze curtains. Unlike Mrs. Baird's, it was so quiet you might have been on a village street in the countryside.

"We were not exaggerating when we said that having your Elementals running about the boarding house could be very dangerous," Lionel said, leaning back in the chair after rearranging the cushions a little. "There are people who have just enough magic that they can see Elementals under certain conditions—as you discovered. The problem is that the Elementals are used to thinking they are invisible unless they choose to be seen. A startled sylph—not such a problem. A startled brownie—simply runs and hides in a mousehole. A startled undine or other Water nymph just vanishes. But a startled Fire Elemental . . . sometimes starts fires."

Her eyes widened, and she forgot to drink for a moment. "Oh . . ."

"Clearly leaving you there was not a good idea. We know you are saving for your divorce . . ." he shrugged, and took a long drink from his beer. "I can afford this. I'll withhold what you were paying Mrs. Baird from your pay packet from my act, if you wish. And believe me, although I would not take it for myself, should supplying this house to you prove to be too great a strain on my budget, there are very, very rich Elemental Masters in London that I shall not hesitate to contact."

He looked down at his beer bottle and laughed a little. "Mind you, these are men who would look at me in horror if they saw me *drinking from the bottle* instead of a proper lager glass. But I will say this much for them; they're prepared to support mages who are less well off than they are, even if they would rather not socialize with us."

Jack snorted. "That's what we were talking about the other day. Nobs. Titles and money or just money alone. They'll spend that money on us because if they didn't, we might not be around to back them up when they need it."

"Oh ..." Now she understood. Well, not the *Tommy go away* reference, but in general what they were getting at. "But ... don't they get resentful, like? And don't they get taken advantage of, or think they might be?"

"Magicians are an odd and independent lot," Lionel told her. "I don't know what it is about us, but we don't like to be beholden. Maybe it's because the Elementals often don't like owing favors, and some of that rubs off on us. Personally, I know I don't like feeling *paid for,* if you get my meaning. But in this case, it would be worth it to minimize the danger to you and those around you. They are well used to providing in cases like this, and they can not only afford it, they probably spend more on picnic hampers from Fortnum and Mason than we would spend on this cottage."

She nodded, satisfied. She wouldn't deprive Lionel for the world—but her people were well used to helping themselves at the expense of those who could afford it. Despite their reputation, most Travelers didn't steal, but they took pleasure in taking advantage of gorgers—what they called the settled folk—who scorned them, when the occasion was given.

She'd never had the occasion to be around anyone who was wealthy, much less with a title. From the sound of things, she probably wouldn't want to.

"Oh, they're not bad," Jack admitted. "Some of them are all-right chaps. They're just used to thinking of anyone that ain't *them* as being someone that don't exactly count for much."

"Feh, enough;" Lionel waved the subject away. "Did Mrs. Buckthorn tell you how to get to the hall from here?"

Mrs. Buckthorn had given her very exact directions, but they were ridiculously easy. "It'll take me a bit longer, but we aren't exactly early risers, are we?" she chuckled. "And I'll make that up at night, not having to queue for a bath, not having to go up and down all them stairs. And not layin' there, listening to the girls going up and down and chattering in their rooms to each other!" She shook her head. "What on *earth* do they have to talk about at all hours of the night?"

"Same things they chatter on about at the hall," said Jack. "What they had for tea and how cheap or dear it was, men, whatever new and objectionable thing they're being asked to do, because even if all it is, is to add a time-step to a routine, it'll be new and objectionable. Who might be keeping time with whom. Who has a fancy admirer and whether or not the gel in question is likely to share in the bounty. What outrageous new act just got introduced . . . you've listened, you know."

She did know, and aside from the fancy admirers—there were no such thing in the circus—it wasn't all that different from the gossip at the circus, or, indeed, at the Fairs that travelers met up at. The Fairs had been a tricky business; before Mary Small, she'd been shunned by the Traveler folks, just as the Traveler folks were shunned by people in houses. Her mother had done the unthinkable twice over; by running away with and marrying a gorger man, even if he was practicing the same sort of life as a Traveler, and by doing so against the will of her father. She'd lost her good name in the Traveler community, and no one wanted to know her. But Katie'd always been able to be unobtrusive and overlooked, and of course she was wildly curious about these people who pretended not to know her mother and father, so she'd done a lot of eavesdropping.

At least she had until it got boring. Once she'd realized how repetitious the gossip was, it had gotten boring quickly.

"I've just never been able to understand how any of that is so important it needs to be brought up again and again like a cow chewing her cud," she said. Both men shook their heads.

"We are mere males," Lionel intoned. "Don't ask us." And at that she had to laugh.

It was so pleasant, just sitting here, in her own place, no worry of interruption or fear that someone might overhear something they shouldn't. The warm breeze carried no foul scents on it as it might in other parts of the city—here the renovations to this cottage and the buildings around it had added all the plumbing into the city sewer system. Suzie had carefully explained the city sewer system, and the flushing loo, and what you could and could not put down there, when she'd first come to the boarding house, and when Katie had been in the cellar she'd seen the great brown pipes that carried away the water—and other things—going down the side of one of the cellar walls. That was a decent, cleanly system. Travelers were fastidiously clean, though they were called "dirty gypsies" by house-folk. They had to be; they'd be sick constantly if they didn't scrub and clean everything in their caravans until it was shining, and keep waste far away. The idea of a chamber pot made her a little ill. Keeping that nasty business *under your bed* until morning when—and she had seen this!—if you were slovenly you might just empty it out a window!

That there literally was no one around at this hour to note that she was entertaining two men without a chaperone—unless you counted one of them as a chaperone—was a not inconsiderable advantage as well. She didn't want to get a reputation . . . or someone might turn up at the door looking for something she was *not* going to give him.

But someone would likely notice when she left for the day . . . and she wasn't exactly going to be dressed in the mode of a respectable businessman's wife. Nor was she going to look like the invalid she was supposed to be. That could be a problem . . .

"Did you say you were going to hire 'your wife' some help, Lionel?" she asked, an idea forming in her mind.

"I didn't exactly say as much, but I did carry away some cards, why?" Lionel replied, looking at her with his head tilted a little.

"I'm not exactly an invalid," she pointed out. "And my gowns aren't—" She shrugged. "I don't look like I'm married, nor to a prosperous man. But I reckon I could pass for a servant-girl."

"But you'd be out all day—" Lionel pointed out. "That's a bit dodgy."

"Ah, not necessarily." Jack put his empty bottle aside and leaned forward a bit to explain. "You'd stay with the lady at night in case she needed anything or took poorly, get her up in the morning, go out to another bit of work by day, then come back to make her supper and put her to bed." He smiled as Katie nodded, liking this explanation very much. "That's if anyone asks. I doubt anyone will."

"Best to forestall it. I'll drop a word or two in the

shop." That would certainly work. "Reckon I've learned a bit of misdirection myself!"

"I would say you had," Lionel applauded.

They passed another hour or two talking about magic—or rather, Lionel and Jack talked; Katie just listened until she got the opening to mention her dreams.

"Well," Jack said, when she had finished. "That's right interesting, that is."

"Is it a real place? I mean, real like magic is real?" she asked.

"I haven't had a dream like that since I was a boy, but yes, it's real enough." To hear Jack confirm her guess made her feel quite good inside. "You've been properly accepted, Katie."

He didn't say anything out loud, but she guessed it from his expression; he knew that she had been "properly accepted" because she had resolved never to exploit the Elementals—and never to allow them to do something that would harm them, however much they wanted to do it for her.

"And the dragon?" she asked.

He shook his head. "Not an Elemental I ever saw myself, but I've heard about dragons, right enough. Them and the phoenixes are supposed to be the nobs of the Fire Elementals. They don't often have much to do with us mages, mostly the Masters, but one could have taken a liking to you. Don't count on it coming if you call, though. And never ask it to do anything for you if it does ever turn up. That'd be like asking Lord Uppercrust to make you a cuppa."

She had to laugh at the image that called up.

"Oh, it's a funny thought, but remember, you're literally

playing with Fire," he cautioned. "Not somethin' you want to offend."

"Then I won't," she promised. It wasn't a difficult promise to make, nor would it be a hard one to keep. She'd known all her life how to be deferential and quiet and appear to be meek.

Not that any of those things had helped her with Dick.

She suppressed a shiver of fear at the thought of him.

Finally it came about time for supper. She stood up. "I'm going to fix a bite, would you care to stay?" she asked. But Lionel shook his head and so did Jack.

"We'll leave you to the last of your settling-in," Lionel said. "And see you at the hall in the morning."

She saw them out, locked the door behind them, made sure that the heavier curtains were shut *quite* tightly, and went down into the cellar for the butter, grapes, a little cheese and an egg and put the kettle on and the egg in it. Then she drew herself a lovely cold bath, and by the time she was done, the water was boiling merrily.

She went to bed after supper, thinking she would never get to sleep quickly. She just noticed the clock in a church somewhere nearby striking ten, and then the next thing she knew it was morning.

It was the arrival of the first of the staff for the offices, combined with the church bell, that woke her; she was in time to count the bells, and discovered she had woken at around seven. Perfect!

This was going to work out beautifully.

13

KATIE had been in the little cottage for three weeks now, and everything had been working out so well it seemed as magical as any of the things she was learning from Jack. Lionel had taken a back seat to Jack in the lessons for the most part, leaving it to the Fire Magician to coax Katie through what he had learned at a much younger age.

It was very hard work. It took a lot of concentration, a different sort of concentration than the dancing and acrobatics took. She had to get her mind trained in an entirely new way of thinking, and it wasn't something that came naturally to her. It wasn't the discipline; she could deal with discipline. It was working out how to balance power and control, because if you had a lot of the latter, the former was a mere little squib, and if you had a lot of the former, the latter became even more difficult, like handling a half-wild horse.

By now, she could ask for salamanders to come and get them reliably, which was a great help in the magic act. She could do the same with Fire sprites. Others, well . . . they came and went as they chose, and that was that. Whether they were smarter than the salamanders, she couldn't tell—a baby hare was smarter than a Fire sprite, it seemed, and they were just happy to dance with her if she fed them afterward.

She felt completely at home in the little cottage now. She had her shopping routine established with Mrs. Buckthorn. She'd dropped her hints at the tiny grocer around the corner—she was completely accepted as the servant who tended the invalid "Mrs. Langford." Being able to sit in a cool tub as long as she liked at night was heaven, and more than made up for the fact that she had to cook and clean for herself. It was even safe to leave the windows open; there was a stout iron grating over the outside of them. She took the 'bus to the hall, but a cab back, at Jack's insistence—he had a friend who operated a cab, who charged her the same as the 'bus would, in exchange for Jack putting him in the way of fares he otherwise wouldn't get.

Even the strike, which had terrified everyone that made their livings off of the holiday-makers, had ended quickly.

Tomorrow was a dark day, and as usual, she was planning to go to Lionel's for food and magic lessons. She thought she was finally making some real progress on her control of those "shields," which was erratic. It was that which was on her mind when she unlocked the door and relocked it behind her—

" 'Ello wifie."

The voice came out of the dark, and she froze, terrified, her worst nightmare suddenly come true. She literally froze; she could not move a muscle, and every thought was blanketed by terror.

She remained as stiff as a statue, as a huge shadow rose up out of one of her chairs and came toward her. It was Dick. It was Dick. It wasn't a nightmare, it was really him. He smelled of beer and sweat, and the violet hair oil he used to make his black locks shine as he loomed over her. One enormous hand grabbed her shoulder, squeezing it painfully.

The next thing she knew, she was on the floor. Not struck—thrown. He'd tossed her half across the room. She looked up at the black shadow looming over her, barely visible in the light from the streetlamps outside. "Wut. Not a single good word f'yer lawful wedded 'usband?" Dick Langford asked.

Then he picked her up by the arm, holding her so her feet dangled helplessly above the floor. "Well. Reckon ye need some remindin', then."

The next hour was a blur of terror and pain, as Dick reasserted his dominance over his "property." But she could tell—and this was even more terrifying—that he was being extremely careful not to damage her in any way that would *show*. Hence, being flung to the floor instead of being backhanded down to it. Pinches and squeezes that would leave her black and blue, blows to stomach and buttocks, pulling her around the room by her hair, throwing himself down on her and pressing his weight on her until she was dizzy from lack of breath—

When he was done—and the cold, calculating fashion in which he beat her was even more frightening than if he had raged—he dropped her on the bed and sat down on the end of it. She was curled on her side, shaking so hard that it shook the bedframe. She was too terrified to make a sound, lest it start him on another round of beating. She ached in every inch of her. And yet—she knew from the past that in the morning she would still be able to dance, do her acts. He never did anything that would impair that. Somehow he knew just what he could and could not do to her that would still allow her to work.

"Now," he said, his voice gloating, rich with satisfaction. "This's 'ow it's gonna be. I loik wut yer got 'ere. I loik this place. I loik Brighton. Plenty fer a feller to do here. Ye got soft livin' 'ere. So, yer gonna go roight on workin' at that music 'all. Yer gonna bring yer pay packet t'me. Oi found thet little nest egg yer had put by, yeah? 'Smine now. Pay me back fer what yer stole from me when yer ran. Yer gonna cook an' clean fer me. Yer gonna do wut I say. An' yer got no choice, roight? Cuz the law's on me side. Yer me wife. I got the license t'prove it. Yer me property, roight an' toight. I'm gonna be in cream, an' yer gonna make it 'appen."

He leaned over where she huddled in a half-curl on the bed. His beery breath washed over her. "Yer ain't gonna run agin, 'cause if ye do, first thing I do is break that there magician's back. Yeah? An' then I'll break th' back uv thet gel Suzie. Then Oi'll fin' me some more backs t'break. Ye get me?"

Weeping silently, she somehow gasped out a strangled "Yes."

"I got some'un in thet hall wut knows all 'bout ye," he said with satisfaction, his hand heavy and bruising on her shoulder. He gave her shoulder a little shake, and she gasped. "'E'll squeal on ye, if ye don' do wut I want. Yeah?"

"I'll be good," she quavered, terrified to think of him hurting Lionel, or Suzie, and thanking God he didn't know about Jack.

"You see thet ye do," he said. "Startin' now."

He left the bed a moment, there was the scratch of a match, and a single one of the gaslights flared on. She huddled on the bed as he went around the cottage, pulling the curtains tight closed. "Get up," he said.

Trembling, she did as he ordered.

"Take them close off," he said. "Expensive. Ain't gonna tear them close. Might wanta sell 'em."

She was shaking so hard she could hardly stand, but she did as he ordered, stripped down to her skin, slowly, one piece of clothing at a time, dropping them into the chair, because that was how he liked it. His eyes were on her the whole time, watching, watching. She knew better than to try to hide herself with her hands. This was an old pastime of his. He wanted to watch her get naked. He probably wanted to watch her shivering with fear, too.

Then she came to bed, and he seized her like an animal.

He did what he wanted to with her, then rolled off her and went to sleep, taking up most of the bed. All she could think of now was the little beds in the loft, beds she wouldn't have to share with *him*. If she just waited long enough, perhaps she could get into one. She would be awake before he was, she always did wake before he did. She could get down out of the loft, and he would never know. She couldn't think to morning; couldn't think past just getting out of the bed he was in and into

another. When she was sure he was sound asleep, she
started to crawl out of bed—

Only to have him wake instantly and clamp one hand
crushingly over her wrist, tightening his grip cruelly until
she whimpered.

"The on'y time ye don' sleep wi' me, wife," he growled,
"Is when I tell ye thet ye don'. Yeah?"

"Aye," she whispered, tears pouring down her cheeks.

He went back to sleep almost immediately. She lay
there until dawn, shaking with fear and crying silently
until her eyes were as sore as the rest of her.

Lionel was awakened at the crack of dawn by impatient
pounding on his door. *What in the name of*—he thought
as Mrs. Buckthorn answered it, then, to his startlement,
he heard heavy footfalls—stumbling, limping in a way
that *sounded* excruciatingly painful, up the stairs to his
bedroom. The door burst open, and Jack stood there, di-
sheveled, looking as if he had just tossed whatever clothing came to hand on, eyes wild, teetering on his wooden
leg.

"He's got her!" his friend wailed. "He's got her!" And
then he collapsed. It was obvious that he had run—or
what passed for running—the entire way from his flat to
Lionel's house.

Mrs. Buckthorn had been hard on his heels, and between the two of them, they got him onto Lionel's bed.
But it was some time before they could get anything co-
herent out of him, and even then, Lionel had to piece it
together, a sobbed word here, a gasp there.

Jack's Elementals had awakened him out of a deep

sleep, and—here Lionel wasn't entirely sure what Jack meant—showed him Katie being beaten by a man. Somehow they had conveyed to Jack that this man was Dick Langford, the dreaded, brutish husband.

"We have to get her away!" Jack shouted, grabbing Lionel by the lapels of his nightshirt and shaking him. "We have to—"

"That'll be *enough,* Private!" Lionel snapped, in his best imitation of a military officer. "Control yourself!"

As he had hoped, the long stint in Africa had instilled an automatic response; Jack froze for a moment, staring blankly at his friend, then covered his face with his hands.

"What, exactly, are we supposed to do, Jack?" Lionel asked, harshly—because he had considered these very things ever since he had learned of Dick Langford and what he was. "The man is her husband. He has every right to do what he likes with her, and the law will support him. If we go storming over there now, he may very well manage to kill us both, and the law will support him in *that* as well. *Think,* man. What do we know?"

Jack was white and shaking at this point, but there was sense in his eyes again. "Nothing," he said, voice rasping.

"And what do you do when you know nothing? You go and find out." Lionel really didn't have any clever ideas at this point, but he did know this much; the best thing he could do, if there was going to be a confrontation, was to stage that confrontation when there were plenty of witnesses, and to go dressed like a gentleman— because Dick Langford certainly would not be. That meant arriving on the door fully kitted out, at the time that the clerks and insurance agents and lawyers and all the other professional men who worked in those offices all around were arriving. "You are in no state to go, and if something should happen, you can't run," he said bluntly. "I'll go pound on the door and demand Kate for rehearsals. *He* doesn't know we don't rehearse on dark day, even if he's found something out about how we do things in the hall on performance days. *You* see what you can find out by means of your Elementals. I can't scry; see if you can."

Jack was still white-faced, but given something to do, he nodded.

"Meanwhile put that first-class planning mind of yours to work. If we're going to get her away from that brute, it'll take both of us." He turned to Mrs. Buckthorn, who, thank heavens, was not in the least flustered by being in the same room as her employer in his nightshirt. "Get him a brandy, would you? It'll steady his nerves. I'll get myself put together."

He retired to his dressing room and kitted himself out as the Professor again. Merely putting the suit on made him feel pompous and superior. He hoped that Dick would react to the façade by going subservient; bullies often did, at least if they weren't drunk.

Now, should I take the trap, or a cab? The trap would be more convenient and less costly . . . but . . . that wouldn't convey what he wanted to convey. A gentleman never drove himself. Dick Langford was from the circus, which was nearly the bottommost range of entertainment. He *should* be impressed by a man who could arrive to scoop up his wayward assistant in a cab.

In theory, anyway.

And right now, theory was all Lionel had to go on. This would probably be the most important piece of improvisational theater he had ever done.

Let's just hope I'm good at it . . .

Satisfied by his appearance, he checked on Jack, to find the man staring intently into a candle-flame. Well good; he was *doing* something. Best for Lionel to do the same.

He headed out into the street to find himself transportation.

The cab pulled up in front of Katie's cottage at exactly the right time, when the street was full of men soberly and similarly dressed making their way to their offices. Instructing the driver to wait, Lionel put on an air of affronted impatience, climbed the three steps to Katie's door, and pounded on it.

Curtains are closed tight . . .

He continued to pound until the door was suddenly wrenched open by a giant in nothing but a pair of trousers with the braces hanging down over his hips. Lionel was assaulted by a wave of stale sweat and beer-smell as the man—stubbled, yet with a crude sort of dark good looks about him—raised a fist—and it was all Lionel could do to maintain his expression of suppressed rage and not turn and run.

Then the man did a visible second take, took in the suit, the air of superiority, and the equally wrathful expression on Lionel's face and lowered his fist again.

"Wot yer want?" emerged from the oddly sensuous face. "'Oo be ye?"

Lionel drew himself up, trying to look as if he'd been insulted by such crude questions. "I am Lionel Hawkins, not that it's any of your business, fellow," he said, in his poshest of accents. He even contrived to look down his nose at the brute, even though the man towered over him. "Where's Kate Langford? She's overdue for rehearsal."

As he had hoped and prayed, the bully responded to this by being taken aback, at least for a moment. But unfortunately, he rallied again, leaning against the doorframe with his arms crossed over his formidable, and bare, chest. "She 'on't be comin'," he replied.

Lionel made himself go pop-eyed, as if with thwarted rage. "What do you mean by that, fellow?" he spluttered. "Who are you? Where is my assistant?"

"Oi'm th' lad wut is tellin' yer she 'on't be comin'," he repeated, with a smug expression on his face. "Dick Langford is 'oo Oi am. 'Tis dark day. Yer got no roights to 'er toime on dark day. She'll be takin' care uv 'er 'usband as she should be." He nodded, as Lionel feigned fuming in impotent rage. "Oi know me roights."

Lionel pretended rage for a few more moments, then shook his finger in the strongman's face. "She had better be at the hall at nine in the morning *on the dot.* I can get myself another assistant like *that.*" He snapped his fingers. "And what's more, I can have her replaced as the Russian dancer quickly enough, just by informing the papers of what she *really* is, a cheap little circus acrobat masquerading as a ballerina!"

Finally he made an impression on the man, who went from smug to alarmed, and put on a placating expression. "'Ere now! No need 'o thet!" he said, and Lionel knew he had found at least one feeble weapon to hold over the brute in this strangest of wars. Money. He'd try to confirm this with Katie later, but he was certain that fear of losing Katie's wages was what had suddenly turned the strongman from arrogant to cowed. "She'll be there. But yer got no roights over 'er toime on dark day, an' a man's got a roight t' 'is woife!"

Lionel tried to make himself swell up. "Just—see that she is!" he exploded, and stamped his way back to the cab.

He held his persona until they had turned several corners, then allowed himself to collapse in the corner of the seat.

Dear god, the man's a monster. Huge. Huge and brutishly intimidating. Like something out of a penny-dreadful. *Think, Lionel. What did you learn?*

Well . . . whatever had happened last night, the brute hadn't killed Katie, and he'd been half afraid that was exactly what had happened. And unless Katie did something to provoke Langford, his lust for money was probably going to keep him from killing her, or even damaging her.

But the clock was ticking, because while this might be true while the man was sober, Lionel had no idea how controlled he'd be when he was drunk—and the smell of beer on him had suggested that the man was likely to be drunk as often as he could afford.

But if he's drunk enough . . . he'll be too drunk to hurt her. That was an idea that had some merit. He tucked it away for later.

By that time the cab had reached his home; he paid the driver and dashed into the house. Maybe Jack had learned something—or thought of something.

Katie huddled in terror on the bed from the moment that the pounding started on the door. In all the time she had been here, there had never once been a visitor, or even someone looking for another address. There were only two people likely to come here and knock with that much urgency, and both of them were going to be in deadly danger from Dick—

She wept—silently—with fear when she heard Lionel's voice. She was certain at every moment that Dick was going to break his neck—right up until she heard Dick's tone abruptly change as Lionel threatened to sack her and get rid of her ballerina act if she didn't turn up at the proper time in the morning.

Then she nearly wept with relief. Lionel had somehow found the only thing he could use to hold over Dick's head. Money. And that was a—not a weapon, but a defense in her hands. Dick would never kill her, and probably wouldn't cripple her, as long as she was bringing in plenty of money.

And at last her mind started working. Just get through today. Tomorrow, she'd find some way to tell Lionel that Dick had an informant in the hall. One thing at a time. Concentrate on the next hour, the rest of the morning. Survive that . . .

She got out of bed as Dick closed the door. "Breakfast?" she said, timidly, not daring to reach for any clothing until he allowed her to. Oh, how she ached! She had gotten used to not hurting . . . the pain of movement came as a shock, and reminded her of what she had to do—keep her voice, her head down. Be meek. Never contradict. Offer every possible comfort. "There's bacon, eggs—"

She glanced up through her hair to see Dick grinning. "Learnt yer lesson, then? Aye. Food, 'oman. Put s'thin' on. Thet skinny carcass uv your's like to kill me appetite."

Given permission to dress, she did, quickly, and hurried over to the stove, where she fried up every rasher of bacon she had, all the eggs, and made fried toast in the grease, and brewed a strong pot of tea. She loaded up two plates with the bounty, and brought it all over to him. She didn't expect to share in the feast, and that was just as well, since he ate every bite, wiping the plates clean with the last bites of toast. "That was the last," she said in a whisper. "I'll have to buy more at the shop."

He was in a good mood after such a breakfast—at the circus, Andy Ball's cook doled out the food with a scrupulous hand, and no use asking for second helpings. Dick had gotten more than anyone else, of course, but she'd still needed to make him elevenses, a big tea, and often a supper after he'd come back from the pub. "Aight," he said agreeably. "Yer kin do thet, while I hev a bit more sleep."

And with that, he turned over on his side and was soon snoring.

When she was certain he was soundly asleep, she quietly pulled down the cabinet-bath and carefully ran cold water into the tub, trying not to let it splash. It was already too warm in the cottage, but she didn't dare open the curtains to let air in, and chance waking him. She stripped herself, soaked in the cold water, and scrubbed and wept, trying to scrub out the vileness she felt in herself.

But she did it all silently. Everything must now revolve around Dick, if she wanted to escape as many

beatings as possible. There was no Andy Ball here to restrain him. He *might* remember that she was the only
bread-earner, but if he was really in a rage, he might not.

Then she did the dishes—he would explode if she left
dirty dishes. There were two kinds of people that lived in
caravans; the scrupulously clean, and the slovenly. Travelers were always scrupulously clean, and oddly, when it
came to the caravan, so was Dick, though he seldom
washed himself. The one and only time she had ever left
dirty dishes for an hour or two, because he had eaten late
and she had been too busy with the show to get to them
immediately, she had been met with the one and only
blow to the face—a blow that left her with half her face
blackened. Andy Ball had had a right fit over that when
he saw her—he'd raged at Dick for an hour because he
couldn't put a bruised girl out in front of an audience,
and Dick had been mightily put out because she hadn't
gotten any pay until she was fit to look at again.

That was when Dick had learned to hurt her where it
didn't show, and he had become almost scientific about
it. He'd also learned never to hurt her in a way that
would keep her from performing. She only hoped he
hadn't forgotten what he'd learned.

. . . and what a dreadful thing, to be reduced to hoping
that her husband "wouldn't hurt her too much."

Maybe it was a good thing that it had taken him so
long to find her. Right after she'd run, he probably would
have murdered her. With so much time passing, the red-
hot rage had cooled enough that when he'd found her,
from what he'd said already, he'd taken the time to find
out what she was doing, and discover that she was worth
a lot more to him alive.

Right now, he was in a good mood. He'd established his ownership of her. He would not have to work as long as she was able to. He was full of good food, he was tucked up in what was probably the best bed he had ever slept in in his life, and he was "in the cream." The longer she could keep him in that mood the better. Maybe she could even keep him happy enough that she could go a full month or more between beatings.

He hadn't troubled to do more than count the money she'd been collecting in the unused toby jug that had come with the oddly assorted dishes left in the cottage. She knew he had counted it, because the money was stacked in groups of five by denomination all across the front of the shelf. He hadn't cared to hide it or take it, because he knew she wouldn't dare touch more than he allowed—and he had just given her permission to shop for food for him. She took more than she thought she'd need, dressed herself with more care, and went out silently with a big shopping basket.

The corner shop was not where she went for "decent" food, but they were well stocked when it came to the sorts of things Dick liked. When she came back, she had all of his favorites; sausages, ham, and lots of bacon. More bread, cheap little cakes, and packets of sweets. Tinned baked beans. Tinned mushy peas. And she had something she hoped would make her life easier; two bottles of gin. Dick was not used to strong drink; he'd not been able to afford it, and it was easier to get a beer or a lager or a cider out of the country-folk at the local pub or inn than it was a bit of strong drink. They'd pay a beer to watch him bend an iron bar. They'd not pay for a tot of gin for the same pleasure. Many of them equated strong drink with sin, anyway; beer was food, beer was something you could (and many of them did) make at home, just like bread and out of the same ingredients, but strong drink was evil, and led to vice—so their preachers told them every Sunday, at least.

When he woke, she already had luncheon ready for him—and she had seen how he had gotten into her locked cottage, when she had taken a chance and peeked through the curtains.

He'd been more than usually cunning, and that suggested he had actually been watching the cottage to plan how to get in. That iron grating over the windows had been no match for his strength. He'd simply gone to the back and pulled the grating for one of them out of the cottage wall. There were no passers-by in the rear to see him and call for a constable, and of course if she had seen a grating gone from a front window when she'd come home, she would *never* have gone in the front door in the first place.

It was just more evidence of how cunning he could be when he put his mind to it.

As he ate she made a careful accounting of every penny spent, just as she'd had to at the circus. He sat there, silently chewing his ploughman's lunch of ham, cheese, and thick bread and butter, his black brows furrowed as he counted up what she had spent in his head. He was very good at counting money, too. He could do sums in his head as easily as she could on paper.

He interrupted her a couple of times. "That's too much—" he'd say.

"It's the shop," she'd reply. "Here's the bill-of-sale, see? It's very dear to shop there. There's cheaper shops, but they're farther away, some of them you have to take the bus to reach, and you didn't give me leave to go that far."

He'd grunt, but at least he didn't cuff her.

Finally she came to the last. "And I got you these," she said, putting the gin bottles on the table. "I thought you'd like some Blue Ruin. I'm making money enough, and you should have good things to drink."

His entire face lit up and she knew that she had pleased him. He didn't say so, of course.

He never gave her anything like praise.

He drank almost half a bottle, then, tipsy, went back to bed after luncheon; she already knew what her duties were. To clean the cottage in complete silence, then make a big tea for him. As she cleaned, she cried, longing with all her heart for the quiet cool of Lionel's house, for the magic, for the things she learned. . . .

. . . .for Jack . . .

But she shuddered to think what would happen if Jack ever came here. He'd die, of course. He'd die, because how could a one-legged man stand up against Dick—an *able-bodied,* normal man couldn't stand up against Dick, and yet she knew he would try to defend her and take her away. She couldn't allow him to do that, even though it *would* free her from Dick. . . .

She'd be free, because Dick would be slapped in gaol and hung.

This wouldn't be the sort of thing where it was just one Traveler killing another, or one lowly circus tramp murdering another of his kind. Dick was nothing more than a circus strongman, and Jack was a respectable man with a respectable job. If it came to killing, the constables wouldn't just ignore it the way they did Traveler killings, and Dick would hang for murder.

Dick might be cunning, but he was under the impression that he could do anything he liked to keep her, even murder, because she was his property. Before Katie had met Lionel and Jack, she had thought the same. After all, the constables didn't *care* when lowly sorts like circus folks did each other in. So far as they were concerned, one bit of trash had got rid of another bit of trash, which was one bit of trash less to watch out for.

Now she knew what Dick did not—that if he did harm Jack over her, it wouldn't matter to respectable society that he'd done it to keep her. Respectable society would howl for his blood, and get it.

But Jack would still be dead, so what would it matter that she was free?

Her only hope lay in keeping him happy—manage to keep him too drunk to get into a rage and beat her, if possible—and endure. Just as she would not soil the innocence of her Fire Elementals by letting them defend her, she would not let Jack be killed by letting him defend her. The two were more nearly the same thing than she had realized before this moment.

She loved them both. She would not let either of them sacrifice themselves for her.

And so, for their sake, she would only concentrate on keeping Dick happy, and bend all the magic she knew to one single wish, a wish that applied to Elementals and Jack alike.

Stay away . . . stay away . . . stay away.

Jack was sitting at the dining table, looking like hell, and no longer staring into a candle. "Did you learn anything?" Lionel asked.

Jack shook his head. "They can't get near her, she's keeping them away, to protect them I assume, and I'm too angry to scry." He didn't have to say who "they" were; the Fire Elementals, of course. So Katie was keeping the Elementals from coming to her aid by keeping them away from her.

As for Jack, he was far more than just *angry,* of course, but Lionel let that pass. "I have a bit of good news. The blackguard can be moved by money, and presumably, by what he regards as a life of luxury as supplied by the money Katie earns. He's cunning enough to have discovered what she does. He's already worked out that he doesn't need to lift a finger, and can live off her. So he's not at all eager for Katie to lose her positions at the hall. I've made it very clear that if she doesn't turn up on time, I'll see she's sacked immediately, and he has no idea that Charlie would move heaven and earth to keep her dancing act. She'll be at rehearsal in the morning at the usual time."

Jack's expression eased the least little bit. "That's something, anyway," he murmured.

"It's more than *something.* It's suggested a way to handle him," Lionel replied. The idea had come to him as soon as he realized how fundamentally lazy and greedy the circus strongman was. "But that will depend on us finding one of the nobby Masters who's deep enough in clover that buying the wretch off for the sake of gaining a Fire Mage is worth the expense." It had happened before that one of the elite had "rescued" someone from a dismal life—although it had generally been someone that one of the Masters had sent off to university, or taken out of an orphanage, or something of the sort. He'd never heard of any case like this one. Nevertheless . . . what was the harm in asking? The worst that would happen would be that his plea would be politely ignored. That was how the toffs were. If they didn't like something you'd asked, they'd pretend you never asked it. "It'd have to be a right royal buy-off too; enough to ship him off to the colonies, or some such, besides setting the swine up for life. That won't come cheap."

"Still . . . it's a good option." Jack drummed his fingers on the table. "I might know one who'd take an interest. And it might be worth me writing to Almsley directly. I've worked with him, and he was less . . . stuffy than most of the upper crust."

"Hmm. And we could remind him of what *might* happen if the girl gets desperate enough and *does* unleash her Elementals." Lionel sighed at that. He trusted Katie. He knew she was a good girl. But how much torture could you expect someone to endure before their resolve broke and they called in everything they could think of to save them from an intolerable situation? "It's damned hot enough, and the buildings hereabouts are tinder-dry . . ."

Jack shuddered. He didn't have to hear anything else to know what *could* happen. As they had both taken great pains to drill into her, Fire was the most emotional of Elements, was the most prone to losing control, and the most prone to allowing emotion to take it over.

"I'll write to Lord Almsley," he said. "You write Alderscroft. But meanwhile—"

"I thought of another thing we might do, but it's risky," Lionel warned. "The man's already a drunkard. We could make sure he stays that way." This, too, had occurred to him once he was out of Dick Langford's presence. There was some danger in this, for Katie. It would depend on what kind of a drunk the strongman was. If he was an angry drunk, it would make things worse for her, unless she could get him to the point where he was an unconscious drunk, and quickly.

"It might not work," Jack warned him. "I knew men who you couldn't tell from sober when they were dead drunk. They get used to it. The only difference between them drunk and sober was that sober they were nastier and meaner than drunk." He stroked his moustache thoughtfully. "I've heard of men that were nicer sober than drunk, too. If he's a mean drunk, that would be bad for Katie."

It seemed they were both thinking the same way.

Lionel shrugged. "I think it's worth trying. We can arrange for deliveries of Blue Ruin to the door. He might drink himself to death and save us all a great deal of expense and worry." Gin was the curse of the lower classes as well as the tipple of choice (with tonic) for the upper. Cheap gin got you drunk faster and for less money than almost anything other than home-brewed beer. Cheap gin was also frequently adulterated, or distilled in apparatus that used lead pipes. It was hard to drink so much beer that it sent a man into a sodden coma; it was easy to do so with cheap gin. So cheap gin could, and frequently did, kill.

"He might well cooperate by drinking himself to death, and gin is the way to do it, if it can be done." Jack nodded.

They both stared at each other. "I can't think of anything else at the moment," Lionel confessed, after a long pause.

Jack sighed. "All right, then. We'll write our letters. I'll tell you where to find the worst gut-rotting gin in Brighton, and you arrange for a jeroboam of it to turn up at Katie's every couple of days. If he doesn't drink himself to death, maybe he'll be poisoned by it."

"Keep at your Elementals," Lionel urged. "They might still be of some use." He already knew his would not; although the sylphs made excellent spies when they chose to do so, they flatly refused to go near the strongman. Dick Langford evidently frightened them as much as he terrorized his wife.

He's so foul he frightens creatures he can't even see . . .

He wondered if there was anything that could be made of that.

Probably not. Except that it would make an excellent line in that letter to Lord Alderscroft.

He went to the desk and brought back pens, ink, and paper for the both of them. "Soon begun, soonest done," he said, and set to work.

Dick woke, splashed some water over himself, drank the entire pot of strong tea Katie had made for him, ate the fried ham and the tinned mushy peas she'd made for him—then went to the carpetbag he'd brought with him and left in the corner of the cottage, a bag she had not dared to touch. He stripped down naked as she averted her eyes, oiled his hair with his favorite violet oil, and began to put on his "best" clothing.

If he hadn't been so big and muscled, he would have looked ridiculous in it. Blue trousers, green shirt, red braces, a bright red scarf around his neck—he was inordinately fond of the peacock outfit, and anyone else wearing it would have found himself the butt of jokes and mockery.

But of course, no one was going to laugh at anyone the size and strength of Dick Langford.

Or if they did, they were soon going to regret it. He'd broken plenty of noses over this clothing, and blacked plenty of eyes. No one had ever laughed at him for wearing this twice.

"Oi'm goin' out," he announced, scooping some of the money from the dresser into his pocket. "Yer stayin' 'ere, yeah?"

"Yes, Dick," she whispered, even though somewhere inside her a little voice was screaming, *Now's your chance! Run!*

But she knew what would happen if she did. Dick was not threatening idly to break Lionel's back.

There were stories all over Andy Ball's circus of how Dick had broken necks, backs, and even killed men who'd offended him, but had been so clever about it he was never brought before the law. Plenty of those men had been in rival shows, or shows Andy had wanted to buy out.

But others had been troublemakers or local bullies among the country-folk; bullies who'd taken one look at Dick and decided to challenge him in some way or other.

This hadn't troubled the circus folk of Andy Ball's establishment; they'd rather taken it as a mark of pride, that Dick would, in a way, avenge them for the often shabby treatment they got at the hands of country-folk, who treated them only slightly better than they treated Travelers. Katie didn't doubt that at least some of the stories were true, because there were villages that the circus would go right around and never stop, and why would Andy Ball ever do that, foregoing a chance at a profit, unless there was a very good reason for it?

So no. She dared not run. For the same reason that she would not allow Jack to come here and challenge Dick, she would not run and put Lionel, Suzie, and who knew who else at risk. Even though Dick would be caught and hang for it and she would be free. She dared only bend her head and whisper, meekly, "Yes, Dick."

"Oi'm gonna hev mesel' a good toime, yeah?" He sneered at her. "None o' yer tea an' cakes. Oi want that Blue Ruin on the table waitin', an' food fit fer a man. An' you be up i' that loft th' minute ye hears me, an' not a peep outa ye. Oi'll be beck i' an hour. Mebbe less."

She almost gaped at him. He couldn't possibly mean what she *thought* he meant. Surely what he intended was to go find someone to bring back to drink with?

But as the church clock struck nine, and she put the cold ham, cheese, bread and gin on the table, she heard him at the door. And the unmistakable giggles of not one, but two women.

She had thought her humiliation was at its nadir. As she scuttled up the ladder and hid in the loft, and Dick led two of the cheapest floozies she had ever seen into the little cottage she had once considered her shelter, she discovered that, when it came to Dick, once again she was wrong.

14

THIS might be the most important letter he had ever written in his life, and Jack had written and torn up a dozen different versions. He was sweating and swearing with the effort, had to stop himself a dozen times from chewing on the end of Lionel's expensive patent pen, and even got up to pace the floor once or twice. Strong tea didn't help. Tea heavy with milk didn't help. Green tea didn't help, and that was his court of last resort for thinking. Finally, though, he thought he had one that would pass muster, and silently handed it over to Lionel to read when they had finished supper—a supper neither of them had much appetite for.

He waited with his heart in his mouth. Lionel was much better educated than he was. Lionel had even gone to public school before throwing over the life of a private secretary to apprentice himself to an illusionist—

fortunately both of his masters, the one he discarded and the one he chose, were also Elemental Mages, so they were far more understanding than "ordinary" men would have been. But he hadn't lost his love for letters, nor his knack with words when he traded the one master for another.

Lionel's eyebrow rose once or twice, but he handed it back to Jack without commenting during the reading of it.

"Well?" Jack demanded, completely unsure whether this meant Lionel approved of the letter or hated it.

A cat fight under one of the windows barely got Jack's attention, he was so focused on Lionel.

"I'm not Lord Almsley, but that letter would probably move me," the magician said. He pulled at his lower lip a little. "You're taking a risk admitting you are in love with the girl, though. Some men might see that as a suspect motive. They might wonder how much of the story of the brutish husband was truth and how much was you trying to come up with an excuse to get her away."

"My father worked more than once with the current Lord's father," Jack explained. "I was in my teens and I met the current and previous Lord Almsley, though young Peter was barely out of the nursery at the time. The previous Lord not only did not criticize my father for marrying a girl with no magic, he said it was a healthy thing, and that all that mattered was that they were happy. If the son is anything like the father, and I think he is, that's not a risk, it's a point in my favor."

"I defer to your judgment," Lionel told him. He carefully folded the sheets, and got up and obtained two envelopes. He wrote something on both—the second address was longer than the first one. He put Jack's letter in the first envelope, sealed it, then put his letter and Jack's in the second. "I'll post these in the morning; I'll enclose yours in mine and ask Alderscroft to send it on." He glanced at the clock on the mantle. "Will you need something to help you sleep?"

"Brandy will probably—" before he could protest, Lionel had gone to the sideboard, poured him a double, and taken one himself. The magician brought both glasses back to the table and shoved one across to Jack. "For God's sake, Lionel, I have my own!"

"And it's nothing like as good as mine," Lionel sniffed his own drink. "If you are going to be unhappy, never drink anything but the best. At least you'll be unhappy with style. Besides, if you leave right after you finish it, this won't hit you till you're on your own doorstep, and then if you find you still can't sleep, you can try a second dose of your own tipple."

Jack had to acknowledge the truth of that. He drank Lionel's excellent brandy with gloomy appreciation, took his leave of his friend, and Lionel escorted him as far as the door before retreating into his own house for the night.

There was one distinct advantage to being just a trifle tipsy on the walk home; his damned stump didn't hurt as badly as it usually did. And he was no more unsteady than usual. Walking on stone, like the cobbled pavement, was hard. If he wasn't careful, and sometimes if he was, the peg leg slipped off the slightly domed surface of the cobblestone he set it on and slid into the join with the next stone, setting him off-balance and jarring his whole body.

It was quiet around his flat when he got there, which was good. He lived in a neighborhood that seemed to have a lot of young bachelors in it, and they were not always the industrious, ambitious clerks he would have preferred as neighbors, the sort of young men who wanted to rise in their firms and went to bed at a sober hour. In fact, for a few of them, he suspected "sober" was a condition they were altogether unfamiliar with.

But he still wasn't able to sleep. He lay there in the dark with the window open to the night air and his thoughts running around in circles, his muscles tense with anxiety, and his mind always coming back to the same place he had left.

His Katie was in danger. At this very moment, she was definitely frightened, and possibly hurt. And yet there was nothing he could do at this moment to help her.

He had to get her away from that brute. He *had* to, in the same way that he *had* to eat, *had* to breathe.

But that brute had every right under the law to do what he wanted to with her. He could beat her, starve her, scream at her, steal her money, even make her work as a whore if he chose. The only thing he couldn't do was kill her. That brute had every right under the law, because under the law she was his property. And there was nothing Jack could do about that.

Finally as he thought, angrily, for the hundredth time, *the law is an ass,* something unexpected occurred to him.

Suddenly, now he saw what the Suffragettes were on about.

He'd never been particularly in sympathy with the Suffragettes—he'd always considered they were making a great deal of fuss over nothing—until now.

Couldn't women already do pretty much what they wanted to? That was the irritated thought that had always crossed his mind when he was encountering one of their marches. Why should they be making such a lot of fuss? Why, look at women like Peggy! They had the best of it. So he had thought, anyway, until Peggy had told him of the three husbands she'd chucked over at immense expense and difficulty—the drunkard, the libertine, and the brute. But still, she had gotten rid of them, right?

But now . . . now his Katie was in the hands of a brute, and she couldn't be rid of him, because she hadn't put her money where he couldn't get at it, and he'd threatened her friends if she tried to chuck him. *And the law was going to let him do that.* Because even if she reported the threat to the police, all he had to do was laugh and say something like "There, you see, women can't take a joke," and it would all be brushed under the carpet—and probably Katie would get a lecture about making false claims to the police.

So now one of the tracks his mind was flying off on was how it wasn't just the vote women wanted. No, now he could see with unhappy clarity that what they wanted was to be treated like equal human beings, and not like someone's possession. Why, he reckoned that there were more laws in place saying what a man could do to his horse or his dog than there were ones saying what a man could do with his wife.

He knew better than to toss and turn in his bed; it served no purpose, it frequently made his stump ache worse. He'd learned long ago that when a black night came, the only thing he could do was to lie there and wait it out.

It wasn't fair to Katie. What had Katie ever done to deserve what was happening to her now?

It wasn't fair to him, either. They had everything arranged! Within months, she would be free, and they could be married! What harm had he ever done—

But then, he knew what he had done to deserve this. Granted, it had been in war, and soldiers were always told that God was on their side, and anything they did in war was for the sake of God and country. But he had known better, and he had never believed that. There were things that were immoral, and wrong, and even heinous, and you didn't do them even if you got thrown in the stockade and court-martialed over them.

He hadn't done those things—but—he wasn't innocent either. He hadn't done harm on purpose, but....

Well . . . harm by omission. I followed orders and said nothing, in Africa. I wasn't the one who was rounding up kiddies and women and burning them out and herding them into prison camps to starve and die—but I didn't say anything either, and I didn't do anything about it. Could I have found a way to make people see the terrible things we were doing there? Probably, if I tried hard enough.

Maybe all of this was his fault, for entangling Katie's life with his....

Maybe if he gave her up ... maybe if he promised God he would be nothing but a friend to her and put distance between them. Maybe God would be merciful and stop heaping punishment on her that was rightly due to him.

The curtain moved in the breeze from the sea; heat and sorrow weighed down every limb like a blanket of stones. Distant noises of people moving through the streets only served to remind him that *other* people were happy, and that he did not deserve to be.

The night stretched on, and despair closed over him like the dark waters of a pitiless sea.

Katie had resorted to pulling a pillow over her head despite the heat in the loft, and trying not to hear the noises coming from the bed. It wasn't just the squeals and the cries and the panting and grunts, nor the thumps and creaking of the bed, either, it was smells she couldn't wall out. Dick's violet hair oil, some cheap, nasty scent one of the women had drenched herself with, sweat, and an intense and unmistakable musky odor that she knew all too well. The smells were actually worse than the sounds, because they seemed to get right inside her.

The heat in the loft was not helped by the embarrassment and shame that permeated her, shame that made her whole body seem on fire. Oh the shame! She hated all of that, and yet, there was a part of her that was going, *but if that was Jack . . .*

But eventually, all the sounds stopped, and she got used to the smells, and once a sort of silence settled over the cottage, she actually dozed off for a little.

She woke, as if shocked awake by a bucket of ice-cold water to the face, to a sickening and familiar sound—the meaty sound of a hand smacking into a face.

Only this time it wasn't her face that was being struck.

There was only a little light in the cottage now, from one of the gaslights turned down low. There wasn't much danger that Dick would spot her, so she wiggled to the edge of the loft and peered over.

There was only one floozy in the cottage now; where the other had gone, she had no idea. The woman was sprawled ungracefully on the floor, wearing nothing but her bloomers and chemise, her face already going black and blue on the side where Dick had slapped her. She was a dirty blonde—literally. It looked to Katie as if she hadn't washed her hair in six months, or her body in three. It also looked as if she never scrubbed off the paint on her face, only put on a new layer over the old. Her underthings were dingy and stained, and the hems were all out and fraying.

Her eyes were screwed up tightly with rage—at least the one that hadn't started to swell closed was—and her mouth snarling under the paint. She made a snatch for something in the puddle of clothing beside the bed. "Ye right bastard!" she spat. "I'll cut ye fer that!"

Before she could make good on her threat, Dick had reached out, with that fast grabbing motion Katie knew so well, hauled the whore up from the floor by her hair, and methodically punched her once in the stomach. That drove the breath out of her, both her hands flew wide-open. A knife clattered to the floor out of the right, and one of Katie's little keepsakes out of the other.

Dick punched her again and she gasped with pain.

But Dick was far from done. This was his cold rage, much more frightening than his hot anger. He didn't say anything, just kept hitting her. It was exactly as he'd beaten Katie last night; the same silent rage, the same methodical blows, with the sole exception that with this woman, Dick wasn't trying to spare her looks or her ability to dance. He was striking her where he pleased, taking care only to not kill her on the spot.

She couldn't even scream, because he had driven all of the breath out of her body, and kept driving it out every time she managed to get a lung-full.

He'd done that to Katie, too. It was his way of keeping her quiet, so no one knew he was beating her.

When he was finally satisfied with his handiwork, he opened the back door, threw the whore out into the scrap of yard back there, and threw her clothing after her. Then he shut the door, dusted his hands like a man who is pleased with a job well done, and turned.

She knew instinctively that he was going to look up, and pulled her head back out of sight before he could. She didn't know if he would be angry to catch her watching, spying on him, or if he would consider the beating an object lesson for her. He had to know she had heard everything. She could only compromise by staying out of sight, and letting him imagine she was cowering with fear in her bed.

It wouldn't be that much of an untruth. She certainly was shaking with terror, chilled despite the heat.

She waited until she heard the sound of a bottle being uncorked followed by noisy swallowing, and looked cautiously down again, just easing her head over the edge of the loft in tiny increments so that he wouldn't be alerted by movement.

As she had thought, he had uncorked the bottle of gin and was guzzling it. She pulled her head back again, just as slowly, before he got a chance to see her watching him. "Spying on him," he would certainly call it, if he caught her now. And despite having worked his anger out on the whore, there would be some sort of punishment for her.

Then he turned out the light and she heard the bed creaking under his weight.

She lay there, staring up at the darkness, her body aching—half from her own beating, and half in sympathy for the one she had watched. She knew exactly what every one of those blows felt like, and although the whore had been caught stealing, surely the theft hadn't merited being pummeled half to death. Katie thought for certain she would never be able to get to sleep after all that.

But exhaustion was too much for her. It had been a long day, full of anxiety, punctuated by dread. She fell into a restless, half-aware "sleep" in which she was conscious of every sound from the room beneath her. The only difference between last night and this was that Dick's heavy body was not beside her, taking up most of the bed, and making her aware every second that she was his slave as surely as if he had bound her with chains.

The sounds of the milkman arriving woke her, and she frantically tried to remember if she had left the money out. Because if Dick didn't have his eggs and butter—

But the sound of clinking bottles as the milkman left new ones told her that she had, and with a surge of relief that made her feel dizzy, she slowly made her way down out of the loft, step by careful step on the ladder, determined not to allow it to creak. She had heard Lionel at the door when he had come to find out where she was. She had heard every word, and if there was a single thing that she was grateful for, it was that Lionel had put on a show, had made up a story of a rehearsal, and had fabricated the persona of the kind of "boss" that Dick would grovel around. Thanks to Lionel, she knew she was expected at the hall at nine, and to get there she would have to leave at eight. Above all, Dick must have his breakfast before she left, and a stack of ham and cheese sandwiches already made in case he wanted them for luncheon. She would have to get very busy.

She opened the back door—the milkman went through the alley, not the main street. This was not the sort of neighborhood where those here wished to be reminded of the existence of tradesmen.

The sun was up in a cloudless blue sky, and it was already as warm as a decent summer day *should* have been, which meant the heat was going to be punishing again. She got the container of eggs nestled in enough hay that they wouldn't get cracked, with a pat of butter wrapped in white paper atop them, then picked up the glass bottle of milk and the smaller one of cream. Until she had come here, she had never seen milk and cream separated before, nor in glass bottles. When she'd gotten milk, you just got a jar or a little pail and went to the farmer, and if you wanted cream, you skimmed it off the top. Well, you did if you knew of a farmer who was friendly to Travelers—and if you didn't, you did without.

Living in the city and buying things from shops had been a revelation. She was glad Mrs. Buckthorn had walked her through it all—passing her off as a new kitchen maid getting training.

The little bit of backyard had a very low wall around it and no gate. It was scarcely more than a bit of lawn surrounded by a knee-high stone fence. In that, it was identical except for size to the other bits of back garden up and down the block. People in offices didn't want to have to tend to gardens too.

There was no sign of the woman that had been tossed into the little yard last night, not even so much as a few threads or a lost ribbon. So at least she hadn't died out there of her injuries, and she'd been sound enough to get away somewhere.

She wondered how badly Dick had hurt the whore. She wasn't going to be the type to go to the law over being beaten, of course; she was a prostitute, and they'd just as likely arrest *her*. They certainly wouldn't take her complaint seriously, and in the unlikely event that someone did come around to make inquiries, Dick would just say he caught her stealing, and that would be the end of it for her—she'd be taken up as a thief. Katie felt both obscurely sorry for her, and grateful. Dick had needed someone to take his rage out on last night, and for once, it hadn't been *her*. In the past, the women he'd bedded had been women he didn't dare beat; wayward wives or daughters, servant girls in love with his oiled hair and muscles. He could take them to bed, but he didn't dare lay a hand on them—they could call it rape, show the bruises and be believed. So all his rage had been worked out on Katie.

But then she felt guilty for feeling glad that it had been someone else, not her, that had suffered.

Then she was shamefully grateful all over again, for she was only half as sore as yesterday, and the bruised places were starting to heal. And the thought came to her unbidden, a wish, almost a prayer—if only Dick would bring home more loose women, every night, and beat *them* instead of her! It would be worth every penny he paid for them, if only—

Then she was appalled at her own thoughts. How

could she wish that on *anybody?* What was wrong with her? She was a horrible person!

But if only—

All the time she was thinking these confused thoughts, she was working, working; she didn't dare stop for a minute, not even though her own stomach was growling at the rich smell of the bacon she was frying. Her hands worked without her even thinking about it, frying the bacon, cutting ham for the sandwiches, working frantically to get the meal ready so she would have time to get herself ready. She knew that the smell of the bacon would wake him, and it did; she felt his eyes on her as she set aside the bacon on his plate, then fried, first the eggs, then the bread in the grease. She turned with two brimming plates, identical to the ones she had served him yesterday, to see him watching her, face expressionless.

He was sitting up in bed, waiting for his food, his hair in oily curls, with a bit of the bedspread over his lap, not for modesty, but to keep his bits from getting burned by the hot plate.

She brought him the plates and then turned to get his tea, when he seized her by the wrist. "I s'pose yer thinkin' Oi'm a wrong 'un fer bringin' them hoors 'ere," he growled, eyes narrowed. The sweat-and-musk smell coming from him was overpowering. It made her feel sick. She fought it back. She dared not show it.

"You can do anything you like," she whispered. "This is your house. It doesn't matter what I think."

The scowl turned to a smirk. "Demned rioght!" he agreed. "Oi say wut goes, yeah! Oi wanta hoor, I gotta rioght t'hev one!"

"Yes, Dick," she replied. "You say what goes, and you do what you like. Let me get your tea before it gets cold."

He let go of her wrist, then, and she hurried over to the stove and the teakettle. Strong enough to take the silver off the spoon, and three sugars, that was what he liked first thing in the morning. She brought him the tea mug. He was already finished with the first plate of food, and she took away the empty to the sink, starting the washing-up. "I made you sandwiches for luncheon," she said, looking fearfully over her shoulder and pointing at the pile on a plate on the sideboard, covered by a glass bowl as she had seen at the pub, so they wouldn't get stale. He began to scowl.

She knew what he was thinking. He had expected her to be here to make him his lunch and his tea. He hadn't thought it through—well, he never thought anything through that he didn't have to. He was accustomed to getting his way in everything.

Except . . . except when a boss was telling him what to do. So that was how she would phrase it.

Before he could say anything, she added "It takes me an hour to go to the hall by 'bus, and I'm only allowed an hour at noon." Then she added, thinking quickly, "The doorman is right there, with his watch in his hand, writing down when we go in and come back for the boss. If I take too long, they take shillings out of my pay."

As she had hoped, it was the mention of having her pay cut that convinced him. He was still scowling, but it was sullen, not angry. "Mis'rable bastards," he grumbled. "Bosses! All alike."

"Yes, Dick," she agreed, and came for his second plate, bringing him a couple of the cheap cakes she had bought that made his eyes light up. He was as greedy as a child for sweets. "The last show ends at nine. I have to make sure all the things are properly put up, and then I have to take the 'bus home. If I hurry and run for the bus, I can catch the one that leaves at ten. I can't possibly be home before eleven. Do you want to wait that long for your supper? There are fish and chips stalls. . . ."

If he had a confederate at the hall, he already knew this; this was something of a test—

"Oi'll git me own supper," he growled. "Jest git here quick. I got plans."

Part of her was dismayed by this—it meant that tonight would probably replicate last night, with the shame that made her stomach churn and the twisted . . . yes, admit it . . . twisted arousal of it. Part of her was glad—it meant that someone else would be enduring him. She resolved to bring home some cotton wool and wax from the hall to make earplugs with, and soak a handkerchief in the lavender cologne that Suzie had given her. Maybe if she couldn't hear and smell what was going on . . .

She had left the cheese, butter, milk, and cream up here rather than taking them down to the cellar. They might spoil, but she didn't want to take them down there. He didn't know there was a cellar, and for some reason she didn't want him to know. Of course, she couldn't possibly *hide* down there; he'd tear the place apart looking for her, and he'd find the cellar right away. . . .

Or he'd go straight after Lionel as he had threatened.

But somewhere in the back of her mind, there was a ghost of a thought. Not even as much as an idea, just a thought, that if he didn't know about it, she could use it somehow.

He wouldn't think to look for it, maybe; he'd never lived in a house before. *She* wouldn't have known it was there if it hadn't been for Mrs. Buckthorn and her explanation of what it was for. So as long as she did nothing, he would have no idea that the rug covered a secret.

And there was another reason to make sure he didn't know about the cellar. He'd take one look at the place and *know* that he could take her down here, drop the hatch, and no one could hear her scream. She had the bone-shuddering feeling that there were things he hadn't done to her yet purely because she *would* scream, she wouldn't be able to help herself, and he knew that screams brought unwelcome attention. He'd have to explain himself. Someone might try to interfere, law or no law.

And what if he saw the cellar and decided it would be a good place to keep a woman captive? Not her, of course, he couldn't do that and still enjoy the money she made. But a whore, or more than one? Whores could go missing and no one would care. He could keep women down there, tied up, made captive—and that *was* against the law. She'd be part of that. He would *make* her part of that. He'd probably make her feed and care for them.

No . . . she didn't want him to know there was a cellar.

"I have to go," she said. "The 'bus is a penny." And she scrupulously took two pennies, no more, making sure he saw that. She took nothing to buy luncheon with, but she had already put a sandwich wrapped in newspaper in her bag. Making an effort not to wince when movement jarred a bruised spot, she hurried out.

It might have felt like freedom to anyone who had never lived with Dick. Katie knew better. This wasn't freedom. It was only a slightly bigger cage, and a long chain around her neck.

At the hall, she went straight past Jack without saying a word other than a murmured "good morning" and a glance that she hoped he interpreted as a warning. Dick had said he had a confederate here, as he'd had at the circus, and she knew she would have to behave as if she was being watched every single moment. She changed into her rehearsal clothing, and went immediately out onto the stage to warm up.

She had gone through her three dances twice when Lionel appeared, signaling the start of the magic act rehearsal. She didn't say a thing to him besides "good morning," "yes, sir," and "no, sir." But there would be one safe time to talk to him. . . .

When she was in the sword basket she hissed wordlessly to alert him, and she was rewarded by a whisper through one of the sword-slits.

"Katie—" Lionel began.

She cut him off. "It's not safe to talk. It's not safe to be too much together. Dick says he has someone here watching me and I believe him. He says if I do anything he doesn't like, he'll know about it. He says if I run from him, he'll start breaking necks, beginning with yours."

There was silence. Lionel slid a sword into place. "Well. That's unsettling."

"He'll do it, too," she warned. "In the circus they said he'd done it before, men that crossed him. They said, circus roustabouts, people Andy Ball had no trouble replacing, and who weren't missed. Some said he'd done in village men who'd vexed him, too, but I don't know about that. He won't do it open, he'll find a time and a place to sneak up on you in the dark and break your spine."

"It's very difficult to sneak up on an Elemental Magician, Katie," Lionel reminded her, as he drove another sword home.

She was trying not to cry and not succeeding very well; tears burned down her cheeks. Why was it men had so much trouble believing that another man could harm them? Why did they dismiss a warning from a woman as if it didn't matter, or was some sort of challenge they had to meet? She turned her arm to take her position for the next sword. "Please *listen* to me, Lionel! Even if he doesn't manage to catch you by surprise, he *will* catch you alone, and you'll be just as dead!"

Silence, the third sword, then "You have a point."

She rubbed her tears off on the shoulder of her shirt. Thank God. He was being sensible. . . .

"He won't kill me as long as I bring him pay packets," she said, despair leaking over into her words as she peered up through the slit. It seemed hideously appropriate that she was trying to tell him all this while contorted around the blades of swords. "He won't hurt me where it will interfere with my dancing. Just—don't do anything. I'll be all right," she added flatly. "I'll manage. I did before and I can do it again."

There was a long silence. "I don't believe that, and neither do you." Lionel said just as flatly. "You know as well as I do there's no 'managing' about this situation. Sooner or later his temper is going to get the better of his greed, and then you'll be hurt or worse. So no more gammon. We'll find a way to get you away from him without anybody's neck getting broken." The fourth sword slid in.

"Just remember he has a man watching!" she reminded him frantically. Damn the man! Why did he keep trying to put himself into danger for *her?* Didn't he even think that if he got hurt because of her, she'd want to die? "Warn Jack! We can't be seen talking outside of what's needed for the act!"

"We'll be careful," Lionel promised as the fifth sword slid home. "But don't you give up hope."

A nice sentiment, but that was all it was. Katie's only real hope was that the craze that had put her on the top of the bill would continue. As long as she could bring home a fat pay packet, Dick would regard her as his golden goose. And that was the *best* she dared hope for. Anything else was fairy dust and rainbows, and nothing would ever come of the hope.

A fat pay packet for him to spend on drink and whores; that was what he needed. That was what *she* needed.

And someone else for him to take his rage out on . . .

There was no other opportunity for her to talk to Lionel, though now she found herself watching every one of the stagehands covertly, trying to see if any of them was paying more attention to her than was needed by his job. Who was the confederate? If only she knew! If she knew, then she wouldn't have to guard herself every single moment!

When rehearsals were over and everyone else had gone off for luncheon, she retreated to her dressing room in a state of drained, nervous exhaustion. All she was expecting was her slightly drying sandwich, and perhaps a chance to sponge off a little of the sweat from the little pitcher of water she kept in there to drink.

Instead, she found a surprise.

Someone had wedged a big basin in here, sticking out from under the lounge, and had left two buckets full of cool water. That same someone had left a packet of fresh cucumber sandwiches and a bottle of lemonade.

It had to be Jack or Lionel, or both. On the face of it, such special treatment could cause more trouble than it was worth, and for a moment, she was terrified by the sight. But then, she realized that they could arrange it all without incurring any suspicion just by saying Charlie had ordered it for her. They might even have *gone* to Charlie and got him to order it. Certainly Peggy had gotten heaps of special considerations because of all the money she brought into the hall—champagne in buckets of ice, boxes of bonbons, and meals brought in for her from outside so she never had to leave the hall except when her taxi came to take her to her lodgings. By those standards, a few sandwiches, some lemonade and a sponge bath was very modest.

It wasn't as good as the big tubs at Mrs. Baird's, or the shallower cabinet bath in the cottage—but standing in the basin, she could get a cool sponge bath without finding herself yanked out of it by her hair, beaten because she was "trying to make herself pretty, and for who?" If she hurried, she could probably even manage a bit of a second bath, getting off the makeup, before she ran to catch the 'bus after the last show.

She locked her door for privacy, sponged herself down, then redressed in her special performing underthings, which were light and tight enough not to show under the tights. Then she ate her luncheon, saving the sandwiches she had brought with her for dinner, and as she heard the rest hurrying back to their dressing rooms, changed into the rest of her costume for the statue dance.

And all the time, she repeated, like a prayer, over and over, what she needed, absolutely needed. *A fat pay packet. Keep him happy. Don't do anything to provoke him . . .*

Lionel had gone to Charlie and told him that Katie was feeling poorly because of the heat. That was all it had taken; the music-hall owner had ordered a big basin, cool water and sponges left in her dressing room from this point on, all on his own. And bottles of lemonade. After all, Charlie had promised everyone could drink beer free at the bar for helping him come up with his substitute ballerina, and since Katie didn't drink beer, a couple of bottles of lemonade seemed only fair. Then, as an after-thought, he sent one of his errand boys for cucumber sandwiches from the tearoom down the street. "That way she don't have to rush out. She can cool down right and tight." He looked very pleased with himself for thinking of it all.

Lionel went to his dressing room in a state of mixed emotions, all of them negative. When he got there, his sylphs buzzed about like restless dragonflies, unable to settle for a single moment. Lionel's sylphs were agitated and unhappy. He didn't blame them. He was pretty agi-tated and unhappy himself. He'd woken with a knot in his stomach, posted off his letters immediately, and got to the theater half afraid Katie wouldn't be there—and entirely unsure what he was going to do about it if she wasn't. His mood hadn't been improved by what she had whispered to him.

He didn't doubt her, when she whispered the threats her husband had made against him if she didn't do what the strongman wanted. His encounter with Dick Langford had left him convinced that the circus strongman was a dangerous man; a bully, yes, but cunning. And very probably with blood on his hands; he didn't doubt that, either. So far as the law of the "good" people of the Kingdom was concerned, there were other people, not "good" people, who were disposable, and if something happened to one of them, well, that was one less trouble-maker to worry about. Circus people came under that category.

There was no way that Langford would get away with killing him—there were too many eyes in the city, and someone would squeal even if Langford thought he was doing it in secret. Police would be involved, and they would look first at people Lionel worked with—and the insanely jealous husband of his magic assistant would be the first suspect on their list. But that would be cold comfort to Lionel, who would be dead. And he had every intention of living to an age where he was a nuisance to those around him with his endless stories and cackling.

So, no. He was not going to provoke this man. He was going to do everything in his power to convince this man that it would be a monumentally bad idea to cross *him.*

The information that Dick Langford had a cohort in the hall was equally unwelcome. That was something he had not even considered as a possibility.

So there was a lot that needed to be discussed, ur-gently, and once he'd gotten Katie sorted out as to the little comfort he could get for her, he went straight to Jack.

Jack had left the arrangement in place for someone to relieve him at luncheon on the door. Lionel dragged him down to the workroom, and bluntly laid out for him everything that that Katie had told him.

Predictably, Jack had not taken it well. But rather than breaking into a fit of angry cursing, as Lionel himself would very much have liked to have done, he drummed his fingers on the arm of his chair for a very long time. Instead of going hot with anger . . . he seemed to have gone cold.

Or perhaps—perhaps the anger was so white-hot by now that it was searing away everything but calculation and logic.

"I don't imagine he's lived in a city before," Jack said, finally.

"Probably not, no," Lionel agreed, wondering where on earth *that* train of thought was going.

"So this morning, dairy and eggs turned up at the door. He won't be surprised if other things turn up too." Jack chewed his lip ferociously. "In fact, I don't think *he* would think twice about it. Look, here is where I am going. A drunk man—drunk past a certain point, that is—is nothing like as dangerous as a sober one. That business about delivering a jeroboam of gin to Katie's door might not be such a bad idea . . . especially if he's asked to pay for it, and it's cheaper than he expects."

"Oh, now . . . that's a good thought." Lionel thought furiously, running through all the possible ways he could get liquor into the hands of the strongman. "I have an idea. Stay here, and think. Let me run over to the pub."

There was, of course, a pub right across from the music hall. This was Brighton, and there was a pub or a chophouse, or both in every block of the entertainment district. After so many years of performing here, the publican knew him very well, so much so that his request to buy the cheapest possible gin in case-lots took him by surprise.

"Cheapest possible Blue Ruin?" The man shook his balding head in disbelief, and polished the bar top with his rag. "I can't do that for you! Master Hawkins, you'll like to kill yourself if you drink that—"

"It's not for me," he said, and laughed. "Or rather, it *is* for me, but I'm working up a new act for winter, and I want a steady alcohol fire for it. We're looking at an Arabian Nights theme, which I can adapt for the panto at Christmas. I fancy the blue flames; they'll look smashing on stage. I tried it today and I reckon I'll need half a bottle for each show, so a bottle a day."

The publican's face cleared immediately. "Well, I can get it by the case, and I can give you a very good deal on it. I can have a case here, waiting for you, tomorrow."

"I don't want to put that kind of temptation in the path of the stagehands," Lionel said. "I don't suppose you'd mind storing it for me?"

"It's not a bit of a problem, and that way I can keep track and order a new case when it's needed," the man replied, and pulled a pint. "Your usual for luncheon?"

Lionel returned feeling as if he had finally accomplished something. Jack was still waiting for him.

"I'm getting cheap gin by the case from Hobson across the street," he explained, as Jack listened intently. "Hobson thinks it's for a new act I'm working out that needs an alcohol fire. I'll have Katie tell the bastard she can get hold of a bottle of gin a night for sixpence."

Jack let out a sigh. "Brilliant. She can build up some money hidden here, and he'll have plenty to get drunk on every night. Let's hope he's a sodden drunk."

At that point, Jack had to return to his post, and Lionel headed for his dressing room, well pleased. Now he just had to work out how to tell Katie what he'd done, get her to understand what her part would be, and then work out how to get the bottle of gin into her dressing room before she left for the night without anyone noticing.

Then he chided himself for being such an ass. *Are you a magician, or not?* he scolded himself.

And it wasn't an Elemental Magician that he meant, either.

Half of being an illusionist was being aware of what other people ignored. And what other people ignored was routine. They got used to how something happened, and as long as nothing occurred to break that routine with something wildly unexpected, they drifted through their routine in a haze of preoccupation, and never saw what was right in front of them.

He knew the routine of this music hall as if he had choreographed it as a trick himself. How hard would it be to make someone disappear and reappear without anyone noticing? And even if he didn't know who the watcher was, he knew who it *couldn't* be.

He waited in his dressing room, listening for the musical cues, until he heard the one that told him Katie's statue dance was over. She would have to make her way through the chorus girls heading for the stage. The next act was putting the finishing touches on his makeup and costume. Every stagehand would be busy with the set change and Charlie supervised backstage like a drill sergeant; if Charlie missed one, or saw one lurking in the corridor to the dressing rooms at this point, he'd fire the man on the spot—and Dick had specified to Katie that he had a *man* as a confederate in the hall. So Lionel listened for the frantic rush to the stage, opened his door as soon as it was past, spotted Katie, and yanked her into his dressing room before she even knew he was there.

"Look—" he said, before she could get out a word. Her face was a mask of terror at being in his room. "You're safe. Right now every man in this hall is doing set-change or in his dressing room. We've got a few minutes of safety. We've had an idea. You tell Dick that one of the bartenders said he'll sell you a bottle of gin for sixpence, but he can only get you one a night without getting in trouble."

Her terror turned to puzzlement. "But—"

"I know, a bottle is twice that, and as soon as Dick realizes this, he'll figure the man is stealing from Charlie and making money off you, but he'll be so pleased at the cheap drink he won't quarrel with it."

She nodded, slowly. "And I can hide the money here."

"It won't add up to much, but it will be enough you can take a taxi if you need to, or take care of some other needs you might have. And you'll be bringing Dick a bottle of gin every night. If we're lucky, he'll drink it dry and leave you alone." It was the best he could offer, but her face lit up with such gratitude that he felt ashamed for not being able to think of more.

"He's not used to strong drink," she said haltingly. "Last night he slept like a dead horse. It might give me some peace."

"Right then—get yourself across to your room. I'll find a way to get the bottle in there tomorrow night." He listened to the music, to the sounds of footsteps—performers were utterly predictable; unless there was something wrong they *always* did the same things at exactly the same time backstage, most of them even timed their actions to the cues they could hear out on stage. Well, they had to. Everything in music hall ran on so tight a schedule that the least deviation could throw everything into chaos. When he knew there would be a moment when no one would be in the corridor or looking out a door, he whisked his door open, shoved her across the hall, and closed his own door silently.

It wasn't enough, dammit. It wasn't *nearly* enough.

But at least it was something.

Katie hurried back to the cottage, running from the 'bus stop, arriving at her own door slightly out of breath. Dick was waiting impatiently, of course, and yanked the door open as soon as she set her hand on it.

She shrank into herself, and let him see her fear. Sometimes that helped. This time, it did.

"'Bout time!" he snarled, and then she saw he was in his favored outfit again, and his hair had been oiled back. "Oi'm goin' out! Just 'bout stifled in here!"

"Dick!" she interjected. "I have some good news. I saw how you liked the gin, and I asked the barkeeper at the hall if he could sell me some, so I could bring it home with me every night. He said he could only sell me one bottle a night, but that it would only be sixpence."

She saw that there were three bottles on the table now, not two; two empty and one full. So he'd been out, and he'd found out the price for himself—

And the stormy look on his face cleared, as if by magic. "Sixpence!" he exclaimed. "That's—"

She nodded eagerly. "It's a great bargain. It's cheaper than beer. Can I take him sixpence a night, then?"

"Aye!" Dick actually patted her on the top of her head, as if she was a dog that had pleased him. "Aye! Fer once't, yer thinkin' sharp!" He barked a laugh. "Yer kin cook, an yer thunk 'o thet! Yer some use arter all!"

He shoved her inside. "Clean up!" he ordered. "Roight 'n toight. Oi'll be back." He closed the door and locked it, leaving her momentarily alone.

She leaned against the closed door for a long, stolen moment. She was alone. There was no one watching her.

Then she cleaned as quickly as she could, immediately discovering what it was he had done for himself for dinner and tea when the sandwiches were gone, for there were greasy newspapers from a fish and chips shop scattered around the bed. At least that meant there were no dishes to wash.

Had he slept most of the day? Probably.

She also discovered that he hadn't been *entirely* idle while she'd been gone. He'd replaced the iron grating over the rear window. Whether he'd done so out of fear the landlord would find the damage, or to prevent her from escaping, she couldn't have said. Probably both.

She swept up the ashes and the butts from the cigarettes he'd smoked, and put them in the dustbin. She cleaned up the teakettle and the mugs he'd used, though a sniff proved he'd used them more for gin than tea. She set the milk and cream bottles out, and left money for the milkman. Then she poured herself the last of the milk—doing without tea, for that would take too long to make—set out food and the gin as she had last night, made herself a sandwich for supper, and took the mug of milk and the sandwich up into the loft. This time she had taken the precaution of leaving the windows open so it wasn't so hot in here, and she shoved one of the trundle beds as far from the edge of the loft as she could get it. Once up there, though there was barely enough room to kneel on the floor and not hit her head, she got out of her dress, into a night dress, and ate her supper. Then she lay down on the bed in a curl so that she fit—it really *was* a child's bed after all—and waited.

She closed her eyes and concentrated with all her might. She wouldn't call her Elementals, but Lionel had said that *wanting* something badly enough was enough to make it happen, sometimes. She wouldn't pray for this—praying for her husband to find a whore was so utterly wrong that even considering it must make Jesus weep. But she could wish for it, and think hard about it. *Just like last night,* she thought feverishly. *Let him find women just like last night.*

This ploy of getting women, of course, was not going to work forever. It might rain, and he would refuse to go out. Eventually, he would discover that word about him had spread, and only a truly desperate woman would come with him. Or none at all. This was holiday time, and the women of the streets had plenty of customers at this season. But for now, he was good looking, in that brutish way, and he had money. He should—

There was only the drunken laughter of a single woman at the front of the cottage this time. The key turned in the lock, and the two of them stumbled inside.

She stuffed the waxed cotton into her ears and gritted her teeth, and pulled the pillow over her head to further block out the sounds.

At some point she fell asleep, worn out by the past two days. When she woke, it was dark.

She eased herself out of the trundle, pulled out one of the earplugs, and looked over the edge. There was only the sound of one person snoring, and there was only the shape of one person in the bed below her. Dick had learned his lesson that if he let a whore "sleep" with him, she was likely to get up while he was sleeping and steal; he must have sent the whore on her way as soon as he was finished with her.

She crept back up into bed and lay there, staring up into the darkness.

So ... this was how life was going to be. Terror that Dick would murder people she cared for, if she somehow put a foot wrong. *Knowing* that if he ever found out how she felt about Jack, he would kill Jack without thinking twice about it. Working to exhaustion to have him steal her money and drink and whore it away. Slaving to his every whim, every waking moment. Being beaten if she didn't satisfy him. Being beaten if she *did,* but not well enough. Being beaten if something made him out of sorts.

How was this life at all?

Dick only growled at her a little in the morning, and when she tried an experiment and brought him the teacup full of gin instead of tea, he drank it and didn't chuck it back at her. He demanded tea with his breakfast, however, and she made it for him. Then she took two pennies and sixpence from the dresser, and escaped.

How Lionel managed to get the bottle into her dressing room, she had no idea, but there it was, after the last show, in a cloth bag. She knotted the sixpence into the end of a scarf that she draped casually across the chair, took her sponge bath, and hurried away to catch the bus with the bottle in the cloth bag at her side.

Dick didn't seem in quite as much of a hurry to leave tonight, which filled her with dread. He waited while she made him some sausages, and sampled the gin, smacking his lips over it. She was careful with the cleaning, internally begging him to leave while he drank his liquor.

"Oi don' see wy ye din' act like this all along," he finally said. "Oi'm yer 'usband. Oi make sure ye don' get mucked about by yer boss'r other fellers. Oi got roights. Oi married yer, even though yer look loike a skinny goat an' yer Traveler get. Oi married yer, when nubuddy else would'a. Oi take care'a ye, yeah? Oi got roights, an' ye niver show no respect fer 'em."

He banged the cup down on the table, making her jump.

"Lissen—" he said, harshly. "Oi'm yer 'usband. Wut'd thet Traveler yer mum say 'bout that? Yeah? 'Usband, 'e's allus roight! 'Usband, yer give 'im wut 'e wants afore 'e asks fer it! 'Usband, ye smile an look noice fer! Yeah? Yer *belong* t'yer favver afore yer married, an' yer 'usband arter! Yer *belong*. Same as a dog or a 'orse. Thet's God's Will!"

He continued on in this vein for some time, occasionally refreshing his mug from the bottle. And . . . it began to wear her down, because she *could* remember her mother saying things like that. That the wife was to utterly depend on her husband. That she was never to disagree with anything he said or wanted. That the husband was to always be deferred to, waited on, and come first in the family.

That all this was God's will, and once God had put two people together, that was it. There was no leaving a marriage, ever.

She had never thought her mother wrong in anything before . . . but here was Dick saying exactly what her mother had said.

. . . was he, were they, right? Was she meant to be a possession? Were Dick's beatings nothing but his right, to drive her back into the path God intended?

Finally he got tired of lecturing her; she was afraid he was coming over to the sink to beat her again, but instead he just grabbed her chin and wrenched her head around, forcing her to look at him.

"God's will," he said, and dropped the cup into the dishwater, turned, and lumbered out the door. "Yer mine. Forever."

She escaped up into the loft, and lay curled on her side like a leaf made of misery.

Did she deserve all of this?

Had she actually been doing what he claimed, driving him to beat her for her own sake?

Was this all her fault because she hadn't been a good enough wife?

Part of her still rebelled, but that part was getting crushed by the weight of Dick's words and the law—for the law said the same thing. That a wife was a man's possession, as his daughter was until she became a wife. That a man could do whatever he cared to with his possession.

So if the law of the land and God's law were saying the same thing—

How dared she even have *thought* about Jack?

There was one way to end this—and end the threat to Jack, Lionel, and Suzie . . . because if she was dead, Dick would have no reason to go after them.

She cried into the pillow so hard she exhausted herself, and was so drowning in bitter sleep that she never even heard when Dick and his conquest of the night came home.

Lionel opened the door to find Mrs. Buckthorn waiting for him. "This arrived by special post, for Master Jack," she said, holding out a letter, "And I knew you would both want to see it immediately."

He snatched the letter from her hand, startled her by planting a kiss on her cheek, and turned on his heel to trot as quickly as the heat would allow to Jack's flat. He actually caught Jack on the very doorstep, and sped up his pace, waving the letter over his head.

Jack gaped at it, as the light from the streetlamp reflected from the white paper. "Almsley?" he asked, breathlessly.

"Addressed to you, so I assume so," Lionel replied. Jack unlocked the door and they both hurried inside. Jack lit the lamps, while Lionel poured a couple of brandies—just in case the news was bad—and placed the envelope on the table between them.

Jack's little sitting room was as tidy as his own would be messy if it wasn't for Mrs. Buckthorn. Everything was arranged with military precision; the two worn leather wing chairs were placed on the hearthrug just so, the clock was square in the middle of the mantelpiece, there was a small table precisely beside each chair. There were magazines neatly stowed in a rack, newspapers neatly stacked on a table under the window, books precisely arranged in bookcases. The little writing desk was firmly closed, the chair tucked precisely beneath it. Not for the first time, it struck Lionel that this sitting room looked more like a display than some place someone actually lived.

Jack lit the gaslights, then stumped over and took his seat, and stared at the letter for a moment. Then, with a shaking hand, he picked it up, lifted the seal with his pen-knife, and opened it.

"My good Master Prescott," Jack read aloud. *"I remember you very well, though we were both scarcely more than boys, and I remember your father as well. You and your father did me and mine a very great service all those years ago, and I am eager to repay the debt I owe you."*

"That sounds promising . . ." Lionel offered.

"We do have some extreme difficulties to overcome, however. I am sure you have thought of them already, but indulge me, for I feel I would be remiss if I did not point them out. The first is, of course, that this young magician is another man's wife. The man is a brute, he certainly does not deserve her, and he will almost certainly trigger the sort of event that none of us wishes to see if he keeps abusing her, but he is her husband, and in the eyes of the law, his rights are absolute over her."

Jack uttered a little moan, and started to put the letter down. Lionel, however, was having none of that. He snatched the letter out of Jack's hand, and picked up where Jack had left off.

"Another great difficulty lies with the man himself. I have known many such cunning brutes in my time; if we attempt to pay him off and send him elsewhere, like the beast that he is, he will smell blood, and open his jaws, and attempt to extract more rather than taking what he is offered and going away. We find ourselves on the horns of a great dilemma, for he will also keep coming back to the same well from which he got such satisfaction, and these days, not even being shipped off to Canada or Australia is likely to keep him from returning. And if we cease to pay, he can easily ruin us all. Society, when being told that one man is paying another man for that man's wife, is likely to place the worst possible of conclusions on the situation."

Now it was Lionel's turn to feel a little faint. Almsley was quite correct. And this was something he hadn't even thought about. This was bad. This was—

But there was still another page to the letter, and Lionel turned it over to read.

"Nevertheless, I am determined to find a way to free this poor girl from the brute. It is not only mandated by real alarm over what she—and her Elementals—may become if she were to lose control. It is mandated by pure decency and honor. I shall be joining you in Brighton as soon as I am able to get away."

"What?" Jack exclaimed, his head snapping around, turning to stare at Lionel with wide, disbelieving eyes.

"It says right here, he's going to help us," Lionel pointed out. But there was more.

"You are a soldier, and your friend is a magician of the stage as well as of the Art. I suggest you put your talents together. There are other ways that may work to rid yourself of this troublesome brute. If, for instance, he was convinced that she was dead, he would have no reason to continue to remain in Brighton. Or, if you were to lure him into committing some act of violence in public, you could have him imprisoned. Neither of these things has to be real of course. Nor do they require the aid of your Elementals. They could easily be mere stage-illusion. I merely make these suggestions and leave it up to you two to see if you can think of an implementation. Yours very truly, Lord Peter."

15

KATIE woke at dawn to the sound of a single bird singing right outside the window. Something had happened as she had slept; she had, as the saying went, struck bottom. It was enough to trigger rebellion in her. And she woke, filled not with terror and despair, but with determination.

Last night, she had thought she wanted to die. She woke knowing that was a lie; she did *not* want to die. And just who was Dick Langford that he could actually make her think she did, at least for a little while? What was wrong with her? Hadn't she learned anything in the months she'd been away from him? How could he so thoroughly have reversed everything she believed in to the point where she was actually thinking *he* was in the right and she was in the wrong?

She had to wonder now if perhaps there wasn't something about *him* that could not be explained by ordinary means. He'd always been persuasive with women—look at all the women he'd gotten into his bed for all these years in virtually every single town and village the circus went to! He was legendary for it. He even had a different sort of persuasion with men; he could make them think he was daring and bold, and make them secretly envy him, rather than thinking he was a filthy cad who took advantage of everyone he ran across.

There were only a few that were immune to his peculiar charm. Andy Ball was one; her father had been another. Andy Ball had taken advantage of that charm for his own ends, however, and—well, at least according to her recollections—had been very well aware of it, if not personally affected by it.

She lay quietly in the trundle, thinking very hard about this as the church clock struck six, indicating that she didn't need to be up quite yet. Was it magic, this power that Dick had? Now that she knew magic existed, it seemed that this might be some sort of magic. She certainly couldn't explain it any other way.

Well, whatever it was, last night's nadir of despair had changed something in her. She'd managed to shake off whatever persuasive power he'd had over her, and she had regained her own spirits.

You've no more power over me, you right bastard, she thought angrily at the snoring hulk in *her* bed. *You'll never get it back again, neither.*

She was, somehow, going to find a way to be rid of him. For good, this time. Lionel had showed her at the theater that there *were* times when they could talk safely. Together the three of them were sure to find some way to thwart Dick. He'd never talk his way around police, for instance, if they found a way to lure him into trouble.

And if Dick had a confederate watching her, well, she had *her* informants, too, except there was an entire group of them, not just one. If it had been him, and not a confederate, she'd have been more worried, but there was no way he could work his magic through someone else. The chorus girls were all her friends, even the couple that didn't get on well with most other girls, because despite her star status, she took care to never put on airs. And—be honest—because when the bounty of chocolates, trinkets, and flowers came in from would-be admirers hoping to get to know the "Russian Ballerina," she shared them with the chorus girl's dressing room, and generally shared the name of the admirer as well. Several of them had eaten well on the bounty of one of those disappointed fellows, and one was still doing so. She could ask the chorus girls quietly—and with obvious distaste—if one of the men working at the hall had been asking about her. She'd hint she'd found some disturbing notes in her dressing room. Every single one of them had experienced, or were experiencing, the attentions of someone they really did not care for or want anywhere about. They'd assume the fellow in question had an unsavory pash for her, and they'd tell her who it was.

But she knew that she would have to be very careful not to betray her newly reawakened spirits to Dick. Any evidence of rebellion would bring a beating. Mind, being meek and cowed would not *prevent* a beating if he was sufficiently determined to find an excuse to give her one, but evidence of rebellion would bring more, and more often.

She came down the ladder from the loft consciously assuming the hunched-over posture of someone suitably humiliated, spirit broken. She had never thought of herself as an actress, but now she would have to put on the best performance she'd ever done, and she might have to keep it up for weeks—months. At least it was a role she was familiar with; her body assumed the posture easily, and she knew she wouldn't have to feign a wince if he looked as if he was about to raise his hand to her.

She managed to get down the ladder so quietly he didn't even snort in his sleep, and started cooking. She made Dick's usual breakfast of bacon, sausages, eggs, and fried bread instead of toast, but this time she brought it all on a single huge metal serving plate she'd found in the bottom of the pantry last night. It had been stored with some dubious pots and pans that looked as if they had been put away with burned food still encrusted on them. The platter, at least, was clean, and was probably meant for serving up a whole roast chicken, or something of the sort, but it was big enough to load down with all the food Dick considered necessary in the morning.

He was sitting up waiting for his breakfast when she turned and brought it, along with a tea mug full of gin. One eyebrow went up at the sight of the huge platter, but he smiled a little. "There's a *proper* brekkie!" he said with approval, and dug in, while she made all the usual preparations to tide him over while she was gone. If he continued to eat like this, without doing anything but lying around in bed all day, would he get fat? She wondered if it would be possible to just keep feeding him until he got so rotund she could outrun him, like the Fat Man in the circus sideshow. It was an amusing thought.

He could set himself up in a Boardwalk stall then. He could live in the stall, never leave, and hire a child to take care of him and feed him on fish and chips.

Thinking of the Boardwalk triggered another thought, one that could have more potential than turning Dick into a sideshow freak. "Have you been down on the Boardwalk or the beach?" she asked quietly as she cut bread and sliced meat.

Out of the corner of her eye she saw his head come up, and he looked at her suspiciously. "No," he replied shortly, his dark brows knitting together in the start of a frown.

"You'd have such a laugh if you did," she said. "It's like the longest sideshow you could ever imagine. There's heaps of people setting out with acts down there. Some have stalls, some just have a rug, and there isn't one strongman that is half as good as you." *There. Let that put a bee in his bonnet.*

She didn't need to add anything to that, for although he was lazy, he was also frugal in a way. She knew he hated having to pay for women, drink, and food if he could get them free, as he had with the circus. He had relied on his circus turn and his personal powers to attract people and his pub tricks to bring them close enough to haul in and get them to pay for things for him. Then he would do a few tricks outside the pub and flex his muscles to get the women. He was a lazy man, but his tricks weren't difficult, and at this point even he had to be getting bored with sleeping the day away and eating. He wasn't going to amuse himself with going to the halls—he'd never see the sense in *paying* for the sort of entertainment he was used to *being* in. He would absolutely never consider doing a regular act in one of the halls himself, not when he had *her* money to laze about on. But going down to the Boardwalk when he felt like it, putting out a scrap of rug, and picking up the odd bit of money *and* attracting women he wouldn't have to pay for? Now that was something he'd enjoy.

He'd also enjoy showing up some of those other strongmen with his tricks. He loved to lord it over other people. That would make him very happy indeed, and the happier he was, the better off she would be.

"There's lots of acts," she continued, meditatively, starting the washing-up. "All up and down, and some on the beach." As one of those acts himself, she didn't have to tell him that he could see bits of them for free just by strolling up when the barker was extolling them. "Fireworks after sunset, and electric illuminations. If you get tired of sleeping, you can just take the 'bus for a penny each way."

"Huh." His brows had unknitted and now he just looked thoughtful instead of suspicious. "Is there foights?"

She knew what he meant; not random fighting, but bare-knuckled brawling matches where men fought for prize money or against all comers, with money for the man who could stay five minutes in the ring. Just before she'd run, he'd started looking for those, and collecting on them too. No one expected a man who looked like Dick to move swiftly, or to fight with any level of calculation, but he was fast, and he had certainly learned the best places to hit by practicing on her and other people he had beaten up.

"I don't know," she said truthfully. "I'm in the hall all

day but dark day, and I never looked for any. But Brighton is big. It stands to reason there are matches somewhere."

"Huh." He was clearly thinking hard about all this. "Lotta toffs 'ere?"

Now, "*toff*" no longer meant the same to her as it did to Dick. To Dick, a toff was a man who had more money than he could reasonably spend, and who liked to toss it around to show off. That was how a Traveler thought, too.

But she had come to think of a "*toff*" the same way Lionel did; toffs had money, all right, but they generally had titles too. When they tossed money around—which many of them did—it wasn't to show off, it was because it literally meant very little to them. There always had been money, there always would be money, so why not spend it to have some fun? They paid very little attention to how much they actually spent.

Dick's sort of *toff* wanted the biggest impression he could buy, but he wanted it at a bargain rate, which was why they spent their money on cheap beer in cheap places. They knew they would never be able to penetrate the circles of noble rank and extravagant wealth, and many of them didn't try, preferring to go after lower-hanging fruit.

Lionel's sort didn't care what sort of impression they made as long as they and their friends were amused out of their boredom for a bit. If the people around them were offended by their attitude, they would neither notice nor believe it—the lower classes were not expected to have any sort of "finer feelings" to be offended. The lower classes were expected to be flattered by having any attention from a gentleman at all. And, of course, the lower classes were expected to wish to do anything for money.

That was the sort every chorus girl dreamed of meeting, for that sort was the kind who might bestow generous presents on them, or even "set them up." It almost never happened of course, and on the rare occasions that it did, the "chorus girl" in question was generally a famous beauty in her own right. But the cheap novels they read were full of such promises, and the girls believed them.

Dick's sort of toff was the kind that would buy an entire pub several rounds, bet extravagantly, and spend most of his money on showy trappings for himself—like a pretty little mistress he could take around to the sort of places he wouldn't take his respectable wife. This was actually the sort of fellow who *would* buy a common chorus girl presents—trinkets of silver and jet, for instance, not gold and diamonds. He *might* "set her up" for a time, but within six months he would tire of her and another would take her place. More than six months together, and she might start to get "ideas" and make demands. He couldn't have that. So she had to go before she got to that point.

Since the showy trappings that *wouldn't* make demands on him might include patronizing a prizefighter, that was the sort Dick was interested in, anyway.

Mind, the ones with the titles were inclined to patronize a fighter too—but they were far more easily offended by someone who was very much their social inferior being too familiar than the self-made "toffs" were. In fact, Dick's sort, sometimes having come up from rough be-

ginnings themselves, often prided themselves on "not
forgetting their roots" and encouraged a certain amount
of familiarity—provided it didn't come with demands of
any sort.

That was the sort of toff that came to Brighton to holiday, sometimes alone, having left the respectable wife
and children at home, sometimes with the respectable
wife and children in tow. It was easy enough to slip off
while the wife was supervising the children at the beach,
or taking them to some of the less-dubious attractions
such as steam-gondolas, roundabouts, and Ferris wheels.
Titled ones went home to their country estates where it
was at least marginally cooler and a great deal less odor-
ous than in the city.

So she knew how to answer Dick's question. "Lots,"
she said. "They don't come to *our* hall often, but I know
they're here. You can see them in carriages everywhere,
they do like to go to the really big halls, and there's some
other posh places they like. I've never been down on the
Pier late at night; they might go there as well."

Since the Pier was where the racy kootch shows were,
it was very likely some of the same people Dick was
looking for were there.

That was what Dick wanted to hear, clearly. "Mebbe
Oi'll do some scoutin' about," he said briefly. But his eyes
were narrowed in speculation and she knew he was
thinking hard. Or . . . perhaps scheming. Thinking things
through was not something he did well; he had relied on
Andy Ball for that. Scheming, however, came naturally
to him.

"I need to go or I will be late," she told him, and got
her eight pence, snatched up her bag, and left. She had to

run to catch the bus, but she was pretty satisfied with the seeds she had planted.

Jack just wished her a common good-morning as she hurried past him. Lionel was nowhere to be seen, but it was early for him. Last night's dismal, overheated attempts at sleep in the loft made her glad to lock the dressing room door and start with a cool sponging down before she got into her rehearsal clothing. Whether it was Charlie who had arranged the water and the basin, or Lionel, she was deeply grateful.

The rehearsal went as yesterday's had gone; only when she was in the basket did Lionel whisper to her.

"I don't want you giving up, Kate," he said, fiercely. "We aren't. We're going to find a way to get you free of this blackguard."

"Be careful," she hissed back. "He looks slow and stupid, but he's awfully cunning. And somehow he makes friends that help him all the time. I don't know how, but he does. Women fall for him, and men want to be his friend, at least for as long as it takes them to buy him drinks. It's like some kind of magic—what do they say? Magnetism? Mesmerism?"

"Both, and it might actually be a kind of magic," Lionel replied, sounding a little startled. "I'll look into that. If it *is*, there could be something Jack and I can do to keep him from making any more 'friends' to help him here in Brighton."

That was all they had time for, but the exchange of words left her feeling encouraged.

After rehearsal, she didn't pause to change out of her rehearsal clothing; instead she snatched up two boxes of chocolates that had arrived last night that she hadn't had the heart to open, and ran down to the chorus girls' dressing room with them before they all scattered off for luncheon. They met her bounty with happy cries.

"Well, these are better than the *notes* someone's been leaving on me mirror," she said, making a disgusted little face. "It has to be someone who works here, 'cause who-ever it is ain't leaving a name. I'd like t'know who it is so I can at least tell Charlie."

Three of the girls exchanged a look that gladdened her heart. "Don't get 'im in trouble with Charlie, and we'll tell," said Bessie Taylor, looking at her plaintively. "'E's new. 'E's a bit greasy, an' a bit uv a suck-up, but 'e's the only one willin' t'let us sneak a fag backstage, an' 'e's got a son. 'E keeps askin' 'bout you, I think 'e's got a pash on you."

Aha. "Well, I won't tell Charlie then," she said crossly. "I'll just give 'im his notes back and a piece of me mind. Who is it?"

"Oscar Nathan," said Bessie. "Don't get 'im sacked, Katie!"

She didn't know the name, but she knew the descrip-tion; a short, balding, greasy-haired fellow that groveled and sniveled a great deal, who'd been hired more to clean up the front of the house than as a stagehand. He really had no business being back-of-house at all, really, but Charlie never made much fuss about where some-one was as long as the job he was supposed to be doing got done. He was *just* the sort that would idolize Dick and be tremendously flattered that Dick confided in him. He'd also be just the sneaky, ratty sort that would think himself tremendously important because Dick asked him to spy on Katie. "I won't get 'im sacked," she replied, with a sniff. "But when I tell 'im I'm gonna hand the next lot of notes over to his missus, I bet he'll reckon that'd be worse than bein' sacked!"

The girls all giggled, and agreed. She went back to her dressing room for another sponge-off and the luncheon Charlie'd had left for her. The sort of heavy, greasy food that Dick thought grand fare was enough to make her ill in this heat. Mrs. Charlie must have ingrained in Charlie's head that "ladies" subsisted on cucumber sandwiches, which at the moment suited Katie right down to the bone. Well, at least she knew there was a way she could pay Charlie back—by giving such good performances that the house would be packed every day.

Now that she knew exactly who to watch for, her anxiety was considerably relieved. She didn't feel as if she had to have eyes in the back of her head anymore, and when she came off her statue dance at the matinee, she had no fears about popping into Lionel's dressing room instead of her own. The greasy little spy would be far too busy cleaning the stalls and sweeping up all the rubbish left on the floor right now to have any time to try and see what Katie was up to. Music halls, unlike theaters, were places you came to eat and drink along with getting your entertainment, and as a consequence there was a lot of mess after each show. People lingered, too, wanting to finish their last drinks in a leisurely fashion, which made cleaning even more difficult. It amused her, thinking of the little sneak getting evil looks and curses as he tried to clean around patrons who didn't particularly wish to leave.

"Oscar Nathan," she said as soon as she was inside. "Hired to sweep and clean the front. I don't know much about him, but once I knew who it was, it was easy to spot him keeping an eye on me when he could sneak backstage. Wish I knew what Dick has told him, because I didn't much like the way he was glaring at me—like it's me that's the bad person."

"It might be nothing," Lionel pointed out. "It might be he was told that you're a wayward wife and Dick wants a sharp eye kept on you, and he thinks he's helping out. It might be almost anything, if Dick is as good at persuading people as you say. It doesn't matter; now we know who it is, we know who to avoid. That's the important part."

That was all they really had time to say. She slipped back into her dressing room, wishing she dared call her Elementals to spy on the man herself. If she dared call them, they could keep her apprised of where he was every moment she was here at the hall. She'd never need to worry that he was spying on her. She could even control exactly what he saw.

But she didn't dare. She could *feel* them, even if she couldn't see them, and she knew that the moment they knew what Dick was doing to her . . . they would react badly. She was having so much trouble controlling herself, as last night's breakdown showed, that she knew she would never be able to exert any sort of control over them. If they had experienced her despair . . . well, she didn't want to inflict that on any other living creature, human or otherwise. And if they had reacted to it by trying to reduce Dick to a pile of ashes, she wasn't sure she'd have had the will to stop them. And that was where everything would go horribly wrong for everyone, not just for her.

Lionel waited until Jack was ready to lock up, rather than going off to his own place as soon as he was changed and the stage makeup removed. He came up behind Jack in the alley, and steered him toward the street. "Until we get Katie free," Lionel said firmly as he took Jack by the elbow with one hand and hailed a taxi with the other. "You are staying with me."

"What?" Jack gaped at him, but as the cab stopped for them, he shut his mouth and nodded. "Of course. I know what you are thinking, and it's a good idea. If that bastard bully doesn't know about me, and it appears that he doesn't, I can act as a sort of bodyguard for you. And if he finds out about me, having both of us in the same place is safer for both of us."

Actually that wasn't what Lionel had been thinking at all, but if that was enough to keep Jack there at Lionel's house, then it was a good enough reason for him.

What he was thinking was a great deal simpler. The two of them could take a single cab to and from the hall, saving Jack a lot of pain and effort. Jack would not have to walk to his little flat from Lionel's after a late night session of trying to plan a way to free Katie—when he was already exhausted. Not that Jack wasn't strong—he was probably physically stronger than Lionel—but Lionel and Katie needed him to save that strength, not waste it on overtaxing himself.

They didn't make much conversation in the cab, but the drive wasn't that long, either. The cabbie set them right down at Lionel's door; the lamp was already lit, and the door unlatched. "Give Mrs. Buckthorn your key;

she'll send the girl over for your things," Lionel said as he opened the door, making it something of an order.

"I'd rather not have the child running about the dark streets with a heavy portmanteau," Jack objected. And before Lionel could say anything, he turned and detained the cabbie before he could drive off again.

Lionel just shrugged, and went into the house. He could see Jack's point. While it wasn't far to Jack's flat, and their neighborhood was relatively safe, a girl with a big bag could be seen as easy prey for theft if nothing else. Mrs. Buckthorn was waiting just inside the front door, as she always did when she heard him coming home. "Jack will be staying here for the next little while," he told the housekeeper. "Have we a room ready?"

Mrs. Buckthorn looked at him over the top of her reading glasses and *tsk'd.* "I always have a room ready, Master Lionel," she said, in a voice ever so slightly chiding. "That's why ye keep me as your housekeeper. I'd be a poor manager if I could not take care of a guest for you at no notice at all."

Properly rebuked, he retired to the sitting room that faced the garden to wait for Jack. Mrs. Buckthorn brought him a gin and tonic, but clearly she was also waiting for Jack; when she heard the sound of cab wheels and the clop of the horse's hooves, she bustled out. Lionel could hear her scolding Jack for trying to take his own bag into the house. He knew that Mrs. Buckthorn would emerge triumphant from that struggle.

They had abandoned the dining room for planning purposes; it was too hot, and the sitting room was far more comfortable to work in. Mrs. Buckthorn did not quite approve of this dining almost-alfresco, but she did acknowledge that at least while it was so warm, perhaps it would be all right to bend enough to be casual. Lionel had pointed out to her that it was perfectly all right and quite the done thing to have tea in the sitting room, so why not supper? She had not had an answer for that, but when he promised that once the summer had cooled off, they would return to eating "properly," she was mollified.

Once Jack had settled in, Mrs. Buckthorn brought them their dinner there instead, making up plates in the kitchen and bringing them in on a tray.

While they ate, Lionel told Jack everything that Katie had managed to get to him that day, including the name of the strongman's confederate, and the bit of information that Dick was looking for prizefights to compete in.

Jack looked a little sour at that news. "Oh...the temptation. It is very hard to be a good man, Lionel."

Lionel nodded. "If ever there was an easy way to be rid of someone you don't want, it's to get him into a rigged prizefight. All it would take would be to find a man who'll cheat for money, and a fight that's being held away from the eyes of the law. Just make sure the trap is sweetened with a sufficiently good prize, and one more fight will end in a terrible 'accident' happening to a man no one will ever miss. But it's wrong, Jack. It'd be murder, just as if we'd turned our Elementals loose, or arranged for him to be coshed in an alley. We don't go down that road."

"No," Jack agreed immediately, and his sour face turned sad. "I—it'd occurred to me that the reason all this has happened to Katie is because she's tangled up with me."

Lionel leapt on that immediately. A few months after they had become friends, Jack had laid out what he *hadn't* done in Africa, and had voiced his feelings of terrible guilt because he had not exposed what was going on. "I've said this before, Jack, don't go down that road either. You're not a murderer."

Jack's face was a mask of uncertainty in the bright gaslight. "No but I let—"

It was more than time to put an end to that particular song. "You know, the last time you brought that up, I decided I'd take a chance that there was someone in the War Office that was a Master or a magician, and do you know, there was?" Lionel interrupted. "I started a correspondence with him. He and I wrote back and forth for a bit, and I finally brought up your matter of conscience to him. Do you know what he said?"

Jack shook his head.

"He said if you'd done *anything,* or even voiced an objection, you'd've been court-martialed and you'd still be in prison now at the least. And if you'd managed to leak the news to the papers?" Lionel shook his head. "You'd have been shot. Then he said, 'I'd rather a man of magic and conscience was walking free in England now, than sitting in a military prison. Tell him from me there was nothing he could have done then, but much he can do now.' So. I don't want to hear anything more about that nonsense of—" He searched for the proper word.

"The Hindoos call it *karma,*" Jack offered helpfully. "Or maybe it's the Chinese. It means paying for things you've done. Or in this case, left undone. Sins of omission as well as commission."

"Well, whatever it is, this is happening for no particular reason other than that Katie was gulled into a marriage with a bad man, and not for any sins of yours." Lionel took a pull of his beer and glared at his friend over his bangers and mash. "And if I hear another word on the subject from you, I will pull off your leg and beat you with it."

He managed to surprise a laugh out of Jack, which cheered him immensely.

They ate in silence for a moment. Both of them were preoccupied with their own thoughts. Lionel kept trying to think of a way that his own skills could help Katie, and so far, he had come a-cropper. "Do you think Almsley has any notion of something we can do?" Jack asked tentatively into the silence.

"Honestly?" Lionel cut a bite of sausage. "I think he's just throwing things out, trying to get us to think creatively. I mean, how could we make Katie vanish, and not end up with Dick Langford coming after me, as he threatened to? Or even after you and me together? The only way would be for all three of us to vanish, and we can't do that to Charlie."

"I don't think Katie would let us vanish her, even if we weren't in danger the moment she went missing," Jack observed, pushing his food around on the plate. "And for the same reason. She won't leave Charlie in the lurch in the middle of the season. Where could he get a replacement for her at this stage?"

"So . . . what can we do, you and I?" Lionel finished his meal and set the tray aside. "If we can't make Katie vanish, is there any way we can protect her?"

"Hrrrmmmm. I wonder . . ." Jack pondered a moment, as Mrs. Buckthorn came in to putter around a bit, cleaning up after them, and left again, taking the tray with her. And leaving each of them with a bottle of beer. It might not be very genteel, but Mrs. Buckthorn knew what men liked on a hot evening. "The first thing that springs to mind is to keep him too busy—or too satisfied—to hurt her."

"He likes women. He likes money. He likes being a bully and hurting people." Lionel shook his head dismally. "Not a great deal there to work with, Jack."

"It's what we have. Maybe we should sleep on it and something will come to us." Jack shrugged. "That's all I can think."

"That's probably the best we can do for now," Lionel admitted.

"At least she's not giving up," Jack replied, after a long silence between them. "We have that much, at least. As long as she's fighting, we have a chance."

16

THE cottage was quiet, and far too warm. It felt as if a storm was about to break, and yet there was no sign of so much as a cloud. It was even too warm for her nightdress; the most comfortable clothing she had in this weather were her cambric chemise and knickers, so that was all she was wearing now, what she had done all the cleaning in, and what she would wear to sleep. Probably a "proper lady" would have been scandalized by such a thing.

Then again, maybe not. Maybe some of them were stifling enough in this heat that they were doing the same.

As the very last thing, Katie laid out the food and gin for Dick, just as she had for the past three nights, and scampered up the ladder to hide in the loft. She wished there was a window up here. You could put a hand to the ceiling and feel warmth coming off of it.

Then she settled into the bed, well out of sight, and started into the mental and magical exercises that Jack had taught her to accept the heat and let it become something that comforted. She expected that Dick would come back long before she was able to get to sleep. But tonight was different.

Tonight was very different.

Dick came back much later than usual, so late that Katie had actually fallen dead asleep. The sounds of him rattling the door broke her out of dreams. She startled awake, and listened, and what she heard did not bode well. It took him three tries to get the key in the lock, and he alarmed her by staggering inside and blundering around, knocking into things, clearly too drunk to properly walk.

Her heart immediately went into a panicked gallop, her mouth dried in an instant, and she began panting with fear. He blundered back to the door and slammed it shut, locking it, then knocked over the paraffin lamp by the front door and smashed it; she heard the glass breaking and smelled the paraffin up in the loft. It was very clear by this point that he was not just intoxicated, he was blind drunk.

It was also very clear that he was in a blind rage. Bestial sounds were coming out of him. She had never seen him like this and it terrified her. He was so drunk that he couldn't even properly roar out her name, bellowing only an inarticulate *"Kaaeee!"* as she shrank into the back of the loft, and hid behind the frame of the bed. She had never been trapped with him in this state, and she had no idea how to react to his bellows. She only knew there would be no appeasing him. She would be an idiot to go down out of the loft now. No matter what happened, it would be her fault—and when he beat her, it would be without any sort of restraint. He wouldn't remember that she was the source of the money he was enjoying; he wouldn't remember that if he hurt her seriously, she wouldn't be able to earn that money. He probably wouldn't even remember that if he murdered her, he'd hang.

Tonight, he might well kill her.

The best she could do was to try to stay out of his hands.

"Kaaaeeee!" The bellowing came from right below her. He shook the ladder, then beat the edge of the loft with it. *"Kaaaeeee!"* She shook like a terrified rabbit, watching the wood of the ladder splintering with each blow.

He started to climb the ladder, but the first, second, and third rungs broke beneath his weight. She heard them "go," and he cursed violently and went back to beating the edge of the loft with the remains of the ladder.

Then, with a final, titanic crash, he actually broke the ladder against the edge of the loft. Bits of wood flew everywhere, and she ducked behind the bed to avoid being hit by them.

He roared with frustration, and threw the bits remaining in his hands across the room. At least, that is what she thought he'd done, all she heard were two tremendous crashes as something flew into the wall and the rear window.

She didn't want to think about how much the damage he was causing was going to cost. Clearly he did not care.

As he raged around the room, smashing glass and crockery against the walls, she somehow managed to muster the courage to creep to the battered edge of the loft and peek down into the rest of the cottage.

At this point, he was reducing part of the ladder to kindling, bellowing like a beast. She had left the gaslights turned up, and the little cottage looked as if a terrible pub-fight had broken out in it.

As if he had sensed her eyes on him, he suddenly looked up. The bright light pitilessly revealed the damage that had been done to him. Not only had she never seen him this drunk before—she had never seen him look as if he was a victim, not the victor.

He must have, for the first time since *she* had known him, and possibly in his life, found himself up against someone who could, and would, beat him as badly as he had beaten others.

His face was bright red, and somewhat battered. His hair, usually carefully oiled and arranged, looked as if someone had been pulling at it, violently. There were bruises around his neck. One ear was twice the size of the other, as if someone had repeatedly hit him on that side of his head. His eyes looked sunken, and piggishly small, as if the flesh around them was slightly swollen.

They were also black with rage.

"Gerrown!" he screamed, stamping his feet and pointing at the ground. *"Gerrown!"*

"I can't, Dick," she said, shaking in every limb. "I can't. You've broken the ladder."

He bellowed again, and flung the piece he was holding at her. She ducked out of the way. He made a clumsy run and a jump for the edge of the loft; she bleated and scuttled back, knowing if he could catch the wood in his hands he had all the strength he needed, even completely drunk, to pull himself up. She expected at any moment to see his hands clutched on the edge, to see his face coming up over it like the sunrise of the damned.

But instead, she heard the crash of him dropping back to the floor, startling an involuntary yelp out of her.

Again and again, he tried and failed to reach the edge of the loft with his outstretched hands. Again and again, he fell back to the floor, howling with pain and anger. Either the loft was just high enough he simply couldn't reach it, or he was too drunk to coordinate his leaps and his catch.

Finally he gave up, and went back to wrecking the cottage. She huddled in the back of the loft, and listened to him breaking things. She wondered if anything was going to be left intact when he was done. He howled words she was certain were curses, but it was impossible to tell what it was he was actually saying.

Her heart pounded so hard she was sure he could hear it down there. How was this going to end? What had set him off in the first place? It looked as if he had been fighting. Had he gone looking for a prizefight and found only defeat and humiliation instead of the victory he had expected? Had he made the mistake of going after a woman who had a stronger man than he was to defend her? Had he run afoul of an entire gang? Even he, with his tremendous strength, could not have held out for long against a gang determined to teach him a lesson.

Whatever had happened, he'd gotten himself in trouble—whether it was before he'd gotten so drunk, or afterward. If only he'd—

Then she heard it; the crash of glass. A strange *whoosh*.
And the inside of the cottage flared with light.

And flame shot up for a moment, visible over the edge of the loft, reaching almost to the ceiling!

The bellows turned to screams of agony, and she scrambled to the edge of the loft to see to her horror that Dick was still blundering around the cottage—but now he was engulfed in fire! He screamed at the top of his lungs beating at his flaming shirt and hair to no effect. There was fire creeping up the wall where one of the gaslights had been, and shattered glass underneath it. A tiny, sane part of her recognized it for the remains of one of the gin bottles. He must have flung it at the gaslight, with predictable results.

He staggered everywhere, flailing, howling in agony—and setting fires everywhere he blundered.

Jack didn't remember falling into bed; he'd been so very exhausted that he'd dropped into it fully clothed. But it couldn't have been long before he was catapulted out of an uneasy sleep by sharp pain and the sense of complete panic. His eyes flew open to find that one of his salamanders had deliberately scorched the back of his hand, while another was biting his nose. Before he could react properly, images exploded into his mind. Katie's cottage, fire *everywhere*, a body on fire sprawled across the back door, Katie trapped in the loft, screaming for help—

He had no memory of plunging across the hall to Lionel's room, but the door opened in his face, and Lionel shoved him out of the way, running for the front door.

He hadn't gotten far down the hall before Lionel was

back, grabbing his arm and hauling him outside, where he found himself being flung into a cab. Lionel shoved a fistful of money at the startled driver and shouted Katie's address. The cabbie reacted by putting the whip to his horse, and the cab lurched forward as the horse leapt into a canter.

"We'll never—" Lionel began, helplessly.

"Send your Elementals," Jack shouted at his friend, grabbing him by the shoulders and shaking him. "I'll send mine!"

He could feel the doubt in Lionel; he was nothing but a magician—and his little sylphs were nothing like strong enough to stop what they both must have seen! Why, not even the firebirds that had protected him and Katie from the runaway rocket were strong enough to damp that conflagration! Lionel shouted back, despairing. "They can't stop the fire, they're—"

"They can hold it back!" he countered. "They can hold it back! And so can she if she'll just think! If she can see ours, she'll know what to do!" Lionel's Elementals were Air; they could steal the air from the fire and keep it from exploding out in all directions. His salamanders could shelter Katie for a little while at least. "Concentrate, Lionel! *Concentrate!*"

He squeezed his own eyes shut, and concentrated on calling his Elementals and showing them what they needed to do in his mind. Keep the fire away from Katie. Absorb it as much as possible. Keep it contained. Don't let it get away and take over the cottage.

He felt his little friends responding; felt still more gathering and following their lead as the cab raced headlong toward Katie's lane. He saw glimpses of the fire through their eyes; saw that they were fighting the battle to the best of their ability, but saw, too, that the battle they were fighting was one they were going to lose, eventually. They were creatures of magic, and weak in the real world. There was only so much they could do—

He heard the cabby shout out a curse, and felt the cab slew sideways as he pulled the horse to a halt. Were they there?

He flung the door open, into the smoke, the heat, the smell of the burning cottage, which had flames coming from every window. The cabby shouted something he didn't even try to understand. He ran as fast has he ever had, even when he'd had two good legs, utterly indifferent to the pain. He didn't even pause at the door; he ducked his head and hit the smoldering wood with his shoulder, breaking it down, and tumbling headlong into hell, into the one spot in the cottage that was still clear of fire, the middle of the floor. He rolled to his feet, heard his name, and looked up into Katie's terrified eyes.

"Jump!" he cried to her, holding out his arms. *"Jump!"*

Without hesitation she grasped the edge of the loft, somersaulted over it, and dropped into his arms, white fabric of her knickers and chemise fluttering around her like wings. They both fell to the floor in a heap.

But in that moment, the flames had gotten out of control of the salamanders; fire sprang up between them and the door, feeding greedily on the wood and the fresh air gushing inside. The back door was already fully engulfed in flame.

With a feeling of despair—and yet, a sort of peace—he tried to hold her closely, to pull her head into his chest so she wouldn't see what was coming.

But she was pulling away from him, crawling a few feet and scrabbling with both hands at something in the floor.

He followed her and saw what she was trying to pull up.

A metal ring? A hatch! There was a cellar down there! Was there a way out to safety?

He joined her, the two of them wrenching the hatch in the floor up with hysterical strength. She fell down into the darkness; he followed, letting the hatch drop down behind him, tumbling down the crude steps to land beside her on a floor that felt like ice after the heat of the fire above.

"Where's the cellar door?" he gasped, thinking there was a way out of here, or why else would she have come down this way. Overhead he heard the flames roaring. He could see the floorboards outlined in yellow glare.

"There isn't one—" she said—then sobbed, and threw herself into his arms. He bent his head down beside hers, and half closed his eyes, feeling her despair along with his own. And yet, a strange peace. They were together. At the last, they were together. "I just—I don't—I didn't want—"

But at that moment, the cellar filled with a clear white light.

For a moment he was certain that the floor had given way and they were dying—they just hadn't felt the pain yet. But she gasped, and he blinked, and turned to look at what she was staring at, and saw—

For a very long moment, he wasn't certain what he was looking at. A wall of diamonds, perhaps. Then he realized that he was staring at a chest and two massive legs that sparkled, as if both were covered with a paving of the finest gemstones that shot off rainbows as the chest moved. And he looked up, and up—

And a long, elegant head on the end of a graceful neck came down, and two bejeweled eyes gazed into his. The whole creature was covered in white gems, and a soft, white light came from it. Two great wings were held closely to its body; the webbing between the "fingers" of the wings looked so soft he longed to touch it.

He held his breath, as Katie was holding hers.

"Do not fear," said a voice like the deepest of church bells in his head. *"Lie as close to the earth as may be."*

What? he thought in confusion. He recognized the creature for what it was, of course. One of the Great Elementals, a drake—something he, as a mere magician, had never expected to see in his life. But—what was it trying to tell him? Had it come for them? Or was this some hallucination their minds were creating to protect them from the hell that was about to devour them?

"She and you are worthy. I pledged her my protection. I will protect you as well, for she loves you. Fear not. Love, and trust."

He turned his head, and looked deeply into Katie's eyes. There was no fear there. No matter what happened—no matter if this was just some dying vision—all he saw in her eyes was love. He gathered her into his arms, and they lay down on the floor of the cellar, and the great wings of the dragon covered them over.

And the fire roared and bellowed as it consumed everything above them.

The heat was incredible; it drove all thought out of his head, it drove even the ability to think out of his head.

All he could do was to murmur, over and over, with lips that were dry, parched and cracking, with a tongue that stuck to the inside of his mouth, was the litany, *"Remember Africa. Remember Africa . . ."*

Was it saying it for himself, or for Katie? Or for them both?

But he remembered. He remembered, and stopped fighting the heat. Accepted it. Made it part of himself. Became the heat; became the flame.

Became the gem-paved dragon lying over them, protecting them from the worst of the flames.

He remembered . . .

And as if something was determined to remind him of his guilt even now, he remembered them. The women, the children of the Boers—remembered them although he had never seen them with his own eyes. Remembered them dying in the same heat, beneath the same sun that was baking him and his mates—and yet, unlike him and his mates, there was no place for them to escape from the sun, scant water, and scanter food. He bore willing witness to their bowed heads, their thin bodies, under the punishing sun, accepting that as he was part of the Army, the nation, that had done this to them, he was responsible for what had happened to them.

And seeing them, he reached out to them.

"I'm sorry—" he told them, eyes too dry for tears, as theirs were too dry for tears. *"I'm sorry. I knew, and I did nothing. I knew—"*

Finally, slowly, they raised their heads; eyes as blue as the pitiless sky gazed back at him. He shrank back into himself for a moment, then steadied himself, and waited. Whatever came, he surely deserved it. They would surely condemn him to the fire here, and the fires of hell afterward. How did he not deserve it?

Just save Katie, he prayed silently. *She never harmed anyone. Just save her.*

But there was no accusation in those eyes. Only peace. Only calm.

Only the one thing he had never, ever expected to receive.

And a thousand, thousand voices spoke wordlessly into his mind.

"We forgive."

It was forever. It took no time at all. There was only the heat, and the strange peace, for the longest time. And then thought came creeping back, and for another timeless time, all he was aware of was Katie lying trustfully in his arms. His eyes were closed, as they had been since the dragon covered them. Slowly, as thought returned, and the ability to move again returned, he opened them.

It was dark. There was shouting. And the great, white weight that had been above them was gone. He could hear someone hoarsely calling their names in the distance.

"Jack! Katie! They're in there, I tell you! Jack!"

Arguing. The sound of scuffling. And suddenly Jack knew who it was that was calling them; he let go of Katie, who stirred and pushed herself up, while he felt for and found the stairs, still uncomfortably hot, and scrambled up them on his hands and knees, and finally shoved and shoved at the place where the hatch had been until, with a groan and a strangely metallic-sounding shattering of half-burned wood, it burst apart.

"Here!" he shouted, and coughed in the smoke that wreathed around him, further obscuring the little vision he had in the thick, dark night. *"Here!"*

There was nothing left of the cottage; he was afraid to move, quite certain now that it would be dangerous to do so. It was still infernally hot; heat washed over him in waves, and Katie gasped behind him.

"Jack!" Lionel bellowed, somewhere off in the darkness. And then there were people stumbling through the still-smoldering remains of the cottage, kicking apart pieces of wood and beams that broke to show coals still inside, making their way through the black and the smoke to where he shouted.

He felt Katie coming up the stairs behind him, and pulled her up, thrusting her into the arms of the first to come to their side. The fireman swung her tiny body up over his shoulder and ran across the ruins to safer ground, while two of his colleagues hauled Jack out by the arms and carried him out between them.

There was a—wagon, or a cart. Someone picked him up bodily and lifted him inside, putting him down on the floor beside Katie. Someone put a bucket of water up to his face and he drank as if he had not drunk a drop for a week, then poured water over his head, then drank again before falling back in a kind of stupor.

He lost track of things again, for a moment. The next time he was aware of anything, he was in a brightly lit room, being cut out of his clothing.

A hospital . . . He recognized the tiled floors and walls, the male aides surrounding him—it wouldn't do for a female nurse to see him naked of course. Most of all he recognized the smell. This was like the hospital in Africa where they'd had his leg off, only it wasn't in a tent. So of course, it wasn't like the hospital in Africa at all. It was all curiously dreamlike, and he laughed. One of the aides looked at him as if he was mad.

"It's all right—" he reassured the man. "It's all right ... brain is just a bit baked ... like a bit of nice cod ..."

And that was when he fell over sideways and didn't have any thoughts at all for some time, as the hospital attendants marveled that he had come through all that, and was somehow, miraculously, almost completely untouched.

"Unbelievable," said Lionel, as he pushed the wheelchair holding Jack out to the cab. "Absolutely unbelievable. I can't wait to hear the whole story. I never would have believed you two would walk out of that inferno hardly touched."

"Act of God, I say," Mrs. Buckthorn said, firmly, as she walked beside them. "Act of God it was! All His Holy Angels were down there in that nasty cellar, protecting you! And neither of you hurt!"

"You will not hear me arguing with you, Mrs. Buckthorn," Jack replied sincerely. "I'd say it was a miracle."

It was true. Aside from being so dehydrated that he drank what seemed like gallons of water, and a few burns that looked no worse than bad sunburn, he (and, he was told, Katie) were fine. The hospital had held them until noon, then let them go since there seemed no reason to hold them any further, and the only reason he was in the wheelchair was because he felt as if he had nearly torn his stump out of his hip socket, what with the running, and catching Katie, and tumbling down the stairs. It wasn't that bad, it was only some torn muscles, they thought, but it hurt like anything and he was very glad of the pills they had given him.

Katie was already in the cab, leaning out, peering anxiously. She was wearing a gown borrowed from Mrs. Buckthorn that was two or three sizes too big for her, and looked like a child playing dress-up. She didn't own so much as a penny or a scrap of clothing now. She didn't look as if she cared. And her face lit up when she saw them finally bringing Jack.

"Careful," Lionel said in a warning tone, very quietly, once he was near enough that she could hear something that was just barely above a whisper. "No demonstrations. You are just friends and fellow workers. There is going to be an inquest, and we don't want anyone deciding that Katie set fire to her husband to be rid of him. It's just as well that the only people that know she wanted to divorce him are us and Peggy."

Katie had been about to rise out of her seat; she sat back down immediately and clasped her hands in her lap, looking frightened. As well she should. There was no telling if the Coroner was going to be looking for a sensational case or not. "It's going to be hard enough to explain why you sent a cabby racing across Brighton just in time to rescue her," Mrs. Buckthorn put in, and Katie paled and bit her lip.

But Lionel winked. "That's taken care of, Mrs. Buckthorn. You see, Jack and I realized she'd left without getting her pay packet, and we knew her husband would be hard on her if she didn't hand it over. That's the thing about my sort of magic. I'm very good at convincing people I've told them something, especially if they already want to believe it. The cabby will back us up."

Mrs. Buckthorn and Katie both heaved sighs of relief, and Lionel and the housekeeper helped Jack into the cab. "I—I don't want to be any trouble, but I don't know where I'm to go now," Katie said, hesitantly.

"That's taken care of, dearie," Mrs. Buckthorn said immediately, patting her knee. "You're all set up at Mrs. Baird's. I saw to it all while you were in hospital. Your old room was still empty and she is glad to have you back again."

Lionel signaled to the cabby by tapping the roof of the cabin, and the horse moved sedately off. "Now that that bastard isn't drinking your pay, and you aren't having to save for a divorce, you'll be all right," he reminded her. "And the girls all did a rummage among their things to find you some clothing that will do until you can buy some pretty things of your own. It's all waiting for you at Mrs. Baird's."

She smiled radiantly at him, and Jack watched Lionel's eyes widen with surprise. He had to smile a little at that. It seemed that only at this moment did the magician realize what a strikingly beautiful little creature she was.

Partly that was because Lionel very carefully *did not* think of his assistants as women, much less pretty, in order to keep things from getting out of hand.

But partly it was that she'd kept all that hidden away under a veil of fear. Now, with the fear gone, she was like another girl entirely, and for the first time Lionel was seeing what Jack had seen all along.

"I don't know what I would have done without you,"

she said, her eyes brightening with tears of gratitude. "I don't know how to thank you."

"It's not over yet," Lionel warned them both. "There's still the inquest. Let's get through that, then you can celebrate. Until that's over, we must be careful, be very cautious—and you, Katie—"

But, full of new self-assurance, she nodded. "I think I know just what to do," she said.

Jack sat stoically in the stuffy, dark little courtroom that had been set up for the inquest. He had put on his best "soldier face" for this, as inscrutable as an Egyptian statue. His patience and acting ability had been severely tried, since the balding, portly Coroner seemed to have taken a dislike to Katie, and from all Jack could tell, was doing his best to try and trip all of them up in their stories.

But Peggy had come to the rescue in advance, by telegram at least, and wired them the name of her solicitor in Brighton. He was thin as a fence-rail, dark, fierce, and sharp. After consulting with all of them, he had managed to find several witnesses of his own.

Some of the key witnesses turned out to be the winner of the prizefight that Dick Langford had lost the night he died, the man's patron, and the owner of the inn where the fight had been held.

The first to be called was the prizefighter. This surprisingly gentle man should not have been a match for the giant Langford, but clearly his skill at fisticuffs must have far outweighed the strongman's size and strength.

"There was no science to him," the man explained.

"Nothing but a bully. I dropped him three times, and the third time he couldn't get up, so he lost the match. And I've seldom seen a worse loser." He went on at some length about Langford's unsporting behavior, and how afterward the strongman had gotten stinking drunk and accused everyone of cheating.

"I threw him out of the bar," the publican testified, shortly, when he was called. "Drunk, trying to pick fights, bullying the patrons. I told him never to come back."

"I had to threaten to call the constables," said the prizefighter's patron. "He was claiming we cheated, making all sorts of ridiculous accusations, then threatening *us* that he was going to get even. As soon as I sent someone for police, though, he stumbled off, blind drunk and raging."

Then it was Katie's turn. She sat in the witness box, quiet, pale, wearing a black gown she had borrowed from Suzie. The Coroner strode up and down in front of her for a moment, then turned on her, and barked out his first question.

"You perform at the Palace Music Hall, is that true?" he said, as if it were a sort of attack. Well, perhaps it was. The jury for the inquest was, of course, composed of very sober tradesmen and businessmen. They would scarcely approve of a woman who exposed herself on a stage to the eyes of strangers. Strange men. . . .

"Yes, sir," Katie replied quietly.

"And you are billed as Natalya Bayonova, the Russian Ballerina!" he crowed, and pointed a long, accusing finger at her. "Yet you are not Russian, you are not a ballerina, and your name is Katherine Langford!" Jack could see what he was doing. Already Katie had a mark against her for being a music hall performer. Now the man was making her out to be a liar.

"The playbills were already printed when Miss Bayonova canceled, sir." Katie was not in the least rattled by the man's belligerence, and Jack marveled at her composure. Then again . . . she'd had plenty of practice in dealing with worse bullies, thanks to her husband. At least the Coroner was not going to beat her into submission. "There was no time to print up more. Mr. Charles Mayhew asked if any of us dancers had an act that could replace her, and I did."

"You've been performing under this . . . pseudonym . . . for the past four weeks. That's plenty of time to print new bills, don't you think?" The Coroner wasn't going to give up this particular bone without a fight.

"I'm just a dancer, sir. I don't know nothing about the business and all. My job is to do my acts, and do them well, and that is the end of it. No boss likes having a girl stick her nose into his business, and it wouldn't be my place to do that. You'd have to ask Mr. Mayhew about all that." She kept her voice steady and didn't flinch as he got right up into her face.

Disgruntled by the fact that he hadn't shaken her, the Coroner stalked away, then turned. "And why were you here in Brighton all alone, taking on jobs, when you should have been with your husband, Richard Langford?" he snapped.

"The circus wasn't doing well, sir," she said, steadily. "Dick and me agreed I was the weaker act for a circus. I reckoned I should go look for work here, where there were lots of places where I could get honest work. That way I could save up money." She shrugged. "I never reckoned on being a headline act. I was just right glad when Mr. Hawkins took me on as his assistant. When Mr. Mayhew give me the headline job, I reckoned I'd fallen in the cream."

Oh, well done. Every word rang true, because it was true. It just wasn't *all* the truth.

"So . . . did you inform your husband of your sudden increase in good fortune?" the Coroner sneered, knowing she hadn't.

But she gave him a long and pitying look, the sort of look you give a child who has given you an answer so completely wrong that you know he didn't bother to even think about it. "How could I," she asked him, "When not even Mr. Andy Ball, the circus owner, knows for sure what the next stop will be? I do be a dancer, sir, not a fortune-teller."

That got a snicker out of the jury, and it sounded sympathetic to Jack.

The Coroner glared at her. "And did your husband tell you *why* he suddenly turned up?"

"I always expected him, sir," she said. Jack clamped his lips tight to keep from smirking. Another truth. "But he didn't tell me why he come when he did." Then she sighed sadly and dropped her eyes. "It didn't take long to guess, sir. It had to be the drinking."

That answer took the Coroner completely by surprise; clearly it was not something he had anticipated her saying. "What do you mean?" he asked, startled.

"He weren't the man I married," she said, still staring at her hands. "The man I married never touched nothing stronger than cider. The man what turned up at my door was drinking a bottle of gin a day. Two, if he could get it."

It was one thing for the other witnesses to have said that the strongman was drunk. It was quite another for Katie to state, matter-of-factly, the sheer *quantity* of alcohol Dick Langford was consuming. There were a couple of incredulous gasps from the jury box.

And Jack knew they would be making up a story to match those facts in their own minds. Langford turning to drink and being tossed out of the circus. Langford coming to Brighton and discovering that his wife was making far more money than either of them had dreamed she could.

Langford, now the slave of gin, falling completely into debauchery. One of the first witnesses that the solicitor had brought in had been the whore Langford had beaten and thrown out—though, of course, she had made no mention of *why* he had brought her to the cottage, nor that she had been trying to steal. Her story had been that "the gemmun offered her a drink, an' 'e beat 'er when she tol' 'im no t' 'is improper advances, an' she didn' know 'e was married."

This was a comfortable story for these jurors, made familiar by dozens of "improving" plays and redemption novels. Jack could almost *see* their thoughts falling into those familiar pathways, and saw their glances as they looked over at Katie soften. She might dance on a stage, but it was "ballet," which was marginally respectable, and she fit the role of "long-suffering wife" a great deal better than "vicious man-killer."

The Coroner saw it too; he had lost them, and he sensed it. From fierce, he turned to crestfallen; his shoulders sagged, and the energy just drained out of him. "Tell us in your own words what happened the night of the fire," he demanded, but he had given up, and his words held no more accusation and no force.

"I had left out dinner for Dick, as he asked me to do," she said. "He said he was going out and would not be back until late. I was having a bit of a lie-down up in the loft, where it was cooler, waiting for him."

The only lie there was that the loft was cooler than the rest of the cottage, but not one of these people would know that.

"I heard him at the door, and he was terribly drunk, the worst he had ever been, and I could tell that even before he got the door open," she continued. She stared down at hands that were clenched tightly in her lap, and her voice trembled as she retold and relived that night. It was not feigned emotion, but it would not be possible for the jurors to tell that it was fear, not grief, that made her shake.

"When he got the door open, he began blundering about, cursing and shouting. He broke the paraffin lamp that was right by the door, and spilled the paraffin all over everything. When I looked down out of the loft, I could tell he'd just ruined his shirt and trousers with it. He was throwing things about and breaking them, and I ducked out of the way to keep from being hit. Then I heard more breaking glass, and there was a huge *whoosh,* and one wall went right up in flames—and screaming, horrible screaming. He was all on fire and running around the room, and setting fire to everything else!"

Now her voice broke on a sob, and there were murmurs of sympathy from the jury.

"He fell down across the back door," she continued. "The front door was already on fire from the paraffin. Then Mr. Prescott broke through the door."

Now she looked up, straight at the jury. "He's a war hero, and a hero twice over to me," she said, her voice ringing with sincerity and admiration. "He charged that fire like the enemy, even though he's only got one leg left from the war. He got me down out of that loft—but by the time he did, we couldn't get out. I remembered there was a cellar, and we got down into it, because going down there was better odds than staying where we were or trying to get out. And that's all."

She dropped her eyes to her hands, but suddenly Jack found himself the center of attention. He looked back at them stoically, and whatever they saw in his expression seemed to satisfy them.

When the jurors finally looked back at Katie, she was sitting there shaking visibly, and it was clear from the looks on their faces that she had gone from Whore of Babylon to Suffering Martyr. The Coroner saw it too, and clearly gave up on any notion of getting her brought up on the charge of murder. He dismissed her, and with a long face, called up Jack.

Jack took his time limping his way to the box with the aid of a crutch. He needed the damned crutch, his hip *still* hurt like fury—but it was a very effective sight, and the Coroner knew it. If he'd gotten the notion that he might cobble up some doubts about why Jack and Lionel had turned up so aptly in the nick of time, he lost them on that long walk to the box.

Jack repeated Lionel's story, that Katie had forgotten her pay packet and that they were afraid her husband would think she—or Lionel—was up to some sort of mischief, and would cause her trouble.

Lionel had already made a very convincing "boss,"

who was already irritated at having lost his last assistant to marriage, and was even more irritated at the notion that his new one would be too battered to perform the next day. "I'm no gull," Lionel had said, gruffly. "I saw bruises on her, covered up by stage paint. I don't care what a man does with his wife in their own home, but if she's my assistant, he'd better leave her fit to work."

Jack backed that up, saying that she was known to be a hard worker, that the Palace *needed* her as the headliner if they were all going to continue to take home pay packets, and that he saw it as his duty to back Lionel up in case Dick Langford got belligerent.

"I'm the doorman," he said. "I'm expected to keep order there, and missing a leg or no, I'm used to a bit of rough and tumble at need. So I came with him and we told the cabby to rush it up. The sooner we got there, the more likely we'd get the blighter calmed down before he did something. But when we pulled up, there the place was, on fire." He straightened his back. "I'm a soldier. I know my duty when I see it. I broke down the door, got in, got the girl down, and by then we couldn't get out again. She thought of the cellar, I thought, well, fire burns *up,* so we might have a chance, so down we went. And that's that." He nodded forthrightly.

And indeed, that was that. The Coroner, deprived of a murder charge, made no further effort at all. The jury declared it a "death by misadventure."

Jack would have liked nothing better than to rush to Katie and embrace her, but instead, he turned his back on her and limped painfully out of the inquest room. Nor did he wait for her to come out; Lionel and the solicitor had been adamant that he must have no contact with her until they were all well clear of the area of the court.

So he took a cab with Lionel back to Lionel's house, which was where he was staying while his hip healed, at both Lionel's and Mrs. Buckthorn's insistence. Katie was going back to Mrs. Baird's with Suzie and a couple of the chorus girls, where they would all have a celebratory tea.

He'd have very much liked to be part of that group . . . but instead, he and Lionel shared a celebratory brandy.

And waited.

And finally, after dinner, after sunset, there came, at last, the sound of a cab pulling up in front of the house, and the sound of Katie's happy voice greeting Mrs. Buckthorn.

She was preceded and accompanied by a veritable horde of salamanders, Fire sprites, and firebirds, who swarmed around her and lit up the room. But nothing lit up the room like her smile.

And then, at long, long last, she was in his arms, as the Elementals wreathed around them both, and all the world was right, as it would be right, from this moment on.